FORBIDDEN ECSTASY

Philip's arms went irresistibly around her, pressing her close. He could feel her softness, the fullness of her breasts against his chest, her surprisingly long, firm legs against his own. Her face was just a breath away from his, so lovely, made lovelier by the willingness in her eyes and the slight, quivering smile on her mouth. He wanted to kiss her, not a brief, restrained kiss such as he had allowed before in his chamber, but the kind of kiss that led to only one form of fulfillment.

In one burst of energy, he held her back at arm's length. "Take pity on me, Alix!" he moaned. "How can I resist taking you—here and now, without a single vow spoken over our heads—when you look upon me this way?"

Also by Maureen Kurr:

NORTHWARD THE HEART

MAUREEN
KURR

LEISURE BOOKS   ✿   NEW YORK CITY

A LEISURE BOOK

Published by

Dorchester Publishing Co., Inc.
6 East 39th Street
New York, NY 10016

Printed in the United States of America

For
my Mom and Dad,
the best parents
any six kids could ever ask for.

Prologue

Late Autumn, 1349

Even from up on the cliff, high above the glowing embers that had once been a thriving village, the cries and shrieks of the dying still echoed. Smoke clouds hung in the stagnant air, a lingering stench left by the fires. Philip de Saines stood at the edge looking down, the sword in his hand so familiar it felt a part of him—like an extended limb, a weight long since accepted as part of his body.

But now, as he looked upon the charred remains of what had once been the homes of numerous families, the blood upon his hands added a burden he could no longer support. His gaze left the destroyed village slowly, and rested upon his sword. Blood, long since dried, still coated the blade. How many had he killed? How many had died because of him? The vow of knighthood taken nearly eight years ago had assigned him a bitter deed this day.

A mist, knee deep, rose from the ground and suffocated the last of the embers below. How long had he stood there, watching the village disappear? It was gone now, swallowed up first by man's torch and now by nature's mist. Gone entirely, except in Philip's mind.

And so were the dead; they were gone, but

hardly forgotten by Philip's tormented mind. He could still see the terror-filled eyes of one peasant mother, struck down after he'd tried to save her. Would he ever forget? Would he ever forget her eyes, or the eyes of the boy-child who cried at the dead woman's side?

They said the village had been inhabited by traitors. Guilty of treason, they said, every one of them, because the villagers spun English wool. Precious French money, pure silver livres, had gone to the hated enemy England in order to pay for that wool. But that was not the worst of their crimes. They housed English soldiers, protected English vessels in their harbor. Surely they deserved to die.

Philip's company of knights, led by one zealous Sir Sidney Paul, had been all too eager to clear France of this English-supporting village. He and all his men would be heroes, he boasted, once the deed was done.

But Philip had not entered the battle with as much enthusiasm as the rest of his company. True, the villagers were traitors and Philip was not hesitant to kill an enemy of France. But this business of attacking them by surprise and in their homes—where their wives and children lived—Philip loathed.

A fight on equal terms would be fair enough, Philip told Sidney Paul. But the older, ambitious knight would not hear of it. France would soon be rid of all traitorous coastal villages if they were shown just what would happen in retaliation for such open support of the enemy.

And so the battle began. The village peasants and the soldiers they housed were taken by surprise; many of them died within minutes. But it was when Sidney Paul turned on the women and unarmed men that Philip committed the greatest crime of a knight. He refused to follow the orders of his liege lord. And he'd gone further than that. A fellow knight felt the edge of Philip's sword. The man had been about to lay his sword to the old woman who even now haunted Philip's mind.

Philip had stopped that knight, but could do nothing when the woman's terror-stricken flight took her straight into the blade of another knight. The child in her arms had fallen at her side, crying for his mother to awaken.

After that Philip could no longer lift his sword in the name of France. He lifted it in the name of all he thought right, moral, chivalrous. It seemed then he fought both sides just to stay alive— peasants attacking him because he was a knight, and Philip defending those few defenseless peasants whom crazed knights unmercifully attacked. But kill he did, on both sides of this insane battle, and that was what sickened him now.

And enraged his liege lord. Sidney Paul's last words, upon their final retreat when the battle was won, were that Philip de Saines would no longer wield a sword in the name of France.

Philip didn't care if Sir Paul carried tales of Philip's treason to the King's ears. He'd given up the sword already.

He stood, his decision made. A gust of wind whipped at his face, and alongside the village he heard the crash of water against the Channel coast. Lifting his sword one final time, he freed the hilt with a war cry of defeat, and let the wind carry the weapon down. It fell into the Channel, and there it would remain, Philip thought, to be washed of its stains and never bloodied again.

1

April, 1352

The rider gripped the collar of his cloak, shielding the lower half of his face from the icy rain pounding into his flesh. Beneath him, the horse floundered on the steep, rocky incline. It had been too many months since his horse had followed this path; in the blinding rain, perhaps the huge beast would not find his way. The rider could barely see enough to direct him.

But he knew, high atop this rocky slope, stood his home—it had once been that. Could he still call it home, this towering fortress that had housed his family for a hundred years?

With the next bolt of lightning, he ventured a glance upward. Yes, it still remained after the score of months he'd been gone. Tall and formidable, perched like a stone lion on the highest hill in the county, so intimidating nary a foe had dared attack its walls in over sixty years.

But it was a welcome sight to this cold, drenched rider. He was home, back in the bosom of his family—even if that family was as void of tenderness for him as the impervious walls of the Chateau itself.

"Oh, Esmerelda, you would eat the kitchen barren!"

The small, furry creature only twitched her whiskered nose and continued nibbling at the yellow cheese set before her.

"And what of you, Beauregard? Will you let your mate eat everything and save nothing for yourself?"

The brown mouse positioned on his hind legs beside Esmerelda sniffed, raising his nose in the air as if searching for some cheese of his own. Alix Beauchamp broke off another corner from the square she herself nibbled at, and set it before Beauregard.

"There you are," Alix said. "That should occupy you for a while."

She watched them work quickly at the offered food, as if they could scarcely believe their good fortune and wished to consume as much as they could before it was taken away. Alix knew just what would happen if she was discovered; if Cook found her feeding the mice again he would undoubtedly forget she had attained the fully grown age of seventeen and give her backside a paddling. It wouldn't be the first time!

But things were different now, she thought to herself. Cook could hardly thrash her, even if she did deserve it. Wasn't she a ward of the de Saineses now? Ward to Cook's lords and masters? It had been quite different when she came visiting from her own, lesser fief, sneaking into the kitchen to play with Arnaud, the huge dog. Now she belonged here, and even Cook couldn't cast her out.

Alix sat back and sighed. How she wished that were true. How she wished she *did* belong. Despite the fact that Alix and her family were under the de Saineses' protection, Alix hardly felt their home was hers.

Familiar anger stiffened her spine. Her home lay in ruins, burned to the ground by marauding Montforts. Oh, no one had accused the Montfort family, and certainly they hadn't admitted their evil deed. But Alix knew. She knew beyond doubt who was responsible for the destruction of her home.

A blast of wind rattled the wooden shutter at the window, and Alix shivered as if the wind had reached her. She heard icy rain tap against the door and shutters, heard the wind howl as if announcing its presence. That's what had sent her from her chambers, the noise of the storm. She'd felt restless on the night a year ago when the Montforts had attacked, just as she felt now.

Arnaud, lying before the cold fireplace, lifted his head drowsily and gazed at her, sensing her unease. But seeing no one else in the room and hearing no one in the vicinity, he wagged his tail once, then plopped his head back down and resumed his slumber.

Esmerelda and Beauregard felt Alix's sudden restlessness as well, and scurried away with the remaining morsels. Alix wished they would have stayed.

It was no use trying to forget her unease; she felt no better in the kitchen. She should have stayed in

13

her bed chamber; at least there she wouldn't feel the cold. Why hadn't she taken her slippers? She'd covered her thinly clad body with a soft woolen blanket but hadn't bothered to cover her feet. Now they felt so cold they were almost numb.

Alix returned her uneaten portion of cheese to its cloth inside a small barrel on the wooden table before her. Then, as she was about to extinguish the candle she'd lit, the flame suddenly died before she had the chance. The outside wind filled the room with a whistle, and banged the door against the stone wall behind it.

Alix's breath caught in her throat. In the darkness, she thought she saw a shadow fill the doorway. But surely she was mistaken! This night couldn't bring a repetition of that other horrible stormy night. It couldn't! No Montfort would be bold enough to attack the de Saineses' home!

Then Alix was sure. Though she could see little in the darkness, and hear almost nothing above the wind, she felt the draft suddenly subside as the door was forcefully closed against it. Terror assailed her. She tried to move, but her limbs failed to carry her in flight. Alix clutched at the table behind her, quivering in fright, and reached behind her for something to arm herself with. There was nothing but an old wooden bowl, but she snatched it anyway. Then—immobile—she waited for the attack.

None came. With her eyes shut tightly against what she did not wish to see, she heard the scratch of a flint and the whisper of a candlewick igniting.

"Well, what have we here? A welcoming party or a nighttime thief?"

Alix opened one eye, slowly, fearfully. But before she could speak, Arnaud rushed passed her and jumped on the tall, water-drenched stranger. At first Alix thought with immense relief that the dog had at last proven his worth and was attacking the intruder. But then she saw Arnaud lick the man's face. His tail wagged fiercely and, despite the man's effort, he would not be put back. The dog was obviously overjoyed to see this lone intruder. Surely this was no Montfort attack. The thought gave Alix courage, and she loosened the bowl she hid at her back.

Standing straight, she demanded, "Who are you?"

At last the man succeeded in shooing Arnaud away. At the tone of her voice he straightened to his full height, and Alix saw that he was much taller than her—quite a feat, since she was considered tall herself. The storm had soaked his hair black; perhaps it would be lighter when dry. His cloak was bulky, made of indistinguishable fur, and tied at his slim waist. Dark chausses clung to muscled calves and thighs, and the boots of leather and fur he wore dripped water into the puddle in which he stood.

After assessing the rest of him, she studied his face. She noticed his eyes first, a clear, bright blue such a stark contrast against the rest of him. His skin was almost fair, but his eyebrows and a few days' growth of beard shadowed his features. His nose was thin and straight, a trifle large; his forehead was wider than his well-defined jawline. And his mouth, just then, hovered in a line somewhere between a scowl and a grin, Alix couldn't tell which.

"I might ask the same of you," the man said in a quiet voice, "although from your dress I would say you live here. A new servant, perhaps?"

For the first time since his entrance, Alix was aware of herself. She'd dropped the blanket at that first frightful moment, and now stood in the thin chemise she slept in. She knew, with a swiftly sinking heart, that it hid nothing from view—not her dark nipples nor the curve of her waist nor the triangle of feminine hair at the apex of her legs. Retaining her pride under his perusal, even in the dim light of a single candle, was nearly impossible.

As if she encountered this situation on a daily basis, she bent in one fluid motion to retrieve the fallen blanket, then swung it around herself with apparent ease. Again, she stood tall, this time with

15

her chin proudly lifted.

"I will ask you again, sir. Who are you?"

He laughed outright, much to her discomfort, then discarded his wet cloak and leaned to do the same with his boots. All the while the traitorous Arnaud sat happily at the man's feet.

"My name is Philip de Saines," he said as he pulled the second sodden boot away. Underneath he wore wool socks, which he pulled off as well and threw by the unlit fireplace. Even his tunic was wet, and for a moment he acted as if he would discard that, too. But then he looked at Alix and asked, "Who are you?"

"I suppose you would competely disrobe if I said I was just a servant," she replied icily. The knowledge that he was a de Saines did not bring the respect to her voice it should have. "You are quite unchivalrous."

"Demoiselle," he said, as if she'd tried his patience, "I suppose it would make a difference, but now that you point it out so vividly, I see the error of my ways. I shall disrobe even if you are a visiting Princess. Will that make you happy?"

"Of course not!" she said, her cheeks coloring. "I am not a Princess, nor am I a servant. I am Alix Evelina Beauchamp, ward to Geoffrey de Saines himself. My family is here as well. And if you dare take off another item of clothing before me, I'll scream until the walls rattle."

He didn't hesitate; he merely lifted the wet tunic over his head, and in a moment it lay beside the socks on the hearth's edge. Then he looked at her again. "Well?"

Alix knew she couldn't scream. And she knew he knew it, too. Since she was indeed a ward, her position and state of dress at this time of night would prove quite compromising. On the other hand, if she *had* been a servant, his disrobing before her would matter to no one. She glared at him, trying hard not to stare at the muscled hardness of his hair-covered chest.

"How do I know you are a de Saines? I've never seen you before."

16

"And how do I know you are a ward of my father's? I had no knowledge of your coming to live with him."

"I've lived here almost a year."

"And you've never heard of Philip de Saines?" Strangely, he gave a short, bitter laugh after that question. "I should have known. Perhaps you thought my father had only one son, Julian?"

"Of course I've heard of Philip de Saines. And Julian as well," she told him. "But I can hardly believe a de Saines would come sneaking in the kitchen entrance at this hour, to be greeted by no one formally."

"I came in the kitchen because I was hungry, demoiselle. As for no one greeting me formally, that is not surprising. I have never been greeted by the fatted calf upon any of my homecomings."

It was true that Eleanore and Geoffrey de Saines spoke more often of Julian than Philip. And somewhere in her memory Alix knew Philip was expected home soon; something about a scandal at Court, where he'd been the last two years, had sent him home. If only she'd paid more attention to the gossip! What had the scandal been about? Hadn't it to do with a woman—a married woman? Hardly aware of her own movement, she found herself a step farther away from him.

The action did not elude Philip de Saines. "I see my reputation—as recently acquired as it is—has preceded me. So you do remember Philip de Saines. The noted rapist of women, defiler of the innocent, devil incarnate." He said the words with barely concealed disgust.

"No . . . I . . ." Where had her courage gone? She hadn't even *heard* the rumors and gossip, and she was quaking under his stare. What was wrong with her? Would words alone frighten her? This man had done nothing to harm her; he hardly looked like a rapist. He might even be handsome, she thought with surprise, if his face were less stern. Once again, she straightened to her full height. "I'm not afraid of you."

Philip gazed at her. By God, he thought, she

17

wasn't. She was either a half-wit or . . . No, he knew she was no half-wit. That sparkle in her eye wasn't madness. It was defiance, bravery, and a touch of boldness. Surprising ingredients for a woman to possess. Not to mention her unusual beauty—his gaze raked over her again, and he remembered what she looked like under the blanket. If he had been a rapist, he thought, this woman would be in serious jeopardy. The sight of her stirred even his bitter blood to boiling; he who'd given up women, sworn them off with good reason.

"I can see you're not afraid," he told her. "But you were, for a moment. And before, when I first came in. Before you even knew who I was. Don't you think you would be wiser to be more afraid now that you know who I am?"

"Because of some stories being told about you? I admit I haven't paid close attention to the gossip and don't know the details, but how do I know they're true? *Are* you a rapist?"

He laughed; he threw back his head and laughed thoroughly, heartily, as if he truly enjoyed her company. Laughter suited him, Alix thought. He was handsome, after all.

"Perhaps I was wrong," he said aloud, to her confusion. "Perhaps you really are a half-wit, standing there half-clad and asking a man who is a total stranger to you—a stranger, but one with a reputation—if he is a rapist."

"I am no half-wit," she said stiffly. "And you are no rapist. If you were, you would have done with it by now. Besides, Arnaud likes you."

"Ah, so the dog has saved my reputation in your eyes. Just who are you, Alix Evelina, that you base your opinion of men on the way a creature greets them?"

"I told you, I am the ward of Geoffrey de Saines."

"Yes, so you've said. You and your family. Why is that? Where do you come from?"

"Our home was destroyed by the . . ." The Montfort name clung to her tongue. Accusations, even to a de Saines and spoken in the still of the night, were a dangerous business. ". . . by fire."

He eyed her closely, wondering what she would have said had she not stopped herself. But he let it pass, his memory of her family returning to him. "You are a Beauchamp? Is your father Giles?"

She nodded.

"And your brother, is he Simon?"

"Yes. He is with the King, under the Order of the Star."

"No doubt he knows Julian."

"Everyone knows of Julian, sire. Especially those with the King." She found herself whispering, almost afraid to say such things, without knowing why. Then she knew: Philip's face once again turned cold.

But the coldness soon disappeared, and he smiled at her. "You are Alix, now I remember. When you were a little girl you used to come here to visit Arnaud. And to steal sweets from Cook."

Alix's memory served her as well, and she recalled seeing Philip at the Chateau once or twice before. But that was long ago, and the little girl she'd been then hardly spared a thought for a fully grown man. Except once . . . when she'd seen Philip on a black charger, looking so handsome that she'd dreamed of him in the innocent way a young girl dreams of a man she wishes would notice her. Aye, that was long ago. She'd forgotten those dreams until this moment.

She said nothing of such memories to Philip. "I didn't steal those sweets," she said. "I thought Cook left the pastries on the ledge for me on purpose."

Philip laughed. "I saw you once, and you didn't look the picture of innocence. As I recall, you were scampering out of here quicker than a saint before the devil, all that copper hair flying behind you. Cook was closing in, waving a wooden spoon, and Arnaud was at his feet trying to protect you."

"By the time I realized Cook didn't mean for me to have the sweets, I'd grown too fond of them to give them up. What could I do? I had no choice but to get them any way I could. It was all Cook's fault, for being such an excellent baker. I told him that once, and do you know what he did?''

"I can guess. He gave you all the sweets you wanted.''

She laughed her admission, but when her laughter died away she felt suddenly awkward. This is insane, she thought to herself. There she was, barefoot and barely clad in a blanket, talking comfortably with a man dressed only in his chausses. She'd never before been so close to a man without a tunic on. And up until that moment, she hadn't been aware of it. After all, he was a man with an unsavory reputation. What was she doing, conversing with him in such privacy, at such an unholy hour of the night?

The silence must have altered Philip's thinking as well, for when he spoke it was no longer as if they shared a careless conversation. "You must be younger than I first thought," he mused aloud. "It seems only yesterday I saw you as a child. You couldn't be more than fifteen."

Her nose tilted upward. "I am seventeen, and fully grown."

His eyes skimmed her once. "I saw that for myself already."

She should have been embarrassed, but somehow the fact that he'd noticed her as a woman—decidedly not as a child—pleased her. But she didn't show it. Feigning offense, she clutched the blanket tighter.

"Perhaps Arnaud is wrong about you, sire, and you truly are a cad where women are concerned."

"Perhaps."

Alix left the room with more dignity than any barefoot, barely clad person had a right to display, and Philip took note of the fact, a glimmer of admiration in his eyes.

2

Early the next morning, well before cockcrow, Philip followed the covered walkway atop the Chateau's outermost wall to the opposite end of the Chateau. To the right, through openings here and there, he could see the villages dotting the de Saineses' countryside amidst a patchwork of farmland. To the left he saw the Chateau, and that was what held his eye. His stride slowed at the sight, for it was far different than he remembered.

Had that wall just opposite the walkway always been cracked? And had the storage houses always been so dilapidated? Surely the stable had never supported such a leaky roof. Even the garden, what he could see of it from there, looked unkempt and sadly overgrown. With all those now living at the Chateau, he'd have guessed his father wanted it in prime condition. Yet Philip had never seen the Chateau so run down. He hated to guess how the mills and granaries looked.

At the end of the high walkway he took the stone steps down two at a time, a lightness in his footing not felt in his heart. There had been many reasons he had not wanted to come home, but the obvious neglect of the place wasn't one of them. In fact, the one thing he'd looked forward to had been the oppulent beauty the Chateau usually sported because of its meticulous care. He'd always loved Chateau de Saines; it was more than home. To Philip, it had all the enchantment of a tangible Camelot, the legendary sixth century Utopia. Its high, impenetrable stone walls mirrored the strength of France itself; the splendor of its halls echoed a hundred years of grandeur. Was that grandeur now gone? Philip wondered. Had the

Plague, the worst of it past by more than two years, left even the Chateau de Saines a mere sickly shadow of its former glorious self? He knew his family had survived the Plague; he hadn't suspected the mortar and stone of the Chateau could suffer from the Pestilence.

At the base of a rear turret Philip halted. The wooden door looked dwarfed by the huge tower above it. A moment after Philip's knock, the door opened to him and an old man stood there expectantly.

"Gustave."

Philip said the name softly, overwhelmed at the changes in his old friend. Had he thought the Chateau altered? But what a difference in Gustave! He seemed to have aged a millennium, not just a few years. The old teacher's hair was completely gray now, and his skin wrinkled and pale, his eyes a watery blue where they'd once been so pure and bright.

Gustave gazed at Philip as though he were a stranger, and for Philip the moment lasted all too long. But then, just as Philip was about to say his own name, the older man's face showed enlightenment.

"Philip? Is it you?"

Philip nodded, and when Gustave reached out, they embraced affectionately.

"Yes, it is I. Philip."

Gustave held him at arm's length, his gaze speaking the words too hard for him to say to another man. But Philip knew. It had been too long since they'd seen one another.

"Do you have a cup of wine to offer?" Philip asked at last.

"Ah, yes," Gustave said, his voice quivering slightly. They went into Gustave's chambers, a dark, cluttered room the circular shape of the turret. On the walls hung every imaginable weapon, from knives and swords to bows and arrows and axes. They didn't shine in the firelight as they used to when Philip had visited as a youth in training, but they still looked in ready condition.

In the center of the room was a small wooden table and three chairs. Gustave found a jug and two cups, and the two sat down to drink.

"When did you get home?" Gustave asked as he poured the dark, sweet drink. His frail hand shook a little with the weight of the full jug of wine, but not a drop spilled outside the cups.

"During the night," Philip answered, and for a moment he remembered the girl who'd greeted him. Alix, he thought with a brief smile, Alix Beauchamp. But he said nothing of her. "It looks as though the family has a full house. How long has this been going on?"

Gustave waved a wrinkled hand. "Time has become irrelevant to me. I no longer count the days. I can say only that it's been a long time. Your father began housing the surrounding nobility when, one by one, they lost their land to waste and neglect."

"It seems to have touched even here," Philip said. "I didn't know."

"There is nothing you can do."

"Doom-saying from you, Gustave?" Philip asked, surprised.

"Realism, my boy. There is no one left to do the work which needs to be done. Those the Plague didn't kill off have fled the area looking for better. Even your father's stubborn hold upon serfdom cannot keep them here."

Philip stood, going to the single window near the door. The neglect was visible from here, too. The bailey grounds were ungroomed, the forebuilding of the Keep weatherbeaten, the wooden grille of the gateway entering the inner bailey broken and splintered in various places. Even the Chapel, once so proud of new colored glass windows, now looked old and tired, with the glass broken in more than one place and left unattended.

"Surely something can be done, even if we have to employ all the guests my generous father has been sheltering the past few years."

Guestave laughed at that, and for a moment he seemed young again. Philip liked the brief reminder of how Gustave used to be. "Your blatant disrespect for nobility will hardly warm you to them now that you're home again, Philip. I heartily doubt any of your father's high-ranking guests would take well to cleaning the dung piles or scrubbing the privies."

"If they want a roof to shelter them much longer, that's just what they'll be doing if I have a say in it."

"And will you? Your father is old, I agree. Almost as old as I've felt—until you walked in here. The times have changed, yet your father does not see it. He lives as though nothing has happened, no Great Pestilence, no inflation, no lack of serfs to work his land and keep up his home. He has not heeded the signs around him, will he heed what you have to tell him?"

Philip's smile held no tenderness. "My father has done a thorough job of ignoring me for two years now; I suppose he'll want to continue doing so. But I have one argument he cannot deny: Chateau de Saines will be mine one day—he will not be able to prevent me from running it forever."

Gustave sighed. "You are young, Philip, despite all you've been through, despite the strength you've shown in the past. You remember the Chateau de Saines as it once was. But I tell you, it shall never live again in such splendor. Your family no longer has the wealth it once had, no one has these days."

Philip shook his head. "*Someone* has the wealth, Gustave. Perhaps not the de Saineses, but someone. True enough, pestilence killed a great number—some say as many as a third of all the people in the land. But with fewer people, there should be *more* silver for those of us who survived. Don't you see? Certainly a third of all the coinage did not die with their owners. And if the de Saineses have lost a portion of their wealth, it should not be impossible to earn it back, with a bit of hard work and thorough planning."

"What have you in mind?"

Philip hesitated. "Nothing," he admitted, adding, "yet." He smiled disarmingly. "But give me time. I've only just arrived home."

Gustave poured them both another cup of wine, then spoke. Already his voice sounded stronger and his cheeks were no longer pale. "After two years, I did not expect to see you here again until after the death of your father."

"I hold no grudge against my father," Philip said. "He is not the reason I've stayed away."

"Nor is he the reason you've come home again now," Gustave observed.

Philip took his seat again. "No, he is not."

"Were you my son," Gustave said, "I do not believe I would act much differently than your father has, with the amount of information you have given him."

Philip flashed the old man a half smile. "Explanations make little difference to Sire Geoffrey," he said. "And you know that since Jean has become King I could have taken up the sword for France again. But I chose not to. Do not bring up this argument again, Gustave. Our generation has already seen far too much death; I have no wish to add to it. I choose not to carry a sword."

No one had approved of Philip's decision to renounce the sword, least of all Gustave, the old teacher who had sharpened Philip's skills for battle. But no one, not Gustave or Philip's family, could ever change Philip's mind.

"And so you frolic your days away at Court," Gustave scoffed. "What sort of life is that for a de Saines?"

Philip did not defend himself, although Gustave's words were far from true. Frolicking was hardly part of the work he'd done at King Jean's side, trying to persuade the impetuous King to rule his kingdom with more caution. But news of the scandal seemed to render Philip's advisory work forgotten.

"I see you have heard the stories already," Philip said.

"Yes, I've heard them," Gustave replied. "And it is a sad truth to learn that you, my prized pupil of knighthood, must be banished from the King's court for your own protection because of an irate husband. And Charles of all people! Your friend; the very knight who trained at your side. Philip, if you never intend to pick up the sword, you should not allow yourself situations in which your name must be defended."

"And if I tell you the rumors were built on a falsehood?" Philip asked. "That it was none of my doing?"

Gustave's gaze held steady for a long moment. "I would believe you." Then he asked, "But does Charles know he has been cuckolded this way? If his wife was faithful after all, then surely he should know?"

"Rachel la Trau is the one who cuckolded him," Philip said sternly. "And my foolish friend has chosen to believe his wife instead of his friend." He smiled rakishly. "Let this show you, Gustave, you've been wise never to marry. Women are an evil lot, every one of them."

By the time the cock crowed the only evidence of the nighttime storm was a puddle here and there and a sweetness in the air. The sun brought welcome warmth, and when Alix woke she threw off the covers and dashed to the window. May!

She hurried to splash herself with a bit of rainwater from the bowl set on the window ledge, then covered her chemise with a brown-colored gown. With a swoop she picked up her oldest pair of leather shoes, but did not stop to put them on until down the stone stairway and out the massive wooden doors at the end of the Banquet Hall.

The sun felt warm on her sleep-freshened features, adding a glow to her already flushed cheeks. Once her shoes were tied, she ran across the bailey greensward, copper hair swinging free in the breeze. The stables were close by, just round the back of the towering keep. She took the turn at a reckless speed.

Only to be stopped stone-still in her tracks. An immovable object stood before her so suddenly she barely discerned it was there but for the blotting out of the sun for that instant before she fell. For a moment she lay still on the muddy ground, wondering what could have happened. Then, slowly, she opened her eyes. A familiar voice spoke through the haze.

"Are you all right? Are you hurt?"

His voice was surprisingly tender, and Alix wished she could see his face clearly. But with the sun so stark behind him, he was only a dark silhouette bending over her.

Alix stood. "I'm perfectly all right," she said, suddenly embarrassed. She brushed the back of her gown, only to come away with muddy hands. "Oh! Look what you've done to my gown!"

Philip de Saines laughed. "*I've* done. Forgive me, demoiselle, but you accomplished that with very little help from me." Then he put a hand on her shoulder while taking a kerchief from his pocket. "Turn around. I'll help clean you up."

On the hip where she landed was a large splotch of black mud, and with impersonal ease he wiped away the worst of the offensive muck. Alix, so stunned at his offhand manner, let him continue his ministrations far longer than was proper. At last she winced away from him.

"You are too familiar, sir," she scolded him, and took a full step back.

Philip did not look at all abashed by her protest. He merely stooped to rinse his kerchief in a deep, clear puddle nearby, then wrung it out to dry.

"You should have your maid rinse out your gown before one of your parents sees that stain," Philip suggested, adding with a teasing lilt, "It looks as though you've been tussling on the ground."

She might have been flustered by the tone, a slight innuendo that the imagined tussling had been shared with someone, but found she felt only

27

good-natured despite the fact that less than a moment ago she'd been angry with him. She knew she ought to return to the keep, at least to change her gown, but instead she fell into step beside Philip.

"Where were you off to in such a hurry?" he asked.

"To the stables," she replied. Then, seeing him look around, Alix guessed why. "I'm quite alone," she told him. "There is no chaperone."

"Is that why you ride when dawn is barely an hour old? So your father won't know you ride alone?"

She laughed. "Perhaps."

"I won't give away your secret, then," Philip said. Once again he was struck by her beauty. In the sunlight, coppery hues danced in her hair and her eyes sparkled green, looking larger than they had last night. Long, dark lashes surrounded them. It was a wonder he'd forgotten, even for a few hours, just how lovely those eyes were. Her skin looked soft as a child's, fair and clear just like a baby's. But he knew she was every bit a woman. "I was going to the stables as well," he said. "Would you object to an escort?"

Alix's smile answered him as they covered the rest of the distance to the stables. There they were greeted by James, marshal of the stables, who addressed Philip happily.

" 'Tis Sire Philip, home at last!" he exclaimed. "I saw your horse in its stall this morning and rejoiced in your homecoming!"

Philip patted the middle-aged man's sturdy shoulder affectionately. "I should have known you could still be found here, James. Even the pestilence couldn't get the best of you."

"How could I leave this earth, my lord, knowing there is no one to see to my children?"

Philip spoke to Alix. "James is the only man I know who can refer to horses as his children and not be accused of sorcery."

"It's because he loves them so," Alix said, and as they entered the stable she went to the tall palfrey

28

in the first stall and patted the horse's nose gently. "My lord Philip, the whole of Chateau de Saines may fall around you, but with James still here, the horses will have the best of care."

James, looking quite humble beneath such praise, bowed his head in embarrassment. Then, eager to have the moment over, he called to a young boy at the far end of the stable. "Ready Morivek and Cedric for riding," James commanded, and the boy hastened to the task, starting with Cedric.

"Morivek has missed you, Demoiselle Alix," James said, watching the palfrey nuzzle Alix's shoulder. "It's been more than a week since your last ride."

"I see the Demoiselle Alix has charmed you into keeping her secret," Philip said to James. "How long have you let her ride unchaperoned without telling anyone?"

Looking properly ashamed, James faltered. "Oh, my lord—"

Alix immediately defended him. "He has guarded my secret well, Lord Philip, ever since I first came to live here. He knows his children are safe with me, and I safe with them."

"True enough," James agreed. "Demoiselle Alix rides like a young knight. You will see for yourself."

Soon both horses were ready for mounting, and without another word spoken it became obvious that today Alix would indeed have a chaperone, Philip himself. James assisted Alix astride Morivek, and then with a wave he bid them a fair ride.

"Perhaps you are the one who should be accused of sorcery," Philip said with a smile as they nudged their mounts to a trot outside the bailey. "James does not trust anyone easily when it comes to these horses."

"I will prove to you, my lord, that I am a capable rider." Her tone was challenging. "Shall we race?"

They were well outside the stone walls, approaching the rise of a gentle, treeless slope. Alix had sped over the distance to the shelter of the forest edge many times, fearful of being caught unchaperoned. Even now she could feel Morivek prance with expectation, only waiting for the nudge to run.

"To the first tree?" Philip suggested, and Alix could not have been more pleased. She was already having difficulty keeping Morivek back.

With a nod the race was on. Alix bent low on Morivek, who sped off with no more encouragement than a loosened rein and a whispered word. Morivek flew the distance, his sure-footed hooves barely touching the ground.

Alix's laughter was lost on the wind. Never once did she look back, so confident was she of her lead. Though she'd never ridden Cedric, the palfrey given to Philip, she believed no other horse could run as free as Morivek.

Cedric proved her wrong. Whether Philip was a superior rider or Cedric a superior horse, or a combination of both, Alix could not tell. In the last moment before nearing the first towering pine, Alix saw the shadow at her side. Morivek obviously had no ambition to win, for Alix felt him slow now that he was so near the cover of the pine just as he always did. Cedric reached the wood first.

The chill morning air showed on the breath of all four of them as they circled the tree, entering the pine forest.

"I stand convinced, my lady," Philip said, a full smile upon his handsome face.

Alix felt exhilarated. She'd never before shared her early morning, secret ride. She'd never wanted to. But now, somehow she knew it would never be the same.

They let their mounts walk the pine-nettle ground at a leisurely pace. Sun rays shot straight and narrow through the branches, setting the green forest alive with light. The air smelled damp but fresh after last night's storm, and some of the branches, still wet, winked sparkling raindrops at them from above.

"Where did you learn to ride?" Philip asked at length. "James was right when he said you ride like a young knight."

"Perhaps because a knight taught me," she answered. "Simon, my brother, used to let me ride with him for long hours when he was home."

"Ah, yes, Simon. The famous Beauchamp knight."

There was something in his tone which caught her interest, the same as it had last night. What was it about knighthood that affected this man? She knew he'd been a famous knight himself once, and now he spoke of the order as if it were somehow less than glorious. But she could not muster the courage to ask; whatever knighthood meant to Philip, it obviously had left some sort of scar. She wasn't sure she wanted to remind him of that.

"Have you been away from home long, my lord?" she asked instead.

"Two years," he said. He gazed back toward the keep, the highest tower and the de Saines flag visible above the trees. "But it seems like much longer. The little I saw of the Chateau seems to have changed a great deal."

Alix sighed, aware of the difference in the Chateau even in the year she'd lived there. "I can guess what you mean. Times have been troublesome for everyone, my lord."

"So they say," he replied, as if that were a poor excuse for the changes.

"Perhaps now that you are home, Lord Philip, you can aid your father in running the Chateau. I have great respect for your father, sire, but of late it seems he would do well with some help."

"The evidence of that is everywhere," Philip said. "Surely he cannot be unaware of how decrepit the Chateau has become."

"The decay has taken over little by little," she said. "To you it seems sudden, but to your father, and even to me, the changes are not so drastic, because we have lived here day by day. Surely there was evidence of the Plague at Court."

31

Philip's mouth twisted in a half smile. "Ah, but there are more important things at Court than pestilence, demoiselle. Chivalrous love, for one. Feasting continued even during the worst of the Plague; the opulence never changed. The King," he added with just a slight hint of disrespect, "wouldn't have it any other way."

They came to the edge of a steep incline which overlooked a small village down below. Two neat rows of cottages stood there, but as Philip gazed at them he saw with surprise they were nearly empty.

"Has the Plague so devastated the de Saines serfs? Where are all the children? And the women doing their laundry in the stream?"

Alix's gaze followed his. "The Plague hit hardest here, my lord. Those who survived, save two families, left the area in favor of freedom."

"My father freed the serfs?" His tone revealed his surprise.

"Oh, no, my lord. They fled."

Philip continued to gaze at the barren village, a thoughtful light entering his eyes. "What about the other villages? Are they as empty as this one?"

She shook her head. "No; this one lost the most. I'm afraid even those who are fully able to work spend their time almost uselessly. Things are not so . . ." she searched for a word not detrimental to Lord Geoffrey's lack of direction. " . . . so orderly any more."

Philip let out a long breath. "Have the times truly gotten the best of my father?" he asked, so quietly Alix was unsure she was meant to hear.

"Oh, no, sire!"

"What other reason could there be?"

She'd never before had need to formulate her thoughts on the subject, but surprisingly enough found she had many. "It isn't only your father, my lord. The serfs themselves have changed. It's as if the Plague left them without respect for life as it was before. They no longer care to work—they see no future in it. They know too well how tenuous life is. Your father simply cannot force them to

32

perform their duties."

"But there is hope now," Philip said. "The Plague has subsided—it's been two years since the worst of it."

"Perhaps they would believe you if you spoke of such things as hope and future," Alix said slowly. "Your father, my lord, does not. That may be why his serfs are not hopeful for the future—they think your father, left with so much more than they, does not believe in a hopeful future for himself, or his family."

"Tell me, Demoiselle Alix," Philip said with interest, "since you have lived here for the past year you must have gotten to know my father well. Would you say my father has given up? Evidence abounds at the Chateau of his lethargy." Philip waited expectantly for her answer, realizing that in the short time since they'd met, he'd come to respect her opinion.

Alix considered her answer first. "Lord Geoffrey does not seem to care as much about the Chateau as he once did, that is true. But he still cares about many things, so lethargy is perhaps too strong a word. He cares very much about his family— about Lady Eleanore, about Julian . . . about . . ." She'd been about to include Lord Philip himself, but in all honesty she could not. Lord Geoffrey had never once uttered Philip's name, although he spoke so often and so fondly of Julian.

Philip gave her an unabashed, knowing smile, seeing her discomfort. "You needn't compromise your honesty by trying to convince me Lord Geoffrey has ever spoken kindly of me. I am not one of my father's favorite people, as I'm sure you'll guess once you see us in each other's company. Lord Geoffrey has never been one to hide his emotions for the sake of a peaceful meal or mere civility."

"You are his son, his heir," Alix said. "Surely he cannot dislike you as you think."

Philip just gave her another knowing smile, as if to say she should wait and see for herself.

Alix knew she was more than lucky in having

parents who had shown her care and consideration. More than once her mother, Marie, had softened Lord Giles's sternness toward Alix. Marie had, in fact, been Alix's best friend since coming to the Chateau. And although Alix's father was quite distant in his behavior toward her, Alix knew he wanted her happiness. How sad that Philip did not know the love of his parents. They could love, that she knew. The way they spoke of Julian had shown her that.

Philip pulled the rein on Cedric, and they turned back in the direction of the Chateau. The conversation had gone on too long, Philip thought. Why had they ever begun talking about parents? He could see all too clearly that the young Demoiselle Alix felt sorry for him. And pity was one charity he could do without, no matter who offered it.

They rode back to the Keep in silence. Alix saw the stiffness in Philip's back, and wondered what she had said to put it there. Though his gaze traveled over the unplowed fields, empty cottages, clogged drainage streams with increasing attention, she knew more than just the needs of the Chateau had drawn him away.

Just as they entered the tall double doorway at the forebuilding of the Keep, a servant bustled up to them, looking quite agitated.

"Lord Philip, your father wishes to see you in the Banquet Hall." Then, as an afterthought it seemed, he added quietly with downcast eyes, "Welcome home, my lord."

The servant disappeared quickly, his slippered feet silent on the stone floor.

Alix followed Philip into the Banquet Hall, hoping to slip along the shadows of the huge room to return to her own chambers.

But Philip whispered to her just as she was about to bid him farewell. "I fear your secret morning rides are about to be discovered. Isn't that couple beside my parents the Lord and Lady Beauchamp?"

Alix looked in the direction of his gaze. True enough, her parents sat beside his at the large banquet table at the far end of the room. The four were alone but for two servants pouring wine, and even from where Alix stood, she could hear Lord Geoffrey's voice echo off the damp walls of the Hall.

When Giles Beauchamp saw his daughter enter the Hall beside Philip, he stood, motioning for Alix to approach.

It was true that Alix had neglected to tell either of her parents she enjoyed a ride early in the morning, but surely it was not a great crime? Nonetheless, seeing her father's stern features, she swallowed hard as she neared the table at Philip's side.

"Philip." Geoffrey de Saines spoke the name as if his son were a stranger—one he was not sure he liked upon first sight.

Philip bowed respectfully, although Alix noticed he did not bend as low as formally expected. Lord Geoffrey did not seem to take notice.

"You should remember the Beauchamps. Lady Marie and Lord Giles."

Philip bowed again, this time a trifle lower.

Alix watched the scene with interest. How odd, she thought. Was this the sort of welcome Philip received upon coming home after two years away? Even his mother, seated across the table, did not greet him. And Lord Geoffrey looked anything but pleased. They did not even offer him a cup of wine.

"It seems you already know Alix," Lord Geoffrey said.

"If I may speak," Giles Beauchamp said, his gaze still upon Alix. "I would like to ask where my daughter has been at such an early hour." For a moment his gaze went to Philip, as if wondering if he could answer the question. But he looked to Alix for an answer.

"I was riding, Father. It is the first of May, you know. At home we always used to ride on the first day of . . ."

"Has the date anything to do with your being outside the Keep with Philip de Saines?"

Giles Beauchamp's voice was quiet, controlled,

but he spoke as if his daughter being anywhere with Philip was a crime too great for words. Alix looked from her father to Lord Geoffrey, and finally to her mother, whose downcast eyes gave away the most. Alix was not mistaken, there was anger beneath the civil tongues of both her father and Philip's. Her mother's submissive posture warned her.

"Demoiselle Alix and I went for a short ride together," Philip said before Alix could respond to her father's question. "I saw that she had no chaperone—"

"And took immediate advantage of the situation!" The irate statement came not from Alix's father, but from Geoffrey de Saines.

Philip stiffened ever so slightly; Alix felt the tension rise in him as if it had reached out and touched her. "I see you have heard the stories from Court," Philip said.

"Who hasn't?" Geoffrey thundered. "My son, the same utter fool who gave up the sword for no apparent reason, has now resorted to raping his best friend's wife!" Then he emitted a long sigh, as if trying to catch his lost temper.

Alix stole a sidelong glance at Philip, hoping to read his reaction. His father left no doubt in anyone's mind; he believed his son guilty of the scandal. But Philip was stoic, without a hint of emotion showing on his face.

"You are home not one full day and already you offend our guests," Geoffrey went on, his voice more controlled now. "Didn't you realize Alix's parents would never have allowed you to escort their daughter because of this scandal?"

"Surely my parents would not prefer I ride alone?" Alix spoke up boldly. Lord Geoffrey had become accustomed to Alix speaking out, and so he did not look surprised that she had something to say now. "I assure you—all of you—Lord Philip was more than courteous and you had nothing to fear, despite rumors from Court. I wished to go for a ride and, seeing I had no chaperone, Lord Philip graciously volunteered so I would not have to give up the ride altogether."

Although it was not entirely true, the words seemed to appease both fathers. Yet why Alix felt compelled to defend Philip, she did not know! Not that he looked in need of protection, she thought with some offense. With a second glance she saw none of his father's ravings had penetrated that untouched countenance whatsoever.

"It seems no harm has been done," spoke up Eleanore de Saines. "Perhaps if Philip were to apologize for not requesting Lord Giles's permission first, everything will be forgotten."

Eleanore looked from Giles to her son, and Alix watched Eleanore's eyes. They were deep, azure blue, not unlike Philip's. But was there no love in those blue eyes, so like her son's? No welcome for him at all?

Philip bowed once more. "My mother is of course correct, Lord Giles," Philip said, affably enough to appease even Lord Geoffrey. "I should have requested your permission first, which I will not hesitate to do next time."

Next time? Alix thought, and she knew her own surprise was reflected by her father. But she put that aside, glad the morning had calmed without too much ado.

Marie Beauchamp stood. "Then I shall see Alix to her room, if we may be excused?"

Marie rounded the banquet table and came to Alix's side, looping her daughter's arm through hers. "There are a few things we must discuss on our own, since part of the blame must rest upon Alix's shoulders." Then, bending her head closer to Alix's, she whispered, "Walk directly in front of me, my dear, or we shall see Hell itself rise up before us."

Perplexed, Alix let her mother propel her forward. Marie followed so closely Alix felt her mother's slippered foot scrape the back of her heel not once but three times over. She felt her mother's urgency, but though she tried could not decipher the cause.

"Alix!"

Her name fairly boomed from her father's lips, and the moment it sounded she felt her mother's grasp upon her arm tighten protectively.

"He's seen it," Marie whispered with dread, and they both turned back to Lord Giles, who strode toward them with two ruddy splotches of anger evident upon his cheeks.

"What is this?" he demanded.

Alix looked down at the dried dirt on the back of her gown. "Why, it's dirt, of course. Whatever is the matter?" she asked innocently. "This is my very oldest dress and I . . ."

Suddenly the truth dawned, and her eyes went to Philip, who looked quite annoyed at the cause for renewed anger. Lord Geoffrey approached his son, every bit as infuriated and distrustful as Alix's father.

"I suppose you can tell us how the backside of the poor girl's dress got sullied? She may be too ashamed to tell all, but by God you shall! Did you have something to do with it?"

Philip scowled, then glanced at Alix and sent his gaze skyward at the ridiculous situation. "Yes, Father," Philip said, "I did contribute to the stain."

Alix almost laughed, and would have had her mother not held her arm so painfully tight.

"Well?" Lord Geoffrey persisted. "Would you care to tell us the details?"

"Are you sure you want to hear the truth, Father? It's quite . . . filthy."

This time Alix did laugh, and all eyes went to her as if she were mad. No doubt the crime against her had rendered her witless, was the thought written upon Lord Geoffrey's face.

"Tell us what happened, Alix," Marie Beauchamp asked pleadingly. "The two of you may get your revenge on your fathers for this unpleasant morning some other way."

"Revenge?" Lord Giles caught the word. "What cause has she for revenge? We've done nothing but concern ourselves with her welfare, and you talk of revenge?"

38

"It's quite easy to see nothing happened," Marie said. "I know our daughter well enough to guess that, even if you don't, Giles. But the way you and Geoffrey behave, it's little wonder that Alix and Philip would like to see you make fools of yourselves over nothing at all."

The situation was intolerable, and even Alix sensed she and Philip had gone too far. So she spoke the truth. "I fell in a puddle—quite by accident. I shouldn't have been running, but I was, and I suppose falling was my punishment for doing such a childish thing."

Lord Giles looked from his daughter to Philip, his skepticism apparent. But evidently he decided nothing worse than his daughter's dunking had taken place, and he bowed to Lord Geoffrey.

"We shall all retire for the time being, my lord," he said. "I'm sure the best thing for us to do is end this vexatious meeting."

Lord Geoffrey hardly seemed to hear. He never took his angry gaze from Philip, and as Marie nudged Alix along, Alix heard Lord Geoffrey speak.

"You dare to come home after the shame you've brought to your name! The King should not have limited banishment from Court and Paris alone—he should have banished you from France itself!"

With one backward glance just before leaving the huge room, Alix saw the scene she left behind. Eleanore de Saines sat somewhat placidly behind the table, looking on with neither compassion for her son nor support for her husband. Lord Geoffrey stood barely a hand's spread from his son, looking so incensed she feared he might resort to physical blows.

But Philip hardly looked worried. He stood taller than his father, only slightly stiff, eyeing Lord Geoffrey in a detached way, as if his ravings were aimed elsewhere. No, she thought, Philip hardly seemed familiar with such an emotion as fear. Certainly it wasn't cowardice which sent him home, away from the scandal at Court.

Alix had never before been interested in scandals and gossip—at least not until she'd met Philip de Saines.

3

"This dress is beyond repair," Marie pronounced with finality. Then she let it fall in a heap, and it was picked up almost immediately by the servant who had just filled Alix's bath.

Alix, from inside the steaming tub of water, eyed the servant carrying her old dress away. She would miss the tattered linen gown, despite its unbecoming, faded brown color. It was the dress she always wore to ride Morivek, for it was by far the most comfortable garment she possessed. She only hoped her mother wouldn't see the shoes she'd worn—each had a hole in its sole. They sat on the floor beside the bed, and with a worried glance she wished she'd had the foresight to kick them underneath.

The serving girl, after discarding the dress, returned with soap in hand and began lathering Alix's thick, waistlength copper curls. Marie Beauchamp stood by the wide window, looking out at the view of the forest some distance off.

"Do you remember Philip from when you used to visit here as a child?" Marie asked, her gaze still directed outside.

Alix wiped soap from her eyes. "Yes, I remember him somewhat. I saw him only once or twice."

"He's older than you—perhaps by as many as ten years. What do you remember of him?"

Alix was thoughtful. "Truthfully, very little," she responded, eyes now closed against further invasion of soap. But behind those lids she saw

40

Philip again, just the way she had eight years ago. He wore the full, shining armor and red crest of a knight, the de Saines dragon emblazoned upon his chest. He was mounted on a black charger, and in his gloved hand was a sword. She remembered it clearly now; he'd been practicing with Gustave, the old teacher who lived in the tower. His face guard had been pushed back and she could see his smile. Such a handsome smile . . . not unlike the one he'd shown this morning, just after their race.

Her mother's voice interrupted the vision. "Do you know anything about the scandal Lord Geoffrey mentioned?"

Alix looked at Marie. All of these questions were most unlike her usually direct mother. Alix knew Marie Beauchamp well; this line of questioning was definitely leading somewhere. And Alix wanted to know where.

"Only that it involved a woman," Alix answered.

Marie left the window's side. She stood directly in front of the bath, gazing at her daughter as if trying to see into her very thoughts.

"Philip de Saines molested his best friend's wife," Marie said bluntly.

Alix gave no reaction; she stared at her mother as unmoved as if they'd been discussing the weather.

"That isn't all," continued Marie. "When his friend, the cuckolded husband Charles la Trau, would have challenged Philip at a Tournament, Philip left Court like a coward."

Alix refused to believe such accusations; Philip de Saines was no coward. "Philip was banished from Court for the scandal," she said. "How could he stay to confront this Charles la Trau if he was commanded to leave by King Jean himself?"

"The King was merely protecting him," Marie told her. "There is obviously very little you know about Philip de Saines."

"Is there some reason I *should* know anything about him? At least all of the reproachful information you seem so eager to tell?"

Marie took a deep breath, fortifying herself.

41

"Philip de Saines has returned home for an unspecified amount of time—perhaps for good. And who knows how long we will be here, sharing his roof. There are few women here who might attract Philip's eye—his plump cousin will hardly warrant a second glance from him."

"Just what are you trying to tell me, Mother?" Alix asked, intrigued.

"Philip de Saines is young and unmarried—heir to this very Chateau and all its wealth and land."

"That much I know of him."

"Then isn't it logical to assume he will be looking for a wife soon? Someone to give him heirs to pass on his wealth?"

"I cannot believe you want me to hold my hopes for fulfilling that position—not after you've made certain I know the worst of him."

"Of course I have no desire for you to marry Lord Philip!" Marie exclaimed. "Your father would never stand for it, regardless of Philip's wealth. Do you think he would allow a man whose name is so blemished into our family? Only our wealth is gone, my dear, not our nobility."

Alix stood, allowing the servant to wrap her in a huge linen towel.

"That is Father speaking through your mouth, Mother," Alix stated. "I know you would welcome anyone into the family if either of your children were in love."

Marie's eyelids fluttered downward, hiding the embarrassed confession her eyes revealed. Nonetheless, she said, "Love is something which comes after marriage, if you are lucky. It did with your father and I. When two people share children, it's hard not to love one another."

Alix waved away the servant combing out her wet hair, and went to her mother's side. She gave her mother a kiss on her fair-skinned cheek and then hugged her close.

"I'm glad for that, Mother," she said. "I'm glad you love Father; he needs someone."

"Alix! You sound as if no one else loves him."

"Simon does, I'm sure of that."

"And you?"

Alix was thoughtful, but finally smiled. "Yes, I love him. But not the way Simon does. Father always seems just a bit uncomfortable with me. He isn't that way with Simon."

The ruffle of worry that had appeared momentarily disappeared from Marie's brow. The possibility that her own daughter did not love Giles was unthinkable. But now she relaxed. "That is because Simon is a knight, my dear. Simon and your father are very much alike. Were you a boy-child and a knight, your father would treat you the same as Simon. But as a girl, you are a mystery to him—even with your hoydenish ways."

"Hoydenish!" she repeated, but her surprise was muffled as the maid dropped a soft, sleeveless chemise over her head to be worn next to the skin. When her head popped through the round neckline, she looked at her mother with a light-hearted grin. "Just because I like to ride horses?"

"Oh, that, and more."

When Alix looked at Marie expectantly, Marie continued, holding up a hand and counting the various points one by one.

"You are a better chess player than any man I know; you would rather be shooting an arrow at a target than stitching a needle through a tapestry—even though I must admit you can stitch far more expertly than I—and you are inherently more out-spoken than any bold knight or lofty lord. Those are just a few of the qualities, endearing as they are, that are not exactly typical of a noble gentle-woman."

"I'm afraid not everyone finds me quite as endearing as you, Mother." Then she added as she tied the bodice of a linen underrobe, "But I'm happy to have at least one friend."

"You could have many friends here at the Chateau, if only you would avail yourself of the others." She looked around the room. "This private chamber, for example. If you returned to the women's bower, I'm sure you would find many friends."

Alix did not remind her mother that she'd tried that already. She enjoyed being away from those others who shared the Chateau, those who laughed too loud, who talked too long, who tried too hard to get Alix to join silly games. Some people, she admitted, were quite friendly and pleasant. But how could she be a friend to anyone when all she thought of was leaving Chateau de Saines, returning home to Beauchamp Estate, where she and her family belonged? Those others might belong here, but Alix did not.

Finally the servant tied a loose chain belt hung low on Alix's hips; the silver contrasted brightly with the deep crimson of her satin gown. At her throat, resting against her skin where the neckline plunged, she wore the string of sparkling rubies her father had given her on her sixteenth birthday. One other ornament completed her costume: a small jewelled dagger hung from her belt, and when she walked the tiny diamonds and sapphires at the hilt caught the light with a twinkle.

Though Alix was now ready to leave her chamber, it was obvious by the look on Marie's face that she had something else to say. Alix waited, pretending to inspect her dress, until Marie was ready to speak.

"I hope you know why I mentioned Philip earlier."

Alix shook her head in all honesty. She hadn't the faintest idea why her mother had made certain she knew of Philip's less honorable aspects.

After a sigh, Marie spoke bluntly. "I saw the way you looked at Philip when the two of you entered the Hall."

"Oh?" Alix turned away, brushing imaginary lint from the back of her gown. She hoped her mother hadn't seen the red stain she felt warm her cheeks.

"You looked at him in a way no woman should look at a man—unless she wants that man to notice her." Marie's voice grew serious. "And I warn you, Alix, your father will not allow you a future with Philip. Philip will no longer fight as a knight, and that is perhaps his greatest crime in your father's eyes."

Alix gazed at her mother with interest. "But Philip fought as a knight many times, Mother. Do you know what happened to make him stop?"

"No, I do not, not fully. I do not believe even Lord Geoffrey himself knows the answer to that."

The conversation echoed in Alix's memory throughout the morning. Not the scandal or the fact that Philip would no longer fight, but that her mother thought it necessary to warn Alix against Philip. What had Marie seen in Alix's gaze when she'd entered the Hall at Philip's side?

Even now, thoughts of Philip made her pulse quicken ever so slightly. Had her mother guessed her pulse raced as well? Was Alix so transparent that she could hide none of these strange new emotions? Not from her mother, and perhaps not even from Philip himself?

Her cheeks burned hotter. Had Philip seen what her mother had? God's blood, she sincerely hoped not! Certainly one scandal involving a woman was enough for Philip right now; surely he did not need another woman in his thoughts. She must hide these new, odd emotions.

And that's just what they were, new and very odd. She'd never before been burdened by such conflicting thoughts. Perhaps her mother had been right to warn her; certainly it *would* be foolish to nurture any fanciful notions of Philip de Saines. Her father simply would not stand for it. She would have realized that by this morning's events even without her mother's reminder. And wasn't she holding herself in store for a knight? A knight just like the one she'd seen on that black charger eight years ago ... And obviously that man was no longer Philip.

Yes, she wanted a knight. Needed a knight, she reminded herself. One who could confront the Montforts for what they'd done to her home, one who could join forces with her brother Simon if necessary and see that the Montforts never again raised their ugly hands in violence.

Each time Philip entered her mind that morning she cast him out, each time more determinedly than the last. But still, by the time the noon dinner was announced by the blow of the horn, she couldn't help but realize this was the first meal she'd ever looked forward to since coming to the Chateau de Saines.

The Hall was always full for dinner, the largest meal of the day. Between the de Saines and their relatives, knights and men-at-arms, guests, village clergy, squires, servants and entertainers, the Hall bustled with activity. Voices echoed off the high ceiling, booted feet tapped a tuneless melody on the mosaic tiled floor. Lighted sconces placed at even intervals between open windows cast out every shadow. The trestle tables were covered with clean, brightly colored cloths and laid out with silver-rimmed bowls, silver spoons and steel knives. The high table where the de Saineses, Alix's uncle Bishop Beauchamp, and the rest of the Beauchamps as highest-ranking guests sat was decorated with early blooming flowers and tall silver goblets. Behind each lord or knight's chair stood an attendant, richly dressed in the colors of his master.

Those who had no attendant or squire were tended to by servants of the Chateau, who now stood with basins and ewers of steaming water and fresh towels for all participants of the meal to wash themselves with. Alix took her seat beside her mother, rinsing her hands as was the custom. But as she did so she noted an empty seat three chairs down, closest by Lady Eleanore. Philip was nowhere to be seen.

The meal did not wait for him. Lady Eleanore signalled for dinner to begin, and Bishop Beauchamp said Grace. Afterward, the procession of servants began, starting with wine bearers and the pantler with bread and butter.

"Word has it that your son has returned home at last," said Richard de Saines, Lord Geoffrey's younger cousin. He did not look like a de Saines; he was short and squat and already balding, although he was still young. Alix didn't like the man; he was forever ogling any female present—herself and even her mother included. At present, however, his eyes were on the sumptuous dinner to be consumed and, Alix noticed, the gleam in his eye toward the food resembled the one he used toward women. "Will Lord Philip be joining us today?" he asked, eyes still coveting the approaching food bearers.

Alix looked at Lord Geoffrey as indeed did all his guests, waiting for a reply to Richard's question. Lord Geoffrey's face darkened with an unmistakable scowl, but when he spoke his tone was civil enough.

"If he's hungry," Lord Geoffrey said, sounding considerably lighter than he obviously felt, "he will be here."

Lady Eleanore's brother-in-law, Sir Roger of Poitou, spoke up next. "My squire tells me he saw Lord Philip at the granary. It seems he's been assessing conditions of the Chateau all morning. I myself saw him at the winery."

Richard chuckled at that, although to Alix his laughter sounded like little more than a cackle. "A likely place for you to run into anyone," he sneered.

Everyone knew of Sir Roger's penchant for wine—wine of any quality. And since coming to Chateau de Saines, where the drink was known for its excellence, he was never far from cup or jug. But nonetheless, Alix thought him a fair and kindly man. Anyone married to Eleanore's sister Jeanne was bound to look for solace wherever it might be found, she thought to herself.

There was no time for further banter between the relatives of the de Saines. At that moment, Philip walked in and all eyes went inevitably to him.

Unlike everyone else present, Philip hadn't bothered to dress for dinner in his finest attire. He looked every bit a peasant—a poor one at that. Dressed in a knee-length tunic bound at the waist by a leather belt, the only evidence of the garment belonging to nobility was a faded row of silver leaves embroidered along its edge. Brown hose and old leather boots covered his muscular legs, and from where Alix sat she guessed he'd been walking by the mill—the muddiest section of the Chateau. He detained a servant carrying a ewer and basin just long enough to wash his hands, then took his seat next to Lady Eleanore, seeming totally unaware the entire meal had stopped for him.

Marie Beauchamp's gaze was the first to leave Philip de Saines. She looked at her daughter, and frowned at what she saw. Alix's green eyes were just a bit wider than usual, but wide enough for Marie to see the difference. There was a blush, ever so faint, upon her daughter's fair cheeks, and an almost imperceptible smile hovered around her small, well-formed mouth. And, Marie concluded with some concern, her daughter had never looked lovelier.

Richard spoke up first. "Does no one welcome Lord Geoffrey's heir?" he asked, his voice somewhat nasal. He smiled, but Alix, who watched closely, thought it was a viperish one.

Philip drank his first cup of wine thirstily, then lifted the goblet for a second cupful. He concentrated on his meal, obviously famished after a full morning's work. He neither responded to nor seemed interested in the conversation around him.

"Perhaps we should have a feast in Lord Philip's honor," Constance de Saines suggested, somewhat shyly, from her seat opposite her brother Richard. She was as plump as her brother but, Alix had learned long ago, displayed none of Richard's malice. Even now, her suggestion was made with sincerity.

But it was ignorant sincerity, Alix feared. She saw a scowl pass Lord Geoffrey's face again, and knew the idea of a feast for Philip did not in any way meet his approval.

It was Richard who spoke. "I certainly did not mean anything so elaborate, Constance. Do you think Lord Geoffrey would hold a feast for any son who returns with the de Saines name disgraced?"

Lord Geoffrey offered no defense for his son. He bit into a large piece of tender mutton as though it were tough as leather, saying nothing.

Constance de Saines looked as if her dinner had taken the wrong pipe down; she turned quite red and quick tears filled her eyes.

Philip's gaze left his full bowl of food to rest on his cousin Constance. He smiled at her, looking friendly and perhaps a bit sorry for her for eliciting the disapproval which so obviously embarrassed her. "It's kind of you, Constance, to want to welcome me. But to be perfectly honest, the de Saines family has no business holding a feast for any reason. We can ill afford it."

Lord Geoffrey sputtered at that. "What! How dare you say such a thing! Even if it were true, you have no business saying such things before my guests."

"But it is true, Father," Philip said, still content to eat although he guessed his father had lost his appetite. Lord Geoffrey laid down his spoon the moment Philip mentioned the poor state of their finances. "The granaries are nearly empty," Philip continued, "the mills in the worst condition I've ever seen them, the lands almost totally un-worked, not to mention that we seem to have lost two-thirds of our serfs. The horses," Philip concluded with a glance toward Alix, "seem to be the only possessions in prime condition, thanks to James."

Alix recalled her own words to Philip that the whole of Chateau de Saines could fall, but with James to see after the horses, at least they would be well cared for. Philip's glance told her he recalled those words as well.

Eleanore de Saines laid a hand on her husband's arm, seeing his ire rising. She spoke calmly to her son. "We have lost many serfs to the Plague, Philip. And many have simply fled, regardless of their duties to us. Times are hard everywhere, as our guests will tell."

There was a murmur of agreement, then Richard spoke up. "Perhaps the young lord has an idea of how to save the Chateau—if indeed, cousin, it does need saving."

"I have an idea," Philip said slowly, pushing aside the remainder of his meal. It was obvious he chose his words carefully. "It is one which should have been done long ago." He leaned back in his chair, ready for a dispute. "Free the remaining serfs."

It seemed the entire room waited expectantly for Lord Geoffrey's reaction. It was true that most lords had freed their serfs long ago—even Alix's father had done so for practical reasons. They had little choice but to let them go when her father could no longer afford to house, clothe and feed them. But Chateau de Saines, with its long-standing wealth, clung to the old ways. They were like a monument to an age that had passed too quickly for the nobility's liking.

Lord Geoffrey spoke surprisingly quietly. "We will not discuss this, Philip."

But Philip would not be put back. "It isn't a horde of coinage we need now; it's men to work the lands and repair the damage to the Chateau. Certainly our serfs would be more willing to stay here than flee somewhere else in search of freedom, money and betterment."

"If we cannot even afford a feast," Lord Geoffrey said somewhat smugly, "how can we afford to pay them all a wage?"

"It's quite simple; we have money, what we don't have are the ingredients for a feast: men to hunt for game, full granaries to supply the Cooks—even the number of cooks and servants is insufficient for a Chateau of this size. What we need now is men and we can afford to pay in coinage so that in the end we'll be paid rents and revenues from them and increase our wealth as well. For now, freeing the serfs is a matter of saving the Chateau."

It was a sound plan, Alix knew, and a simple

one. But she could see Lord Geoffrey did not agree.

"If those remaining serfs were freed they would flee before morning," he stated. "And then we would have no one at all to do the work which needs to be done from day to day." He took a long draft of wine, setting his goblet down firmly. "Now I'll have no more talk of this."

Alix spoke before she'd even considered the consequences. "But, Sire Geoffrey, I'm sure if there were a way to attract more workers here, you would take it. Surely Lady Eleanore would like to see the Chateau restored to its former beauty. The gardens, the greenswards, the fountains. If the serfs have fled looking for better, why not give them better right here? They would no doubt be happy to work your land if you promise something more than life as it's been since the Plague."

Lord Giles interceded before Geoffrey could respond. "It's preposterous, my lord," he said hastily. "You must forgive my outspoken daughter for voicing an opinion that is neither warranted nor asked for." He spoke while glaring at Alix, his eyes commanding her silence more than his words.

But Lord Geoffrey, who now looked less angry than before, waved away Lord Giles's apologies. "It is not the first time I've heard your daughter's opinions, Giles, and no doubt it won't be the last. But you should caution the young Demoiselle Alix, my friend. Few men want a wife with so many opinions."

Alix's unmarried state seemed of great interest to Lord Geoffrey of late, Alix thought. Just a week ago he'd looked her way at dinner, smiled his stiff, unfamiliar smile and asked how old she was. Well past the marrying age, he must have concluded from her reply, and perhaps there was something which could be done about that. Since that day he'd given her father countless bits of advice concerning the various faults she revealed at the dinner hours. On several occasions she'd been late, which he said nary a husband would tolerate, and on others she'd been too quiet, unsociable, something the Lady of a manor must never be. Once he even commented on her attire. She'd worn a veil which covered her forehead and hair; she'd put it on before her morning ride, for it had been a windy day. Lord Geoffrey asked her to remove it, reminding her only married women were required to cover their hair and that her time would come soon enough.

This present reference, however, was one with the specific design to change an unpleasant topic of conversation.

"Perhaps you would rather discuss the attributes of wifery than the affairs of the Chateau," Philip said to his father, "but I warn you, if something is not done, and done soon, the very walls of this place will come tumbling down just like Jericho's."

Lord Geoffrey caught the disdain in Philip's voice which his angry features revealed. "You will assume control over the Chateau soon enough when I am gone, Philip. And then you will learn you are fighting a losing battle. You will try your schemes and plans, but you shall learn, as I did, that the Plague left its blight on the very walls of this place."

The haunting words brooked no response, not from Philip nor anyone else, and the remainder of the meal was spent in a melancholy silence. Not the type of homecoming Alix would have expected for the heir of the great de Saines fortune.

4

The hallway leading to Alix's chamber above the kitchen was completely dark tonight. Alix didn't mind the darkness, although she knew she would have to retrieve a few of the smaller candles forgotten by the steward in the banquet hall. Blanche, Alix's servant, often expressed her fear of the total darkness and Alix hated to have the young girl scampering down the hall as if the demons of hell were right behind.

Alix grimaced, wondering if taking those candles was in some small way considered thievery. She never wanted to request more candles or refilled sconces along her hallway, fearing even so small a detail might prove an excuse for her father to have her returned to the women's bower.

It was an unending topic of conversation with Lord Giles, although not one to cause anger any more. Alix had requested permission to move her bed to an unused storeroom long ago, but even now her father had not quite accepted it. At first he'd resisted, saying it was unnatural for a young girl to sleep alone. Marie, too, had opposed the idea; she wanted Alix to befriend the women of the Chateau, not set herself apart from them. But eventually Alix convinced Marie to agree, and Marie had convinced Giles. After all, Alix argued, what harm could come from having a chamber of her own?

Even when Alix learned that Hugh, one of her father's oldest and most loyal retainers, had set up his pallet at the base of the single stairway leading to her new chamber, Alix's pleasure at her privacy was not diminished. She knew her father would never have allowed her complete freedom. Hugh's presence was for her own protection, she could still hear her father say. But she didn't mind. It was enough to have her own chamber.

Since this hallway led nowhere but Alix's chamber, there was little possibility of losing her way, even in the blackness. At last she reached her room, and stepped inside, closing the solid wooden door behind her. She welcomed the silence and darkness. Through the single window opposite her shone silvery moonlight, and she could see the furniture clearly outlined. On one wall was her bed, large and soft, piled high with no less than four quilts. Next to that was a stand with ewer and basin, and beyond that a huge box of sewing material that would only have collected dust had not Blanche seen to it. A dressing table and chest full of clothing adorned the wall across from the bed; upon the dressing table were Alix's combs, two boxes of jewelry, and a small cask of perfume her mother had given her long ago. The jewelry and perfume were all that had survived the fire; they'd been in the single storeroom that remained untouched when the Beauchamp Estate suffered its fatal inferno.

Lonely, indeed! She remembered her father's prediction that she would be lonely having no one to share her chambers with. But here was all she needed. She fingered one of the boxes upon the table. Here before her were the only reminders of home. She didn't want to be with all those other women who didn't care that they'd left behind their own homes for one reason or another. How could she be lonely when all she wanted to do was escape the company of every inhabitant of this crowded Chateau? Her father had forgotten that she used to sleep alone at their own, less populous Estate. It was there, as she was growing up, that her independent spirit had been born.

Alix sat on the stone ledge at the window. Did she truly wish to escape the company of every inhabitant? She surprised herself with the question. Wasn't she happy to be alone tonight?

She'd left the full banquet hall just after the evening meal because she'd felt unutterably bored. Philip had not shown up at all for the meal, although she insisted to herself that it hardly mattered. Each time her gaze went to the hall entryway, as if searching for the sole latecomer, she silently scolded herself, admitting what a fool she was. What did it matter that Philip had not come for dinner? It didn't matter. It couldn't possibly.

Rather than stay behind and listen to the

evening musical or linger over of cup of mulled cider, as she'd often done in the company of her parents, she left the room saying she was tired. But she wasn't; she just could not sit there on that hard, unyielding chair any longer, succumbing to that undeniable but unwitting feeling of waiting.

How strange she felt! As she gazed outside, the vastness of the Chateau only intensified her restlessness. With so huge a dwelling, why did she feel as though she were trapped in a cage? She saw the thick stone walls that enclosed the Chateau; they were meant to protect, she told herself, not to confine.

Soon Hugh would be laying his pallet down at the end of the stairway. And she would be in for the night.

Just then, as she was about to turn her gaze from outside, an unfamiliar light caught her eye. High above, on the far end of the Chateau, a small window glowed bright. Strange, she thought, for someone to be up in the abandoned tower. The one opposite that was lit often, for Gustave, the old teacher lived there. But no one lived in the highest tower—no one ever had, at least since Alix had been there. For what reason? It used to serve as a lookout point, but Gustave's smaller tower served almost as well. There was hardly reason for a lookout these days; the de Saineses, though not without enemies like the Montforts, were so powerful it seemed ludicrous to imagine anyone attacking their walls.

Alix turned her back on the outside as the restlessness rose once again. She reminded herself that Hugh would be settling soon; if she was to do anything about her discontent she must do it now.

She left her chamber, taking the dark passageway down to the kitchen rather than back to the Banquet Hall.

Three scullery maids huddled over large kettles of water, elbow-deep in suds. Nearby, Cook sat eating a late supper. When he saw her he grinned a familiar grin and greeted her.

"Ah! So you've come for a second helping of my

55

pastry! I knew the strawberries would appeal to you, Demoiselle Alix."

Alix laughed. "I had two pastries already, Cook, and enjoyed every bite. I'm off for a walk."

Cook raised a fatherly brow. "Out the kitchen way, Demoiselle Alix?"

"Yes, Cook," she said, a bit firmly, then continued toward the door.

Cook's tut-tut did not give her pause; she'd left this way before, and each time Cook asked if her parents knew of her late-evening, solitary jaunts. But Alix knew she need not answer; Cook guessed the truth anyway. So far, however, he had not given her away, but Alix was well aware he disapproved.

The night air felt cool, with a gentle, western breeze. The scent of roses and honeysuckle, long since grown wild, beckoned to her. In the light of the bright half moon, the garden resembled a dark, miniature jungle, natural and untouched by man's cultivating hand. Long branches of untamed bushes reached out, tentacle-like, and swayed in the breeze as if to touch Alix with a will of their own when she passed. Except for the tall stone walls, some grown thick with ivy, Alix could have imagined herself far away . . . Far from this Chateau de Saines which had never been her home.

Idly, she glanced up at the deserted tower. It appeared to be abandoned once again, for the light which had shone just moments ago was now gone.

The path down the center of the garden was almost too narrow to navigate. Thorny boughs snagged her surcoat and scratched through her long sleeves. One jagged bristle caught at her palm with a sting, but she wasn't deterred. She knew in the center of the garden was a stone area clear of the brush, with a bench just waiting for company. It was by far the most private place of the Chateau out under the stars. She liked to sit there during the warm summer evenings, watching the sky, enjoying the flower-laden air, feeling the cool breeze. Last summer, her first summer at the

Chateau, she'd spent many a night alone out there. She'd even fallen asleep on that cool stone bench; but of course neither Lord Giles nor Lady Marie knew that!

The bench, as always, was deserted. She sat down, brushing rose bush leaves from her skirt and hair. Just then she noticed a scratch, rather deep, across the palm of her hand, and remembered the pierce of that tall, prickly bough. She hadn't given it a thought until now, seeing three drops of blood fall to her lap. It gave her little pain, just a tingle where the blood now oozed. Taking advantage of the omen, even if it was superstitious and against Church teachings, she closed her eyes and wished upon the triple drops of blood.

"Wishes, wishes, upon this blood grant my desire by early morn . . . I wish for three things, one for each drop of blood," she whispered, eyes closed, face upturned to the sky. "That we—my family and I—may return to our home, away from all of these brash de Saineses. And I wish . . . for the end of this feud, to see the Montforts brought to task for what they did. And for my last wish, a purely selfish one." She hesitated, sighing. How could she put into words this last, most personal desire? "I wish for an end to this new loneliness—"

A gentle rustle in the bushes behind her halted Alix's wishing. She stood, for it sounded again, and she turned expectantly in the direction of the interruption.

"I thought it best to make my presence known, Demoiselle," came a voice from the shadows, "before I eavesdrop any further."

"Who is there?" she demanded.

Philip de Saines stepped forward. "I could not help but overhear," he confessed.

Alix was glad the blush warming her cheeks would not be seen in the dim light of the moon and stars. "I—have never been discovered in this place before," she said. What else could she say? That she was happy to see him? Embarrassed he'd overheard? That only he, of all the Chateau inhabitants, would be a welcome intruder in this secret place of hers? It was all true, but she could hardly tell him so.

"Little wonder no one has ever found you here," he replied, nearing her while brushing leaves off his tunic. "The pathway is so overgrown it's invisible. Few of my father's guests probably know this stone center even exists."

"I suppose it was lovely once, trimmed and cultivated," she said, looking around. "Your mother mentioned she used to sit in the center and simply watch the flowers grow—that is how I knew this bench was here."

"So the garden has been in this condition since before you came here to live."

She nodded. "But truthfully, I still think it's lovely. I remember how it looked—vaguely—from my visits here as a child. I suppose I never paid it much attention, but I do remember the summertime profusion of flowers. Perhaps the rose bushes have turned wild, and there is no longer any defined shape or symmetry to the way it all grows now—but the flowers still smell as sweet."

He smiled that same, handsome smile that made Alix's heart behave so strangely in her breast. Then he, too, looked around, as if trying to see the beauty she saw.

"It helps if you close your eyes and simply breathe in the scented air," she suggested. "Then, when you open your eyes again, you'll know this isn't so far from what a garden should be."

He did as requested, taking a deep breath, and when he opened his eyes again he looked directly at her. He was standing close, so close she felt the air emitted from his deep sigh as it brushed a strand of her hair.

"It does smell sweet," he said, "and yes, I do see the beauty."

Suddenly aware that his scrutiny seemed aimed more at her than the surrounding garden, she stepped nervously away and took a seat once again on the bench.

Philip sat beside her. "I intend on working to restore the Chateau. But the garden, I fear, must wait until the very last. Do you understand?"

His words were spoken as if to comfort her in some way which, she admitted to herself, *should* have made her angry. Improving the Chateau was important work, and although she fervently wished to return to her own home, she could still remember the grandeur of the Chateau from years ago. And she wanted to see it restored, eliminating all reminders of the troublesome times. Yet he must imagine she wanted him to abandon the granaries, the cropfields, the storage houses and countless other vital aspects of the Chateau just to improve a garden of no earthly value except its beauty. But she could summon no anger, or even offense. Not when he seemed to speak only out of kindness. After all, he hardly knew her—and, if he expected her to be anything like the other women of the Chateau, perhaps such comfort would have been necessary.

"I will tell you a secret," she said with a half-smile. "Because the garden offers me privacy, I prefer it the way it is."

Philip beheld the smile and, quite without effort, he returned one in kind. Yet you wished for an end to your loneliness just moments ago, he wanted to say. But could not. Instead, he said, "I've invaded your privacy in more ways than one, then, Demoiselle. From above, in my tower, I can see the center of the garden. In all chivalry, I must tell you this place no longer offers you privacy from all who live here."

So it was Philip who inhabited the tower, she thought. But more than that, she realized she didn't mind it was Philip who had discovered her secret place and would know whenever she was there alone.

"I should confess, too," Philip continued, "that I saw you moments ago and came here because of that."

"Because you . . . saw me?"

He nodded. "I had no chance to speak to you

59

earlier, but I wished to commend you for speaking up during dinner this afternoon. No one else—except my father, of course, seemed to care one way or the other."

"But everyone *must* care," she quickly replied. "The Chateau is their home, and it is indeed in dire need. It is like a knight, my lord, this Chateau. A knight who has all the chivalry and strength to be the greatest, but his squire has neglected his tools: his armor is tarnished, his sword dull. With a bit of work—perhaps more than a bit—the Chateau will again be the fortress it once was."

Philip ignored the uneasy thoughts her comparison inspired, he who might be in the same condition as this Chateau. His tools of battle had become tarnished long ago from disuse. Her words had revealed a greater discovery: she, who only moments ago wished to leave the Chateau for her own home, seemed to care more for its welfare than all the de Saineses within in the Banquet Hall who had far more reason, by right of their heritage, to care for its restoration.

"It seems my father is correct about one thing," he said, "you do have your own opinions, don't you?"

She must not have caught his teasing tone, for her eyelids cast a shadow over her eyes and she said, "Yes, much to my father's disappointment."

He laughed then, and she relaxed, recognizing his enjoyment.

"I guessed this morning on our ride that you are a woman with a mind—and I owe you an apology for thinking, even for a moment, that you would be like others of your sex and believe a garden more important to a Chateau than its working functions."

"You sound almost cynical about others of my gender," she observed.

"Let us just say I have reason to beware."

"Because of the scandal at Court?" The moment the words were out, she regretted them. Would she ever learn to hold her tongue? Perhaps Sire Geoffrey was right—no man would ever see past her faults to ask her to wed. Surely her wayward tongue would lead her to a convent, or worse.

But Philip, thankfully, did not appear offended by her candor. "Yes, that has much to do with it. The scandal has made it seem a crime for me to be alone with any woman, as you must have learned this morning from my father's behavior."

"My own father acted no better," she said. "And it was all a silly misunderstanding."

"Perhaps, in part."

"Then I suppose I should not be here alone with you now."

Philip's gaze caught hers, and he saw a contradiction in her eyes—a desire to stay that belied her words. Could it be, he wondered, that she was as loath to leave as he was? Despite such thoughts, however, he said, "No, I suppose you should not. My father, and yours, too, would not approve."

"It seems to me you are paying for a crime before you've even been proven guilty."

No one else had ever given it a moment's doubt; Philip was glad this woman had. "That, Demoiselle, makes little difference now. I am here, away from Court, away from an irate husband instead of facing him with the truth. That is all that matters; my father could not have judged me any other way."

"He might have at least considered your innocence," she said softly, touching his forearm with a gentle caress.

Philip stiffened so considerably Alix wished once again she'd learned to control her tongue. But she hadn't meant to sound pitying! That, however, must have been how it sounded to Philip. "You *are* innocent, though, Lord Philip." She had to say it, to let him know she believed in him.

Instead of responding, he stood, bowing formally before her. "Good-night, Demoiselle Alix. And may the wishes I interrupted earlier all come true for you."

Alix watched him go, regret, confusion, even relief jumbling within her as he disappeared into the thick, overgrown garden shrubbery. Regret

over her own words, confusion over his, and relief
that it was over and her tongue could make
matters no worse.

What had he meant when he hoped her wishes
would come true? She'd wished for an end to her
loneliness, and for revenge against the Montforts.
But she could not forget her first wish, that her
home be restored. Was that the wish Philip
referred to? Because *he* wished she would return
to her home?

5

Sire Geoffrey watched the strong back of his son,
muscles laboring under the weight of a huge
wooden beam. Philip dragged the beam along the
grassy bank with four peasants at his side. They
were outside the central citadel of the Chateau, at
the edge of the river which ran along the north
side and behind the de Saineses' fortress lands. From
here, Geoffrey could see the town's church steeple
amidst rows of cottages and various merchant
stores. Save for the free merchants, all within the
town owed Geoffrey de Saines fealty. And one day
to Philip. But, thought Geoffrey as his gaze
returned to his toiling son, that time had not yet
come. Not yet! Perhaps when Philip was seigneur
of the vast de Saines estates he could do as he
pleased, but by God, not until then!

Geoffrey watched his son a moment longer, his
mind intent on the words he would use against his
ignoble behavior. The watermill wheel, sadly
limping on one side, was in dire need of the
support beam Philip was, with all his might and
with the help of the peasants, hauling to the river.
Beads of sweat glistened on Philip's face; and his
tunic, so like the serf workers' at his side, was

drenched and stained. Knee-length leather boots were covered with mud from the soggy ground around them. But the support beam, once it was locked into place, would no longer succumb to the soft earth. Not the way Philip's intricate wooden structure was attached to the solid stone mill-house; Lord Geoffrey could guess that from where he stood on a rocky incline above them.

The huge beam snapped into place with a re-sounding thud. Before his eyes, Lord Geoffrey saw the mill wheel stand straight and tall—something which had not been beheld for nearly two years now. The wheel once again turned freely with the force of the water, and from within the millhouse he could hear the churning mechanism ready to grind the de Saineses' crops. That is, Geoffrey thought with a grim twist to his mouth, if the un-worked land around them would ever prosper again.

Then he called to his son, who stood wiping his brow, still breathing heavily from exertion. When Philip heard his father, he looked up, shielding his eyes from the bright mid-morning sun. Seeing Lord Geoffrey, he told the serfs to take a rest, then walked up the short incline to his father. Three of the serfs, without shedding a garment, tossed themselves into the cool river water upon which the millwheel now stood.

Lord Geoffrey leaned heavily on the carved silver and wooden cane he gripped in his hand. Rather than look his approaching son eye to eye, his gaze remained on the water wheel beneath them, and beyond to the overgrown fields and quiet village in the distance. A fly buzzed at his ear, which he chased off with a wave of his hand. Under the full sun, Lord Geoffrey's skin looked pasty-white, Philip noticed, and his hair quite gray, almost as silver as the cane's handle reflecting the sun above.

Philip waited for his father to speak.

"Your mother wishes to know why you chose to sleep in that dilapidated old tower last night," Geoffrey said. "Surely it's full of every imaginable vermin. She wishes—that is, we have made ready your old chambers in the east wing. You will sleep there henceforth."

"I prefer not to, Father."

A moment went by without the slightest indication Lord Geoffrey had heard. But then he spoke, quite calmly, still not meeting his son's gaze.

"You may sleep with whatever vermin you care to, Philip," Lord Geoffrey said. His lips were now whiter than the rest of his pale skin. "It seems that was a habit you learned at Court. But for the sake of your mother, begin the Chateau's restoration with the Tower, if you insist upon staying there."

"I've cleaned it already," Philip said. "Mother can rest her mind; I do not sleep with vermin. Here," he added, staring intently at his father's averted gaze, "or at Court."

That it was obvious neither were speaking of the mice inhabitating the Tower, and possibly Court, they did not acknowledge. It was all too clear just how deeply Lord Geoffrey believed his son guilty of the scandal Philip left behind.

"This," Geoffrey said, pointing to the wheel with the tip of his cane, "this improvement you've nearly broken your back to achieve. Do you think it necessary given the fact that nearly all our lands are unplowed this year? Hand grinding has been well enough recently."

"Hands which grind our grain are needed elsewhere," Philip answered curtly.

To that Sire Geoffrey did not reply. To their left he could see the Chateau high on the hilltop, completely surrounded by massive stone walls topped with battlements. In siege, the mighty fortress could house nearly a thousand. And yet, Geoffrey himself had to admit if they were attacked in the Chateau's present condition, the enemy could not be held off for long. But who could attack? Geoffrey thought defensively. The whole world had been left almost destitute by the pestilence, not just the de Saineses. Was Philip so pompous to believe he could reverse what the scourge had done?

"You have grand plans for the Chateau," he stated.

"Not grand," Philip said, "at least not more grand than the Chateau once was. I merely intend restoring it."

"The Chateau still runs," Lord Geoffrey said. "We are housed, we are served, we are well fed. Which, I might add, is tenfold more than most of France's nobility these days. Do not press the remaining serfs too far, Philip, or they, too, will flee."

Philip braced himself with a stiffened back before issuing his reply. "The way to keep them is to free them, sire. Free them and pay wages."

Geoffrey waved his hand at the subject, not unlike the way he'd waved away the pesky fly just moments ago. "I came not to argue with you but to speak my mind on your behavior since returning home. Would you reduce the honor of the de Saines name by laboring like any peasant?"

"I'm well aware nobility loathes manual labor."

"It is not mere loathing you refer to as though it were laziness. Our work is for the civilization of France, to add to its refinement and grandeur. Our knights and our fortresses protect it. Our wealth sustains it. And just as our clergy must see to its spiritual needs, and our King to its unity, so our peasants are here to work and feed our populace. All but the clergy are born into their slot—and the clergy God Himself chooses later on. We all have our purpose, and yours is *not* that of a peasant. You were not born to such a place."

"Hasn't the Plague tested the purpose of each of us, Father?" Philip asked. But he knew already his argument would do little good. Sire Geoffrey de Saines hadn't been pleased with his eldest son's manner or speech since that day two years before, when Philip had thrown down his sword.

"Have you added philosopher to all of your present ignoble titles?"

Philip would waste no more time on argument. "The Chateau needs work, that no one can deny."

His tone was curt. "And since you, as seigneur, have shown little desire to keep this fortress in its glory, then I, as the next seigneur, will do whatever needs doing. If that means laboring beside the peasants, then I shall do so. If it means freeing the serfs, that I shall also do, if it needs to be done. Do you understand, Father? I will do what needs to be done."

"You go too far, Philip," Geoffrey said, in an even, iron-edged voice. "You have brought shame upon this family, first in giving up the sword and then proving your cowardice in leaving Court with an irate husband on your tail. And now you've abandoned entirely all vestiges of knighthood and nobility by taking up the work of a peasant.

"Listen well, Philip," Geoffrey continued, "if you choose to remain my son. You must return to your senses." His voice took on an almost pleading tone, and for the first time his gaze sought Philip's. "You must resume the life befitting my son. You are a noble from noble breeding, Philip, the son of a long line of noble fathers. Run the Chateau if you wish, but do it through the proper channels! Call my stewards, take them to task where I have been lax. Organize them, order them, see the plans through. Only give up this peasant work!"

Philip lay a hand on his father's shoulder. It had been a long time since they'd had even that much contact, but his father's request had invoked within Philip a response that gathered a lump at the base of his throat. Alone as they were, without vassal or relative to overhear, Geoffrey could speak freely. But Philip knew it wasn't his work on the Chateau which so angered Geoffrey.

"I know I've brought you nothing but grief in recent years, Father. I wish to please you . . . as much as Julian does, but I . . ." His hand dropped, his search for words lost.

"Yes, Julian pleases me!" Geoffrey exclaimed. "He is the grand knight now, every bit as brave and famous as you once were. And may God protect him from the insanity which blighted you in your decision to drop the sword! Ever since then it seems I have lost you as my son."

Philip said nothing; he had no defense. He could try to explain, again, what had made him give up the sword. But that explanation had brought no understanding from Geoffrey two years ago; little would that change now.

How could he tell his father of that battle which even now haunted his nights? The screams of the innocent still woke him from slumber. Try as he might he could not forget. Too many blameless people had lost their lives in that quiet harbor village, all in the name of France. He wanted no part of France's sword even now.

"Father, I know the true complaint you have against me is my refusal to fight. It isn't this supposed scandal at Court, or where I sleep, or the way I've worked like a peasant that wears on you now. I can only believe that if I were still that knight—the kind that Julian is now—then these other complaints would not be held against me, at least from you."

"I doubt we shall ever come to an understanding about that," Geoffrey said, his eyes once again turned away from his son. He stood erect, and Philip felt the constraint rise again like a tangible element between them. There would be no more pleading, no further wish to find any understanding. At least, Philip realized, not from Geoffrey.

The whistle of an arrow was quickly followed by a dull thud as it struck its mark: the narrow trunk of a tall pine at the opposite end of the back courtyard.

"Bullseye, Dob!" Alix swelled with pride as she lowered the firmly strung bow to her side. "That makes four sous you owe me!"

Dob, his blond head shaking in wry disbelief, said, "Four or found hundred, demoiselle. You know I cannot pay. You must give me a chance to earn back my loss."

She handed him the bow without further ado,

but just then they heard the distant approach of Gustave. His voice sounded stronger than ever, Alix noted, and she wondered at the new vitality in a man who hadn't shown interest in anything since Alix came to live at the Chateau. Even his gait, usually slow and burdened with age-hardened limbs, seemed quicker.

"Dob!" Gustave called. "Why are you here wasting your time when you should be off with Lord Philip?"

As Gustave neared, his tone grew quieter. "The young lord needs all able bodies," Gustive said. "It's shame enough he's been doing the labor of a dozen men himself."

Dob, at the same age as Alix, was strong and healthy, and not averse to hard work—that is, thought Gustave, until he'd one day discovered the young Demoiselle Alix. Now it seemed more than a few times a week Gustave had to prevent him from spending too much leisure time with Alix.

"Surely Dob isn't wasting his time practicing his shot," Alix defended him. "He's to be knighted soon."

Gustave looked at Alix. She was a spirited one, all right. He could hardly blame Dob for preferring to spend his time with this one but—God's teeth!—the Lord Philip was almost breaking his neck putting the Chateau in order. If Lord Philip couldn't rest then, by the Wrath of Whomever, no one else would, either!

He kept his righteous anger hidden, however, when addressing Alix.

"The bow is for youngsters, demoiselle. Look around you." Gustave held up his hand, motioning toward the various mechanisms dotting the inner courtyard set aside for training knights. "There," he said, pointing to a wooden horse upon which sat a stuffed dummy, "Dob has learned to joust with lance in hand, facing the opponent in direct combat. And there." He motioned to large leather balls dangling from a row of wooden posts. "He learns to use his sword on horseback—to thrust his blade directly into the heart of any enemy. Tell me, demoiselle, do you see any of a knight's traning which includes bow and arrow? A knight demands physical contact, not the distance of bow and arrow."

"But surely being a fine shot cannot detract from his skill as a knight," Alix argued. "The King himself has allowed his tournaments to include bowshot. Where is the shame?"

"There is no shame," Gustave conceded. This young lady was forever brandishing her tongue in someone's defense! "Would you keep this boy from serving the son of his liege lord?"

Against that argument Alix could not win, and all three of them knew it. "I did not mean to keep Dob from his duty," Alix said, eyelids lowered in uncommon submission.

"Then go, Dob. You will find Lord Philip at the west drainage canal."

Dob was off after a cordial farewell to Alix. Gustave returned with her to the Keep. With his old, stiff limbs, he was no help to Lord Philip; the least he could do was assure himself that Philip had all available help.

"You must have trained Lord Philip in the ways of knighthood," Alix said as they passed the training yard.

"Yes, Demoiselle Alix. He learned, along with a dozen others, in this very courtyard. A shame the Plague has left us with so few for our former way of life."

There were only a few of Sire Geoffrey's knights in the yard now, either honing their own skills or working with their squires. And, Gustave thought, the yard had never looked lonelier.

"It is like a nest without a bird," he said aloud.

"Do you know why Sire Philip gave up his sword?"

Gustave cast her a surprised look at her boldness, but answered her nonetheless. "I doubt anyone can answer that question but Lord Philip himself. I know no more than the stories which are told."

"And what are they?"

"Some say he went mad during a battle and killed so many innocents the blood upon his hands sickened him with remorse."

"I do not believe that!"

Guestave smiled. "Nor do I. Not that tale. There are others. Some say he disobeyed his battle liege lord and his sword was taken from him for his act of treason."

"He must have had good reason to disobey, if that was indeed the case."

"But King Jean favors Philip," Gustave reminded her. "Would the same King forbid him use of his sword, if Philip wished to use it?"

Alix was thoughtful. "You are right, of course."

They reached the gate to the inner citadel, where Alix would head for the Keep and Gustave to his small tower. But rather than bid him a quick farewell, Alix gazed up and him and said, "You seem different somehow, Gustave. Younger. And now that I think on the subject, you've made this miraculous change since Lord Philip returned. You care for him a great deal, do you not?"

"True, Demoiselle Alix. He has long been my favorite de Saines. And now he is home again, where he belongs. Do look around you." He lifted his hand, wrinkled and lean, covered with a faint showing of gray hair. His wave included the surrounding area. "It is not just myself looking better on only the second full day of Lord Philip's return. The Chateau itself already seems to shine more fair beneath our sun, just knowing one who cares is back."

Alix looked around. True, the Chateau *did* seem more fair. Despite its intimidating strength, it had always been a lovely Chateau. Philip's work was already showing in the repaired grille of the gate, and inspired serfs mending the inner stable's roof, and the battlements above being cleaned of ages of dried leaves and other such signs of disuse.

"It seems Lord Philip has wasted no time. But I wonder," she added softly, "how the present seigneur views all of this?"

* * *

"Sheer lunacy," Sire Geoffrey exploded. His wife sat at her embroidery table, passively listening to her husband's tirade. It seemed this morning's talk with their son had only added more fuel to the fire between Sire and heir. And Eleanore was grateful for only one thing: they were in the privacy of their inner chambers where none of their myriad guests could hear Sire Geoffrey's irate ranting.

"He'll continue to work like a peasant regardless of what I say," Geoffrey continued. "Imagine what France will say about our mad son. Never before have I wished to be anything but Sire Geoffrey de Saines, lord to the de Saines domain—but today, knowing if we were no more important than the town baker, at least then our son's madness would be of no consequence. As it is, the whole of France will look to us and laugh."

"The idle chatter of others has never rattled you before, my dear."

"It will be no idle chatter, woman! Who will trust the future of the de Saineses while it rests in Philip's hands? A man who doesn't even know what it is to be the son of a nobleman?"

"Perhaps he will return to his senses," Eleanore said, although her tone did not suggest much hope.

Geoffrey paid no attention to his wife. He spoke aloud, but as if to himself. "No doubt Cousin Richard will toy with this for the remainder of my days, and taunt me for the addle-brained heir I've produced. Even *this* Chateau isn't large enough to be spared from the tongues of those like Richard." He sighed, taking a seat opposite Eleanore. "I've had enough of well over half our guests, and the worst of it is they'll undoubtedly be with us for the duration of our lives or theirs. It wears on me, Eleanore."

"It's been almost two years, Geoffrey. Our lives seem no longer our own. But," she added, sighing with a superior air, "it is our role, as nobility, to house these folk left poor by the scourge. You would not see my sister turned out, would you, or the Beauchamps?''

"Of course not," Geoffrey answered, although to himself he admitted he could do very well indeed without the overbearing presence of Jeanne, Eleanore's elder sister.

But the Beauchamps were a different matter entirely. Giles was a dear friend from childhood; his father and Giles's had been close as well, past the bond of lord and high vassal. And that daughter of his . . . an annoying twit, sometimes, he confessed, what with that unladylike boldness of hers. But she was a beauty, all right, and it would be well if her spirit were passed on to male heirs. Yes, he thought, he had plans for the young Beauchamp girl. Plans she herself would undoubtedly welcome with gratitude.

"You should not bemoan Philip's behavior overmuch," Eleanore was saying. "In truth, this is the most active you've been in years, my dear. Perhaps this homecoming will do us some good."

"Hmph," Geoffrey snorted.

Eleanore breathed again deeply for she, too, wondered what good Philip's homecoming could bring. He was such a mystery to her! He always had been, even as a child. And he was a burden to dear Geoffrey, by bringing shame upon shame to the noble de Saines name.

"If only it had been Julian," she said wistfully, hardly aware she spoke the words aloud, "to return home."

"Only that," Geoffrey said with equal longing, "would make all else bearable."

6

"Why don't you join in the games?"

Alix only smiled and shook her head at her mother's suggestion. The Banquet Hall was filled with Chateau inhabitants, knights and squires dressed in the de Saines colors, lords and ladies attired in rich silks and brocades. Interspersed here and there were somberly dressed servants, brightly dressed jesters and jugglers, and a pair of tumble dancers in their parti-colored tights.

Smoke from the center hearth floated in the air, wafting toward the two huge windows which let in the afternoon sun. Tables had been cleared of dinner debris, except for the occasional mug where someone sat who did not participate in the games.

It was the typical afternoon repast of nobility: games for the amusement and entertainment of all. Most of it was quite silly, Alix thought, such as hoodman blind or other such masked games, or the circle game in which a kerchief was dropped before a knight of the lady's choosing. Young, unmarried folk usually participated, and many knights. On occasion Alix had joined in a game of chess with her father or Sir Hugh, or on a larger scale she'd joined the word game, writing on a small scrap of paper any particularly truthful trait of those around her, such as Sir Hugh's outspoken honesty which she so admired, or Richard's boorish nature, or Constance's gentility. Her scrap of paper then joined the others, and Fate decided which trait matched the participants when the folded scraps were chosen at random and then read aloud. It turned quite risque at times, for once she herself had picked a scrap that read, "As lovely at the board as in the bed." But she'd only laughed, for it was just a game. Those of a more sensitive nature, Constance, for one, should not participate. Constance had more than once left the word game with tears of embarrassment spilling from her eyes.

But today they played the kerchief game, and Alix thought it a foolish way to be flirtatious. It was one game she'd never yet participated in.

Soon the minstrels and musicians took up their instruments and dancing began. Unwittingly, Alix's gaze went to the Hall entryway. What would it be like, she wondered, if Lord Philip came

73

through that entry, walked boldly to her and requested a dance? He would hold out his hand, and she would accept . . .

How silly! she chided herself. Her thoughts were still those of that eight-year-old child who once viewed Philip on his charger. Certainly she had outgrown such childish fancies!

"You look quite lovely this afternoon, child," Lord Giles said to his daughter. His glance took in her appearance. The close-fitted surcoat she wore complimented her slender figure well, the Baghdad silk following every curve. The bodice was square cut in front and back, low as was the fashion, showing her white underrobe beneath. Long, full sleeves were trimmed with ermine at the wrist, and tippet streamers fell from her elbows. Her hair was her finest adornment, Giles thought. Like the color of a warm fire, long and thick and inviting to touch. "Why aren't you dancing?" he asked after a moment. Having just reminded himself of the beauty his daughter possessed, it seemed odd indeed that no one came forth to ask her to dance.

Marie answered for Alix. "After refusing the young unmarried men so many times, they've grown tired of asking."

Giles eyed Alix. "Is that true?"

"I've danced many times."

"Why not now?" he persisted. "You should have a partner for every dance, young lady. You're the prettiest girl here, aren't you?" He motioned for Kay, the young boy who served as squire to Sir Hugh. The boy responded at once, bowing formally to his lord.

"Go, boy, ask Sir Thomas to come here and dance with my daughter."

"Wait!" Alix called quickly, for Kay was already off to do Lord Giles's bidding. The boy stopped expectantly, and Alix turned to her father. "Father, you wouldn't subject me to this humiliation!"

"What humiliation is there to dance with young Tom? He's a likeable young man; a grand fighter, too."

"But to ask him to dance with me!" Alix was mortified, and looked imploringly toward her mother.

Marie spoke up. "Perhaps Alix is right, Giles," Marie said gently. "It would appear as if Alix has no admirers by her own merit, and can get no one to dance with her except at your command."

"That appears to be the truth, wouldn't you say?" Giles said.

Marie's laughter brightened the dim situation, and Alix began to relax when Marie waved Kay away. "Now, Giles, just because no one has asked Alix to dance today doesn't mean half the men in this room aren't smitten by her."

"If that's the case, why isn't she at least betrothed? We should have seen to this long ago, when that young boy she was promised to died."

Alix knew this conversation would have to take place sooner or later. At the age of eleven she'd been betrothed to marry Peter Courbet. Both families were satisfied with the match, even Alix herself hadn't objected. Peter was a childhood friend and at least he would be a tolerable husband. She'd known some girls who were betrothed to men or boys they didn't even know, or old men more than twice their age. She had been content, if not happy, with Peter as her father's choice. But when Peter died of one of the many wintertime illnesses, Alix's family had not named another as betrothed out of respect for Peter's family. Once the grief was forgotten, they'd planned to see to that aspect of Alix's future. But the pestilence had begun shortly after that, and then the Beauchamp Estate was destroyed. In all of life's changes, the matter of Alix's betrothal had been laid aside. Until now, Alix feared.

"Your father is right, you know," Marie said to Alix. "You should be betrothed, and soon. What do you think of the matter? Have you anyone in mind, for your husband and I to consider?"

She'd been about to give her negative reply just when her gaze was caught at the Hall entryway.

Marie exchanged a worried glance with Giles as they saw their daughter's attention stolen by the newest arrival to the Hall.

Philip paused at the entryway, perusing the festivities which were so like those at King Jean's court. He was able to squelch his sneer, but his thoughts knew no bound. Even his father's steward, Sir Henry, danced like a careless fool, no doubt without thought to the crumbling walls around him.

No matter. Sir Henry would soon mend his ways, Philip vowed, or he would never dance again—at least not at this Chateau.

Since it was obvious he'd once again missed the meal, Philip had no wish to linger. He certainly had no desire to join the merrymakers frittering their time away. Or see his father's disapproval, even though Philip had tried, hadn't he, to join the family at mealtime?

His gaze touched Alix's just as he was about to turn away. The entire room separated them, smoke from the hearth clouded the path in between, dancers spun in and out of the way. Yet Alix's gaze met his, and there it held. For a moment Philip caught his breath.

The south field needed checking; the roof of almost every granary needed mending; countless other tasks demanded Philip's attention. So why didn't he turn away? Why even consider this absurd desire to ignore all else so he could do something as inane as dancing with this lovely woman?

Instead of moving, Philip merely stared. He felt like a besotted fool! He had to do something, either leave the room or enter it. No more standing on the edge. And entering it could possibly be one of the most idiotic decisions he could make.

Which is precisely what he did.

Alix's heart beat almost painfully hard within her. But certainly he couldn't guess, although he did look at her as if he could see into the very depth of her being. Her gaze could not leave his,

76

even when she tried to look away. Surely he headed this way.

"Philip!"

Alix watched, her rapidly beating heart spiraling downward to an uncomfortable spot at the base of her stomach. Philip's path took an unexpected turn as he responded, somewhat slowly, to his mother's call.

"You must remember Marguerite," Eleanore said, with an introductory wave of her hand toward the young woman at her side. Marguerite sent Philip a dazzling smile, her face alight with welcome. She was not much older than Alix herself. Alix had spoken with her many times; she was friendly, Alix had to admit, and pretty as well. And at this moment Alix wished she would simply disappear.

Alix heard Eleanore continue. "Marguerite is the daughter of Marquis de Boigne. She is staying here while her father manages their Estate in Burgundy."

Alix didn't want to listen, but she wasn't able to help herself. More than once she wished she possessed the strength—or the pride—to leave. But she listened, shamelessly.

"Marguerite is with us for just a short time, Philip," Eleanore went on. "Why don't you take advantage of this opportunity, at least to dance?"

Although Alix told herself it would be impossible for Philip to refuse—he may have given up the sword, but one could not ignore all chivalry—she could not dismiss the weight still at the bottom of her stomach, pulling down her every imagined hope. Marguerite looked lovely beside Philip, her slim, petite figure a feminine contrast to his strong masculinity. Today Philip did not wear the garb of peasantry as he'd been wont to wear on previous days. He wore a walnut-colored doublet with embroidered silk attached to his chest, stitched in the de Saines herald of the star constellation Draco, the dragon. His chausses were black, and his leather shoes for once clear of any trace of the morning's work. He was, by far, the most handsome man present.

And, Alix thought, the musicians played far too long.

Lord Giles had not forgotten the former topic of conversation with his daughter. But as he watched her pay such avid attention to the de Saines heir, he felt a frown tug at his mouth. True, a match with the de Saines wealth would see his own financial state greatly improved, but he could not tolerate the thought of that treasonous scoundrel joining his family. No daughter of his would marry a man who would not fight, who could not even defend his own name. How could he defend and protect a wife if he could not defend and protect his own name?

Something would have to be done about betrothing Alix to a worthy man, Giles thought, and it must be done soon.

At last the dancing ended and a vocalist stepped to the center of the mosaic floor. Most took their seats to listen to the song. Philip escorted Marguerite to her chair, spoke a few words Alix could not hear, then stood at Marguerite's side through the performance of a May song extolling the beauty of Spring. Alix heard barely a word, although she forced her gaze to remain fixed on the singer as if mesmerized by each note.

"Wouldn't you rather view Spring for yourself than listen to a poet sing of it?"

The whispered words startled Alix, and she turned round with widened eyes. Philip stood behind her, a smile upon his handsome face as warm as the Spring sun in the singer's verse. "Seeing is always better than hearing about anything," she whispered back.

The vocalist had begun another song, but Alix had no desire to stay to listen. Philip held out his hand—oh, so like her fantasy—and Alix did not hesitate to accept it. She glanced briefly at her father and mother, who watched with equal amounts of disapproval forming on their faces. But Alix looked away quickly; she wouldn't be stopped now. And she knew her parents well enough to guess they would let her go rather than forbid her the company of the son and heir of their host before all his guests.

No one gave them pause as they walked along the wall of the Great Room, behind those seated around the tables. The attention of most was still, thankfully, upon the vocalist.

Alix squinted under the bright Spring sun, so stark in comparison to the dusky hall. They walked the few steps down to the inner bailey and, Alix noted with ressurrected hope, Philip seemed as loath to loosen her hand as she was to loosen his.

"I want to show you something," Philip said, and they headed toward the stable.

It took a few minutes for the grooms to saddle two horses, but before long and without many words spoken, Alix was mounted and following Philip from the bailey. They left the high Chateau, passing the outer courtyards and, as they had just the day before, headed toward the pine wood.

"Your homecoming is missing one ingredient, Lord Philip," Alix said as her horse trotted at a relaxed pace beside Philip's.

"And what is that?"

"Your presence," she said with a smile.

"I seem to have forgotten the dinner hours since returning home," Philip explained. "As you can see," he said with a hand indicating his formal attire, "I fully intended to be present this afternoon."

"You must be hungry, then," Alix said, suddenly distressed for him. "Perhaps we should return—"

"Not just yet," he said. "We're almost there."

"Where?"

Philip gave no answer until he slowed his horse on the very incline they'd stood upon yesterday morning, overlooking one of the nearly empty peasant villages.

Today, however, the village was not quite so quiet. Few as they were, the serfs inhabiting the village were no longer hiding in their homes from any lingering pestilence. Women were at the riverside with their laundry once again, and beyond, in the field, a few serfs behind horse and plow tended the earth. With so few to work and so large an area of land, the progress seemed minimal. But, Alix thought, it was so good to see people working again! So like it had been before all the sickness began. And Philip, she realized as she turned her gaze on him, was responsible. Admiration filled her and for a moment she thought it must have shown on her face, for when he glanced her way his gaze held hers, as if he saw something there he couldn't quite believe. Alix looked away, suddenly embarrassed.

"I wanted to remind you what this looked like today," Philip said, somewhat huskily. "Because in two months' time it will once again be what it was before—before we lost so many."

"Two months?" Alix repeated, unable to conceal her surprise. Even for Philip, the task seemed impossible. Why, to fill the village alone would take generations!

"Today I will take the first step in filling those little homes down there," he said, as if she'd spoken her thought aloud. "I'm going to free the serfs."

Her brows raised in interest. "Your father approves?"

By his hesitation, Alix knew the answer without a word spoken. "Let us say he is prepared for what I'm about to do."

Alix could not keep silent. "And he makes no objection?"

Philip smiled that brilliant smile of his and Alix found herself returning the gesture even though somewhere inside, undefined as yet but creeping steadily to the forefront of her mind, was a warning that Sire Geoffrey would not be as indifferent about this as he'd been about the Chateau itself for the last two years.

As they reined their horses around, Alix realized the disappointment of missing a dance with Philip had evaporated. How much more important it was to share this hope, see his dream, know his plans.

Somehow she knew it would all be reality; Philip would free the serfs, and Geoffrey would see it was for the best. Paying wages would soon attract more villeins and the Chateau and surrounding villages would once again work to fullest potential. Alix had no doubt Philip would succeed in fulfilling that dream.

"I will see Sir Henry when we return," Philip said. They let their horses walk slowly back toward the keep; Philip was in no great hurry to return. His smile had faded, leaving behind the determination that went with working to see his dreams become a reality. And although he spoke aloud, Alix sensed he was speaking as much to himself as he was to her. "My father's council has done nothing in the past months. No doubt they'll prefer to continue their dancing and foolishness, but it's time they worked for their titles and lodgings."

"My father's castellan, Sir Hugh, would be more than willing to help you," Alix said. "He always worked very hard with my father at our Estate. And since coming to Chateau de Saines, he feels as displaced as—"

Philip's attention focused on Alix. Philip knew what she'd been about to say, he remembered too well her wish in the garden last night. It was Alix who felt so displaced. She undoubtedly missed her home yet, selfishly, he realized if she hadn't lost that home he might never have gotten to know her. And if that home was restored to her, she would leave the Chateau, possibly for good. The one guest out of the hundreds who inhabited the place who seemed to enliven the entire Chateau. And she felt displaced.

"How badly damaged was your home?" Philip asked.

"Destroyed entirely. It's unlivable."

"By fire, you said?"

She nodded, not looking at him.

"Do you know how the fire started?"

"They say it was a kitchen accident."

Disbelief riddled her statement.

81

"You would rather return there, wouldn't you, Alix?" he asked, somewhat gently. "Rather than stay here with all of these de Saineses?"

No one, not even her mother, had ever voiced that suspicion, even though Alix was sure her mother knew how she felt. But since there was little likelihood of ever returning there, it seemed everyone, including Alix herself, avoided speaking of that fervent wish of hers.

"I doubt that could ever be possible," she said. "Only the outer stone walls still remain. Much of the Keep was wood-hewn. It burned to the ground."

He heard her sadness and could only guess at the depth of her loss. Before even giving it much consideration—only for a moment did the fear of his own loss mar the unselfish thought—he spoke. "When the Chateau is running again," he said slowly, "there will no doubt be more than enough workers to keep the Chateau going smoothly. And, as the Beauchamp Estate is one of the de Saineses' fiefs, it would behoove the de Saineses to see it restored. Would that . . . please you?"

Alix gazed at him in unabashed wonder. "You would do that?"

Philip nodded even while inside he called himself a fool. It would be far preferable to keep this woman here, he thought. But as he observed the unadulterated joy flooding her lovely features, he knew he could do nothing else but follow through with this promise.

It wasn't only that the Estate was a de Saines fief—true, it was valuable, but it was far easier to let it rot than rebuild. The land was still the property of the de Saineses, and someday it would be profitable to rebuild. But the way times were now, it would take some very shrewd planning to find the men and materials for building. Lord Geoffrey must have decided that a year ago when taking the Beauchamp family into the Chateau.

They finished their ride in companionable silence. Alix could think of nothing to say, but she felt no need to fill the peaceful air between them with needless chatter.

A lone rider coming from the east interrupted the calm. As they neared the Keep, the rider passed by in such haste he took no time to see whose path he cut short. His black cape whipped in the wind, and the horse's mane and tail rippled long and black from the speed they traveled. As the horse's hooves clapped loud upon the lowered drawbridge, Alix heard the call of the sentry and the gate's grille was raised. Alix and Philip nudged their mounts onward, and in a moment they followed the rider under the portcullis.

The sentry's horn had alerted those in the Keep, and as Philip and Alix dismounted, others emerged from the forebuilding of the inner citidel. Sir Oliver, Geoffrey's castellan, reached the rider just behind Alix and Philip.

"It's young St. Clair, squire to Sir Fredegar," Sir Oliver told Philip. The boy nearly fell from his horse into Philip's arms.

"A battle," began St. Clair, breathless but eager, "along the d'Aussy lands."

"Between whom?" Philip asked, holding him up in a strong grip spanning the boy's chest.

"D'Aussy and . . ." The boy nearly fainted, but Philip pulled him up straight and that revived him. "The Montforts."

"Who was the victor, boy?" demanded Sir Oliver.

"The Montforts," he whispered. "There were few survivors."

"Surely the family is left?" Alix asked, unable to hold back the question.

St. Clair shook his head weakly.

"But Countess Adele . . ."

"Killed at her husband's side," the boy finished, then he collapsed against Philip, and no amount of Sir Oliver's questioning could revive him. He was carried off gently by de Saines attendants, the Chateau physician at their side.

"Sir Oliver, send as many men as you can spare to the d'Aussy Chateau. See what needs be done; bring back any survivors, whether they are

83

d'Aussy or Montfort."

Sir Oliver hesitated. "Bring a Montfort . . . here?"

Philip did not answer; he gazed at Sir Oliver and before another moment passed, his order was carried out.

The circle that had formed around the messenger soon dispersed, leaving Alix alone with Philip. She stared at him, surprise, dread, and a tiny bit of awe conflicting within her.

"You would have them bring a Montfort here?" How could he allow such a thing? Even suggest it?

For the first time since meeting her, the look on Alix's face brought Philip no delight; quite the opposite, in fact, it annoyed him. The look matched Sir Oliver's; she was thinking of the Montfort family as nothing more than an enemy. An enemy to mercilessly let die.

"Last night you wished for an end to the feud," Philip said, face concealing any emotion. "There are more ways than annihilation to achieve that."

Alix said nothing; she could tell he thought her heartless, even cruel. But he didn't know the truth! He didn't know what the Montforts had done. How could she show mercy toward a family responsible for destroying her home?

Before uttering a word, even in her own defense, she turned on her heel and was gone. He thought her bloodthirsty; her accusations against the Montforts would make little difference. For that's all they were: accusations. She had no proof, no evidence that the Montforts were to blame. But would Philip even care if she did have proof? Would he raise his swordless hand against anyone?

Let her go, Philip told himself as he watched her flee from him. Running after her would do no good, he knew that. To do that he would have to use words to comfort her, and he had no such words. She wanted no charity shown for the family who had been a thorn in the side of Brittany ever since they'd acquired their wealth a few years ago. A family who wanted nothing more than to become part of the nobility they alienated with their angry acts of violence.

So he let her go, unable to remove the thorn that had just risen between them.

7

Sir Oliver and his men returned after sunset. They brought with them only those well enough to travel. The others were left at the d'Aussy Chateau with several Holy Sisters of the Beatitudes to care for them under the guidance of a de Saines physician. There had been no Montforts to return with; the only Montforts left on d'Aussy land had been dead long before Sir Oliver ever reached them—at least that is what he told Lord Philip.

By the time Alix reached her bed chamber that night, it was quite late. She'd tended the wounded at her mother's side, all the while refusing to think of Philip. It was just as well they had realized their differences so soon, she said to herself as she slipped out of her clothes and in between the quilts on her bed. No doubt he would not be asking her to ride with him ever again, and she was glad. Why had she ever allowed herself to resurrect that childhood infatuation for him, even for a short time? Her mother's warning that her father would never accept Philip as son-in-law was needless. After all, Alix had always imagined herself married to a knight, and now she wanted that even more. The man she married would do something ending the feud the Montforts stirred in this land. Certainly he would not offer shelter to someone responsible for so much violence.

But as she shifted and turned in her bed, unable to sleep, she gazed out her window more than once. And when she saw the light in the once-abandoned tower, she could not deny her heart skipped a beat as she imagined Philip there, readying himself for bed. Soon the light was extinguished and she thought he must be sleeping. If only she could do the same.

Several days went by before Alix saw Philip again, although she insisted to herself she was not looking for him. She went for one of her early morning rides, intent only on the exercise and fresh air, despite the threat of rain in the dark clouds hanging overhead. She happened to ride past the incline overlooking the village, and though it was just after sunrise the villagers were already up and about. A new family had joined the village, Alix saw, for one of the formerly empty cottages now had children playing in the yard.

She rode on, drawing out her ride longer than she'd ever dared before, especially on such a dreary, cloudy morning. She went by the watermill, the wheat granary and the smokehouse, going the long way by the winery back toward the Keep. It was there she saw Philip. He was with the steward, Sir Henry, and from the distance she kept she could not hear the words spoken between them. But it was obvious Philip pointed out various repairs he wanted Sir Henry to oversee. It seemed a strange sight, for Philip was once again dressed little better than a peasant, and Sir Henry, to whom Philip gave the orders, looked far more noble in his dark doublet, gold belt and forest-green chausses.

When Philip saw Alix he waved at her, bidding her welcome. As he drew near, an impulse told her to leave before he reached her side, but she stayed immobile, holding steady the frisky palfrey beneath her. Sir Henry disappeared within the winery.

"Unchaperoned, I see," Philip greeted her, smiling. "Do your parents know you're out?"

She shook her head.

"You've kept very much to yourself the last few days," Philip observed. "I've finally gotten into the habit of the regular dinner hour, and you have yet to be there when I am. Do you often take your repast alone in the women's bower?"

"No...I...I do not sleep in the women's bower. I take my dinners in my own chambers."

He raised a brow, then said, "Would you like an escort back to the Keep? It looks as though it'll storm soon."

She shook her head before letting her heart answer for her. Yes, she wanted to say. She'd been doing a poor job of hiding her feelings from herself the past three days; though she kept to her chamber, her thoughts strayed to Philip. And this morning's ride... How could she deny, even to herself, that she'd extended it in hope of seeing Philip? And now she'd seen him. Part of her said it wasn't enough. She wanted him to escort her back to the Chateau. But she couldn't, she wouldn't, let him. She would end this hopeless infatuation.

"No," she told him. "I'll go back alone."

"And risk your parents finding out about your unchaperoned rides?"

"I've risked it before."

It was all too obvious she didn't want his company, but Philip persisted. The words coming from her mouth didn't seem to match the look in her eye. And what was she doing at this end of the Chateau lands, with a rainstorm approaching? If she'd begun this morning's ride just after dawn as she had before, then she must have been riding for more than an hour. It hardly made sense that she'd been looking for him, since she clearly did not want his company, but that possibility did cross his mind.

A clap of thunder sounded above, and the first raindrops fell from the sky. It was no short ride back to the Keep, and Alix knew she would be drenched before long. But the prospect of being soaked by fresh rainwater seemed far less dangerous than spending another moment alone with Philip.

He caught her rein just as she was about to direct the palfrey away. "You can't ride all the way back to the Keep in this weather," he said, loud enough to be heard over another peal of thunder. "Come into the winery until this passes."

Surely there was no harm in taking shelter in the winery, Alix thought. It was full of workers overseen by Sir Henry. She allowed Philip to assist her off the horse, and together they ran to the wide door of the winery.

It was a huge building, with a multitude of vats and barrels taking up most of the space. But though voices echoed from the opposite end of the high-ceilinged room, Alix could see no one else around.

Philip led her to a small room which boasted the only fireplace in the building meant for comfort. It was a pleasant chamber which served as a tasting room for steward or lord to sample the winery's product. The fireplace was cold, but Philip bent to ignite it while Alix looked around. To one side was a padded couch, covered in rich scarlet satin. Two large, ornately carved chairs with leather seats were placed opposite, with a small table in between. Light filtered in from the glassed window, where raindrops marred the view outside. Alix was still standing in the same spot when Philip stood, a healthy fire crackling behind him.

"Come and dry yourself," he invited.

"All right," she said, somewhat stiffly, and moved closer. But she did so only because it was the sensible thing to do.

He stood at her side, and both were silent, not looking at one another. At last, Philip said in a quiet, knowing tone, "You're uneasy."

Alix did not look up; she stared at the fire, holding out her hands to feel its warmth. She neither admitted nor denied his observation.

Philip leaned on the mantel above the fire, watching Alix. He knew he was right; this was the first time she'd ever avoided looking at him eye to eye. And he'd never known her to be so quiet! Philip knew why. She was still uncomfortable about his offer to shelter wounded Montforts. That, after all, had been the last time he'd seen her. Undoubtedly it was that action that caused her to avoid him.

For a moment he considered what he should do. Ignore her uneasiness? Pretend it wasn't there? Seek to ease it, understand it, be rid of it? But to do that he must settle one nagging suspicion.

"How did the fire start at the Beauchamp Estate?" he asked directly.

That was enough to bring her gaze to his. Though she made an effort to hide her surprise, it was too late to keep from Philip.

"I told you," she said. "It was an accident."

"An accident ... perhaps caused by a Montfort?"

She turned away, knowing she could not help but reveal the truth in her eyes. She said nothing, not even trusting her voice.

"Is that why you hate the Montforts so?" he asked to her turned back. When she refused to answer he continued. "Surely it cannot be simply because the Montforts have wished for the past few years to be accepted as nobility. Or even the fact that they've petitioned King Edward of England for a title should he succeed in winning Brittany in any future battles between our warring countries."

Still, she kept silent. So he said, "Would you have me believe you hate them so passionately simply because they might one day be enemies of France, the way Sir Oliver hates them, the way any knight would hate them?"

"Shouldn't all citizens of France hate our enemies?" she asked, skirting the truth.

He shrugged an answer to that, saying instead, "The other day, when I offered to give shelter to any Montforts, the feelings you showed were far more personal than as just a citizen of France acting in the best interest of King and country. And now you're decidedly cool toward me, for one reason I can only guess: I offered shelter to wounded Montforts. Tell me the truth, Alix."

"Why?" she asked at last. "What good will it do?"

"Perhaps none," he admitted, "except to let me

know you. Understand you."

Pulse racing, she turned her gaze back to the fire. "Why would you want to do that?"

With one step he was behind her, so close she felt his breath where her upswept hair bared the back of her neck.

"Because we share the same Chateau," he said.

It was a silly reason, both knew, but Alix welcomed it nonetheless.

"There are many living at the Chateau whom I hardly know," she said, hoping her voice didn't sound as tremulous as she felt.

He cited another reason. "Because as heir to the de Saines seigneur, I will one day be your lord. And I command for us to know one another."

Such a command was easy to obey, Alix thought. She was tired of pretending to herself she wanted anything else; it would be impossible to forget that infatuation she had for Philip, she knew that now. It had grown into something more than that—although into what, she dared not define. Not yet.

With him so near, it was almost impossible for Alix to think clearly. And when, gently, he touched her shoulder, she turned and faced him with widened eyes and racing pulse.

His gaze seemed fixed on hers, and Alix knew she could not, would not, look away. Not when those eyes as blue as the clearest summer sky gazed at her the way they did. As if she were all he wanted to see, as if he were content to fill his vision only with her.

She knew then she was not the only one experiencing this underlying tension—a delicious excitement, anticipation of sorts. Though exactly what she anticipated, Alix did not know.

In that gaze, all else was forgotten, at least for the moment. Forgotten was the fact that Philip was no closer to knowing for certain just what it was Alix believed the Montforts had done. Forgotten was the importance of this subject, the very reason for Alix's former self-imposed cool-ness. She could hardly be cool to the man who set her blood afire.

Run from here, part of her said, but as his embrace encircled her she let her own arms slip around Philip's neck. And when he lowered his mouth to hers she willingly accepted his kiss.

She hardly knew what was happening. That childish infatuation she harbored exploded into a desire that was anything but childish. His kiss melted away every trace of resistance, leaving in its place an almost tangible need forming somewhere in her middle. She felt as hot as the fire just behind them, her skin tingling as if the flames licked every spot where her body met Philip's.

She felt the hard muscles of his shoulders just beneath the thin layer of his peasant-like tunic. He was warm and strong and wonderfully masculine, and Alix knew she wanted nothing but this.

His kiss deepened, and Alix felt desire, sweet and incredibly new, spring from some unfamiliar well deep in her being. Like a warm fire, it spread throughout her veins, down her limbs, to her fingertips, making her dizzy. She clung tighter to Philip's embrace.

His hand reached into the neat chignon at the back of her head, and in a moment it was free of its restraints. Philip luxuriated in the softness of her hair as it tumbled down, his fingers lost in its thickness. And he pressed her ever closer, the desire in him threatening to burst free from deep within where he'd kept it hidden.

Alix didn't want it to end; she wanted this kiss to go on forever, and lead where it may. She didn't stop to question those thoughts, to wonder at her own sudden fall into sin. In fact, if she did not hurry she would miss morning Mass with her family and the rest of the de Saineses. But how could she leave? How could she pull away from this kiss that had made her discover something within herself she hadn't even known was there?

Philip was the first to pull away. His hand came to caress her face, a hand she could have sworn trembled just a bit, as hers did. Was he feeling this same wave of desire? Was he holding himself

91

back, as she was, from a need that threatened to overwhelm all senses? It couldn't be possible, she thought. It couldn't be that her inexperienced kiss could ignite the same flame in him as he ignited in her.

Philip let her go, and she felt a chill sweep over her when he took a full step back. Surely there was some mistake! Philip looked at her as though she had slapped rather than kissed him. His face was cold as he stared down at her, made colder by the sudden and inexplicable contrast to the way he'd looked at her just before kissing her.

"I'm sure that's why Lord Giles and my own father thought it improper for you to be alone with me," Philip said. "Fearing just this sort of thing might happen."

The bewilderment on her face made Philip want to withdraw those foolish words, to retract the last few moments and end the kiss the way he wanted to—with a second one equally ardent. But it was too late.

Philip knew she would not understand. How could she, when he didn't understand himself? He knew only that for a moment he'd had the almost irresistible urge to take this first, passionate kiss farther than even he was prepared to go. And here, in his father's winery! Had just a few days with this woman made him forget that another woman was responsible for a scandal that had sent him home in disgrace? Hadn't he sworn to himself that no woman would ever get the best of him? And here he was, his resolve cast away, his control and his judgment at her feet.

Alix turned from Philip, wanting to hide her face from him. Confusion assailed her, but that warred with the overwhelming embarrassment coursing through her. No doubt he thought her shameless, not only allowing such a kiss but so obviously enjoying it. And now he had the audacity to remind her of their disapproving fathers, as if that would restore her decorum if she could not summon it herself.

"You're right, of course," she said stiffly. "I

should not be here—at least not alone with you.
I'm sure Sir Henry has need of your advice . . .
elsewhere."

He was out of the room within moments.

Vivid images of the kiss played in Alix's mind all
day. It was the kiss which filled her thoughts
instead of the words her uncle the Bishop said at
Mass that morning. And later, when Marie asked
her to join the other women working on one of the
Chateau's huge tapestries, it was Philip Alix saw
rather than the stitches she sewed.

How could she have been so foolish? she asked
herself again and again. She had let Philip kiss her
without the slightest hesitation. And she had
enjoyed it! Surely he knew, surely he'd guessed
just how deeply his kiss had stirred her. Even now,
waves of lingering passion sometimes erupted
within her, causing her hands to tremble so
fiercely she fumbled over more than one stitch.

Certainly this was no way to forget Philip de
Saines!

"Word from your brother is that many knights
will be coming home soon," Marie said, seated at
Alix's side. Her needle worked faster than Alix's,
but no one, not even Marie herself, denied that
Alix was a more competent needleworker.

When Alix said nothing, Marie repeated herself.
At last, Alix turned her faraway gaze on her
mother.

"Simon is coming home?" she asked, then
amended her statement. "Simon is coming here?"

Marie sighed. "That isn't exactly what I said, but
it's close enough. You've hardly heard a word I've
said all morning. What ails you today, child?"

Alix only shrugged. She didn't want to lie to her
mother, she never had before. But she couldn't
bring herself to tell her precisely what the trouble
was.

"Then what exactly did you say?" Alix asked,
seeking to change the subject. "Is Simon
returning?"

"The King has allowed several of his lords to let

their knights return home, at least for a while. With the current truce between France and England, the men are whiling away their time at camps and getting themselves into all kinds of trouble—from sprinkling their bastards here and there to murdering innocent folk for lack of any enemy to kill. So King Jean is dispersing the most troublesome of the lot and that, fortunately—or unfortunately—includes your brother's company."

She would be glad to see Simon again, she thought. Perhaps, since he would not have to fight for France, at least for a while, he could do something about the feud here in Brittany. Alix was sure, once Simon realized his family no longer had a home of their own—just a borrowed bed at a charitable lord's Chateau—he would do all he could to see the Montforts pay for what they did.

Simon, it seemed, was her only hope in that respect. She sighed. If only things were different; if only her father was not quite so content to accept Lord Geoffrey's hospitality. If only she herself had someone to whom she could go, someone who could rally all of the knights, just spoiling to take revenge upon the Montforts. If only she *herself* could do it—but of course that was impossible. How could she, when her father would not willingly allow her even to ride unchaperoned? No, for this she needed a man. It was the closest Alix ever came to wishing for a husband.

A husband, she thought with grim determination, who would fight. She must forget this morning's kiss . . . she must!

8

Cheering voices competed with the snarls and growls of the pair of dogs fighting in the center of the circle formed by the surrounding men. The dog's feral battle appealed to the baser instincts of the knights who watched, for they saw this as an encapsulation of the struggle they themselves faced so often in clashes with the enemy. The dogs were evenly matched in weight and belligerence, making the contest all the more fascinating for those who looked on. And when blood was drawn the cheering intensified with the powerful intoxication of witnessing the strong achieve victory. It was the dream of every knight, conquest over a worthy enemy.

Julian de Saines looked on with the rest of his fellow knights, a flask of bitter wine carelessly held in one unsteady hand. He was more than a little drunk, he knew, but to endure this battle to its end he needed to be. He far preferred cockfights; at least the death of a worthless bird did not unsettle his stomach the way the death of a dog did.

But he shouted along with the others, as loud as anyone for fear of being found out. It wouldn't do to have the bravest knight present labeled a milksop simply because he had an aversion to watching a silky-coated dog eaten alive for the sport of man.

Soon it was over, though none too soon for Julian's liking.

"That was the best one yet, wouldn't you say, Claude?" he said to the burly, slightly paunched fellow at his side. Claude was twice the size of

Julian, who was tall and broad himself, but Claude's brawn was as much from overeating as from muscle, unlike Julian's lean sinew.

The two went to one of the many fires of the encampment, where their young squires were ready to serve dinner. Smoke from the fires wafted above the crowded camp, mingling with a late evening fog trapped between the surrounding trees. Julian took another long draft of the vinegary wine before letting his squire fill a bowl with roasted fowl for him. The smell of the beaten dog's raw, bloody flesh still rankled his nostrils.

"Pity we have to depend upon the fight of beasts for our entertainment," Claude said. "It's been nearly four months since our last skirmish, and that hardly warranted a scratch on any of us."

It was true; even in the unrested territory of Flanders, nary a battle could be found to fight in the name of France. It was enough to set the men squabbling between themselves, as had happened so often in the past few weeks.

"There will be a bit of excitement soon enough," predicted Julian with a secretive smile touching his sensual mouth. Claude looked at him with interest.

"Have you heard of renewed battle?" Claude asked, excitement ringing with each word.

But Julian only shrugged, biting into the burned flank of roasted chicken. Instead of looking at Claude, he watched the broad back of Gene Bazille as he strutted past them to his own carefully tended campfire. Claude, seeing where his young friend's attention lay, watched as well, knowing something was afoot.

Gene accepted a fully laden bowl from his squire. He stood for a few moments, holding his bowl in one hand and choosing the largest cut from the cooked bird. Julian continued to watch, saying nothing, and Claude did not ask why. Knowing Julian, there were a multitude of guesses to choose from. Nothing swayed his attention.

Gene bent to retrieve his flask of wine, taking huge gulps to wash down his food. Then, as he neared the intricately carved chair that he had sent for all the way from home some weeks past, Julian's eyes sparkled with anticipation.

Gene's roar resounded throughout the entire camp when he landed ignobly upon his backside, the chair beneath him collapsed into a pile of carved wooden rubble. For a moment the entire company of knights did not utter a sound as they watched first in amazement, then in obviously suppressed humor. When one knight lost his battle against laughing aloud, the rest joined in, none more avidly than Julian.

"De Saines!"

His name bellowed from between Gene's lips, and the laughter halted—all but Julian's. He watched, unafraid, as the fiercest of their troupe scrambled to his feet as quickly as his large girth could accommodate. The very ground beneath him seemed to rumble as he strode toward Julian.

"That little prank has the stamp of a de Saines on it," he accused, looking down at Julian like a frenzied beast about to pounce. Quicker than a flash he did just that, and Julian barely had a moment to thrust his dinner away before standing to defend himself.

Unlike the dogs, these two were not evenly matched in weight, or in belligerence. Where Gene was nearly bloodthirsty, Julian felt the exhilaration of a prank well done, and this fight merely topped it off. He dodged Gene's punches, squirmed out of his bone-crushing armlocks, out-maneuvered Gene's heavy footwork. Before long, Gene tired of fighting an opponent so slippery, and he heaved a great sigh of annoyance.

"You fight like your brother," said Bazille in disgust, "which is not at all."

Gene knew those were the words to incite this stripling; mention of his brother—in any manner —and the younger de Saines went berserk. Gene had seen it happen many times.

Sure enough, Julian's response had been predictable. Fury covered his youthful, handsome face, and with one powerful burst of energy he bent and rammed himself into Gene's wide frame; his rock-hard shoulder struck Gene somewhere in the middle, knocking the wind out of the older man.

But that was precisely what Gene had wished for. The fight was on, and the same knights who had just witnessed the dog fight now circled the two combatting men. It was a real fight now, not just the amusing fun Julian had made it before, and so every knight around was attracted. Their cheering voices sounded very much like they had just minutes earlier when watching the dogs.

Julian's dexterity aided him well. He landed three well-aimed punches on Gene's jaw before the man had even regained his lost breath. But Bazille was stronger than Julian, with longer arms to better land his pommeling fist to Julian's face. And his blows had more impact than Julian's; more than once the younger, smaller man swayed and staggered under Gene's attack. But he continued to fight, pure rage rendering worthless whatever sense he possessed.

At last, Gene's fist landed a blow that sent Julian sprawling. Then, his anger spent, Gene walked off, tall and proud, his brawn challenged by no one. He looked like a pompous sea lion who had just defended his harem.

Soon the crowd dispersed, leaving Claude and their two squires alone at Julian's side. In a moment Julian revived, and started to rise, as if to continue the lost fight. But Claude held him down.

"He's gone," Claude said, then told one of the boys to fetch cool water from the nearby creek. "You could use a better nursemaid than I, my friend, but I'm all you've got."

Julian grimaced, then moaned at the pain such facial movement caused. The welts along his jaw were quickly heightening to ugly bruises.

Claude dipped his kerchief into the bowl of water the squire had returned with, then wiped Julian's face carefully. "You should be careful of angering that one too often," Claude warned. "He needs no reason to fight, and you've given him ample cause often enough."

Julian tried to laugh, though his smile was decidedly crooked. "But no one else is quite so much fun to irritate," he said. "Take you, my friend. What good is making mischief against one who simply will not be ruffled? You're too even-tempered—which is probably why I admire you so."

He took the wet kerchief from Claude's hand, wiping the rest of his face himself, then sitting up. "I'd say that was worth the sight of Bazille landing flat on his back," he announced, then laughed more heartily, and the other three, Claude and the two squires, joined in, though Claude not so heartily.

"There would have been no fight at all had he not mentioned your brother," Claude said. Then, seeing Julian's eyes flash with renewed anger, he held up a protesting hand. "Now, don't lose yourself again just because I mentioned . . . Philip. You've got to realize one thing, Julian. Any man here tonight could whip you as badly as Gene just did if they only mention Philip's name. It's not any superior strength that whips you—it's your blind anger. It makes you the worst fighter here, even though I know, when you're levelheaded, you could beat the lot of us."

Julian said nothing; he just reached for the dinner he'd discarded before the ruckus, and chewed, somewhat gingerly, upon the same flank he'd started before.

"It's true, Julian," Claude continued. "You've one thing to settle in yourself: either accept your brother as he is now, or hate him and discard him."

"I do hate him," Julian said suddenly, but his voice cracked, betraying his real feelings. He threw down his supper once again.

"How many times are you going to let yourself get trounced simply because you can't bear to hear him ridiculed? You certainly don't hate him—but it might be better for you if you did."

Julian stood, walking away from his friend and

his dinner and his warm fire. I do hate him, Julian said to himself. I do.

"There he is!" Alix exclaimed from atop one of the battlements. "Simon is coming!"

She raced to the stone stairway that would take her down below, halting at her mother's side before the iron and wood gate of the inner bailey. A squire had arrived half an hour earlier to announce Simon's approach, and both Marie and Alix had waited expectantly ever since. Lord Giles was still in bed, for he was suffering from one of his recurring stomachaches. Nothing helped him when the unpredictable pains attacked; physicians tried to ease the symptoms with herbs and teas, even blood-letting, but nothing as yet had ever proven successful. So he remained in bed, eating nothing and accepting no visitors. But of course with the arrival of his son, he'd commanded the boy brought to him the minute he set foot within the Chateau.

At last Simon came through the gate, along with two squires, four attendants, two wagons of supplies and possessions and three horses in tow. He looked every bit as dashing as any of King Jean's knights, wearing the crimson color of the Order of the Star upon his resplendent black doublet. He did not sport full armor for his arrival home; instead the only hint of his usual uniform were the gauntlets covering his hands and the dark hood usually worn beneath a helmet.

Upon seeing his mother and sister, he was off his traveling horse within moments and embracing both Marie and Alix in one affectionate swoop.

"Mother!" he said with a kiss, then kissed Alix as well. "It's good to see you both." He squeezed them tight, then stood back to scrutinize his sister.

"Why, she's grown to a beauty, Mother! I'll no doubt have to defend this one from too many swains. It's a good thing I'm home."

Alix glared at her brother in mock severity. Inside, though, she did not feel quite so lighthearted about such a subject. There were no "swains" in her life. The one man she spent so much wasted time on with her silly daytime dreams sought only one thing: to avoid her. It had been two full weeks since Philip had kissed her; two weeks of trying to forget, two weeks of reliving that kiss despite her resolve to forget. Two weeks of turmoil. She'd seen Philip at a total of three dinners; the rest of the time he was as absent from her company as he was from everyone else's. And during those three dinners he spoke not a word to her; he barely glanced her way.

They went inside the Keep, following the wide central stairway to the chambers occupied by Marie and Giles. All three of them entered the inner chamber, but while Marie approached the huge curtained bed, Alix stayed back at Simon's side.

"Father has had one of his stomach ailments since yesterday," Alix explained.

Simon looked worried, and Alix hastened to assure him.

"It's nothing too serious; he's had it before, and will no doubt have it again. It lasts only a few days, then disappears as suddenly and mysteriously as it came."

"How long has Father suffered from this? I always remember him perfectly healthy."

"Since we came to live here . . . over a year now."

"Has it been so long?" he whispered.

Alix nodded. "And now that you're here, perhaps you can do something about our future—away from here."

She no longer counted on Philip's promise to restore the Beauchamp Estate; he'd been so cool toward her since they'd kissed she doubted he would fulfill any previous promises made.

Simon had no chance to respond, for Marie called them both to Lord Giles's bedside. She had pulled back one of the heavy curtains, and in the center, underneath a pile of thick quilts, lay their father, somewhat pale, but with a clear smile on his face as he gazed upon his approaching son.

Alix watched as Simon accepted Lord Giles's outstretched hand. Simon sat on the bed, Lord Giles's smile reflected on his youthful face.

"My son," Giles greeted Simon. "Wearing your colors, I see," he proudly observed.

Then Giles raised his free hand toward Alix and Marie. "Go, both of you. Simon and I have things to discuss, between father and son."

Marie led Alix to the antechamber, a small room she and Giles used as their own private sitting room. The furniture was comfortable there, two long couches richly upholstered in multi-colored brocade, polished tables interspersed here and there, and a small, round window which brightened the room considerably. They sat on one of the couches in the spill of sunlight.

Marie pulled one of the tables toward her; it had tiny wheels attached to its legs, and so it hardly made a sound. On the table was a book, paper, ink and quill, and she began writing almost immediately. She often copied the letters and words from the Chateau library of books; it helped to pass the time, time when most women either sewed or stitched, things Marie had never been fond of. She hoped one day, if they returned to a home of their own, their library would equal that of the de Saineses'. Alix often helped her with the task, and in the year they'd been the de Saineses' guests, they'd copied seven. The de Saineses owned twice that many, and Marie had saved the longest for last.

"Father was very glad to see Simon," Alix said, pulling forth another table so she, too, could write. "Perhaps it will speed his recovery this time."

Marie nodded. "Perhaps."

Soon both were bent over their writing tables, neither saying a word. Writing was the only pastime which took enough of Alix's concentration to keep away thoughts of Philip.

The two had not been working long when the

door to the bedchamber opened and Simon entered.

"He fell asleep," Simon said as he took a seat opposite his mother and sister.

"No doubt with a smile on his face," Marie said, putting down her quill to focus full attention on her son. How handsome he looks, she thought with pride. Tall and strong, sandy-haired like Marie's father. And that smile was decidedly Giles's. It was a happy one, Marie thought, but more than mere contentment at being reunited with family. There was more to this smile that touched Simon's eyes.

"How long will you be able to stay with us, Simon?" Marie asked, going to sit beside him.

Simon welcomed her with an arm about her shoulder, pulling her close. He winked at Alix across from them at the same time. "For a while."

"Does the King demand all of you?" Marie complained, even though her voice wasn't much louder than a whisper.

"France is in need of anyone who can help restore order to its cities. Do you know there are people, so mind-aflicted by the pestilence, they roam the streets naked, beating themselves because they believe the wrath of God has descended upon us? There must be those who can keep such insanity from spreading."

"I am lucky, I suppose, that he let you come home at all," Marie said grudgingly.

"But I thought," Alix said, tempted to tease her brother, "with the truce between our country and England, that all of your feisty knights were getting into every manner of mischief, with lack of any enemy to fight."

"Ah, so you know the true reason for my visit home, do you?" he said with a laugh.

"How long do you have with us?" Marie asked.

Simon hesitated with a hefty intake of breath and long exhale. "It isn't only the king who takes me away, Mother."

"Oh? Where are you off to, then?"

"To Burgundy. I've met a young lady, someone

whom I'm entirely unworthy of, but who has—miraculously—shown an interest in me. Her father has lands in Burgundy, and so I'm off to claim his daughter in marriage."

"Marriage!" Marie and Alix said in unison.

Simon grimaced at their faces. "Is it so incredible that someone has agreed to wed me?"

All three laughed, and Marie embraced Simon from where she sat.

"I won't be leaving for a while, however," Simon continued. "Before I go, I'd like to see about restoring the Estate. I cannot very well bring my bride home to the de Saineses' Chateau."

"Oh, Simon, you will rebuild our home?" Alix asked breathlessly.

But Simon held up a warning hand. "I don't know if I can. I must petition Lord Geoffrey for help; I myself have only a few servants and two horses won in tournaments, besides my own charger and palfrey. Hardly enough manpower to do the job. And as I recall, Alix said the place was devastated."

"Simon, perhaps you should just bring your bride here," Marie said. "There are so few serfs to be found anywhere these days. How will you get the job done in any reasonable amount of time?"

"How can you say that, Mother?" Alix said excitedly. "If Simon brings his bride here, all incentive for him to rebuild will be gone. Don't you want us to go home, where we belong?"

"Of course," she said. "But will Simon's bride wait as long as that?"

"Surely Sire Geoffrey can spare the serfs it will take to rebuild in a timely manner," Simon said. He hadn't seen the damage to the Estate, and secretly he believed his sister's tale of utter destruction was grossly exaggerated. Alix was always so passionate, so dramatic! Surely the damage was not so great.

But both women were obviously skeptical that the Estate would be liveable very soon.

"Look around you, Simon," Alix suggested. "Even this Chateau has fallen near to ruin. Lord

Philip is doing all he can to restore this place, but with such a shortage of workers—"

"Lord Philip?"

"Yes, he's come home."

"I knew he was here," Simon said. "I saw him before he left Paris. But isn't Lord Geoffrey the one overseeing his serfs?"

Marie and Alix exchanged glances. "Since Philip returned, he's acted more as seigneur than Lord Geoffrey himself," Marie said.

Simon smiled. "Than I shall see him about my needs."

He stood to leave, but before he reached the door, Marie called after him. "Wait! You haven't told us who your bride will be."

Simon's eyes took on a softened glow. "Marguerite de Boigne, daughter of Marquis de Boigne."

"But she is here!" Alix exclaimed.

Simon looked puzzled. "Here at Chateau de Saines?"

"Her father left her here while he settled his affairs in Burgundy," Marie told him. "But just for a few days—"

Marie was uncertain her son heard her final words; he was out of the room and down the hall before she'd barely had the chance to utter them.

9

From his window in the high tower, Philip saw the light in the room above the kitchen. It had glowed for nearly an hour, and in that time his concentration had been sorely tried.

He laid aside the books he'd been reading, the charts and graphs he'd drawn in comparison to those in the copies of ancient books on astronomy.

It was no use tonight. He would log the movements of the stars as he always did, but he could not study Ptolemy's works. Not tonight. Not when the glow of someone's candle, not the glow of the stars, captured his attention.

Why didn't she just go to sleep? It was quite late—past midnight. What was she doing?

It hadn't taken Philip long to discover which storeroom Alix occupied. He knew the Chateau well, and was aware that the room now regularly alight at bedtime had been deserted since his childhood. He'd seen Alix on several occasions in her favorite garden spot, and minutes after her departure the once-empty storeroom would glow bright. He knew the room; he used to go there as a child, for it was the only empty room of the Chateau with a window of its own. The room, he suspected, had been deserted long ago because it got too little sun and too much wind. But to Alix the cold had obviously been preferable to the company of the many females sharing the bower. Somehow, the knowledge that Alix slept alone, not amidst a crowded women's bower, made Philip all the more conscious of her.

God's teeth! he was angry with her. And for what reason? Simply because she so unwittingly distracted him? There was nary an hour when she did not enter his thoughts. During the day, when he worked so hard nothing should have been able to penetrate his concentration, he found himself more than once scanning the horizon for her presence. But it seemed she'd given up riding—at least on any rides which would take her near him. And at night, when pure exhaustion should have made him too tired to think of more than the astronomy he delved into for pure enjoyment, thoughts of her inevitably interfered. He remembered that kiss too vividly, the kiss that had ignited all of these wayward thoughts of her. Surely before that kiss he'd been content with his work and his astronomy.

Philip had never been one to waste his time dreaming of a woman. He'd had his share of bedmates, that was true—some might say he'd enjoyed more than one man's share. But that was all they'd ever been: bedmates. He'd never once wanted a woman as friend; he found the intellect of most women as interesting as a dark sky void of stars.

Until meeting Alix. He found himself wanting to discuss everything with her, all of his plans for the Chateau, including the decisions he made regarding its future. Even the steward, Sir Henry, had not seemed as interested or concerned as Alix.

Was he fighting a losing battle? It certainly seemed so. Why even fight? he wondered. He'd kissed her that day because he wanted to kiss her, and thought she wanted it, too. And hadn't she? Didn't it seem as though she enjoyed that kiss every bit as much as he did?

But he'd been scared; he, who had once faced as many as a half-dozen armed men in combat with little more than his wit and his sword. He'd been afraid of one mere woman. So he froze. He fled. He avoided her. And what good had it done, except to make him realize what a fool he was?

There was no reason to continue in this way, was there? After all, Alix was certainly marriage-able. Marriageable! He'd never even considered it . . . but why shouldn't he? He should have wed already; he'd just never gotten around to it, not with his attitude about women being what it was, especially since the scandal had stirred. But Alix had changed that in a miraculously short span of time. Here was a woman who would not be just a bedmate; she would be a partner, one to share more than only the pleasures discovered between the sheets.

Philip stood, going to his window and staring at the glow from the room across from him. He never supposed he would consider marriage with quite so much anticipation. He'd expected to marry one day, of course, and had always imagined the prospect with as much trepidation as any other ingredient when fulfilling the inevitable. It was quite a shock to realize he found the idea of marriage to Alix quite pleasing. More than that: he thought it quite possibly the only solution to his present misery. He would at least be settling the battle waging within himself.

Just then the light extinguished in the room opposite him. Sleep well, thought Philip. Soon, he hoped, her nights would not be spent alone.

Alix patted Morivek's neck. Both were slightly winded after speeding along the open greensward to the shelter of the forest, winded but invigorated. It was a lovely spring morning; the sun was brilliant up above, the air warm and fresh. Early wildflowers were already in bloom, and the grass beneath them a very bright green. Alix especially enjoyed the seasons of change, Spring and Autumn; both were contemplative times, Spring a hope of new things to come, Autumn a reflection on time past.

Alix had spent the past two weeks cooped up like a young bird too afraid to leave the nest. What had she been afraid of? More aptly, whom? Philip? There was no reason for that; he had not forced upon her the kiss they'd shared; she had no reason to fear he would ever force her to do anything. So was it herself she was afraid of? Afraid of the feelings that kiss had stirred? Perhaps. But not any more. She fully intended to go about her days as though that kiss had never taken place, as though Philip de Saines did not even exist.

She came to a glen she'd often sought in the past. It was a secluded spot near the deepest part of the river which ran through de Saines land. Once or twice last summer, on unbearably hot days, she'd stripped to her chemise and gone swimming—a delightful secret she'd shared with no one, not even her mother for fear of being forbidden any future opportunities.

It was too cool to swim today, but she did discard her soft leather shoes and linen hose to test the water with her toes. It was shockingly cold, but she delighted in it, holding her gown immodestly high above her hips. In a frolicking mood after so many days spent indoors, she splashed Morivek who stood nearby, and he whinnied and pawed at the waterline.

Alix sucked in the fresh air. On such a lovely Spring day, it was nothing but a sin to be confined indoors. She had half a mind to skip morning Mass. Why, she wondered, couldn't the service be held outdoors, right under God's eyes? Surely to see and feel the wonders of God's earth would only increase the reverence of all worshippers. She would have to speak to Father Fantin about such an idea.

Just then something grabbed her about the ankle. She screamed, trying to free herself, and in the process almost lost her balance. But she did not fall, for just as suddenly as she'd been grabbed, she was set free, an she heard a huge splash behind her as a tall shadow emerged from the water.

"Philip!" His name, minus his title, poured off her tongue as easily as the droplets covering his wet body. He smiled a huge smile her way, looking so boyishly mischievous she couldn't help but laugh. "You frightened me!" she scolded nonetheless.

He bowed formally. "I beg pardon then, milady. But, upon seeing such a delectable ankle underneath the water, I couldn't help but try to capture it."

He was dressed only in a pair of dark chausses, his chest completely bare and glistening in the sunlight. The chausses clung to his wet legs, defining every muscle of his thighs, revealing all, right down to his mid-calf where the rest of him disappeared into the water. Suddenly conscious of staring at him, Alix forced herself to look away. How could they be standing here, laughing like a couple of children, when they'd spent a better part of the past two weeks trying to avoid one another?

"I didn't know anyone was here," she said at last, slightly breathless. She still held her gown up around her thighs and, realizing the unseemliness of her position, she backed out of the water,

109

letting her skirts fall to the ground once she was on dry land. But she was still conscious of her bare feet.

"This place, for me, is like the center of the garden to you," Philip said as he followed her from the river. "Peaceful and private. I used to come here often as I was growing up."

"I didn't mean to intrude," she said, looking at him in earnest.

He smiled at her. "I'm glad you're here." Then, clearing his throat somewhat awkwardly, he added, "Besides, I intruded on your private place the night I joined you in the garden. The least I can do is share my own favorite place with you in return."

Alix stared at Philip. He was so different! He was entirely at ease, happy to be in her company, it seemed. Then why had he ignored her for the past two weeks? She wasn't naive enough to think she'd been entirely successful in avoiding him the whole time unless he'd given her a bit of help by avoiding her as well. Yet now it was obvious he welcomed her company. Certainly she had not imagined the coolness he'd shown her on the few occasions she'd seen him at the dinner hour. Why the change? she wondered.

Philip gave her no time to ponder the question, or to voice it, although she doubted she would have had the courage to do so. He spoke again, just as friendly and at ease as the first moment he'd popped up from underneath the water.

"Have you been to the village lately?" he asked. "The one I have such hopes for?"

He seemed so anxious for her answer, Alix hated to issue her disappointing answer. "No, I haven't. I've . . . kept to my room of late."

Philip was only too aware of that, but he made no reference to that fact.

"Since the de Saines serfs have been freed, not one family has fled, as my father feared. Not only that, with the wages we're paying, two more entire families have joined us with the promise of sending for relatives in Burgundy. The south field

110

is planted, as well as the north. Soon we'll have the de Saines grain fields as prosperous as they always were."

Alix found it so easy to admire this man. He was pleased with the results of his labor, that was certain. And he had every right to be. Although Alix had kept to herself recently, she wasn't oblivious to the signs of Philip's work. Even within the Chateau things had begun to change. Repairs had been made on every dilapidated rooftop, all broken windows had been replaced, each and every dusty corner had been swept clean. Even the dark corridor leading to her chamber had been miraculously supplied with long, brightly shining tapers to light the way. The Chateau de Saines, in an amazingly short span of time, was swiftly becoming all it had been before the bleak destitution of the Plague had marred its beauty.

"Lord Geoffrey must be very proud of all you've accomplished," Alix said. She wanted to say she was the proud one, but she knew she had no right.

Philip laughed as if she'd said something extremely amusing. "Lord Geoffrey has found no pride in me, his eldest son, for quite some time. He saves all that for Julian."

"Perhaps Julian will be coming home soon," Alix said. "My brother is here, you know. Perhaps the King will send Julian home as well."

"Simon is here? I haven't seen him."

"I think he may seek you out, my lord," she said. "He wishes to borrow some of your serfs to restore the Beauchamp Estate. Simon wishes to be married, and live there with his new bride."

Philip raised his brows. "Then it's good that I sent Sir Henry to the Estate this morning to assess the needs. I was planning to ride there myself after my swim. Would you care to join me? Perhaps we can find Simon as well."

"You will start work on the Estate?" She was plainly surprised.

"I promised you I would. Didn't you believe me?"

She felt herself flush. "I . . . I wasn't sure . . .

after the last time we saw each other." She started to turn away in embarrassment, but he touched her shoulder gently, preventing her from moving.

"I acted foolishly the last time we met," he stated matter-of-factly.

"You regret it, then?" she couldn't help but ask.

He laughed briefly. "Yes, I regret it. And it won't happen again."

Alix felt her heart sink in utter disappointment. How foolish she'd been! She thought that kiss had meant something to him . . . had at least some effect on him. Even his avoidance of her in the past two weeks seemed to show the kiss had not left him indifferent. Not until today. Now she knew why he'd avoided her; it wasn't because he was afraid he would feel tempted to kiss her again, as she'd secretly hoped. Isn't that why she'd avoided him? Because she was afraid he would somehow see that she wished he would kiss her again? No; he had avoided her because he regretted what must have been an unpleasant experience for him.

When he stepped closer, so close she felt his legs brush against her skirt, she looked up at him, bewildered. He acted as though he would kiss her again . . . when he'd just said . . .

When his lips came down on hers she was totally unprepared. She offered neither welcome nor resistance; she merely stood, her pulse racing, lips parted, eyes not even closed. But when his arms came around her and she felt his strong embrace, her own arms encircled him with a will of their own. Her fingers felt his skin, cool and still slightly damp, smooth and hard on his back. His lips were warm, and when his tongue entered where her mouth had been parted in surprise, she felt a thrill of excitement. There was no hesitation in this kiss, no uncertainty or quarter given. He held fast, his mouth pressed to hers with such assurance and sudden, irrevocable passion that Alix could not hold back.

She welcomed the intimacy of his kiss, and shyly, she moved her own inexperienced tongue against his. She felt his hands move against her hair, smoothing it gently down her back. His other hand moved down her side, along the curve of her waist, sending little tremors throughout the body. And when that hand moved higher, up along the curve of her breast, Alix almost moaned aloud. But his kiss prevented it. She reveled in the touch of his fingers, gently teasing her sensitized skin through the material of her underrobe and gown. How she wished she was as devoid of clothing as he was! How she wished she could feel his chest, so strong and solid, against hers without the interference of clothing.

For Philip, the desire to rid her of her garments created an almost overwhelming struggle within him. Her breast, soft and full, felt wonderfully warm and inviting. As inviting as her kiss. He wanted to take her right here, right now, regardless of the hard ground beneath them, regardless of the bright sunlight shining down on them, regardless of the possibility of intrusion, either human or animal here in the middle of the forest. And what of all his plans? He wanted this woman as a bedmate—oh, so much—but more than that. What of the vows that should be exchanged before exploring this bliss?

And he knew, if he didn't stop this moment, then surroundings be hanged, vows be hanged. He would take her. And he doubted he would find much resistance. How tempting she felt, so pliant under his touch, so obviously aroused. Her kiss was almost as eager as his own, her body as welcome to his touch as he could possibly hope for. And he felt her hands on his back; they moved gently, slowly, as if discovering his body through touch in a way only a lover could. He wanted her to discover all of him, each and every inch, without hesitation, and with all the freedom and unhurried motion he himself wished to use to discover her in just as much detail.

When Philip let her go, Alix did not want to open her eyes. She dreaded what she would see, perhaps a repetition of that first time, when he'd

113

looked at her so coldly after igniting such an inferno within her. But she knew she must face whatever Philip offered. She knew what she wanted to see, a fire in his eyes that matched her own. But she dared not hope for that. So, when she did open her eyes, she kept her head bent like a coward. She was not yet ready to look at him.

One of his hands, ever so gently, touched her chin and urged her to look. She knew then she must.

What she saw both thrilled and delightfully discomposed her. There was a fire—a fire burning stronger than her own. In his eyes she saw a passion so real it made her own passion for the unknown pale in comparison. But she knew it was Philip she longed to have show her.

"I behaved foolishly last time," he repeated himself, "because I fled like a coward. But never again."

He kissed her once more, not quite so thoroughly, for if he allowed himself that pleasure he knew it would be impossible to break away. And so he did not hold her quite so close, nor did he allow his hands to stray from her back. It was hardly a chaste kiss, however, for his lips traveled from her mouth to her smooth cheek, to the tiny lobe of her ear and on down her neck. Then, for one long moment, he simply held her, completely unmoving.

"I've thought of little else since that day in the winery," he confessed.

"But you gave no clue of that! You hardly spoke to me."

"More foolishness," he said. "But now that is all over."

He held her at arm's length. "I want us to know each other, Alix. Would you grant me that wish?"

She nodded, eyes wide, unable to hide the pleasure she would have in granting such a wish. "I do want to know you, Lord Philip."

He frowned at the use of his title. "None of that," he told her. "A moment ago you called me simply by my name, and I found it very nice to hear."

"All right . . . Philip," she said, a slight smile trembling on her lips.

"We'll start today," he told her briskly. "Would you accompany me to the Estate? I'd like you to tell me exactly how it looked before the fire." He frowned then, ever so slightly, and continued. "I'll be going there every day for a while, at least until much of the work is begun, so I doubt we'll be seeing much more of each other than we have the past two weeks. But don't," he added firmly, "think today's kiss had anything to do with it. If I had it my way I would have you there beside me every day."

Alix could hardly believe his words and, because if she was anything she was impetuous, she said, "Why can't I be?"

He looked at her, surprised. "It would hardly be very much fun, watching a bunch of men working."

"I could help . . . couldn't I? Somehow? Besides, I truly do want to be there."

He saw her sincerity and knew he was unable to resist. He nodded before he even considered what he was doing. Blast, he thought after he'd consented, how was he to get anything accomplished having her within reach?

Alix hugged him so impulsively it surprised them both.

"Meet me at the stable in an hour," Philip said. "I'll find Simon and bring him along. Go now—I can't escort you back to the Keep looking like this."

Alix fairly floated back to the Chateau. Could it be possible? Could every dream she'd ever imagined be fulfilled by Philip de Saines? Would her home be rebuilt by the man she was so quickly coming to love?

The thought of loving Philip no longer frightened her the way it had those two weeks she agonized over all the time spent on thoughts of him. She hadn't wanted to love Philip then; she'd been certain it would bring only pain. And now? She knew one thing: Philip wanted her. He wanted her every bit as much as she wanted him. Surely love played a part in that?

She found Simon before Philip had the chance. As she approached the Chateau, she passed the training yard and saw her brother atop his prized charger. He looked resplendent in his full armor, so tall and invincible. And for a moment her breath caught in her throat. How like Philip he looked, just for a moment. Like the Philip she'd fallen in love with when she was just a child. The Philip that no longer was.

What silliness, she thought. Just moments ago she'd come from his embrace, an embrace that still sent tremors of desire along her spine.

Alix longed to understand him, to know why it was he would never again mount his own charger, and take up battle armor. Perhaps, if she understood that, the image of the brave knight of her childhood could be put behind the image of Philip today.

10

From the hilltop on which the de Saines Chateau was built, the Beauchamp Estate could be seen far in the distance. In between were various newly planted fields, a dozen or more tenant cottages, and one of the largest villages on de Saines land. The colors were already vibrant for so early in Spring, with green budding trees, dark rich soil, yellow rooftops, and the azure sky sparkling up above.

Alix used to cross the distance often as a child, but as she traveled it once again today, she felt a new excitement, one she hadn't felt as a child. No doubt she had always loved her home, but she hadn't realized how much until losing it. And now, because of Philip, it was being restored.

But, strangely enough, the loneliness she'd felt at the Chateau—the same loneliness that had made her pine for her home—was disappearing with the company of Philip. That, however, did not diminish her excitement at having the Estate rebuilt.

Philip rode Cedric at her side, and on his far side rode Simon on his fine palfrey.

"So you are the one who taught Demoiselle Alix to ride like a knight," Philip said to Simon.

Alix had the good sense to say nothing, in defense of either herself or Simon. But Simon looked exaggeratedly sorrowful with a shake of his head and a frown that tugged at his handsome mouth and wrinkled his forehead from his dark hairline to his somewhat bushy black brows.

"I lament the day," he said with melodrama. "More than once my father has reminded me ladies of quality do not take pleasure in such a sport. And, I must add, Alix has not made it any easier for me. Do you know, as soon as she realized her love for horseback riding, she would sneak out at dawn and ride alone? Unchaperoned?"

Alix exchanged an uneasy glance with Philip, who merely looked amused. It was obvious Sir Simon was totally unaware that Alix had never given up the habit.

"Those were the days when the Estate bred the finest mounts in all of France " Simon continued, somewhat wistfully. Alix welcomed the change of subject, particularly since it went to the Estate. "It was sad news to hear the stables were lost along with the home. Odd, don't you think, Alix, since the stables were set quite far from the main building where the accident was to occur?"

Alix hadn't thought it odd. Why should she, when she knew the fire in the stable had been set just as intentionally as the one that destroyed the

117

home itself? If the stables had been left undamaged, the valuable studs and mares within left unharmed, then the Estate could easily have raised the funds it needed to rebuild itself without having to depend upon its overlord. The Montforts had been thorough in their destruction, a destruction sure to effect the de Saineses.

Philip saw the hard line of her mouth—the mouth that was usually so soft, so inviting, so eagerly smiling. Now was the time, he thought, to speak his suspicions. He wanted to know just what it was that affected her each and every time the fire was mentioned.

"It wouldn't be odd," Philip said, "if the fire were no accident."

Both Alix and Simon looked at Philip with surprise. Simon spoke. "What do you mean?" he asked.

"Only that I believe there is something suspicious about this fire," he said evasively, looking at neither of them. All he truly knew was that Alix believed there was something suspicious about it. That was enough.

"My father said it was an accident," Simon pointed out calmly. "He was here at the time—and since neither you nor I were, we should trust his judgment."

"But I was here," Alix said firmly, angry her brother could dismiss her so easily. "And I do not think it was an accident."

Simon seemed hesitant to accept her opinion. "Who do you think responsible?"

Alix breathed deeply, ready to issue her accusation even if her brother was not prepared to believe her . . . One glance at Philip told her he had more faith in her. "There is only one family capable of it: the Montforts."

"Have you spoken to Father about this?" Simon asked.

Simon's calm question was hardly welcome. He sounded just like Father! "After the fire I told Father what I thought."

"And?"

118

Alix shifted in her saddle, looking away. But she spoke the truth. "He disagreed. He said he would have taken vengeance upon the Montforts immediately—even though their numbers are greater than ours—if he had any evidence. But he blamed the kitchen maids; he knew them to be careless and believed it was their fault."

"What about the stables?" Philip asked.

"The air was dry that night . . . My father said the wind carried the fire from one roof to the other."

"It sounds very logical, Alix," Simon said. "I am surprised you still disagree."

It was entirely obvious she remained unconvinced of her father's opinion, and the fact that Simon so easily agreed with Lord Giles did not rest well with her either. Philip could see that written plainly upon her lovely but troubled face.

Soon the Estate lands were in close view. Alix used to ride here often when she first left it to live with the de Saines; it was her escape, her refuge away from the crowded Chateau. But eventually she realized coming to this place only made her miss it all the more. Seeing it look so destroyed and empty only multiplied the pain. And when her mother so often discouraged her hopes of returning there to live, Alix finally stopped coming altogether. It had been more torture than pleasure.

But there was no trace of unhappiness in her today. Her gaze traveled the familiar landscape lovingly. Gentle hills, already green with new spring life, surrounded the Estate like a mammoth, greatly stuffed quilt. There were tall trees here and there, a cluster of pines, a lone oak, and many beech. Many of the outbuildings had been left untouched by the devastating fire, and so upon the initial approach the Estate looked the way it always had: gracious, welcoming, and above all others in beauty. Even the wildflowers growing on the hillsides bade welcome as they swayed gently in the breeze.

"It looks the same from here," Simon said hopefully as they rode. He'd been off fighting the English when the Estate had burned, and various tales of its destruction had reached his ears. But none had been so awesome as Alix's. She'd told him of utter destruction, not of a mere fire. But she'd always been prone to dramatics, he'd consoled himself. Never once had he imagined the Estate with the damage she'd described.

Silently, all three of them urged their mounts to a slightly faster pace, and they nearly trotted as they traversed the weedy road that led to the center of the Estate lands.

Finally they reached the crest of the last hill. All three came to an abrupt halt. Beyond lie the Estate in all its misery and desolation.

Alix held her breath. It had been so long since she'd seen it; could she have forgotten the complete devastation? Nothing was left, not even a chimney. They must have crumbled along with the rest of the old place.

She could see several men standing in the shade of a tall tree, their horses tied and off to one side. They just stood there; no one had even begun.

But where to begin? The question was written all over Philip's face. Alix saw disbelief written on Simon's, and for a moment she submitted to the impossibility of the task. They obviously already had. It would take months alone just to clear all of the debris. Charred ruins of what had once been a three-story, double-winged structure lay in a black pile, a few tall beams still standing here and there but so obviously unstable it would take the bravery of every man involved just to remove the waste before even attempting to rebuild.

Beyond where the house had been were the ruins of the stable. Once, the Beauchamp stables had boasted the best horses in Brittany. That had been the greatest tragedy of that awful night, Alix remembered. All inhabitants of the home had escaped, but many of the best chargers and palfreys, bred for the finest knights in France, had been trapped and met a horrible death. She could still hear their cries.

Alix looked at Philip, and what she saw burdened her more than Simon's obvious distress. But she had told him! Hadn't she said, on that very first night, that her home had been destroyed? What had he expected?

"It's useless, isn't it?" she said softly. "There aren't enough men in all France to haul away all of this debris."

Philip did not answer immediately. It did seem useless, he thought for the briefest moment. The ruins were stacked higher than the height of four men, spanning an area almost as wide as the Chateau itself. Nothing of value was left, not even a lone chimney! And his men *were* limited. It had taken seventeen years to build the Chateau, stone by stone, and the Estate, even though it had been made of wood, had been remarkably huge. It was even older than the Chateau, for the nobility that owned the land before the de Saines family acquired it had been tied to that Estate since the time of Charles the Fat. Generations had passed since then, adding and restoring, always keeping the original charm by adhering to the wooden beauty. And now it was gone; all of it, every stick.

But the desolation on Alix's face was almost as great. He'd been foolish, he realized to promise something without knowing the full extent of what that promise entailed. But, by God, he would not abandon his word.

He reached out and touched Alix's hand, ever so briefly for they were not alone. If that had been the case, he thought, if they *had* been alone, he would have swept her into his arms and soothed away every line of worry. He would promise her anything, he thought, just to have some measure of this morning's happiness restored to her.

"It isn't useless," he said, forcing himself to believe his own words. "It'll just take a little longer than I thought." He turned to Simon. "It seems I spoke too soon this morning, Simon. I hope your bride is patient. It'll be more than a few short months before this place can welcome your new family."

Alix turned her gaze to Simon as well, her eyes plaintively wide. "I'm so sorry, Simon," she said. "I've been so anxious to have our home rebuilt that I've selfishly disregarded all you've counted on. Surely Marguerite will wait?"

"She needn't, you know," Philip reminded them. "You have a home at de Saines Chateau as long as you need it. I doubt my parents, or even yours, are quite so anxious for this place to be rebuilt."

Surprisingly enough, Simon laughed. "You're right, I suppose. Marguerite likes it at the Chateau; I'm sure she'll be happy there. But it isn't Marguerite I worry about. Her father is one of the wealthiest men in all Burgundy. He doesn't yet know of my wish to marry his daughter. What will he say to a man who cannot even offer his only child a home of her own?"

"He will be lucky to have you as son-in-law," Alix said vehemently, her fierce loyalty apparent. "And living at the Chateau is only temporary from now on. Everyone will know that once work here begins."

Her eyes met Philip's then, and for the first time she realized what it meant to have the Estate rebuilt. She would no longer be sharing the same home as Philip. Just yesterday that thought might have consoled her; today, after this morning, it threatened to bring only a great sense of loss. After all, she had no idea what Philip wanted from her. He'd said he wanted to know her—but why? For what purpose? As a friend? A lover? A mistress? She gulped hard. As a wife? She dared not hope.

Simon was smiling at her. "You've always been the one to offer me assurance and see the best—perhaps that's why I wasn't prepared to accept all your dire descriptions of the damage done to the Estate. At the very least, I suspected you of typical female exaggeration."

Philip laughed, too. "I must have been guilty of believing that as well, even though I learned very quickly that your sister's mind is hardly like any other female's."

Simon's gaze shifted to Philip, thinking he sounded suspiciously like Simon himself when speaking of Marguerite. Could it be, he wondered, that his sister had stirred the interest of Philip de Saines—heir to the great de Saines fortune? Not that his fortune would matter, least of all to Alix. Or to Lord Giles. No amount of money could rectify the fact that Philip no longer lived the life of a knight. Philip didn't have to fight, that was true. He owed his sword to none but France itself. Not like Simon, who had to sell his sword and his might behind it to the highest bidder, who at this time happened to be the extravagant King Jean himself. Not Lord Philip, though. He didn't need to fight for money. But he was a knight, and in Lord Giles's mind, Simon had no doubt, that meant he must wield a sword. Every able-bodied man was created for that purpose; isn't that what Lord Giles had taught him?

Simon might not agree with his father's attitude about Philip, but he was wise enough to know beyond a doubt that if Alix was to encourage this interest shown by Philip, she would have Lord Giles to reckon with. That is, he thought, if she herself could ignore the fact that Philip no longer acted as a knight. He knew his sister well, so well, in fact, that he knew if she'd been born a man, she herself would be as great a knight as any. But then, he smiled to himself with wry amusement, if Alix had been born a man, there certainly wouldn't have been any attraction to Philip de Saines to concern themselves with!

The three of them descended the gentle incline to join the de Saines steward and his men. Sir Henry greeted Philip in a less than enthusiastic manner.

"These men," he said as he referred to the handful of men behind him, "are all we can spare from the Chateau. I'm sure I haven't any need to tell you how long it would take to rebuild here with so few workers."

"No, Sir Henry, you needn't," said Philip, his friendly tone hardly responding to Sir Henry's obvious lack of dedication to the arduous task ahead.

"Then should we return to the Chateau?" he asked, obviously ready to abandon the job before it was ever begun.

Philip eyed Sir Henry. "Now why should you want to do that when there is so much to be done here?"

Sir Henry's scowl showed he was displeased, and he was hardly one to keep his feelings hidden. "Sire, there is much work left at the Chateau, you said so yourself. Not only that, how can you leave the Chateau undefended? With so many men here doing the labor of mere peasants, what would happen to the Chateau should the Montforts attack the way they attacked the d'Aussy lands?"

Simon had no idea there had been fighting in the area. Nor had he any notion that the men Philip hoped to use to rebuild the land were anything but peasant workers. But now that he looked more closely, he recognized a few of the men as pages and squires to some of the de Saines men-at-arms. Surely none were knights, for no knight would ever do the labor of a peasant. But he doubted any of these men present had ever imagined service to their lord would include rebuilding a noble's estate.

"My father's men-at-arms will see to the defense of the Chateau," Philip reminded Sir Henry. "You, as steward, should see to the domestic needs as well as the other interests of the de Saines family."

"I'm aware of my duty, my lord," Sir Henry said stiffly.

"Good," Philip said, smiling congenially. "Then let us all see how best you may perform that duty." But he knew the duties of steward were not the ambition of Sir Henry. Would he never change? Philip asked himself. Henry had been Geoffrey's steward for nearly eight years, but all knew just how eagerly he longed for the position of castellan. Sir Oliver had held the coveted position longer than Henry had been steward, but nary a day had gone by when Henry had not made his hopes known. He was a knight with great aspirations—and who could rule a finer army than that of Geoffrey de Saines? There were few, save of course the King, who could claim the quality of the de Saines men-at-arms. And Henry was just rapacious enough to want that position.

Alix continued to listen as Philip issued orders and assigned tasks to begin removal of the debris. Several men were sent back to the Chateau for sturdy war horses which were accustomed to pulling the heavy wagons of battle paraphernalia. They would find pulling wagonloads of crumbled chimneys and charred beams little different from the disassembled tents and bulky camp utensils which followed the knights from battleground to battleground. Other men were sent straight to the task at hand: hauling away debris. Philip dismissed a suggestion of Sir Henry's to rebuild the keep elsewhere and in so doing avoid the onerous task of removing the remains of the previous home. It was obvious this hilltop was the only clearly defensible place in which to rebuild. The forefathers who had first chosen the spot had chosen well. To one side was a sheer, insurmountable cliff. To the other lay the slopes leading to the fields and village and, eventually, to the Chateau. It was not as invincible as the Chateau on its higher, steeper hilltop, surrounded entirely by a manmade moat, but it was by far the most defensible spot this far east. That even Sir Henry could not deny. And, knowing he might one day he asked to defend this fief of his lord's, he did not argue long when Philip resisted his task-saving suggestion.

Soon everyone was immersed in the labor at hand. Twice Alix was led away from the dangerous remains when she came too close to a precariously balanced beam. But she could not remain idle and, finally, when for the third time Philip asked her to remain outside the ruins, he suggested accompanying her back to the Chateau.

"How can I hope to work with the others if I

have to worry over your welfare?" Philip asked when he saw protest forming in her expression.

"I cannot sit idle while everyone else is working so hard—on *my* home."

"This isn't work for a woman."

"Nor is it work for pages and squires," she countered. "But you let them work."

He let out a long sigh. "Alix, I am quickly coming to realize you are the most unusual woman I have ever met. You speak as boldly as any knight, you're willing to work like a peasant, and you're about as obedient as an untrained pup. But won't you admit one thing? This work is too heavy for you—you may compare favorably with any man in boldness and intellect, but our Creator made man the stronger of the two genders. Let us at least be truthful about that."

"I have no argument with that," she said.

"Then let me take you back to the Chateau while we remove this heavy debris."

Alix could see she had lost the brief battle. But there was no reason to take him away from the work just to act as escort.

"I can ride back alone," she told him. "You, of all people, know I hardly need a chaperone."

But he was already walking alongside her as they headed toward the horses. "There are two reasons I have no intention of letting you go back alone. The first is your brother: I brought you here properly accompanied and I have no intention of stirring his righteous wrath by letting you return alone. Part of that has to do with your dress—if you'd look at yourself. The last time I returned you to the Chateau with a soiled dress, all manner of Hell broke loose."

Alix gazed down at her gown for the first time. He was right, the gown was covered with soot and grime. No doubt beyond repair, as her mother would say.

"I will not have you facing your parents alone when their imaginations get the best of them again."

"Those are not very strong reasons to send me

126

away," she pointed out.

They had reached the horses and, before assisting her astride Morivek, he smiled that same smile that still did not fail to make her heart jump.

"Those reasons are combined as one. The second and more important reason is that I would like to accompany you back to the Chateau. Alone. Do you object?"

Her smile answered him.

They paused only long enough to tell Simon where they were going before leaving the Estate grounds. Simon, working alongside two squires who were every bit as filthy as he was, just watched them go, neither smiling nor frowning. He wasn't quite sure how to respond to the relationship growing between those two. But he was hardly worried. He'd learned long ago not to be concerned over his feisty, if somewhat head-strong, sister. Not only did she take care of herself, he knew well enough she resented anyone worrying over her as if she were a child. And, as Philip de Saines no doubt realized, Alix certainly was no child.

Alix and Philip let their horses slow down once they were out of sight of the working men. Philip did not want to be gone too long, considering the huge amount of work to be done, but he could not ignore his wish to linger in Alix's company. Even with soot spattering her yellow gown and a smudge of cinders streaking across one smooth cheek, she was lovelier than any woman he'd ever seen. Her hair had come loose from its chignon, and it seemed to float in the gentle southerly breeze. Her green eyes sparkled in the sunlight, the color of polished emeralds, and her smile was as fresh as the spring air surrounding them. Yes, he thought, it would be very easy to forget every responsibility and just while away the day at her side.

"Perhaps I should have my maid smuggle a fresh gown from my room for me," Alix said lightly, "so my father will not see me wearing this one."

127

"He has reason, I suppose, to fret. He no doubt imagines he'll be spending a whole year's revenue replacing your gowns."

Alix frowned as she looked down the dark stains covering her front. "This gown truly is ruined, as the other one was. I really ought to be more careful."

"Your father may want to marry you off just to avoid replenishing your wardrobe himself. Leave that expense to the prospective husband."

That he was teasing seemed obvious, Alix thought, but when their eyes met she couldn't help letting her gaze stay a moment longer than necessary. Philip, too, let his gaze linger, and she felt warmth rise from her middle and spread throughout her entire being.

"I was betrothed once," Alix said, forcing conversation when the length of the look between them threatened to embarrass her. "I was very young, no more than eleven. I was to marry a boy from another of your father's fiefs."

"What happened?"

"He grew sick and died before the wedding could take place. And, because my family respected his, they did not betroth me to anyone else out of respect for his memory."

"Surely they cannot expect you never to marry?" Philip asked, a trifle too quickly.

"Oh, no. I believe the years have simply crept up on us all. I should have been wed long ago, even my father said so just the other day." Now why had she said that? It sounded so brazen, as if she were hinting at her own thoughts on the subject. But surely she had no overwhelming desire to wed!

"My father said the same of me not long ago," Philip told her. He watched her closely, wondering if the topic of conversation had any effect on her. But she hid her emotions well, although he did suspect she was a bit nervous. She held the reins more stiffly than usual, and from Morivek's sudden restlessness he guessed she hugged him rather tight with her knees. Then he said, "But with the scandal still so fresh in everyone's mind, I doubt any woman of honor would have me."

"Oh, that's not so!" Alix hastily assured him. "I do not understand why people are so eager to spread tales of one such as you . . . I mean, someone of your title and lineage."

Her protest warmed him. "My family has always been the source of gossip; our fortune seems only to enhance the stories, I suppose. Even my father is not above reproach. Everyone wonders why he doesn't petition the King for the coveted title of Duke; everyone knows he is certainly powerful enough to warrant such a title."

Alix could only smile knowingly. "Anyone acquainted long with your father could guess the reason for that. What does he need with a title? He's so like a king in his own domain that the title of Duke could hardly matter."

Philip was pleased that Alix was so perceptive in her observation of his father. Geoffrey was the only person, aside from Alix, who had warranted any amount of Philip's attention in the past few weeks. He seemed so changed from the man he'd been before Philip had left home. Once Geoffrey de Saines had been the strongest seigneur in the land. Now he was indecisive, indifferent to the needs of his Chateau, and in too many ways empty of the care needed to properly oversee a Chateau of any size. Philip had expected a fight when issuing freedom for the serfs. Instead, Lord Geoffrey had said and done nothing. It seemed all he wished was that Philip conduct himself in a manner more befitting the de Saines name. So, Philip had made a concerted effort to attend many meals, and to be less conspicuous about the manual work he did by dressing properly whenever entering the hall. But of course none of this had much impact on Geoffrey, who barely spoke a word to his eldest son. Philip was not foolish enough to believe anything he did—short of taking up the sword again—would bring him any closer to his father. The disappointment Geoffrey felt in Philip obviously outweighed whatever pride he felt for the Chateau and the work Philip did for it.

"Tell me, Demoiselle, do you know every member of my family so thoroughly?"

She laughed. "I know very little about your family, really," she said. "I hardly know your mother at all—she is reserved and quiet in her dignity. And your brother Julian . . . I barely remember him from our youth. And you . . . I have a great many unanswered questions about you. I suppose everyone does—that is why they gossip about you. But eventually the gossip will end," she added brightly. "Once they have something else to talk about."

"Perhaps they will have a more pleasant topic to discuss regarding the de Saines name," Philip said, his tone hopeful. He watched her closely. "A betrothal announcement would certainly occupy their tongues for a while."

Alix did not have the courage to look directly at Philip, although she could feel his gaze on her. "A betrothal?" she said, thankful her voice didn't sound as nervous as she felt.

"Is it time, after all. My parents long for grandchildren, and I . . . have need of heirs."

Though his words referred to marriage for what it was—a contract within which to create heirs—his tone was soft and sensual. Alix said nothing, as if knowing he would continue. Morivek danced nervously beneath her, sensing her excitement.

Philip pulled rein on Cedric, at the same time reaching over and gently doing the same with Morivek. Then, just as gently, he put a fingertip beneath Alix's chin until she had no choice but to look up at him.

"I said earlier today I would like us to get to know one another better," Philip said, his unblinking eyes staring at her so intensely she felt under a spell. "Perhaps . . . after we do that . . . there can be a betrothal announcement."

He wasn't precisely asking for her hand in marriage—it was not his place to ask Alix's permission, but her father's—and yet Alix felt as if

130

the world suddenly spun around her. Marriage was obviously the goal Philip had in mind, provided what they discovered in each other was to their liking. It seemed too wondrous to be true. Most men would have simply gone to her father, asked for her hand, then introduced themselves. It was hardly Alix herself they seemed to want to marry—rather some image they had of her, built on the way she composed herself at dinner or the way she danced or the way she laughed at anyone's joke. Philip wanted to know her first, and let her know him. How much more wonderful a marriage would be if they didn't have to spend the first moments of it just learning each other's full names!

"Will you let us know one another better, then?" Philip asked her at last.

Smiling tremulously, she nodded. "Yes, Philip. I would like that."

Philip seemed relieved; he let out a breath and smiled, and a wrinkle disappeared from his forehead.

"We'll let it be our secret for the time being," he said. "Living under one roof along with our parents, they would undoubtedly put strains on us we'd be better off without. Do you agree?"

She nodded wholeheartedly. She didn't want to face the prospect of her father's response just yet.

"Then shall we seal the pact?" he asked.

Alix's green eyes widened, anticipation forming so readily she should have been ashamed. But she wasn't. Would they dismount for a kiss? The same sort of kiss they'd shared this morning, or in the winery? How she would enjoy that! she thought boldly. Even now, the beginning of desire spawned deep within.

But Philip made no move to dismount, and it was his lead Alix felt she must follow. Instead, he took her hand, sliding his fingers through hers and squeezing ever so gently. Then, leaning close, he pressed a kiss . . . to her cheek!

11

Sire Geoffrey listened to those around him with an expression he knew revealed none of his inner thoughts. Lord Giles sat beside him, and from his old friend's face he could see the ravings of Sir Oliver, Geoffrey's castellan, were met with the same amount of ambivalence Geoffrey secretly felt. But, by God, he'd rot in Hell before he let anyone know he was tempted to shy away from a fight. Not when his own son had put that shame on the de Saines name twice too often—once when first laying down the sword and again just recently, when running from that blasted scandal at Court.

"The d'Aussys must be avenged!" Sir Oliver pronounced, and continued in a tone that resounded to the farthest corner of the Hall. "The Montforts should be thrown from their stolen lands, and murdered in the way they murdered the d'Aussys."

"Word has it, my lord," joined in Georges, one of Oliver's most zealous followers, "that the Montforts have built up their arms and are preparing to attack the Chateau itself."

At that Geoffrey simply sneered. "Let them try," he said with quiet confidence.

"Oh, there is no doubt they would fail, Lord Geoffrey," Sir Oliver assured him, "but why let them go so far as to attack this mighty fortress, one whose strength alone has diminished any enemy's notion of attacking for more than sixty years? And now we have true reason to fight: the d'Aussy lands lay open and unprotected because of them. Their next move will no doubt be to simply usurp that land the way they usurped the lands they now possess. And they must be stopped—not only for the enemies they are, but also so that their deeds won't inspire others to follow in their stead."

Though Geoffrey would admit it to no one, he was not eager to fight. The pestilence had left him with less than half of his men-at-arms, and for the time being at least, he preferred to wait until their numbers could be built up once again. "How many is this Montfort family said to have protecting them?"

"Their gold—stolen gold—has been able to buy the allegiance of mercenaries from both France and England. And everyone knows, my lord," Sir Oliver added with a cunning note, "that King Edward himself is behind any plot that embroils France in bloodshed. It would suit his purposes well to have us so occupied with each other that he may pounce upon us unawares and conquer."

"So Montfort's arms are fairly unlimited from England," Giles stated from Geoffrey's side.

Georges answered him. "That is so, my lord, which is why we should act now, before he has time to raise a larger army. Let us attack as soon as possible, rather than be attacked later."

Geoffrey held up a cautioning hand. "I would know more before escalating this feud into a full battle between the two families. The Montforts have been a thorn in the de Saines side some four years or more, but it has never amounted to much more than bitter words flying back and forth because they are quite obviously jealous of our, and every other noble's, lineage. They have the wealth of a noble, but not the breeding with their peasant stock. I had always believed they would eventually petition the King of France for a title and that would be the end of it; they would have their claim to nobility and have no further reason to instigate trouble to prove their growing power."

"Perhaps they've chosen to prove just how powerful they've become by conquering the most powerful family in Brittany—the de Saines," said

Sir Oliver. "That would certainly gain the attention of the King of France—and the King of England. They could easily appeal to either of them for a title as great as Duke, and which King could ignore them? If the war with England is resumed, King Edward would be only too glad to grant the Montforts whatever they desired. And King Jean can hardly ignore a family mighty enough to thwart the ancient de Saines dynasty. How could he, when one of his fears would logically be that the Montforts' next target might be in Paris itself—and Jean's throne?"

Geoffrey considered all Oliver said. He did not want a full-scale war between his men and the Montforts; he had to admit, even though it was true he'd scorned his son for so many things, one of them being his obvious distaste for war, Geoffrey himself was enjoying the results of Philip's work—work he could not do if he took up his sword. Philip had renewed the sense of prosperity the Chateau had been famous for. And if Geoffrey ordered all of his men, knights and freed serfs alike, to do battle, it would put a quick end to all Philip's endeavors. But, by God, he would not shy from battle simply because he welcomed the renewed taste of opulent life. If that was true he was no better than his son, who in Geoffrey's opinion fully deserved the malicious gossip following his name. Perhaps, Geoffrey thought with some hope, Philip would even have reason enough to take up the sword again—if he saw the threat to all the work he'd done in the past weeks.

"Sir Oliver," Geoffrey began, "I want you to find out exactly what resources Montfort has at his disposal. How many men, both knights and foot soldiers, and how well armed they are. And send as many as you can spare to the d'Aussy lands. See that it is protected from the Montforts henceforth."

Sir Oliver's eyes glittered with anticipation. "I will see to these matters myself, my lord." Then he bowed formally and left the room without delay.

Oliver passed Philip and Alix as he left the Great Hall. Because it was expected, he bowed respectfully as he passed, but he never lifted his eyes to meet Philip's.

Philip paid Oliver little mind. He saw Lord Geoffrey at the far end of the hall seated on the huge chair on the raised dais. He was surrounded by the remaining knights.

"Looks like a council of war," Philip said with a hint of disfavor touching his tone. Sir Oliver, still within earshot and obviously without thought to possible consequences, spoke insolently.

"Something you no doubt are quite happy to be excluded from."

Philip eyed Oliver before issuing any reply. He knew the ambitious knight well; he'd been his father's castellan some nine years. In many ways, the older man reminded Philip of the zealous Sir Sidney Paul, the one knight that to this day tempted Philip to touch his sword just once more. But that was just his pride speaking, and he knew how to control that. Just as he knew he must control it now.

"Quite," he said congenially enough. Then, when Oliver smirked, Philip added, "I learned long ago that mad dogs are best left to themselves."

Oliver literally sputtered at that. "Mad dogs? You accuse me . . . and your father of being mad dogs?"

Philip said nothing, offering neither denial nor admission. Oliver stared, his dark eyes blazing angrily, but at last, obviously dismissing Philip as something akin to a coward, if not a total coward, he uttered one low oath and strutted from the hall.

Philip watched him go, his expression changing to what Alix thought was pity. "Will they never realize?"

"What?" Alix said, her voice barely a whisper.

Philip let out the breath he'd held back. He glanced at her, ready to change the subject, but upon seeing her earnest interest, he explained his thoughts. "One day, when our world is more

135

sensible than it is today—more civilized—perhaps we'll tire of the glory of killing. The pestilence killed thousands; does that have glory? Perhaps someday men will want to understand our world instead of just making it one huge battleground."

Alix stared, unabashed. Never in her life had she heard such words, not even at Mass! And part of her rebelled at such thoughts; noble, they might be, but simply not logical! How could one man strive for peace when the whole world around him battled? He would simply be crushed and the world would have no knowledge of his existence.

But another part of her welcomed the words, for more than just the true nobility of his thinking. Here, she thought, was the reason Philip laid down his sword. Not because he was a coward—she'd never believed that. But because he was sick of it, tired of all the killing. The pestilence should have made us all tired of death, she thought to herself.

Still, she was not entirely convinced Philip's thinking was right. How could it be, when the Montforts lurked, unrepentant, ready to renew any manner of killing if it served their purposes? A man without a sword would hardly stand in the Montforts' way.

As they walked farther into the hall, the group of knights surrounding Sire Geoffrey and Alix's father began to disperse. Alix would have slipped through the crowd, hoping for anonymity, but her father spotted her and waved her to his side.

"I suppose he's readying himself to scold me for the new wardrobe I shall need," Alix whispered to Philip.

Philip accompanied her to Lord Giles' side, thinking both Lord Giles and Geoffrey looked far too stern to be worried about the cost of a new gown.

"Alix," Lord Giles began, "I have reminded you many times that you are not to leave the Keep without an escort. There are those who roam the countryside who have little care that you are the daughter of a nobleman. Henceforth, you are not to leave the Keep or bailey—unless accompanied. That is," he added with a disparaging glance directed Philip's way, "by a man fully armed."

"I assure you—" Alix began boldly, but her father would not let her speak.

Giles continued, his tone firm, his countenance set in an unmistakable scowl. "Philip de Saines is hardly a fitting protector. Without sword or weapon, how could he protect you from any form of danger?"

"I feel no jeopardy when in Lord Philip's company," Alix said. She would have said more, but cautioned herself against speaking too vehemently in Philip's defense—and not only because they wished to keep their relationship a secret for the time being. She sensed Philip himself would not welcome any defense—whether from her or anyone else. He'd made the decision to give up the sword, and lived with that decision far more comfortably than anyone else did.

Sire Geoffrey spoke up, not in defense of his son, but to open a new topic of conversation. It was obvious by his restless position he disliked the previous topic. "It is just as well you are here, Philip. I would have sent for you before the supper hour anyway. I understand you have persuaded several of my men's squires and pages to work for you."

"That is true."

"It must stop; such men were not born to labor in such a manner."

"There is much work to be done, both here and at the Beauchamp Estate. Every idle hand should be employed."

Geoffrey waved away Philip's logic. "Those hands are hardly idle when doing the services of their knights."

"But, Sire," Alix spoke up, "if you could only see just how much work there is to be done on the Estate! Even my brother has been working there today—he sees what a task it shall be to rebuild."

Lord Giles leaned forward in his seat. "Simon is there, working like a peasant?"

Immediately Alix regretted her rash statement. "Yes, Father. He is most anxious, as we all should be, to have the Estate rebuilt."

Giles glared at Philip. "I would like to speak to you, Lord Philip, after your father has spoken to you."

Philip looked at Giles, his face barren of emotion, looking neither defensive nor alarmed that Giles obviously wished to reprove him.

"You may say right now whatever you wish, Lord Giles. My father will most likely agree with whatever you have to say."

Giles glanced from Philip to Geoffrey, who nodded assent for Giles to speak freely to his son. Giles did not delay. "Having my son work like a peasant is no doubt your doing, with the example you've given since your return. We've all seen how you've ignored the ways of nobililty in order to work like a common serf. Perhaps that is the way you ignore the scandal everyone still speaks of—by avoiding those of your rank who are your judges." He raised a hand, pointing from Philip to Alix and then back again as he spoke. "You are to stay away from my son, and my daughter as well. I'll not have your influence affecting either one of them—for my son to work like a peasant or my daughter to associate with a man who cannot clear his name of scandal."

"Father—" Alix began, aghast at his words, but Philip spoke over her protest.

"I realize we disagree on a great many things, Lord Giles," Philip said. "But I would hope, with time, you and I might understand one another better. As for influencing either one of your children, my lord, I doubt I could do that even if I tried. They both think very well for themselves, without looking elsewhere for instruction."

The coolness so apparent in Lord Giles did not melt away, despite Philip's calm logic. "I do not think we shall ever understand each other, Philip," he said, "but out of reverence for your family, I'll speak no more of our differences, or of the scandal. It is not my place to disapprove of my lord's son, except if you affect my children. I think that is all we need to understand."

Geoffrey sighed deeply and, sensing no more would be said between the two, he resumed what he'd begun to speak of moments ago. "You noticed, did you not, Philip, the council which just dispersed?"

Philip nodded.

"We discussed what must be done regarding the Montforts."

Alix couldn't help but listen with intense interest, despite the fact she wished to let herself sort out exactly what had transpired between her father and Philip. But such thoughts were put off while Sire Geoffrey spoke.

"I will need the full services of my men-at-arms, which includes their squires and pages. Indeed, some squires are nearing the age and experience for knighthood, and we shall need each and every one of them."

Geoffrey waited for his son's response, hoping he would ask for the details, hoping he would show at least some small regard for the matters of the Chateau's defense. God's teeth! Philip was concerned enough with the Chateau's other workings, with its plowed fields and revamped roofs, how could he completely ignore its protection?

Philip said nothing.

At last Lord Giles spoke. "Alix, you can see why it is more important than ever that you do not leave the Chateau unprotected." Then he added, knowing only too well his daughter's obdurate disobedience, "If you disregard my wishes in this, Alix, I shall see you locked within your chambers. Do you see this is only for your own good? Even your mother will agree; she will see I do this only out of love and protection for you."

Alix did not look at her father. The possibility of being confined to the Chateau—and to her chambers if she did not follow that order—made her feel as though she were a small child being threatened with a thrashing if she did not obey. How she hated for Philip to witness such a thing!

Especially now, after they'd confessed their interest in one another—interest as fully mature adults!

"You will find your mother in our chambers," Giles said, "copying manuscripts. If you find my wishes so confining, you may ask your mother to help fill your time—she does not find it necessary to go outside the Chateau walls for entertainment; I'm sure she will occupy your time as well."

Bristling once again because she was being dismissed like a child, Alix found she wanted to go—to be away from this unpleasant feeling before Philip's eyes. She wanted to escape, at least for the moment, until she could recompose and once again feel like the woman Philip saw in her. Not the child her father was making her at this moment.

Philip watched her go, wanting to follow but knowing he mustn't. He wanted—no, needed—to speak to her about the consequences of what had just taken place. How much more obvious could it be that her father would not willingly agree to a betrothal between them—at least for now? But how long would it take before their wish to become man and wife would be accepted by Lord Giles? Philip was aware Giles would be an obstacle, but until this moment he hadn't realized just how great an obstacle he was.

Time was their only ally, he thought. He knew Alix had wanted to reveal to her father just how far their friendship had grown—he'd guessed that easily enough by the tone of her voice. But now was not the time to reveal what their plans were. Giles would only be stronger in his resistance, particularly if their hopes for marriage were revealed in the midst of an argument in which Alix felt compelled to defend him.

No, he thought, better to reveal their relationship once the resentment in Giles had a chance to wane. Philip had no intention of taking up the sword again just to please Lord Giles, but he did think, in time, Giles would look past that difference and see he had far more to offer Alix than a bloody sword at his side. Despite what Giles seemed to think, Philip would protect Alix with his life, he need have no fear on that count. And would Giles forever ignore the fact that Philip would one day be seigneur—and if Giles outlived Geoffrey, Giles would owe his fealty to Philip himself? It was a low plan to hope for, waiting until Philip was Giles's lord, and Philip by no means planned to wait that long. But certainly Giles must be aware of that on some level of thought.

But Philip would not be able to speak to Alix about all of this . . . until when? Because they'd lingered so long at the Estate this morning, they'd missed the first meal of the day, and meals would from now on be the only possible place for them to talk—he frowned at that. A crowded hall was hardly the place he'd envisioned getting to know Alix. Not with both sets of disapproving parents there to watch. It would have to suffice, however, since she was no longer allowed to leave the protection of the inner Chateau. Not that he blamed Lord Giles for his order; Alix *would* be safer within the impenetrable walls of the Chateau. And even though it meant he would see her far less, for he had looked forward to seeing her ride out to oversee whatever work he was doing, he had to admit this feud with the Mont-forts wasn't something to be ignored, as much as he wished they could. Would he have been able to rest easy knowing Alix was riding the countryside alone? And then, upon arriving at the Estate, what would have been different from today? She no doubt would insist upon working alongside the others, and he would have to return her to the keep as he'd done today. It might be worth it, he thought, to be able to spend time with Alix, but the risks were undeniable and at least he would not have to worry over her.

He wished he could speak to her about all the thoughts filling his head—those and more. He realized with the squires and pages recalled to their duties, work on the Estate would be lagging even more. But he wished to assure Alix this by no means meant the end of his plans to rebuild. She would have her home back, he wanted to tell her. Even if she never returned there to live, at least her home would be restored to match her fond memory of the place.

He, too, excused himself from the hall. As he left, he had one consolation. The garden, Alix's favorite place, was within the Chateau walls. She would not be deprived of at least one of her pleasures and, he thought with rising hope, perhaps that secret place would provide the means for them to talk in more privacy than the crowded hall would ever allow.

Boisterous conversation filled the halls at the last meal of the day. The knights were in higher spirits than they'd been in many months, and their gaiety spread to the others—that is, to most others.

Alix was seated between her mother and Father Fantin, Gustave's brother and the one Chateau priest who had penetrated Alix's reserve to become her friend. She watched the happy antics of the knights with an odd mixture of cheer and melancholy. Philip was nowhere to be seen; she knew, with half his workforce gone—the pages and squires were once again with their knights, for the time being carousing in the same fashion as their masters—Philip was probably once again trying to find a way to do the monumental tasks which lie ahead.

She knew she was doing a poor job of hiding her conflicting emotions, for she felt the gaze of both her mother and Father Fantin upon her more than once.

Father Fantin whispered to her in a tone only Alix could hear. "How many times have you confessed to the Almighty your uncharitable wish for revenge upon the Montforts?" he asked. "Here before you is the beginning of that wish fulfilled. Yet I see ambivalence upon your face. Have you listened to God's word, child? Do you see now that vengeance belongs only to Him?"

The Father's words made Alix think of what Philip had said earlier. "Tell me, Father, would you have all of France lay down their swords to achieve peace?"

His brows lifted at such a direct question, although he'd said to himself often enough that Demoiselle Alix could no longer surprise him with that unbridled tongue of hers. But somehow she never failed to amaze him. He sighed, wondering how best to answer. "My allegiance is first to God's kingdom, and He has told us to use the Sword of Truth."

"Do you take that to mean a literal sword?"

"Oh, no, not his priests. But because of the analogy, I cannot help but think he does not mean for our knights—call'd to defend our faith and our earthly kingdom—to lay down their swords. If I thought that, all the saintly men who died in the Crusades would have died in vain. And my brother Gustave would be in grave danger of doom, being the master-at-arms here at the Chateau. I do not believe that."

"Then it is right for a knight to wield a sword?"

"It is their duty," Father Fantin said. "They are called to fight the battles of angels."

A frown wrinkled Alix's brow, and Father Fantin spoke again. "With what do you wrestle now, Demoiselle Alix? Your vengeance upon the Montforts or ... perhaps the decision Lord Philip made two years ago to give up his sword?"

Alix's gaze flew to the Father's, but he consoled her with a gentle pat to her hand.

"Do not worry, child. No one knows you as well as I—except perhaps your mother, who, though she does not look this way, is straining to hear each word we say. And perhaps, since your mother does not know Lord Philip as I do, she has not guessed. But I have seen the way you both have acted—merely by avoiding one another, and that has given me reason to wonder."

"There is really very little to wonder about," Alix said, trying to sound lighthearted. She had agreed with Philip they would keep their interest a

143

secret, at least for now. And Alix wanted to honor that agreement, even if it was difficult to keep anything from Father Fantin. And her mother. "We became friends because he offered to rebuild the Estate. And you know how I've longed for that, Father. Is it so odd I should be grateful to him?"

"That does not explain why his company has been so hard for you to bear that you have locked yourself in your chamber for the past days. But do not worry, I require no explanation. If I am to be truthful about my thoughts, I hope for a union between you two. I have never known two people more suited to one another—you with a tongue only a man like Philip could match, and he with an intolerance for stupidity only a woman like yourself could rise above. But, child, do not suffer so over his decision to lay down the sword. He himself made no great battle of it. When it was done, it was done, and I do not believe he's regretted it for a moment."

"No, I do not believe he's regretted it," she admitted. "But Father, how can I be the wife of a man who will not fight? Me, with a lust for vengeance upon the Montforts only a knight should possess?" She shouldn't be speaking in such a manner, she warned herself silently, even to her most trusted friend Father Fantin. But she hadn't really admitted anything. It was Father Fantin who spoke of a match, and she was just responding to his idea.

"I can only believe your wish for vengeance and Philip's aversion to fight will be met halfway by you both. In a sense you are both wrong in your thinking. Vengeance is no reason for bloodshed, God's word tells us that. Yet we still have need of skilled knights for other battles, battles angels themselves would fight if God allowed it. And my brother has known much sadness since Philip laid down his sword. God bestowed upon Philip unmatched excellence in knighthood and all it entails. He does not believe God meant for Philip to lay down his sword."

"Do you?"

Father Fantin lifted a hand, as if indecisive. "I know only that Philip believes it was the right decision. How can one argue, if a man seems to know his own soul?"

Alix was thoughtful, silent. Soon Father Fantin gently touched her hand, and said, "Perhaps God Himself has brought you two together. The differences you have will melt in your unity, and you will be like two colors blending into one on the painter's brush, new, unique and vibrant."

"Father Fantin, stop filling my daughter's head with such fanciful notions," Lady Marie said, a trifle harsh for speaking to a priest. Then, seemingly repentant, added, "You are such a poet you could no doubt make a snake appeal to a mouse."

"There is no need to be cautionary, Mother," Alix said, taking her mother's hand. "I was about to remind Father Fantin again that Lord Philip and I are merely friends. As I said, I am grateful to Philip for offering to rebuild the Estate. Surely you both understand that, knowing how I've longed to return there to live. But now, it seems, that work will be halted. I'm sure you're both aware that Lord Geoffrey has ordered many of the squires to increase their training in order to be knighted soon. And the pages are to prepare as foot soldiers alongside many peasants. Since they will not be able to work for Lord Philip any longer, I'm sure work on the Estate will be forgotten."

"Simon is training his squires even now," Marie said. "He did not seem overly disappointed rebuilding the Estate will be delayed. Marguerite has made it more than clear it is Simon she wants, not his home."

Alix's gaze followed her mother's down the table to Marguerite, who sat on the far side of Lady Eleanore. Marguerite caught their look and returned their smiles with one of her own dazzling ones.

"Have you spoken to Marguerite since learning of her relationship to Simon?" Marie asked.

Alix was glad the subject had been changed.

"No, I haven't yet. Perhaps when the meal is ended I will speak to her. Has Simon spoken to Father about their intentions?"

Marie shook her head. "But I'm sure Giles will approve."

Father Fantin was not so relieved to see the subject switch from Alix and Philip. Alix, in Father Fantin's opinion, was exactly what Philip needed. A woman with spirit and one, he did not doubt, who might just be the impetus for settling that decision Philip had made two years ago. For though Philip had made the decision to lay down his sword without regret, Father Fantin had the distinct belief that, while Philip might be through with the sword, the sword was not through with Philip.

12

Philip appeared in the hall just when Alix was about to retire for the night. He looked weary and, Alix noticed, though he was dressed in a resplendent doublet and chausses with a silver belt at his slim waist, he wore no crest or amulet marking his family name. Nor was his hair properly combed, letting the obvious be known: he'd hurried to make it to the dinner board once again.

Whatever disappointment Alix might have felt that he'd missed the meal melted upon sight of him. Perhaps he wasn't quite so anxious to see her as she was to see him—if he were, certainly he would have shown up earlier to share what time they could together—but it didn't matter. He was here, at last.

He passed her on his way to his chair at his mother's side. He paused just long enough to whisper a cordial greeting which, Alix saw, included her mother as well, who was watching.

Alix was glad, then, that she hadn't said her good-nights as of yet. It wouldn't do to have her mother know she'd changed her mind only when Philip appeared.

Philip was served and he ate quickly, without enjoying the sumptuous fare. His gaze went more than once down the table in Alix's direction, but their eyes met only twice. For him, it was enough to read all he hoped for. She was happy to see him.

He hadn't intended to be so late for this meal. After all, the dinner board would be the single place where he could be assured of seeing Alix. But he'd been determined to make visible progress at the Estate, and with only a half-dozen peasants there to help, the task was impossible. He gave in only when the sun sank low in the western sky, reminding him of the hour.

Beside him, his parents sat in silence, and down the board Alix, too, was quiet. As he finished the last bite of spiced herring, a new dilemma occurred to him. If he were to show Alix the amount of attention he wished at the dinner board, surely both his parents and Alix's would see what was developing. That bothered him for only one reason: he was sure both sets of parents would object to their betrothal, at least until the heat of the scandal cooled.

Philip was no fool. He knew his father greatly favored Alix; he would undoubtedly welcome her into the family. It was not Alix he felt Geoffrey would object to. No; it was Philip himself whom Geoffrey would believe not good enough for Alix. That might well be true, he admitted, for Alix's family was old, respected, and though moneyless for the present time, they were not without their own power. Alix had undoubtedly received many requests for marriage, including those which would prove advantageous. While Philip would certainly be able to bring money to her family with such a match, for the present time he offered little else that was of any honor. He knew Giles

147

Beauchamp had been a zealous knight in his youth, and he'd heard Giles speak often of Simon, swelling with pride when referring to the battles he fought. He doubted Lord Giles would heartily welcome into his family a man who would not touch his sword. Lord Giles had made that perfectly clear already.

But, given enough time, Philip was sure those obstacles would disappear. He did not forget Marie, whom he was convinced wanted Alix's happiness. And if that happiness included Philip himself, and Philip certainly hoped it would, then she would be a force in their favor. A formidable force, given the fact that Lord Giles held her in high esteem.

Many of the guests had departed for the evening, and Philip had one amusing thought to lighten his mood. Perhaps he and Alix could simply wait until everyone had gone to bed . . . But no, that would hardly do considering the majority of men-at-arms had bower closets within the hall. There was no privacy to be found here. All who were left just now were his parents and Alix's, Father Fantin and Philip's uncle, Sir Roger, who lingered over his wine. And of course Alix. The fact that she was still present must have surprised her mother, for Marie was saying for the third time in the last half hour that she had never known Alix to stay in the hall so long.

"Are you not tired?" Marie continued. "You are usually abed long before this."

Alix could think of no further excuse for tarrying. Her mother had thought it strange almost an hour ago; what could she say now? Her gaze went to Philip in silent entreaty, but she knew there was nothing he could say to offer her a chance to stay. There was but one thing to do: ignore her frustration and retire for the night. What a vexatious meal this had been! It had fulfilled none of her hopes and had, in fact, only inspired an exasperated feeling of discontent. Having Philip nearby and yet being unable to speak to him directly without drawing attention

148

was more than irksome. It was intolerable! She must speak to Philip about the importance of keeping their interest such a secret, even though she knew her father would not welcome the news. Surely facing her father's possible displeasure was better than this frustration!

Alix said good-night, casting one last glance in Philip's direction to include him in her farewells for the night. And as her steps carried her from the hall, her heart sank ever lower. Would tomorrow be any different?

Alone in her room, sitting in darkness, Alix had never felt so lonely. The silence was so intense she wished for the very first time that she hadn't moved her bed from the women's bower. At least there the women chattered until late night, and it might have helped to keep her mind from Philip. As it was, she relived all they'd said that day, the early morning kiss, even the chaste peck on the cheek he'd given her when discussing their desire to know one another better.

Before long, a light shone in the tower opposite her room, and Alix's frustration only grew. How could she sleep, knowing he was so near?

Philip woke late the next morning, which was most unusual for him. But half the night had been spent watching the garden, hoping to see Alix there so he could meet her. At last he'd fallen asleep, vowing before another night went by he would get a message to her to meet him there come sunset.

Though the morning went quickly because of his delayed start, Philip was not late for the noon meal. In fact, he came early, in hope of finding Alix before everyone was served. His plan was fruitful, for just as he entered he saw her come through the kitchen entryway, obviously just down from her chamber. He went immediately to her side, taking advantage of the absence of most Chateau inhabitants.

Alix quickened her step when she saw Philip approach. She'd spent a near sleepless night, but

149

upon sight of him she felt entirely refreshed. When they met just behind the trestle tables the servants even now were setting with utensils, she could not help but offer her hand. He took it, squeezing it gently.

"Was it a long night?" he asked, "Or was it just me?"

She shook her head. "It was the longest night of my life."

They both laughed, but when several servants glanced their way, Philip let go of her hand. He knew only too well how fast tales spread, and servants played a vital part in the vine of gossip. They were everywhere.

"Perhaps the day won't be any better," he said in a whisper. "But at least we might have something to look forward to. Do you think you could come to the garden tonight? If we are to talk at all freely, it obviously cannot be at the meals. Last night proved that."

The prospect of being alone with Philip in the garden made Alix's eyes glisten with anticipation. "I'll be there . . . tonight, just after the evening meal."

"So will I," he said, then, glancing around and seeing that the servants were on the opposite side of the large square of trestles, he pressed one quick kiss to her palm.

Alix did not think it was possible for time to move any more slowly than it had last night, but she was proven wrong. The day seemed interminable. And she could not even enjoy her favorite pastime in hopes of occupying herself. Confined to the keep, riding was out of the question. So, after the noon meal—in which she'd exchanged nary a word with Philip—she sat in her mother's antechamber, diligently copying a book of prayer. Thankfully, her mother was with Eleanore. Alix hated to keep anything from Marie, but she knew these budding feelings for Philip must be kept secret. At least until she spoke to Philip. Tonight, she consoled herself. Tonight.

The evening meal progressed much as it had the

150

night before, only Father Fantin did not mention any hopes for a match between Alix and Philip. Alix was glad he didn't, for she doubted she could keep herself from giving away what she felt inside. Both Father Fantin and her mother knew her so well, they might guess almost anything just by her manner of speech or heightened nervousness when speaking of Philip. It was best not to speak of him at all.

Eleanore de Saines obviously had no idea Simon wished to marry Marguerite, for she called Marguerite to sit beside Philip and share his trencher. Every time they sipped wine out of the same cup or took a bite from the same almond-roasted beef, Alix felt her own meal rise like a sickness from her stomach. She knew she had no reason to be jealous; Philip cast her more than one smile and something in his manner told her he wished it was her he shared his meal with. And Alix had no doubt Marguerite would have preferred Simon's company, for she watched him almost as closely as Alix watched Philip. And, poor Simon! He barely ate a bite, his gaze never leaving Marguerite. More than once he looked as though he would rise; once when Philip sipped the cup precisely where Marguerite had—quite by accident, Alix was sure, for she knew Philip was aware of Marguerite's feelings for Simon. And then Simon had almost risen again, when Marguerite had followed custom and broken the bread and fed it to Philip with her fingertips.

Eventually Simon left his place with the other men-at-arms and came to his mother's side for a brief moment. Alix heard him whisper Marie should do something for his sake, but of course there was nothing to be done. It was Eleanore's board they shared, and it was up to her where everyone sat.

Lord Giles looked on with confused interest, but he said nothing. Simon simply returned to his seat, a frown so apparent on his face that even Lord Geoffrey noticed.

"Is something amiss with the meal, Sir Simon?"

Simon forced a smile, then held up his cup. "Not at all. I was just saying how I enjoyed your wine."

Immediately a wine bearer refilled his cup, which he drank so quickly all who watched wondered how he could enjoy anything he consumed in such a manner. Wine was to be savored—even Sir Roger knew that! Alix knew her brother was well on his way to drunkenness.

She, on the other hand, controlled her bouts with jealousy more privately. Though she felt sick within, she had enough pride to see her through the meal without mishap. Common sense told her not to be jealous; after all, Marguerite loved Simon and Philip . . . well, he might not love Alix yet, but he hoped to know her better, didn't he? And it was with Alix he'd set up tonight's tryst. She consoled herself with those thoughts throughout the meal.

After the meal, alone in her chamber, she gazed out the window just waiting for total darkness. The western sky had a rosy hue, and the first stars of the night were just peeking out. Soon, she thought, it would be time.

She went to her dressing table, taking up her brush and combing through her long hair. Then, taking two ornate combs, she pulled her hair away from her face, letting the wavy tresses fall down her back. She pressed a small amount of perfume to her throat and bodice, then, assuring herself her surcoat was free of wrinkles and positioned just right, she went to the door. She knew this surcoat was her most beautiful, and also her most seductive. It was a rich, sapphire blue with a fine design of green edging the deep V of the bodice. Beneath, her pure white underrobe was barely visible, for the eye was caught instead by the fullness of her breasts. And though she'd chosen the surcoat earlier precisely for its display of her feminity, second thoughts made her wonder if it was too obviously intended for Philip's attention.

But she scolded herself. Not only was the neckline in fashion, but Philip had seen her in it already at dinner. She hadn't been embarrassed there, had she, with so many others around? But perhaps that was just it; now they would be alone, and she didn't want him to think her brazen.

Such foolishness! she chided. It was only because she was so aware of what he did to her inside. Perhaps she stirred nothing of the kind in him; after all, that simple kiss upon the cheek yesterday hardly spoke of a man who couldn't control his passion for her.

She left her room, glad that Hugh was nowhere to be seen. It was far too early for him to retire, but she'd been looking forward to this rendezvous so intently she'd been afraid something would go awry. Nothing had, so far, and she was thankful for that.

Not even Cook was there to give her pause with his disapproval of her solitary walks. The kitchen was empty but for Arnaud, and she assumed it was because the hour was early yet. The hall was still full, but the meal already over. Cook could not supervise a cleanup, separating leftovers for the poor from leftovers for Arnaud and other Chateau creatures, until the hall was empty. He more than likely was with the steward, making sure of the satisfaction of every guest in the hall.

Alix could hardly believe her good fortune; she met nary a soul all the way to the garden. There had been times she'd waited before entering the garden in order to be totally unnoticed. She wanted no one knowing where she was and going after her. But tonight she suffered no such delays, and followed the overgrown pathway more hastily than ever.

Philip was already there when she pushed away the last bough and entered the secret center. He was seated on the stone bench but, upon seeing her, he stood and walked the few steps to her. Before a word was spoken by either of them, he took her hands in his and pulled her close. Then, quite without warning, Philip's lips came down on Alix's, gently at first, then more firmly, until Alix thought she might swoon. Though from her own suddenly erupting passion or the unexpectedness

153

of his, she knew not which. His lips felt warm and smooth against her own, his embrace strong and sure. Alix pressed herself against him, her thoughts suddenly swirling, with only one overwhelming reality filling her: Philip wanted her—and she wanted him.

Philip held her at arm's length, smiling ruefully. "I didn't mean to do that quite so ... thoroughly," he explained. "But seeing you, I couldn't help myself. You're very lovely, Alix."

He was so much taller than her she had to tilt her head upward to look at him, standing at this close angle. "Thank you," she said, far more confidently than she felt. "But there isn't really any need for an apology. Did you not notice? The kiss was hardly met with any resistance."

"I noticed," he said softly.

Then, fearing he thought her shameless, she said hastily, "I should not have said that, should I?" She frowned. "I should be a lady of nobility and slap you with my kerchief for being so bold."

He laughed, and again she misunderstood.

"Am I foolish?" she asked.

"No, Demoiselle Alix, you are anything but foolish. You are honest, and outspoken, and I admire you greatly. You should know that already."

"Then you should know, since I have no kerchief and thus cannot act the lady, that I have never allowed a man to kiss me that way. To be honest, no one has ever kissed me in such a manner."

"Not even your first betrothed?" he asked as he led her to the bench for them to sit down.

She laughed at the idea. "We had more fun playing hoodman blind."

"Then I am honored to be the first," he said truthfully. He continued to hold her hand once they were seated.

"Why did you not kiss me that way yesterday, when sealing our pact?" she asked. She was no longer concerned about behaving like a demure lady; Philip knew better than to expect that.

Philip did not answer immediately, and in the

154

dim starlight she could see his frown. His dark brows drew together and his mouth—such a sensual mouth—curved slightly downward at one side. Then he spoke, and the frown disappeared. "I do not want you to be wary of me, Alix, or to think I might hurry a carnal relationship before first establishing a friendship. But at times—more often than not, I'm afraid, I cannot help myself. Yesterday, when sealing our pact, I kissed you the way I thought an honorable man should kiss a woman—chastely. I don't want to be less than honorable in your eyes."

Alix was thoughtful. "I would not have you thinking ill of me, Philip, but to be truthful . . . I enjoy your kisses."

There seemed only one way to respond to that statement, and Philip did not hesitate. His free hand went around her shoulders, pulling her closer, and his mouth pressed to hers. This time, his tongue begged entrance between her lips, and she willingly responded by opening her mouth to him. He held her firmly, and Alix's arms crept about his wide, strong shoulders. It was so good to be this close to him, to feel his heart beat against hers, to know with his kiss that he wanted her. And though in her innocence Alix was uncertain just what this desire entailed, she knew she wanted him every bit as much as he did her. She returned his kiss, shyly letting her tongue tease his, delighting in the intimacy.

Her heart pounded within when his hand loosened hers to caress her. Slowly, his fingers explored the softness of her skin, barely touching yet setting each sensitized spot afire. His thumb rubbed lightly below her chin and on down her throat, so tenderly it would have tickled had it not aroused desire instead. Then, at last, his touch reached the bodice of her gown, and there he hesitated, as if uncertain he should continue. His kiss deepened, and Alix responded in kind, her lips against his urging him on with renewed fervency.

Philip felt the lure of her answering kiss and let his fingers resume their exploration. The wide, low V left her smooth fullness open to his caress, and without any difficulty his thumb found the sensitive tip just below the soft material of her underrobe and flickered sensually until rewarded with the response he sought.

Alix's body was quick to respond; it took less than a moment, for even with her innocence she was already so susceptible to his touch her body seemed to anticipate what he would do. Strange, secret parts of her longed for his caress, and she realized if he wished to know each and every detail of her body, she would open herself to him. He had only to ask.

But he didn't. Not verbally or with silent entreaty. Gently, he tore himself away from her all too willing embrace, hearing his own unsteady breath and knowing he'd almost gone too far. Another moment, and it would have been too late to turn back, to draw away even though, sensibly, he knew they should wait. They weren't even betrothed! Not yet.

His gaze sought hers, and even in the dim light he could see her eyes filled with a desire that matched his own. Oh, to show her how deep that desire went! But he couldn't. Why, they were in the middle of a garden, on a hard stone bench, without even the preliminary betrothal vows spoken by either one of them. He couldn't let this go any further, for he knew, as much as she wanted this now, when the light of day revived their rationality, they would regret being so impetuous. Temptation was strong, but they must be stronger. Philip had done enough ignoble things in the past without adding a stolen virginity.

He gave her a decidedly lopsided grin. "I believe, Demoiselle, that we could spend the remainder of the evening enjoying one another's kisses. But that, remember, is not why we agreed to meet."

"Isn't it?" she asked.

Philip almost laughed; she was so innocent, she didn't know how he tempted him! Instead, he said,

"Didn't we agree to get to know one another? Wasn't that what our pact was all about?"

She nodded, but was obviously disappointed. How he wished to dispel that feeling! But the only way to do that led to behavior that would be scandalous if ever discovered . . . and though they were alone and he was sure neither one of them would spread tales of their activities, it would hardly do to have their nest full before their wedding! His name had been attached to too many scandals already. But more important than that, he didn't want Alix's name attached to one.

Alix took a deep, steadying breath. "You're right, of course," she said. "And you must think me very bold."

"I think you're very beautiful," he assured her. "And my struggle to end that kiss could have been lost in another moment. I want you, Alix, make no mistake about that."

She smiled tremulously. "You're very honorable, Philip. And of course you are right; we should wait until it is proper." Then she added, and he could see the twinkle in her eye, "But I shall look forward to our wedding night—or perhaps the night after, when we are alone."

"Not more than I," he said. "And perhaps, if we are lucky, I can convince my family to dispense with the witness of our wedding night. It's been done before, and I believe we should have that choice."

Suddenly Alix laughed, so delightedly Philip was tempted to join in without even knowing the reason for her mirth.

"Listen to us, Philip," she said. "We are talking about our wedding night before we are even betrothed! Didn't we agree only to know one another first?"

"And that, Demoiselle," he said lightly, "is why we should restrain our kisses. To let us know one another in more ways than one—for it's obvious in that way we are already compatible!"

Alix stroked his cheek, a brief, gentle caress that felt wonderful. "I do want to know you, Philip. In all ways."

He almost kissed her again, but he held back. Instead, he cleared his throat, one hand going to the collar of his doublet and pulling it away as if it were suddenly constricting. Then he said in a voice that betrayed none of the continuing struggle for control, "Do you know why it is best for us to wait before going to our parents with our intentions?"

"Yesterday you said we would have more freedom this way, without everyone looking at our every move. But," she added, somewhat unhappily, "I do not think we have so much freedom as it is; after all, we cannot even speak to one another at the dinner board, and this evening, when your mother had Marguerite share your trencher . . ."

He kissed her cheek, ever so briefly. "I wished it had been you instead," he told her.

She welcomed the words. "I, too. But surely if your mother knew how we felt, she would not ask such things of you."

"You are right, of course. Yet both of us know betrothed couples are watched more closely than individuals. And, I fear a betrothal announcement would not be welcomed by either my parents or yours until the scandal has cooled."

"I have not heard so much gossip about it," she said idly.

Philip guessed what she hinted at. "You haven't been listening, then, for it's still on the tongues of almost all. My servant warns me of it; my parents' behavior reminds me of it. But," he added, "you would like to know the details of it, would you not? If any of it is true, and what exactly happened?"

She hid her eyes with her lids, fearing he would see she was indeed anxious to know the truth. She believed in him, she knew, no matter what he would reveal. But surely it was best to know what was being said, and how it differed from the truth.

"You know it involved a woman," he began, remembering the very first night they'd met. "She is the wife of my friend—my former friend, I should say. Rumors started that she and I . . . were unfaithful to Charles, her husband. At first I ignored it; love affairs are widespread, even habitual at Court and there is always some tale of affairs being told. In this case, it was false, and so I assumed were many other tales. But when I learned Rachel herself contributed to the stories—in fact, had initiated them—I denied them all for the lies they were. It was an ugly scene; in front of a handful of people she alluded to the gossip, adding some very definite comments to let the others think it was all true. I suppose I did not act gallantly by speaking the truth, but—God's teeth—Charles is my friend, and he deserved better than to think his wife would cuckold him with his best friend."

"She must have wanted you a great deal," Alix said quietly, without looked at him, "to stir up so much trouble."

"Perhaps . . . or else she just wanted to hurt her husband." He shrugged. "It was hardly the way to go about seducing someone, in any event."

Alix's gaze flew to his. "Do you mean, if she'd gone about it differently, you would have . . . ?"

He laughed at the thought. "No, I would not have bedded her, regardless of the circumstances. Even," he added, "if she was not wed to Charles. Rachel is a cold-hearted woman used to manipulating people. She thought she could manipulate me as well."

Alix could not help breathing a sigh of relief; at least the scandal did not involve Philip's heart. That would have been harder to bear.

"The rumor eventually spread to Charles, who was off in Flanders on campaign with a company of other knights. It was said when he heard what was happening back at Court between his wife and his best friend, he disappeared into the Forest for three days and nights, refusing to speak, talk, or listen to those who would have brought him back to the comforts of camp. And when he returned, he vowed before his troop that he would see me dead

159

when he returns to Paris."

"But surely he will listen to reason! It was all a lie!"

Philip shook his head, his countenance hard, and somewhat sad. "He will believe his wife; he loves her, despite all her faults." Then, after a pause, he continued with the tale. "When King Jean learned of the trouble brewing, knowing he could not keep Charles away from Paris—away from his wife—forever, he chose to act the guardian angel and send me away—for my own good, so he said." His mouth twisted in disgust. "Like the naughty little boy I'd been, sent home."

"But he wanted to protect you," Alix reminded him gently. "Surely there is no great crime in that?"

Philip only shrugged. "I suppose not." Then he smiled, but there was no happiness to be seen. "I could not have fought Charles in any case, no matter how he tried to provoke me. King Jean knew that, since I'd told him two years ago the sword would never again grace my hand. And, for better or worse, the King favors me enough to want me alive, if I will not protect myself. But," he added, "I would have been better off staying in Paris. The scandal would have been no different from any other then."

"And have Charles kill you?" Alix asked, aghast.

"I do not believe it would have come to that. Charles is a reasonable man."

"He does not sound so reasonable to me," Alix said. "At least when it comes to this Rachel. Would a reasonable man disappear for three days and nights, and vow to kill a man he once cared for?"

"He believes his wife was compromised."

"Which only proves he is daft when it comes to her. He believes her lies."

"Still, if I had stayed in Paris, I believe I could have convinced Charles of my innocence, despite what Rachel said. And even if I couldn't, the shame of having run from an irate husband is hard to bear without having stood up to him in some way."

"But you didn't run," Alix said. "The King banished you from Paris. How could you have stayed, even if you wanted to?"

He smiled at her faith in him. "Not everyone can look at it as you do, Alix. My father, for one. He believes me a coward—but he began believing that long ago, when I first laid down the sword. He knows, as do all others, that King Jean would not have banished me if I'd been able to protect myself, if I'd proven willing to take up the sword again. And that, I cannot do."

Alix did not question the reason for that; she felt Philip had revealed as much as he wanted of himself for one evening. She knew already that he'd laid down the sword because he was tired of all the killing; she could learn the details from him later. There would be time, she thought hopefully, to learn all about each other.

"Until my father—and yours, I suspect as well—can forget the gossip attached to my name, I doubt our betrothal will be approved, no matter how we feel about one another. And there is no choice but to have their approval." He took her hand, kissing it once. "Will you wait, then, Alix?"

She squeezed his hand in hers. "I will wait," she told him earnestly. "As long as it takes."

Soon afterward, they said good-night, not trusting themselves even to one last kiss.

13

It hardly seemed like morning. The sunless sky was heavy with colorless clouds, and a misty drizzle penetrate Julian de Saines's bulkiest cloak. He didn't bother any longer to scan for familiar landscape. It all looked the same: the ground brown and muddy, the outskirts of the horizon shrouded in white vapors hanging between the cool, rain-laden sky and the Spring-warmed earth.

Julian's spirit was as low as the clouds enveloping the land. He should be happy, he told himself again and again. He was going home. And after a full year and a half away, that should make him happy. No more campaigns, no more sleeping in the mud, eating half-cooked, half-burned meals, no more a victim to the whims of nature with its one day rain and next day cold. And, he would see his parents again. That thought did bring some measure of cheer. His parents were dear to him, and he to them, he knew.

"We're coming to a forest up ahead," called back one of Julian's men. Surrounded as he was by his retinue of companions, from squires and pages to his horse marshal and private falconer, some twenty men in all, Julian was a tempting target for any villains lurking in the shadows of the trees. He was laden with the many prizes he'd won at tournaments, like the half-dozen or more prime destriers, complete with their tooled saddles and silver bits. Julian also possessed rewards earned from the impetuous King for fine service, like the pair of falcons and three prize hunting dogs, along with an even more precious gift, a box of gold coins. And of course he had the fruits of his own personal wealth such as the large emerald set in the center of his shield, and the jewel-encrusted doublet he wore beneath his cloak. The design on his doublet was shaped in the de Saines dragon with sapphire eyes, diamond nostrils and ruby flames spewing from his pearl mouth. Julian always wore it when traveling; it was by far, he thought, the safest place to keep it. He would die before giving it up, and no opponent, no matter how fierce, could take it from him. Julian feared no man.

The sound of clanking chain mail, the rubbing of

leather saddles, the whinny of horses and an occasional cough from one of the men echoed off the thick-grown forest trees. The fog was thickest here, almost blinding. Bushes and undergrowth took on phantom-like life, unmoving in the stagnant air yet changing shape as the shadowy mist wafted between the boughs and branches.

Julian knew what rankled him, yet, even now, hated to face the truth. In two day's time, what it would take to reach the Chateau, he would see Philip again. He hadn't seen him since . . . since that day, two years past, when Philip had come home without his sword.

"What happened to you?" Julian had asked. He was the first to see Philip that day. Julian had been outside the Chateau exercising one of his falcons when he spied Philip's approach. But when Julian rode up to greet his favored older brother, he was put off first by Philip's somber demeanor, and then by his lack of a weapon. "Where is your sword? Did you lose it in battle?"

Philip said nothing; he just shook his head.

"In a tournament?" Julian presisted as they rode slowly toward the Chateau. Julian hoped to discover exactly what had taken place before they reached the Keep; once there he would have to share his brother with his parents, and they no doubt would have just as many questions.

Still, Philip did not answer.

"Where is it?" Julian asked. After all, didn't he have a right to know? The sword had been in the de Saines family for generations; it would have been Julian's if he'd been first born.

"At the bottom of the Channel," Philip said, somewhat serenely.

Julian's mouth dropped open. At the bottom of the Channel! A sword that had been passed down through the family, polished and cared for, cherished as though it were a family member, lay at the bottom of the sea? Surely Philip jested.

But he hadn't. Philip had refused to elaborate, to explain, to give any clue to what had sent that precious sword to its unnatural grave. No one, least of all Julian himself, understood Philip's actions and refusal to disclose the reasons for his insane deed. That he had put the sword there, intentionally and without coercion from any enemy, was the only fact the family could discern. And that was inconceivable.

Julian shook himself, not from the cold or the gloomy forest, but to rid himself of the memory. He didn't want to think of Philip, not now, not ever. His brother who refused to fight.

But Julian knew he must confront Philip upon his arrival home. The brother who was the cause of more hatred in Julian than any other factor in his twenty years of life. How many times had he needed to prove himself, to convince everyone, most especially himself, that he wasn't like Philip? That he wouldn't back down in battle? That he would carry his sword till his dying day?

He pulled the collar of his cloak tighter, but it did little good. The damp reached to his very bones, and these somber thoughts did nothing to brighten his mood. He would do his best, he decided, to live under the same roof as Philip and never, ever, see his brother's face. He couldn't bear it. He knew the memory of Philip from long ago was still too fresh. The Philip who had taught him to wield a sword, to outmaneuver an enemy as slippery as a snake—God's blood! Philip had even taken him to his first woman, on his thirteenth birthday when Philip decided Julian was old enough to know the pleasures of the flesh. Those were the years, Julian thought wistfully, that Philip had been nothing short of a demigod. And Julian had wanted to be just like him.

No more. Philip had grown into nothing but a coward, and Julian must now spend his every waking moment proving he was nothing like his older brother. Nothing like him.

For the past year or more, Julian had purposely requested campaigns away from the Chateau, away from Paris, away from anywhere he knew his brother might be; it was bad enough to share the same name with his brother. He didn't want to share the same home.

A rustle from the surrounding underbrush curled through the air, and Julian shivered under his cloak. But there was no wind. Strange, he thought. For a moment, it sounded as though a breeze had stirred the forest.

Suddenly a cry cracked the dull quiet, and the neighing of a hundred horses. Or was it only one, echoing in the eerie air? Julian had no time to learn, for he, along with his retinue, was bombarded by both sides. Shouting men on horseback appeared from the white shadows, and Julian could not count them for he was busy fighting off two of the aggressors who attacked him. His sword flew like magic, thrusting here, swinging there, always reaching its mark. All of his men were armed, even the page who drove the wagon, and all were expertly trained. Julian himself had taught the young page and several of those younger than him how best to fight the enemy. He and his men fought off the attackers and, one by one, the outlaws tasted defeat.

Julian, spying one of the attackers making a hasty retreat, nudged his horse into a quick sprint after the man. He would show these bold outlaws, Julian thought with malice, what would happen when careless of just whom they attacked.

He reached his prey within moments, and with one hand he thrust back his shield and sword, while with his free hand he reached and grabbed the quarry's collar. With surprising ease, the outlaw came free of his mount and landed in Julian's lap.

Julian laid his sword against the man's throat. But no, he thought to himself, this was no more than a boy, judging by the slight build and weight. With one fluid movement he pulled back the heavy hood that concealed the outlaw's face. And in his surprise—just one moment of uncertainty was all it took—the prey squirmed free of Julian's grasp and slid to the ground, running after his horse so speedily he reached it in seconds. Then, without even a glance back, the outlaw sped off, disappearing into the forest and fog.

For a moment Julian did not move. He was unsure of what he had seen, and for more than one unsettling second he thought he must have imagined the face of that outlaw. He was no more than a boy, as Julian suspected by the weight, perhaps eleven or twelve at the most. But it wasn't his age that rendered Julian powerless; instead, it was his eyes. Huge and blue-green, a color he'd seen only once before, when the summer sun struck the clear pond on de Saines land. Those eyes held no fear, just defiance and anger at being held in so ignoble a position. For the barest moment he'd thought the child might even be a girl-child, but of course that was preposterous. What would a young girl be doing with a band of outlaws?

Julian dismissed the incident easily enough while he returned to his men. It wouldn't do to admit the outlaw had gotten away, so Julian said nothing upon rejoining the rest of his travelers.

"There were seven in all," said Edouard, Julian's chief man-at-arms. "Three ran off, including the one you chased, and the other four are there." He motioned to the bodies, each lying in their own warm bloody pool. "One's still alive, though barely breathing. Shall I kill him, or let him finish dying on his own?"

"Leave him," Julian said. "We owe neither help nor a clean death to any outlaw."

After Julian assessed the damages to his own troop, just three wounded men, only one seriously—who was placed in the wagon, they remounted and continued on their journey. The child outlaw was entirely forgotten.

The excitement filling the halls of the Chateau was almost tangible. Everywhere servants bustled about, polishing wall sconces, replacing rushes, shaking the dust from tapestries which had graced the walls for years. Much of the initial cleaning had already been begun, weeks ago under Philip's instruction. But today's efforts were at the command of Sire Geoffrey himself; the entire household was preparing for a feast.,

When Alix left her chamber that morning and entered the kitchen on her way out to the bailey, she heard Cook counting the sacks of flour and murmuring in between that he feared only half the required number of pies could be squeezed from the amount at hand.

"We'll have to buy at the market," he complained, speaking to no one in particular. "And pay the price."

"Surely there are enough sacks of flour here to feed the Chateau for days," Alix said, surprising Cook from behind.

Cook frowned at her, one hand coming to rest on his large belly. "Only on a normal day," Cook said. "But we're to have a feast—one so great, even the poor of the villages are to celebrate with us. Imagine that!" he complained. "We have barely enough to feed our own, and the Sire sends word he is opening the Chateau to the entire County to welcome home his son."

Alix's brows lifted in surprise. Surely this feast was unexpected—and late. Philip had been home for weeks. But then the truth dawned. Sire Geoffrey certainly would not hold a feast for Philip. Julian must be coming home.

"When is the feast to be?" she asked.

"That is the worst of it!" Cook replied. "In two days' time. Impossible!"

As Alix wandered through the Chateau, passing the hall and various antechambers, she saw more activity than she'd seen since arriving at the Chateau. Servants fussed everywhere, and more than once she felt in the way.

She left the inner keep, feeling all too strongly the boundary imposed upon her by her father. How she wished she could ride away from this bustling activity! More than that, she wished she could ride away from all it meant. It was painfully clear just how favored Julian was—and how disfavored was Philip. The entire Chateau was preparing for a feast that should have been Philip's.

She wondered if he knew what was happening.

With one glance back, she guessed her father and mother were still within their private, inner chambers. How was her father to know, she thought to herself, if she went out just one last time? She'd gotten away with many early morning jaunts before, why shouldn't she this time?

She hurried to the stables, without allowing much thought to the consequences of her disobedience. She would worry about that only if she were caught, she said to herself.

"James!" she called, once inside the dark stables.

He did not appear for several moments, and when he did he did not look at all pleased to see her. He stood nervously before her, shifting his weight from one foot to the other and then back again.

"I'd like to ride Morivek, please," she said, going to the mare's stall and greeting the palfrey with an affectionate pat on the nose.

James stood still, an unusual frown creasing his brow. The fact of his hesitation sent a twinge of worry to Alix's mind.

"I cannot," James said, without looking her in the eye.

"But why ever not?" Alix said. "You've always kept our little secret, James. Surely nothing's changed?"

James ran a trembling hand through his wiry black hair and uneasily he picked up a brush and began seeing to the horse in the stall opposite Morivek.

Alix followed him, watching him from the stall gate. "James, if you won't saddle Morivek for me, then I'll simply call someone else to do it."

He faced her, his skin paling under her threat. "No, Demoiselle Alix. We've all been given our orders—by the Sire himself. You're to stay within the Chateau, unless accompanied by one of the men-at-arms."

"But I've left alone before, James. What's spooked you?"

"The Sire, Demoiselle," James confessed. "He said if . . . if anyone aids you in riding out alone, we'd be put from the keep. Every last one of us, no matter who it was who helped you."

Alix was tempted to curse Sire Geoffrey's orders and saddle Morivek herself. And for a moment her thoughts must have been revealed on her face, for James looked at her with ever increasing worry. But she knew she wouldn't. She couldn't jeopardize James's job—it was more than just that, to him. These horses were his children, his life. And she couldn't be the cause of having him lose that.

Nonetheless, she chafed under the thoroughness of her father's and Sire Geoffrey's order to keep her within the Chateau. And all for her own good!

"All right," she said at last. "I won't press you further, James. You've been too kind already. I suppose our secret couldn't have lasted forever."

James brightened immediately, even saying hopefully, "Why don't you ask one of your father's men to escort you? Surely having someone tag along is better than not going at all?"

"Perhaps I will," she said aloud, though to herself she realized staying at home would be better. There was only one reason she wanted to leave the keep today, and that was to find Philip. It wouldn't do to have anyone knowing that.

Alix spent the morning at Mass, along with many others. She prayed and sang, and listened to the melodious voice of Father Fantin as he spoke. And she tried not to think about her confinement.

She lingered after Mass to speak to Father Fantin, and together they went to the hall for the noon meal. Alix knew she would not see Philip there today; he'd told her last night he planned to spend the day at the Estate and preferred to return to the Chateau for only one meal rather than both. Neither expressed any disappointment at the time, after being so frustrated at the evening meal last night. But today she wished he had decided to attend all meals just so they could see each other, even if they couldn't exchange many words. Without him to anticipate seeing, she was in no great hurry to join the others at the dinner board. They were all in such high spirits with the coming of the feast.

The usual games and festivities were not announced after the dinner was cleared away. Instead, many servants appeared with bundles of sewing articles which they distributed to the women.

Eleanore stood at her place on the raised dais at the far end of the hall. "I am asking all charitable women of the Chateau to participate in sewing garments for the poor," she announced. "My husband, in his generosity, has decreed that all visitors of lower station attending the feast in honor of our son will be given fresh new garments."

Cheers extolling Lord Geoffrey's goodness rung through the hall. How kind he was, how noble. Alix, however, did not raise her voice with all the others. Kind, he might be, but also somewhat foolish, at least in his treatment of his eldest, his heir.

"Alix!" Marie called to her daughter. She motioned to the empty seat beside her at the smaller sewing table servants had erected.

Alix went to her side, passing through the squires, pages and men-at-arms as they vacated the large room.

"Isn't this generous of the Sire?" Marie said excitedly. She, who hated to sew, had a generous heart of her own to be so enthusiastic about a task she normally loathed.

Alix nodded, automatically taking up the needle and thread supplied by a suddenly appearing servant. "One would think Julian to be the de Saines heir," Alix said quietly, without looking up.

Marie chided her daughter. "We should all welcome this feast, no matter what the cause. After so much loss and death the past few years, any manner of gaiety is welcome."

"Still," Alix said, "I cannot help thinking none of this would be possible but for the work Philip has been doing to restore bounty to the Chateau. And yet when Philip returned home he was greeted by no one but the family dog."

Marie raised a brow. "Were you there when Philip returned?" When she received no verbal answer, she said assuredly, her needle held in midair. "You were, weren't you?"

"It hardly matters, Mother. But yes, I was in the kitchen when Philip returned that night. No one even greeted him, and certainly there was no talk of a feast, before or after his return."

"There are entirely different circumstances," Marie said, sewing once again. "Julian is coming home in great favor of the King. Word has it he's won at least a half-dozen Tourneys in as many months. How can his parents not be proud of that?"

"I do not begrudge Julian."

"Nor should you think less of Sire Geoffrey for holding no feast for Philip. After all, look at what Philip returned with. A single horse and still no sword upon his belt. The only thing he brought with him is a shameful scandal attached to the noble de Saines name."

"A scandal that was none of his doing," Alix couldn't help but say. She knew she treaded dangerous water, but she could not stop herself from proclaiming Philip's innocence.

"What do you know of it?" Marie asked, her voice low so the other women could not hear. There was gossip enough without adding to it the suspicious way Alix protected Philip.

Alix shrugged, unwilling to go into detail for fear that Marie would press her further. It wouldn't do to have her mother learning how she came about her information—in an intimate conversation under the starlit sky.

"Has Philip spoke to you of the scandal?" Marie persisted.

"Just briefly," Alix said evasively.

"Then he's said more to you than anyone else," Marie said. "Eleanore tells me her son refuses to speak to anyone of the details—even to her or Lord Geoffrey. He's as secretive about this scandal as he was about the ludicrous decision to give up the sword."

"Why do you call it ludicrous when you know nothing about it?"

Marie gazed at her daughter, letting her sewing wait. "Don't tell me he's told you about that, too? Just how close have you come to Philip? And when did all of the conversation take place? I haven't seen you with him."

Curse her candid tongue! Would Alix never learn control? But that was extremely difficult when harsh words were spoken of Philip; she must defend him—even if he would not defend himself.

Nonetheless, she had said too much already. She must rest her defensive tongue. "In truth, he's said almost nothing of why he put down the sword," she was able to say in all honesty. "He gave me no reasons; I can only guess that he had good reason, since he gave up so much."

Obviously accepting her daughter's word, Marie took up her needle and thread once again, turning under a collar on the simple tunic design. Under Eleanore's command, servants had worked through the previous night measuring and cutting the fabric so that all tunics, of similar size and style, were practically complete. The women of nobility added only the finishing touches, like hems and connecting seams. Work simple enough not to tax their concentration with the more tedious aspects of sewing, yet a definite contribution to allow them the joy of charity.

Marie sighed, then, because she was careless with the needle, winced when she hit her fingertip rather than the garment. "I pity the poor peasant unlucky enough to receive this gift," Marie said in annoyance. On the collar was a drop of blood, and when she held the garment up for closer inspection, found the collar was undeniably crooked.

"Give it to me, Mother," Alix said gently, adding as she traded her own handiwork, "Just finish this seam instead; you cannot possibly harm it if you follow the straight line I've begun."

Marie grimaced, but did as her daughter bade. Alix snipped off the stitches her mother had made to the uneven collar and started anew, all the while silently thankful the previous subject had been forgotten.

Because of all the work being done in preparation for the coming feast, the second meal that day was spare. The Sire and his Lady announced they would sup alone in their chamber, and because of that so did most others, including Alix's parents. And without her mother and father there to be seated with, Alix could not join those who did opt to eat in the hall. She was required to either sup alone in her chamber or share her meal in her parents' antechamber. She chose to eat alone.

Alix barely tasted any of the raisin-stuffed quail. She knew Philip would be looking for her, and now, more than ever, she wished she had a chance to speak to him. He would learn of the coming feast for Julian and, although she was certain he would try to hide any insult this made him feel, she knew he was bound for some amount of pain. How could he not feel the pain? His parents' favoritism was so obvious the entire County would know of it, if they didn't already.

When Blanche came to remove the dinner tray she found her mistress pacing the room restlessly.

"Is Hugh abed yet?" Alix asked, her tone curt.

"No, Demoiselle. He is in the hall, lingering over his supper."

"Very well. Just take the tray, Blanche. I will not require aid in changing my garments this night."

Blanche disappeared as quietly as she had come,

shaking her head at the small amount of food her mistress had eaten.

Alix went to the window, her gaze traveling longingly to the tower just opposite her chamber. It was dark. Was he in the hall, waiting for her even now? But surely he would know she could not join the others without the proper escort of her parents. If only she could speak to him, just to ease whatever sorrow his parents' slight might have caused.

Her gaze went to the garden, although from her vantage she could not see the center. She knew she must see him; perhaps, if she were to wait for him in the garden . . .

She was out of her room within moments, flying down the stairs and through the kitchen at such a pace even Cook barely noticed her passing, for she was little more than a breeze as she hurried through the room.

The sun had barely set, so she knew it would be some time before Philip would even look for her there. Then it occurred to her; she would see him all the sooner if she went to his tower, would she not? He would undoubtedly go there after his meal, to wait there until after sunset when they could go to the garden without being noticed. She could wait for him in the private comfort of his tower chamber, and see him at the soonest opportunity.

The wind whistled through the battlements, rustling her skirts as she traversed the high walkway toward Philip's tower. She could see the setting sun best from here, lighting the few puffy clouds up above a startling deep pink. But she paid the twilight beauty only sparse attention; her thoughts were intent upon her destination.

Perhaps it was not the wisest thing to do, this idea of hers to wait in Philip's chamber. After all, they were not legally betrothed as of yet and if she were discovered in his chamber all manner of Hell would spew forth with her father's wrath. But Alix knew she could not turn back now. Her heart wouldn't let her.

14

The sound of the heavy wooden door shutting behind Alix echoed up the tall, dark tower. For a moment the utter blackness gave her pause; she waited until her eyes adjusted to the dimness. Then, graced only by the light passing through a pair of cross-shaped arrow slits up above, Alix found her way to the base of the winding stairway.

The wooden structure hardly looked stable. Its inner railing had long since given way, and though the stairs themselves were supported by beams cemented in the mortar of the tower itself, Alix hesitated with each creak and groan as she climbed ever higher. Round and round she went, losing count of the stairs as she passed the first arrow slit. The sun was just a pale rose glow in the western sky, its global shape sunk beneath the horizon. In a moment she would be in total darkness.

At last she reached the top, finding herself in the center of a circular room. One huge window and, opposite that, an open doorway leading to a balcony let in the lingering sunlight. But before taking notice of anything more, she scanned the room for candle or sconce; all too soon she would not have even the pallid glow from the disappearing sun to give her so much as a hint of her unfamiliar surroundings.

She found a pair of candles on a table which stood near the window, and lit one with the flint beside it. Then, turning to inspect the room, she found it scrupulously clean and as spare of furniture as a monk's den. The bed was narrow and hard, with the thinnest feather-stuffed

175

mattress Alix had ever touched. Only two coarse blankets covered it. Beside the bed was a table, and next to it an open chest filled with neatly folded clothing. The room had no floor coverings, no rushes or carpeting, just the rough cut oak as old as the tower. The only other furniture was the table; it was littered with a myriad of books and papers, inks and quills. Looking closer, she saw the papers were covered with drawings, with certain points and connecting lines. Each point was given a name, strange names like Alkaid and Mizar and Phad. She could make no sense of them and so, out of curiosity, she studied the leather-bound manuscripts.

She sat on the single chair, finding it hard-backed and extremely uncomfortable. So she went to the bed, book in one hand and candle in the other. The book was inscribed in Latin, and after several moments she deduced it was a study of the stars of heaven. The drawings, then, were of various constellations, for the book itself had similar sketches with the name of each star cluster.

For the most part, Alix understood very little but, because this was obviously of great interest to Philip, it intrigued her. Her education, while more extensive than that of most men who were required to spend their time in the training yards rather than a tutoring room, nonetheless did not include astronomy. The Church feared it too closely linked to astrology, the pagan belief, and so her training had not extended to the literal heaven, only the ethereal one.

Before long the complex script began to blur before her sleepy eyes. In search of comfort, she lay upon the bed, holding the book beside her. Philip would be returning soon, she thought to herself. Perhaps then he could explain some of these complicated points. She felt so obtuse ... And sleepy.

Philip sat in the garden with steadily sinking spirits. He'd waited for Alix over two hours, but

176

there was nary a sign of her—either in the garden, or in the hall. For long moments he gazed at the window of her room, hoping to see light, some evidence of her presence, but it remained dark. He could only guess she had supped with her parents in their inner chamber and was still in their company.

Perhaps he should go to his chambers. At least from his tower he could still watch their secret garden center, and when she came, if she came, he could hurry back and meet her. But rather than leave, he remained. Just a few moments longer, he thought to himself.

When he'd first gone to the garden he had little doubt she would be there. He understood that she couldn't have attended the evening supper in the hall without her parents, and so he'd rushed through the meal in hopes of finding her in the only possible place they could meet. But the stone garden center had been abysmally empty. So he'd waited.

Time passed slowly from the start, but his hopes remained firm. He was sure she would want to see him, for they hadn't seen each other since the night before—so long ago!

He sat on the unyielding stone bench, thinking of Alix, hearing an occasional voice from the keep to distract him. The servants still bustled about, preparing for the feast to be held the day after next. For Julian.

Philip didn't want to think of his younger brother; he far preferred thoughts of Alix. Nonetheless, Julian did penetrate his mind's eye. It would be good to see the young sibling; no doubt he was quite grown. Philip wished, briefly and irrationally, for a miraculous change in his relationship to Julian, but knew the air would be the same as it had been two years ago when they'd last seen each other. The tension would no doubt be as tangible as it had been then, and Philip did not look forward to the sense of betrayal he was sure to see in Julian's eye.

At last, seeing the dim sliver of the moon rise

ever higher and the stars take shape, Philip concluded Alix would not come. He stood, his steps slow and heavy, taking him reluctantly away. Philip did not want to imagine the reason for her absence; he only hoped he would see her in the morning. He would not ask, he promised himself, why she did not come. He would be glad just to see her.

His behavior might have surprised him just a few short weeks ago, he thought to himself on his way to his tower. Tonight he had sat, like a lovesick youth, waiting for his ladylove under the starlit sky. He, who'd vowed women were good for one purpose only. And, when she'd failed to come, he felt only sorrow, no amount of anger. After all, he said to himself, they'd made no previous arrangement to meet every night. He'd just assumed she would want to, as he did.

He closed the door of his tower behind him, automatically reaching for the candle and flint he kept on a protruding stone beside the door frame. Then, with his way dimly lit, he took the steps with no great hurry.

In his room, the candle beside the bed, burning so low it would extinguish itself before long, warned him of another's presence. He didn't see her at first, for her back was to him, and her dark hair blended with the blanket she'd covered herself with. But he knew before aproaching who it was, and his heart leapt from the depths it had sunk to earlier.

"Alix." He said her name gently, little more than a whisper. And for a moment she didn't stir. He gazed down at her under the light of the two flickering candles, his and the one at the bedside, and thought he'd never seen a lovelier sight. Then, as if feeling rather than hearing his presence, her eyes fluttered open.

"Oh!" She sat up, the book in her arms dropping beside her on the bed. "I fell asleep," she said, rather stupidly. But in her embarrassment no other words came to her.

Philip smiled. "So you did. But I can't think of a

more ideal person to share my bed with."

She shifted her legs over the side of the spare feather mattress, not looking at him. He'd teased her before, but she still was not accustomed to it . . . not when he used that sensual tone of voice that hinted he meant every word he said. Then she remembered why she had come.

"I imagine you know about the feast everyone is preparing for," she said softly.

He nodded, still looking down at her so intently she wondered if he knew the reason for the feast. He acted as if her presence in his chamber were more important!

"I . . . wanted to be with you," she told him.

At that he looked intrigued. "You sound concerned about me."

Then she knew he must not be aware of the reason the feast was to be held. How could he be so unconcerned, when his parents treated him so unfairly?

"Do you know that Julian is coming home?" she asked, her voice still quiet. "And that he is the reason for the feast?"

He nodded, looking so indifferent to the news that she felt quite foolish. It truly did not matter to him! So she laughed, for there was nothing else she could do.

"I thought . . . I worried you would be unhappy," she said at last, responding to the puzzlement upon his face. "You are obviously not afflicted with the petty vices I am, such as envy and sibling jealousy, Philip." Then she sobered, and reached up to caress his handsome face. "You are too noble for that, I see it now. I should have known."

Philip sat beside her, still holding the candle with one hand and taking her hand with his other. "I cannot say I am entirely indifferent to what is happening," he admitted. "Part of me wants to bemoan the whole situation . . . that I have never had such a feast to honor me. But it would solve nothing, would it?"

She shook her head, her heart warming to his

wisdom. "I was foolish to think of you in such a way. I suppose I worried because I myself would have behaved much less nobly."

He loosened her hand to turn her face to his. "You were concerned about me, and that makes me happy. I was hoping to see you tonight . . . and I cannot think of a more perfect spot than right here."

His lips sought hers, gently at first, then more firmly. And how good she felt, so inviting and sleep-warmed. And upon his bed! But, mindful not only of propriety but also of the burning candle in his hand, which dripped hot wax upon his fingers, he lifted his mouth from hers and, after setting the candle beside the other on the bedside table, simply held her in an innocent embrace.

Philip knew Alix had come to his room impulsively. He knew he must think for them both in this matter—she couldn't possibly have considered all that might happen if she stayed with him. He could, oh, so easily take her right here and now. He knew, without doubt, she would offer no resistance, only sweet openness.

But dare they? Without even a betrothal? Should anyone learn of their indiscretion, there would be harsh repercussions. A marriage would most likely ensue, but under such circumstances as Philip was eager to avoid. He was tired of scandal, tired of people whispering behind his back, tired of bringing more shame to his father's name and seeing Lord Geoffrey look upon him with such disfavor.

And, he didn't want Alix to suffer the gossip and scandal. He wanted her untouched by all of that.

So yes, he must indeed think of them both, for it was obvious by her willing kiss that rational thought had not entered Alix's mind. He, for the first time in his life, must cool the passion between himself and an all too desirable woman. At least for now.

But he couldn't let her go.

Then he noticed the book beside them on the bed. "Were you looking at that?" he asked.

She nodded. "But I don't make much sense of it."

"Come here," he said, standing and leading her to the balcony doorway.

Outside, the air was balmy with a western breeze. From here they could see down the sheerness of the chateau's outermost wall, but not far beyond, for it was a dark, almost moonless night. There was barely any glow from the thin sliver hanging in the sky above them.

"It's a good night for stargazing," Philip said. "The moon's light won't cast a pall on the stars. Did you notice the drawings in the book?"

"Yes, and strange names like Merak and Dubhe."

He pointed above, in the northern part of the sky. "Do you see that star, so bright? And those two, there, just below?"

Upon her nod, he continued. "Merak and Dubhe point to Polaris, the brighter star. If you're ever lost, and don't know which direction you are headed, look to the sky. In daylight you have the sun's position to direct you. At night, Polaris always points to the north."

"When I was a child I thought the stars were eyes of people who had gone to Heaven," she said, leaning on the stone rail of the balcony. Her gaze remained skyward. "And when my grandfather died, my mother's father, I used to creep outside onto my window ledge—forbidden because of the steep drop to the ground below. But from there I could see almost the entire sky, or so I thought at that young age. From there, I used to talk to my grandfather." She pointed to two stars in the eastern sky. "There, do you see those two stars, so close together?"

He nodded.

"Those two are the ones I spoke to. Even though I never knew my grandmother, grandpapa always told me he would join her when he died. And when he did, I saw those two bright stars, so close, so beautiful, for the first time. I thought they must certainly be my grandparents."

Then she looked down, suddenly embarrassed. "I was very silly to talk to the stars, to think those particular stars had just appeared once Grandpapa died."

"It wasn't silly," he defended her. "You must have missed your grandfather a great deal. And you must have been lonely." He did not remind her of the night he'd overheard her wishes, knowing it would only add to her embarrassment. But he longed to take her into his arms, and assure her she would never be lonely again. He had vowed, however, only moments ago, to control his passion, and embracing her would no doubt threaten that control—perhaps to its limit.

"Do those stars have names, too?" she asked, still looking at the two she'd once talked to.

"All the stars have names," he told her. "Those are Castor and Pollux, the Twins."

"Twins!" she repeated, surprised. "Then of course they cannot be my grandpapa and his ladylove, my grandmother!" She laughed at her own silliness, and Philip joined in.

"How do you remember all the names of the stars?" she asked after a moment. "There must be hundreds."

He shrugged under her admiration. "I remember the names of stars better than the names of people. Probably because I have more interest in knowing the stars—more than most people, that is. Not more than you."

They gazed at each other then, and Philip once again had the urge to draw her into his arms. But he held back, remembering the promise he must keep to himself. God's teeth! It was difficult.

"Perhaps I should escort you back to the keep," he said, his voice sounding strained even to his own ears. "At least as far as the kitchen."

"There is no hurry," she said lightly, looking up at the star-filled sky once again. "Hugh is no doubt settled for the night, believing me to be safely tucked in my own bed." She smiled mischievously. "I could be gone all night long and Hugh would hardly miss me. I slept in the garden, and he never

182

even knew it. He isn't the most astute of guardians
—he made the fatal mistake of trusting my good
behavior."

Philip thought those were hardly words she
should be saying to him, he who could so easily
plead with her to stay the whole night in his
chamber. Why must she make it so difficult?

"Tell me more about the stars," she asked. "I
saw the drawings on your desk, of a bear and a
hunter with bow and arrow, and a lion—and even
the de Saines dragon. Tell me abut the dragon."

It was obvious she would not leave unless he
asked her to, and Philip had no intention of doing
that, even if it would make his struggle more con-
querable.

He spoke in an even tone, trying to keep his
mind on the galaxy above, not the woman beside
him. "The de Saines dragon is from the star constellation Draco, there between the dipper constellations." He named each star, pointing out
each one, first the head and all the way down the
dragon's tail.

"It's why I first became interested in
astronomy," Philip said, at last becoming more at
ease now that he was caught up in the subject.
"Father Fantin took me out to show me the
constellation when I was a small boy. He knew
about the stars, even though he kept that
knowledge secret from the Church. He's even led
me to believe—and I've the charts inside to add to
his theory—that the world is round, not flat. By
measuring the length of a noon shadow at
different points upon the land or sea, it's obvious
there must be a curve to the surface. Of course,
this sort of idea cannot be spoken of freely, what
with the Inquisitors all too eager to search for
those spreading the Devil's ideas. And even if the
earth truly is round and this is no Devil's
deception, the Church teaches the world is flat.
Who are we to say otherwise?"

"But how can the world be round?" she asked,
aghast at the extraordinary thought. "What keeps
us from . . . from rolling off, into oblivion?"

183

"There are many things we cannot understand," he said, adding without looking at her, his gaze going in the direction of the knights' training yard, just below, "which is why I wish we could spend our energy learning to understand such things instead of destroying one another." He turned to her then, his voice growing steadily more enthusiastic. "If men could devote themselves to learning, as I would like to do, rather than killing, think of all we would discover! We cannot depend only on the Church for our enlightenment. We need the freedom to learn all things, not only that which the Pope and clergy deem proper and godly. And there is so much to learn . . . about the skies, and our earth, even about our own bodies, all God's creations. I think He would be more pleased with that than with us killing one another, don't you agree?"

She nodded, her eyes wide and her mouth smiling. She couldn't help stepping closer and, very gently, kissing his cheek. "You really are the most unusual man."

Alix wanted to be close to him, to share in his eagerness, to see his dream. She wanted to forget her own, less noble desires, like the revenge upon the Montforts she'd wished for so often, or even the more recent wish to see Philip on his charger once again, sword in hand. Right now, hearing him speak this way, sharing this time with him under his stars—for they seemed like his—it was easy to forget her own hopes and see only Philip's. His were far more noble.

Philip's arms went irresistibly around her, pressing her close. He could feel her softness, the fullness of her breasts against his chest, her surprisingly long, firm legs against his own. Her face was just a breath away from him, so lovely, made lovelier by the willingness in her eyes and the slight, quivering smile on her mouth. He wanted to kiss her, not a brief, restrained kiss such as he had allowed before in his chamber, but the kind of kiss that led to only one form of fulfillment.

In one burst of energy, he held her back at arm's length. "Take pity on me, Alix!" he moaned. "How can I resist taking you—here and now, without a single vow spoken over our heads—when you look upon me this way?"

"Must we resist?" she asked, the question slipping out before she could call it back. Hadn't she known they would be sorely tempted if she came to his tower? She had known he would find her there, and, heaven knew, she had meant for him to! Hadn't she known, even before she set foot into his chamber, that before she left it again she would be a maiden no longer?

At her question, spoken with such innocent desire, he let his hands fall to his side. "Do you know what you're offering?" he asked, thinking her innocence must have blinded her. "It's not just a kiss I hold myself back from. Not even a kiss like the one we shared in the winery or at the pond. If we allow ourselves that, here, now, neither one of us will be satisfied to stop with that. Do you know what that means?"

She stared, wide-eyed, her gaze as pure as a saint's. "I do not know all it entails . . . but I am not entirely ignorant of mating. The animals in spring—"

"Forgive me, Alix, but do not compare our mating to that of the barn animals!" he said. "They mate and separate, having fulfilled their need to propagate the species. For us, once having shared each other, it will only be harder to keep apart."

"Will it be so much harder than it is right now?" she asked.

Philip moaned. He wanted to shake her, but more than that he wanted to kiss her, to make her his in every way. But again, he held himself back. He looked at her squarely, trying hard to continue the conversation and not simply scoop her up into his arms and take her to the bed.

"If we let ourselves do this, without betrothal or marriage vows, it could mean an even greater scandal than I am involved in already—for it would be fact, if discovered, not a lie."

She did not seem at all perturbed by that possibility. "But who could discover what we do here, where no one but you and I know we are together?"

"You could get with child, and be walking down the Church's aisle to me, thick for all to see."

At that she looked aghast, but for reasons other than the scandalous thought. "Surely we won't have to wait so long? It takes months to show a child growing in a woman!"

He smiled and stroked her hair. "I don't know how long it will take to convince your father I am a worthy man for you—perhaps I never shall."

"Oh, but you are! You are a de Saines, the son of his liege lord!"

"Are you forgetting he does not even think me fitting as an escort for you? Why should he entrust your whole life to me, when he will not entrust me with your safety, even for a ride in one of the villages?"

Alix did not want to think about the sense of Philip's words. She wanted to end this whole conversation; she didn't want to talk, not any more. And the easiest and surest way to accomplish that was to step closer and kiss his lips, which is what she did. "My father cares for my wishes," she told him while she placed her arms up about his neck. "I believe he will let me marry whomever I wish."

It was impossible for Philip to hold her back, when his own arms moved about her with a will all their own. And how could he resist her kiss, when she'd learned so expertly to tease him with her tongue, darting against his lips? Had he taught her that, with just the few kisses they'd shared? He returned her kiss with the passion she evoked, holding her so close he could feel each of her curves against him.

To Alix, the kiss released every desire she'd felt building inside her. A need, growing ever stronger, started somewhere in her middle until it seemed to permeate her entire being. She felt hot from head to toe, and her limbs felt unsteady and her fingers trembled. She was eager for this, yet a little afraid, too, of the unknown.

Alix did not know the details of how a man mated with a woman, but she did know her clothes would be in the way. And so, trying to regain control of her quaking fingers, she untied the knot at the side of her belt. In a moment her small scissors, jeweled dagger and single key to her jewel box fell to the floor in a jingle. And, because the belt had kept the low bodice of her surcoat in place, it gaped open with the lack of restraint.

Philip gazed, seeing the fullness of her breasts, the rose-hued tips peeking out just beneath the thin layer of her lace-edged underrobe. He knew then whatever battle he'd waged was entirely lost; there would be no stopping the rush of desire, no matter how hard he tried.

In an instant he swept her up into his arms, carrying her into the dimly lit room. The smaller of the two candles had extinguished itself, leaving only the meager light of a single taper. Philip let it glow, wanting to see the splendor of Alix's body, wanting her to see him.

But Alix did not lie at his side. Instead, she sat up, pulling at her surcoat until it was over her head in one swift instant, and on the floor in another. She sat in her thin underrobe, its gauzy material scant covering for her feminine body. In a moment she would have removed that as well, but Philip took her in his arms, stilling her anxious movements.

He could feel her embrace, slightly more urgent than it had been on the balcony, and thought it was not entirely due to their passion. She desired him, yes, but she was uncertain, too. And in her uncertainty she sped ahead, wanting to know the unknown. But he must restrain her, or else the pleasures might be wasted in haste.

He pressed her back down upon the bed, lying beside her and gently embracing her. Slowly, he bestowed light kisses on her face—her cheeks and eyes and nose, near but not on her mouth. His kiss roamed then, to her throat and to her ear, lingering at her lobe and teasing her with his tongue. She shivered.

Then, just as lingeringly, he moved his free hand, for the other still held her close, to stroke her hair. The combs which had pulled back her hair fell to the pillow, but neither paid them any mind.

At last Philip's kiss returned to her mouth, probing and intimate. She still seemed eager, though somewhat anxious, for her kiss was not as soft as it had been on the balcony. And she clung to him, her arms about his shoulders a bit too firm.

"I won't hurt you," he whispered into her ear. "Most of what we share will bring nothing but pleasure."

"Most?" she cast him a wide-eyed glance.

He smiled. "This is your first time—and though I've never had a virgin, I've heard it said there is some pain. You know, don't you, that there will be some blood?"

She nodded. The blood they were supposed to show on the morn after their wedding, as evidence of her purity.

He seemed to read her thoughts. "Would you rather wait? Until this is proper?"

She shook her head. "No, Philip! I do want you . . . even if I am just a tiny bit afraid."

She wasn't sure from where that fear stemmed; fear of pain? Perhaps. Or was it a fear of losing herself? Of losing herself forever, completely, to Philip, never to be her own self, ever again? But she'd already lost her heart to Philip; losing power over the rest of her seemed only fitting.

He kissed her again, gently, as if to prove he meant to give her no pain. And slowly, the passion reignited in Alix, making her forget her uncertainty of what was to come. Her arms about him relaxed, her lips softened. Her tongue teased his. But she was still eager.

Her hand went to the latch at his belt, and after a moment he assisted her in removing it. His tunic came off next, and Alix let her fingers gently caress his taut skin, pulled firmly over the muscles of his shoulders, back and chest. But she did not linger; instead, her inquisitive fingers went to the string tying his chausses. She wanted to know all of him, and she saw no reason to hesitate.

But Philip stilled her fast-moving hands. He took both her hands in his, bringing them to his mouth. He kissed the knuckles, then the palms, surprising her by sliding his tongue along one wrist. It tickled, sending strange shivers up her arms and a tremor across her shoulders. Then, her hands still tenderly imprisoned in his, he placed a kiss, sure and quick, directly between her breasts, at the top of the valley separating them.

His kiss traveled sensuously, pushing aside the top of her underrobe, until he took her nipple into his mouth. A sigh escaped her at the intimacy, and, without quite knowing for certain, she guessed Philip's motive. This mating would be no quick thing, like the animals in spring which were Alix's only basis for comparison. He meant to know all of her, not just with a swift glance before joining, but intimately, with every sense imaginable.

He released her hands, and she held him close, her fingers now exploring. He had many scars from his life as a knight, one that traveled from his bottom rib up under his arm. There were more on his chest, a few hidden by the dark hair that grew into a single, tapering line, disappearing into the top of his chausses. He may no longer be a knight, but his body displayed the truth that he had been one once—and a mighty one at that. To have survived so many injuries, he must indeed be strong.

And his strength had not diminished, even though he no longer lived the life of a knight. His arms were powerful, his chest and back corded with flat, hard sinew. She felt slight beneath his hard bulk, but safe within his arms.

His fingers were like the rest of him, long and lean, as they gently caressed her breasts. His kiss pleasured her other nipple, leaving no part unexplored. Then, without any word, he knelt above her, leaning down and removing first one of her shoes and then the other. Next, as if accustomed to undressing her, he eased her stockings down her legs, letting them fall beside her discarded surcoat. And finally, when his mouth once again sought hers, she felt him tug gently at the single garment between their upper bodies. Her underrobe came loose, raised over her head, and she was completely unclothed to his sight and touch.

To say she was as lovely as he expected seemed to minimize her beauty. She was indeed lovely, but far more than even Philip had imagined. Her skin, under the single candle's glow, was pure white, without blemish. The rich rose hue of her nipples, standing with desire from his kiss, contrasted with the ivory of the rest of her, but not so much in contrast as the dark triangle where her legs met. It might have been easy to hurry this coupling; to go there, directly to the source of desire, but he would not let himself. That might have been well enough for others; not so with Alix. This was her first time, and he wished to show her all the pleasures she could delight in.

This time when Alix's hand went to his chausses, she met no resistance. But her fingers, trembling ever so slightly, needed the deft assistance of his. It took Philip a moment too long as well, for his own hands were not quite as steady as usual, but in a moment the chausses were free and the fact of their nakedness was all that mattered.

Philip pulled her beside him until she was almost above him, and it made her feel bold. She lowered her mouth to his, teasing his lips with her tongue. Then she kissed his shoulder, and, before a moment's thought might have made her shy, she let her kiss travel to his masculine nipple, where she touched him with the tip of her tongue. She could not suckle him as he had her, for there was no softness to be found, but she knew he found pleasure nonetheless, for when she looked up at him he smiled at her open willingness to bring him as much pleasure as he'd given her.

She had not let her gaze roam too far since he'd discarded his chausses, but now she did. She looked at the length of him, seeing with such stark

190

clarity just how much he desired her. She wondered that he did not burst, and hoped he found no pain in the delay their exploration forced, which left him so ready and swollen. Curiously, she longed to touch him, and her fingers moved slowly, following the hairs of his chest tapered into a line leading the way.

He was smooth and hot, firm as she'd guessed, and at her caress he took a deep intake of breath. At first she feared she'd hurt him, but then she saw the pleasure in his eyes and knew he welcomed her touch. He was so full, she wondered if perhaps there might be blood each time he used that shaft upon her body, but she gave no heed to such fears. In her middle, pulsating from between her legs, was an emptiness she knew he could fill.

He shifted his weight to his side, and she lay back, letting him explore her body as she had explored his. Her breasts, already sensitized from his kiss, seemed to swell at his caress, and though she wished he would linger, other parts of her body cried out for attention. That need, that spring erupting from her very center, felt so hot she thought she would have demanded his touch had she not felt his hand, after hesitating upon her hip, travel to just that spot. She felt his fingers and for one moment dizziness assailed her, her desire was so fierce. He was sure with his touch, finding a spot which quickened her breath, changing her body into a maelstrom of yearning. Her hips moved sinuously under his caress, an invitation as primeval as life itself, and as instinctive as breathing.

Her need was so clear it brought an urgency to Philip's own, restrained passion. He moved atop her, still holding back, thinking that to go too quickly might bring her pain. Gently, he eased himself nearer, holding himself rigidly above her so not to crush her with his weight.

But the rein he held on himself almost broke when she clung to him, pulling him closer. Her breasts, soft beneath his hard chest, were warm, and moving delightfully against him with her ragged breaths. He lowered himself, seeking and finding her entrance that would make them one. But still he held back, only allowing the very tip of him to tease at the opening.

"I want . . . all of you," she said, her voice unsteady, pleading.

In the dim light, he saw the passion in her eyes, knew he could hold back no longer, and did as she asked. With one quick thrust he gave her all of him, and watched as her eyes closed briefly, if in pain he could not tell. When she opened them again, the passion was still there.

She met his every plunge, answering his need with a need of her own. He seemed to fill her to the very core, and yet she thrust her hips upward at each of his withdrawals, so he was always deep within her. Faster and harder, and deeper he seemed to penetrate, until the need grew into an intense fulfillment, which also grew and grew, sending her to the very sky they'd studied before.

Philip did not entirely loosen the rein he'd held; his desire was so urgent, filling him so intensely he thought certainly he must send forth his seed. But still he thrust, waiting, holding himself back in a struggle that threatened fatigue more thoroughly than anything he'd ever known. Then, when he felt a shudder pass through her, a sigh so sweet escape her lips, he let forth that surge of himself. And the release was more vital than any he'd known.

His arms, which still held most of his weight from her, threatened collapse. With one deep breath, he moved beside her, laying still, feeling her lethargy as sure as his own. Still, one of his hands held hers, his thumb gently caressing her palm.

At last, once his breath was regained, he propped himself up on one elbow, and looked down at her. Surprisingly, her eyes were open wide, and she smiled. One hand raised to caress his cheek.

"I fear you were right, Sire," she whispered. "Knowing this only makes it harder to think of doing without, no matter how long or short the time until our wedding."

He nuzzled the soft skin of her shoulder and throat. "Fine time to realize that," he teased.

She laughed, but then, suddenly, she held him tight, pulling him close and half atop her. "What shall we do? I cannot be parted from you . . . not now, not ever. In my mind . . . surely in God's eyes, you are my husband already, after what we have shared here tonight." Then she said again, her voice desperately unsteady, "Whatever shall we do?"

He looked at her, stroking back her hair, relishing even now in its softness. "I will speak to your father," he promised. "I will ask him for your hand. Tomorrow."

That was promise enough. "Then perhaps we can make the coming feast one of betrothal . . . that would save us the trouble of having one separately." She grinned. "Rather timely, wouldn't you say? Perhaps we can be wed by month-end."

"With only a few short weeks to wait, it will not be so unbearable."

She hugged him close again. "But it will be, for me!"

"And for me," he admitted, returning the intensity of her embrace. Then, even though exhaustion from their first coupling still left its weight upon him, one of his hands came to caress her breast. "Tonight," he told her between a rain of gentle kisses upon her sweet nipple, "must live in our memory and carry us through. Let us make the most of it."

15

Alix waited until Hugh went off to the training yard before returning to her chamber. Philip had wanted to accompany her, to be with her in case she was discovered, but Alix dissuaded him. If she were discovered, it would be far less dangerous for her to be discovered alone.

She was tired, but too lighthearted to pay her fatigue any mind. Blanche was in Alix's chamber when Alix opened the door but, as other times when Alix did not sleep in her bed, the loyal servant said nothing.

"I'd like a bath this morning," Alix said cheerily. "And I think I shall wear my green surcoat today." She smiled to herself at the choice, remembering one of the things Philip had told her in a late-night, whispered discussion. They'd been too exhausted to make love again yet too excited to sleep, and so, recouping their strength, they lay in each other's arms, exchanging intimate conversation rather than intimate caresses. He'd told her he loved the color of her eyes, a green so clear he felt he gazed at spring itself. She had laughed, telling him his eyes were the first aspect of him she had loved. Silently she had marveled, remembering that first night when she'd met him in the kitchen. She hadn't seen just how handsome he was, not yet. But now, she thought there wasn't a more handsome man in all the world, and she told him so.

The green of her eyes would be enhanced by the surcoat, she thought with satisfaction as Blanche retrieved it from the chest.

The bath felt wonderfully soothing to her exhausted muscles—muscles she'd never used before. She felt a bit sore between her legs, and the muscles of her thighs were the ones which cried out most clearly, but with each twinge she smiled. The slight pain now hardly compared to the pleasure of last night.

Blanche lathered Alix's hair, and the gentle, circular massage felt so welcome it almost put Alix to sleep.

"Are the fixings for the feast complete yet?" Alix asked, eyes closed.

"No, Demoiselle," Blanche said. "Cook is still strutting like a rooster under attack, offended the Sire would demand such a feast with so little time to prepare."

Yesterday the feast hardly mattered to Alix, but today, because its purpose would no doubt be shared by her betrothal, she welcomed it. Like Sire Geoffrey, she wanted it to excel all others. That is, she thought with one tiny wrinkle forming on her brow, provided her father agreed to Philip's request.

But why should he not? she asked herself, leaning back and letting Blanche minister to her. Did her father really think the small matter of Philip's inactive sword enough reason to forbid his daughter a marriage she desired? There was no real reason for Philip to fight; most knights serviced their lord for the best reason of all: it was their only means of support. But there lay the true fact. Philip hardly needed to sell the services of his sword. He was a de Saines! Surely that meant something to her father—the impoverished Beauchamp family should welcome a marriage bond that would link them more closely with the wealthiest family in the land.

The timing was perhaps the only problem. With the scandal from court still so fresh, Alix's father would no doubt hesitate to let his daughter be open to any repercussions from Philip's involvement. But Alix was confident she could convince her mother that Philip was Alix's only choice for a husband. And if Alix could convince Marie, Marie could convince Giles. It was as simple as that.

Philip removed the blanket from the bed with tender care, folding it so the blood staining the center was hidden. Then, turning to the chest laying open against one wall, he removed enough articles until he saw bottom. There he placed the blanket, irrefutable evidence of Alix's purity and that he alone had taken it, and covered it with layers of clothing. For safekeeping, he said to himself.

Philip did not relish the thought of facing Alix's father. Lord Giles had made it all too clear exactly what he thought of Philip, and Philip wasn't fool enough to believe his position as the de Saines heir would negate Lord Giles's disregard for him. But the notion that Giles might stand in the way of Philip's only chance at happiness tempted Philip to promise anything, just to have Alix as his own.

Indecision tore at his insides. He would promise anything, he said to himself, except taking up the sword again. He would restore the Beauchamp Estate in more splendor than it had ever seen, he would restock its stables, replenish its grain fields, fill its vaults with every treasure imaginable. And pray all the while that Giles would be satisfied with that.

But something warned him, a small, nagging voice, reminding him that Giles might hold a service-bloodied sword more precious than any amount of gold. Could Philip buy Giles's daughter? Or would he have to break the vow he'd made to himself two years past, a vow he swore nothing could ever make him forget?

By God, he wouldn't! He would sooner steal Alix away than take up the sword again.

Philip knew that was insane. His father would never let him go, and even if they did run away, Geoffrey had the power and means to find them and bring them back like the two wayward children they would be. If his father had any intention of letting Philip give up his place as heir, he would have done so the moment Philip returned to the Chateau without his sword.

Lord Geoffrey respected the fates, God's will, more highly than any other value. Or perhaps he feared God's wrath if he were to disown the son God had given him. Geoffrey, Philip knew, was not one to question God's purposes. It was because of that, and nothing else—certainly no love for Philip himself—that Philip was still the de Saines heir, when all who knew the de Saines family could easily guess it was Julian who was so highly favored.

Julian had always been Eleanore's favorite, Philip knew. Even when they were children, Eleanore would call Julian to her side and greet him with an embrace and kiss. She seemed always to want him near, as if no other person on earth could give her such pleasure just with his presence.

As for Sire Geoffrey, Julian had become his favorite the moment Philip told him he would no longer carry his sword. Before that, Geoffrey had been proud of both his sons. But since that time it was clear to all he found nothing but shame in his heir.

The scandal had only made matters worse although, with time, Philip hoped that salt in the wound between them would wear away. There was little he could do to rid himself of the vicious names being linked to him, of caitiff and coward, being labeled a man who chased women only in the most villainous manner. He knew the King had sent him from Paris only out of affection and respect for Philip's decision never to touch the sword again, but perhaps if Philip had stayed, weathered what was being said, faced Charles in person—somehow convinced him he had not been the disloyal friend Rachel said he was . . .

But he knew Charles. Words would not have appeased him. Philip knew, sensibly, that if he had stayed he would have been forced to take up the sword again. Or die. Charles would have seen to that.

And taking up the sword again now was the only way to put an early end to the scandal. But he knew he could not; how could he face Charles with a sword, over a woman who had deceived him? Charles did not deserve that, to fight a battle for a woman who obviously cared so little for him. It would be better to let the scandal die of old age. And that, Philip feared, would take more time than he had.

God above, Philip prayed, let Lord Giles value the revitalization of his Estate and title more fervently than he did the reputation of a prospective son-in-law!

Philip did not go to the Estate to work that day. He sent as many peasants as he could spare, but he himself stayed close to the Chateau. He wanted to see Lord Giles at the earliest possible moment.

Just before the noon meal, Philip went to the hall. Alix was already there, seated beside her mother. When Philip entered, Alix's eyes met his and, with a smile passed between them that brought back every image of last night, Philip approached.

He bowed formally, and addressed Marie.

"Good-morn to you, Lady Marie," he said, still smiling. But now his eyes held only cheer, not the tender sensuality he'd sent Alix's way. Then he bowed to Alix, but Philip could see she had lost the initial happiness she'd greeted him with. He thought with growing concern that she looked almost worried.

"Good-morning to you, Lord Philip," Marie said congenially.

Even Marie looked somewhat reserved. But then, he thought, she normally did when in his company. He knew only too well that Marie agreed with her husband: Philip was not a fitting match for any woman, least of all her daughter. He could only pray that would change, and soon!

"I believe this is the first time you have arrived early to one of the meals," Marie added.

"I came with good reason, Madame," he admitted. "I hoped to have words with your husband, Lord Giles."

Marie sighed. "Giles is in his bed once again,

saving his strength for the feast to be held tomorrow. You know that he was ill just a few days past."

Then Philip understood the disappointment in Alix's eye. Lord Giles never accepted visitors when he took to his bed, other than immediate family.

"I had hoped he was better," Philip said, then, hiding his own disappointment, he extended his wish. "Please tell Lord Giles I hope for his speedy recovery."

"He will be well by the time of the feast," Marie promised. "He has told me it is very important that we all be there."

"No doubt my brother will appreciate that," Philip said sincerely.

Philip wished he could have left then, and taken Alix with him. He did not want to sit through an entire meal, one which would serve no purpose, so close to her and yet unable to touch her. But his father approached from behind, and after a cordial greeting to the ladies, invited Philip to his seat.

Sire Geoffrey took his seat beside his son. Then, quite directly, he said, "You will be at the feast tomorrow."

Philip smiled despite the bristle of resistance stiffening his spine from his father's tone of voice. He was no stripling to be ordered about in such a manner. "Yes, Father, I have every intention of being there."

Geoffrey relaxed visibly. The deeply etched wrinkles upon his brow seemed to ease somewhat, and he leaned back comfortably in his chair. "I had thought . . . the last time you were home with Julian, the air was not pleasant between you two. I feared there would be a lasting effect."

Philip shook his head, although secretly he feared it was Julian who would not so easily forget. After all, it was Julian who felt so betrayed, not Philip. Hadn't Philip taught him so much of what he knew as a knight? Hadn't Philip taken him under his wing, shown him the ways of knighthood, only to renounce them later on? Julian had become the knight Philip had shown him how to be; as a boy, Julian had spent his every waking moment trying to please his older brother, to perform every skill with as much prowess as Philip himself, or more.

Philip knew Julian had idolized him. Long ago, it had brought him a certain satisfaction: Julian might be his mother's favorite, but he, Philip himself, was Julian's. For a time, it seemed to give him a place in the family, this family that he'd never really felt a part of. He'd never been as carefree as Julian, as likeable. Philip had never even enjoyed the family's vast wealth, not the way Julian did. Philip had preferred studying the stars, even as a child. Perhaps it was his quiet nature, his preference for solitude that kept his parents, most especially his mother, so distant from him. But whatever the reason, once Julian no longer worshipped him, Philip had lost his place in the family. The recent scandal had merely filled the existing chasm between Philip and his family with very icy water.

The noon meal was sparse in comparison with other meals; the servants were, understandably, still very busy with preparations for the feast to be held the next day. And for the second day in a row, the typical afternoon games were forestalled. The knights were wont to go to the training yard, for their squires were to be knighted soon and the Montfort feud still threatened. They would need all their skills, and strove to keep themselves finely honed. And the women resumed their sewing; if every peasant was to receive a tunic, their nimble fingers would have to double the number they'd created yesterday.

Alix watched Philip leave the hall, her heart sinking with each step taking him farther away. She longed to go with him, to sneak into his tower and relive those memories of last night which tinted her cheeks with a blush of remembered passion. But she knew she could not. They had been lucky enough already, she knew, not to have been discovered last night.

200

Alix sat beside her mother at the sewing table, and, to her pleasant surprise found Marguerite taking the chair to her left.

"Demoiselle Marguerite," Alix greeted her with a smile. "My brother has been very unattentive to you, I fear. I have not seen you together since he returned."

Marguerite smiled, but her eyes seemed to hold a secret. "Only before an audience, Demoiselle Alix," she whispered. "He wishes to speak to my father before making our intentions known."

"Has Simon not even spoken to my father about your betrothal?" Alix asked, surprised.

Marguerite shook her head. "Only you and your mother share our secret. But it will not be long," she added. "My father is arriving today, and Simon will speak to both fathers tomorrow, after the feast."

"What are you two whispering about?" asked Lady Marie.

Both young women laughed, and Alix said, "Secrets, Mother." But only Alix knew just how well she understood Marguerite's.

16

"He is here! Sir Julian is here!"

Alix stood back, making way for the excited servant to pass with his news. From atop the battlements, horns blew the proclamation of Julian's coming. Alix heard the creaking draw-bridge as it was lowered, and watched as the procession of men-at-arms, guests, vassals and every de Saines relation—all but Philip—took places on the outer stone steps of the forebuilding in anticipation of Julian's arrival.

Sire Geoffrey and Lady Eleanore stood at the

center, dressed in such finery even King Jean himself would have been impressed. Eleanore's surcoat sparkled with silver and gold threaded in intricate designs, a small de Saines dragon emblazoned on each cuff. Beside her, Sire Geoffrey was resplendent in a doublet also designed in the dragon; but his was studded with precious jewels that glistened under the late morning sun.

Alix stood between her parents, just behind the Sire and his wife. She scanned the area for Philip, wondering where he would be if not beside his mother and father. But a moment later her heart tumbled at the sight of him as he approached from the direction of his tower. He, too, wore the dragon upon his chest, plainer than his father's, for his was stitched only in crimson thread. But it stood out proudly against the black of his doublet. The sole sign of wealth he wore was a cross medallion, in its center a diamond glittering like a single eye. Alix had never seen Philip dressed so splendidly. But, she thought with a smile, he looked handsome to her no matter what he wore—and even in nothing at all. Most especially then. She also noted with a touch of possessive pride, she was not the only woman looking Philip's way. He attracted many a female glance.

Philip took his place on the far side of his father. Sire Geoffrey noted his eldest son's arrival, for Alix heard Geoffrey say, "I feared I would have to send Oliver after you, despite your promise you would be here today."

"My word is still good, Father," Philip said, confident yet cool that his father obviously doubted him.

"You would have had such a feast as this to welcome you," Geoffrey said quietly, yet loud enough for Alix to hear. Then he added, "Had you not needed to come home under the cover of darkness."

That he still believed his son guilty of the scandal was obvious. But Philip said easily, "There was no need for me to return at night,

Father. It simply happened that way, since I traveled without resting the nights."

Philip's face still seemed placid, despite the unpleasant exchange with his father. Philip was void of the excitement so obvious on every face around him, but, Alix noted, without a trace of resentment. He was, she thought to herself, the only one present with reason to be indignant over this joyous reception. Yet he showed no sign of such a feeling. Sire Geoffrey's words had reminded her of the lonely welcome Philip had received upon his homecoming. If she herself had not been there, and quite by chance, then only Arnaud, the dog, would have even known Philip had returned.

But Philip's face softened when he glanced her way, and sent her a smile that made her tumbling heart leap with joy. There was no chance to speak, to exchange even a few quick words, but his smile had said enough. Today's feast might have a dual purpose—not only to welcome Julian home, but to announce their betrothal. And with that thought, she returned his smile with every bit as much joy.

Cheering voices competed with the trumpets playing from above on the high walls. At last Julian's procession began to pass through the raised portcullis. First came Julian's men-at-arms, then his squires, and, just ahead of a cheering mass of peasants, poor and merchant alike, came Julian himself, heralded by the many villagers invited to the feast to welcome him home.

Alix watched Philip's young sibling as he neared the keep's forebuilding. So this was the person who stole the love of Philip's parents. She remembered Julian from childhood; he'd always been in some sort of mischief, and, because of that, he'd reminded her of her brother, for Simon, too, had a penchant for a prank when he was young. Once Julian had set a trap for Sir Oliver, who at that time had not yet been castellan. Julian must have known the knight always rode his horse to the village at the same time each day—some said he met a young peasant girl for a tryst in her father's barn. Julian had waited for him, with a rope drawn round one tree trunk and holding the other end from the opposite side of the road. When Sir Oliver approached, blissfully unsuspecting, Julian pulled the rope at precisely the right moment to startle the highly sensitive destrier beneath Oliver. The horse, as expected, immediately whinnied in fright and reared, sending Sir Oliver sprawling.

The story went that Julian hadn't fled but, confident of his position as the Sire's son, came out from hiding in a fit of mirth, holding the rope in his hand to reveal how he'd played his trick. And Sir Oliver could do nothing, for even though Julian would have deserved a thrashing—startling an excitable destrier could have proved dangerous for both the man and the expensive beast—he knew that, if Lady Eleanore ever heard of it, Oliver would be banished from the Chateau.

But surely Julian had changed since then, Alix thought. He was fully grown, resplendent as everyone else present, and wearing a doublet that was startlingly like his father's with a jeweled dragon decorating the chest. He was laughing and smiling, obviously pleased at the festive welcome. When he saw his parents he jumped from the horse and rushed to their side, embracing his mother first and then, while still holding her hand, kissing his father's cheek in affectionate reverence. Cheers resounded everywhere, seeing the happy reunion.

"How good it is to see you both!" Julian said, the smile upon his face and love in his eyes reflected by both the Sire and Lady Eleanore. Then, with a kiss for his mother, added, "I've missed you."

"Surely not as much as we've missed you," said the Sire, patting Julian's back.

As Julian's gaze then traveled to those around them, it halted upon Philip. His back stiffened, and he let go his mother's hand. Upon his face, for the barest moment, was a strange mixture of emotion, a gamut from a glimmer of happiness to the more visible sign of unease—and was that pain? Finally, animosity was plainly evident upon his handsome, youthful face.

"Welcome home, Julian," Philip said, stepping forward and clasping one hand upon Julian's shoulder. He gazed at Julian closely, feeling the hostility as apparent as the tension in the shoulder beneath Philip's fingertips. "It has been too long."

"I see you still wear no sword at your side," Julian said between lips that barely moved.

"Only because I haven't forgotten the lesson my bloody sword taught," Philip told him.

"Which was?" Julian asked, his blue eyes like ice as he stared at his older brother.

"That blood begets blood. It must stop somewhere."

"This is no time for philosophizing," Sire Geoffrey said as he stepped between the two brothers. "Julian, you have many others left to greet."

Philip watched as Julian turned away. Hadn't he expected Julian's aloofness? Julian was the one who felt so betrayed when Philip gave up the sword. After all, he had taught his brother so well how to use it—and then he renounced the very tool Julian had become such an expert with under Philip's tutelage. To Julian, it must have been like the god renouncing his own religion, the teacher denying the worth of all his knowledge.

Philip frowned. This was one more lesson he wished he could teach his young, glory-seeking brother. But Philip knew, at least for now, Julian was just too young to listen.

Others stepped forward, surrounding the honored son, but Geoffrey called Lord Giles and his family to Julian's attention. Geoffrey took Alix's hand, bringing her from behind her father and mother.

"And this beauty is Giles's daughter, Alix." Sire Geoffrey introduced her to Julian. "Do you remember her, my boy?"

Julian's gaze traversed her length as if trying to place her—a gaze so intimate it seemed to penetrate her clothes. His eyes, blue so like his brother's and yet so different, cast her a look she would have welcomed had it come from Philip instead. But from Julian, she was tempted to scold him for his boldness. After all, they would be brother and sister-in-law soon—and with leftover memories of their childhood, Alix already thought of Julian as a brother.

Julian was not as tall as his brother, or as lean. His shoulders were perhaps a trifle broader, or it could have been padding in his doublet, his muscular bulk was so great. There was no doubting his handsomeness, for his blue eyes were clear, his nose narrow and straight, his teeth white and uniform. His hair, also dark like Philip's, was every bit as thick, waving away from his face. Yes, he was handsome, Alix thought, perhaps even more so than Philip, whose nose was as narrow but somewhat larger, his waist thinner, and his height almost an inconvenience. But there was no one more pleasing for her eyes to behold than Philip; she knew that without doubt.

"How could I forget one so lovely?" Julian said after a lengthy assessment of her. He took her hand and kissed her palm, letting his lips linger a bit longer than customary.

"How kind of you to say so," Alix replied, somewhat coolly, as she pulled her hand from his. She knew from the manner of his evasive statement that he had indeed totally forgotten her, and she was amused that he would try to cover that fact with flirtation. She was surprised at herself; she'd wondered what she would think of Julian when she met him, and feared she would dislike him because he received the honor Philip deserved from their parents. Besides that, the only childhood memories she had of him were unpleasant. He'd once frightened her with one of his falcons, for he had trained it to land on one's head at a single command. Fortunately she had been wearing a hat which protected her from the bird's sharp talons, but having the predatory bird swoop down out of nowhere had given her a fear of birds that lasted to this day.

But now, seeing him, she found none of that childhood animosity toward him. Perhaps it was Philip's welcome that had given her this release from such feelings. After all, it was obvious he welcomed Julian. Could she do less, when Julian had done nothing to offend her? If Philip still cared for Julian as a brother, she would try to do so as well.

Julian greeted all of the other high guests, vassals and de Saines relatives he obviously hadn't seen in years, for he said so. And while he did that, Alix gazed at Philip, noticing happily that he headed in her direction.

"Good-morn to you and yours, Demoiselle Alix," he said with a bow. Then, to Lord Giles, he said, "It is good to see you up and about, my lord. I hope your health is restored."

"I am well enough," Giles said stiffly, but a cough belied his words. But he smiled when his gaze rested on Julian, who had just kissed his cousin Constance and said something which made all around laugh. "No doubt you are well pleased to have your brother home at last."

"Of course," Philip said, then, "Lord Giles, I wish to have words with you before today's feast closes. It is a private matter."

Giles looked at him, eyebrows raised in interest. "Oh? Yes, all right. But it must wait until after the final course; I have another matter on my mind that will demand my attention until then."

Philip bowed formally, but before returning to his mother's side, he exchanged a glance with Alix that made him wish he could have his intentions known here and now, without delay. In her eyes he saw her love, so real, and something else, too. A hint of the fire he'd discovered in her last night, a glimpse of remembered passion that stirred him deep within. Yes, he thought, he was eager! He felt like a besotted youth, but didn't care. Their love was so tangible, there between them, even in this crowd, that he knew nothing could keep them apart for long.

With the sound of trumpets, Lord Geoffrey led the way into the hall, with Eleanore on one side and Julian on the other. Only the high guests would sup within; the rest would be served outdoors. Not that it mattered to the poor; most had not seen a full meal in years, some not at all, and that coupled with the fine new clothes being given to each and every one of them made this feast beyond compare.

Indoors, people took their places. Alix went to a seat beside her brother, who for once took his place next to his mother rather than with his men-at-arms. But before Alix could be seated, she heard Sire Geoffrey call to her.

"Demoiselle Alix, come sit here with us," he invited congenially. "As the daughter of my lord high vassal, you shall share the trencher with my son."

For a moment her heart raced, and her gaze went yearningly to Philip. But too soon it was clear Sire Geoffrey had not meant Philip, but Julian, for Geoffrey waved his hand in the direction of the favored son.

Alix knew she could hardly refuse to feed Sir Julian, especially if her liege lord commanded it. She approached Julian slowly, forcing a smile to her lips so as not to appear rude. How she wished she could go to Philip's side instead! She found sharing a trencher with any high guest almost an intimacy, using the same cup, eating from the same cut of meat, using her very fingertips to feed her partner. Why couldn't Sire Geoffrey have asked her to share Philip's trencher instead?

But she quickly resigned herself to her fate; she must share this meal with Julian, and hide her preference for the present. After all, it wouldn't be long before Julian was her brother-in-law; it would do to get to know him.

Julian took her hand in a brief squeeze, leading her to the chair beside his. "I am the most fortunate man here, Demoiselle," he whispered, "to be serviced by one such as you."

As Alix took her seat, she did not feel so

fortunate. She found she could hardly see Philip, for he sat down the table, with his mother on one side and Constance de Saines on the other. Constance, Alix saw, had a trencher of her own and would not be sharing Philip's. Not that Alix had reason to be jealous! Constance was certainly of marriageable age, but she was Philip's cousin— even if she did look at Philip with wide eyes. Philip might have lost favor with his father, but it seemed scandal and the intrigue of laying down his sword had only made him more fascinating to the women of the Chateau.

Alix pushed her chair as close to the table as possible, pleased that afforded her a better view. She might have to share her meal with Julian, but that did not mean she could not gaze often upon the person she longed to be with.

Servants came in at the call of the horn. Wine and food bearers moved about in an order that served all in short time, starting with the Sire and his immediate family and then all others. From every direction food abounded, from the roasted meat taken from dozens of slaughtered cattle, suckling pig, and hunted deer, to the hundreds of fowl dishes from quail to swan. Fish, too, was served, pike, crab, eels and herring. Vegetables steamed with herbs, bread was topped with mustard or butter, and pears, peaches, and apples were either cooked in cinnamon or honey or offered fresh. Wine flowed freely, a better quality indoors than out, but nary a cup at any table was empty, at least for very long. And everywhere laughter resounded; spirits were high at this feast, for it had been far too long since the last.

In the center of the hall, tumblers and jugglers appeared. Dressed in their parti-colored tights, they were as colorful as the jester whose task it was to always speak the truth to his lord, and to make even the harshest truth a subject to laugh over. The jester sat at his lord's feet, telling amusing stories, laughing at the jugglers even when their tricks were on the mark. And in the background, hardly discernible over the conversations and laughter, a harpist played.

Then, just after the Bishop's deep voice echoed above all others in a call for the food's blessing, the meal commenced. Though Bishop Beauchamp was her uncle, Alix barely knew him. Her father's brother was an important man in the Church, as evidenced by his high station and the fact that he'd long been able to choose where he ministered—which of course was his homeland Brittany. And what Chateau in Brittany was more comfortable than the de Saineses'?

Alix broke the bread she was to share with Julian, placing the first morsel between Julian's smiling lips. She was startled when his mouth closed around her fingertips for the barest moment. Her eyes flew to his, but he only smiled innocently.

"I can see you are quite famished after your travels," she said with prim self-restraint as she dipped her fingers in the small bowl of water beside her cup.

"Quite," he said, still smiling as if he knew what he'd done and was glad she'd noticed.

The fact that he'd touched her fingers intentionally, and with the very first bite, set an annoyingly intimate precedent, one Alix was determined to circumvent.

"Then you should enjoy today's meal," she said. "Cook has been threatening rebellion the past few days, he's been working so hard to have the feast all it should be."

"Ah, Cook," Julian said fondly. "Now he is one servant I've missed. And not only because of his skills. He acts as though he's a member of the family—and I think he's gotten us all believing him."

"Cook said to me more than once he would be better off with locks on the cellars if you were coming home. It seems he remembers the day you stole flour for some devious purpose."

Julian laughed. "So he's told you about my criminal past?"

"Hardly. My brother was in on that particular

prank." She remembered how Julian and Simon had covered themselves with the white powder to frighten every woman in the bower into believing the Chateau was haunted. "How did you ever find your way into the women's bower without being detected?"

He grinned crookedly. "A secret, Demoiselle. One I shall never divulge, for it may still serve a purpose one day."

Alix shook her head, thinking though Julian might look grown up, he obviously was very much like the devious little boy she'd known as a child.

Then, as Julian chatted on about various childhood memories, she let her gaze wander to Philip, seeing him speaking to Constance. Did he know, she wondered, why Constance looked so flushed? Not because of the warmth of the two burning hearths, but because she was seated beside Philip!

But when Philip saw her look his way, he smiled. And her heart moved within, knowing how lucky she was that it was she, rather than any other woman present, who had caught his eye. She was able to tend to her own meal with a buoyed spirit.

Philip watched Alix as she deftly cut the meat upon the plate she shared with his brother, then offer it to Julian. From where he sat, it looked as though the piece was rather large, and he smiled to himself wondering if perhaps she'd cut it that way intentionally to quiet her voluble partner.

"They look well together, don't they, Philip?" his mother asked, seeing where his gaze lingered.

Philip turned his attention to Lady Eleanore. "Julian and Alix?" he repeated.

"Of course. That's where you were looking."

Philip cleared his throat, then said, "Demoiselle Alix is a very beautiful woman, Mother. She would look well with any man at her side."

"Then you would welcome Alix into our family?"

"Of course," he assured his mother, wondering if she could have guessed, somehow, of his relationship with Alix. Then he asked curiously,

"Wouldn't you?"

Eleanore laughed. "Your father and I are very fond of Alix—of all the Beauchamps."

Though this was no new knowledge, Philip nonetheless was warmed by his mother's words. At least there would be no challenge there, once his intention to marry Alix was known.

He looked once again at Julian and Alix, seeing Julian still speaking eagerly. He certainly did not look tired from his travels, Philip thought, noting the spirited way he upheld the conversation. Philip would have liked to tell his father immediately, upon the announcement that Alix was to share her meal with Julian, that there was reason for Alix to be Philip's supper partner instead. But he held back, forcing himself to be patient. Until he had a chance to speak to Lord Giles alone, Philip must not cause any commotion that might complicate matters. And certainly sharing a dinner trencher with Julian was something they all could endure.

Alix cut the meat she shared with Julian, passed the cup, and gave him the choicest portions, always showing proper deference but not often letting her gaze meet his. She let Julian do most of the talking, knowing he was enjoying the entire meal far more than she was. She was content to let her gaze, and her thoughts, roam farther down the table. If Julian knew her better—or if he were more observant of where her gaze went so often, he might guess why she was more than a little distracted. But it was hardly important that Julian did not know her well enough to guess the source of her preoccupation. She had no intention of letting Julian know her any better—except as his brother's wife!

At last, after a lengthy pause during which Alix distinctly felt Julian's penetrating gaze upon her, he whispered, "Your shyness is very refreshing after knowing just the brazen camp followers for this past year or more."

"Shyness?" He'd caught her attention with that statement. "Sir Julian," she told him quite bluntly, "I am not shy."

He lifted his brows. "But you have grown so quiet." Then, as if an idea just dawned, he asked, "Or is it—could it be—that I bring out some sort of coyness in you?"

Alix almost giggled but, seeing his earnestness, spared the insult to his pride. "I apologize if I have not done my part in our conversation, Sir. I shall try to do better. But coyness has nothing to do with it. In fact, you remind me greatly of my brother. One is not coy with a brother."

His hopeful expression died quickly upon hearing those words, and Alix feared she had succeeded in bruising his vanity anyway. But in a moment he was smiling every bit as sensuously as before, and said, "I hope to see much of you here at home, Demoiselle. Perhaps then I may rid you of this brotherly image you hold of me."

"I doubt that will be possible," Alix said, seeing to the meal once again by cutting more of the tender beef. Perhaps she could appeal to his knighthood; she must think of something else to claim his interest. "Your father has not had a chance to speak to you of such matters, but our County is embroiled in a feud which needs every available man."

"Not the Montforts again?" he asked, then accepted a piece of the meat from her.

She nodded. "Just days ago they attacked the d'Aussy land—and killed the lord and his lady. They must not go unpunished."

Julian was thoughtful, and Alix was glad she'd been able to steer the subject to one less personal. Perhaps she could even get him to do something about the feud. At least his homecoming would serve some real purpose, she thought uncharitably. But, God's teeth! This whole feast should have been Philip's! And the honor Geoffrey and Eleanore paid Julian should be paid to Philip! Even if Philip was noble enough to set aside such thoughts, she herself could not, not entirely.

"I will speak to my father about this," Julian said. "You are correct, of course. The Montforts must not go unpunished."

That gave some small comfort to Alix, and the remainder of the long meal passed without speaking of personal matters. Julian did not touch her fingers with his lips again, but he did refuse several of the choicest cuts for her to take instead, showing her consideration that should have been paid only to a wife or betrothed. And Alix accepted his kindness, only because she guessed Julian would have been offended if she had not.

Just after the final course of an array of pastries and cakes was served, a half-dozen minstrels joined the harpist and the music became bold and inviting. But rather than calling for a dance, a vocalist was announced by Sir Henry the steward. Conversation dulled in respect for the entertainment.

LET ALL LOVERS HEED
HOPE IS NOW CLEAR
A BETROTHAL IS RIPE
WHAT ALL LOVERS NEED . . .

The betrothal song! Alix's joyful gaze bolted to Philip's. Had he already spken to her father? But how? When? Her heart fluttered within, making her pulse race with delight. She hadn't expected it to be quite so easy, but—praises!—she was glad it was.

But when Philip's eyes met hers, he looked plainly bewildered. And with a shake of his head, for he must have seen in her happiness the conclusion she jumped to, her hopes were arrested. Alix gazed at him, his bewilderment now reaching her.

With an idea, she glanced Simon's way, wondering if perhaps he had spoken to their father about his intentions to marry Marguerite. But he did not look her way, and, Alix had to admit, he hardly looked as if he expected his betrothal to be announced. He was in deep conversation with Father Fantin beside him, seemingly oblivious to the betrothal song being sung.

At last, the vocalist grew silent. And when

conversations never resumed, even Simon's attention was piqued. All eyes went to Sire Geoffrey, for it was he who was expected to direct the attention of all to the father about to make any betrothal announcement.

Sire Geoffrey stood, cup in hand.

"No doubt you are all wondering what shall be announced here today—each and every one of you, even the betrothal couples themselves, for they do not know their parents' kind intentions. This feast, as grand as it is, shall serve two purposes. One is no less important than the other, for both show the love Lady Eleanore and I have for our son. For both our sons," he added, somewhat less boisterously, glancing at Philip.

"It is time the de Saines sons expand our family," Sire Geoffrey continued. "With that in mind, I should like all of you to share our joy in announcing the betrothals of my two sons."

Alix's gaze once again sought Philip's, but he was looking at his father with a suspicious frown carved deep on his face. That Philip had no idea of what his father would say was obvious to Alix. And the worry so clearly interspersed with that curiosity sent a shiver of concern across Alix's shoulders. Suddenly the anticipation of having Sire Geoffrey announce the betrothal of his eldest son was something she dreaded instead of welcomed, as she would have at the beginning of this feast when she was sure their intentions would be known.

"Philip," Geoffrey said, looking at his eldest son who sat beside Eleanore, "you shall have a wife as beautiful as any man could ask and enter into a family who admires and reveres the de Saines name. For you, my son, my heir, I have chosen Marguerite de Boigne, with the full blessing and happiness of her father, Marquis de Boigne."

Philip started to rise, a protest so close to the edge of his tongue he barely heeded the thoughts running through his mind. But he said nothing, his mind working quicker than his erupting emotions. What would he have said, there before all? Surely

215

denial of his father's intentions would only add further scandal to his name—when he already had one too many scandals attached to it already. And at the same time he thought of Marguerite. He had no doubt she was as shocked as he was, and received the announcement with as much disfavor. Hold back, he told himself. Wait. At least until this could be cleared up without another scandal. He had no intention of fulfilling this betrothal wish of his father's, but now was not the time to announce his refusal.

Alix was stunned. She did not look at Philip; she could not. She saw nothing, for her heart seemed to freeze within her, blinding her, making her wish she was prone to swooning. At least in a faint she would not feel this pain. But she simply sat, unmoving, seeing nothing, hearing nothing. She wanted to protest, to scream a denial. This could not happen! But she did nothing. She felt immovable, as if, at least for that moment of astonishment, a part of her mind had rendered her powerless in a form of self-preservation.

After cheers of approval for the fine match—approval!—Sire Geoffrey called attention once more. Alix did not want to listen. She wanted only one thing, and that was to leave. And not alone; she wanted Philip at her side.

Only the sound of her name penetrated the miserable haze engulfing her. The Sire's hearty voice continued. "Alix Beauchamp, daughter of my lord high vassal and lifelong friend, is beyond doubt as beloved of Eleanore and me as a daughter of our own would be. And, as Julian's wife, we welcome her into our family with happiness matched only by that of her own family. It is a match that brings joy to us all to be joined in such a way."

Registered somewhere in her mind, she knew Julian took her hand and pressed her palm to his mouth for a kiss. She felt slow, obtuse. She was being betrothed? Had the Sire announced her name, linking her with *Julian*? But it must be, she thought, for she's felt Julian's kiss on her hand, saw the welcoming smile upon his face, and knew it was true. She, too, was betrothed, not only Philip. How could this be? How could it be they both were being promised to others?

Alix could muster no response to the obvious happiness Julian displayed. She wanted nothing but to be alone with her pain, to release this welling of tears she felt dammed behind her eyes. And more than that; she wanted to run, to flee, to use up this pain inside her and leave only exhaustion, so she could truly feel numb from fatigue.

But she could not. Automatically following Julian's lead, she stood with him. Pressing her hand upon his forearm, he led her past the edge of the table, and she saw Simon, still seated between their mother and Father Fantin. For a moment she saw her own pain reflected there, her desolation recognizing his, for his eyes were riveted to Marguerite, who stood in the center of the mosaic floor . . . with Philip at her side. Julian directed Alix there as well.

Then her eyes met Philip's, and the tenuous hold she kept upon sanity nearly loosened. His eyes had never been so blue, she thought—they were darkened by a pain she herself knew as well. But quickly he smiled at her, a forced one, she could tell, but one meant to give her strength, and something else, too. Courage. He was not resigned to this awful circumstance. Neither should be she.

Her smile, weak and tremulous in response, nonetheless gave Philip the will to hold himself back from her. When he'd seen her walking toward him, holding Julian's arm, he'd wanted to rush toward her, to hold her and assure her this would all be cleared up. To erase the confusion and shock his father's announcement had caused. If only he could touch her, he'd thought to himself, she would know this announcement changed nothing between them. A temporary obstacle! He certainly had no intention of marrying anyone but Alix, and would never, never allow her to marry another! Could she doubt that, after last night?

But the smile they exchanged had been as effective as a caress. And though her own smile was a meager one, he knew she was as strong as he needed her to be. Strong enough to know they would overcome this obstacle.

Good wishes began with the bishop, Alix's uncle, in a prayer spoken over their bowed heads. But, Philip thought as the Bishop's prayer went on, the only wedding that would occur, by God, would be his wedding to Alix.

At last the prayer was over, but just when Alix looked once again toward Philip, for he was the source of the strength keeping her standing, the musicians began playing again and Julian swooped her into a dance.

"It looks as though I shall have my wish, after all, Demoiselle Alix," he said happily. "And I shall be able to spend much of my time here at home at your side."

Alix felt like stone beside him, stiff and un-yielding, following his steps with great effort. Soon others joined the dancing procession, and, because she could not help herself, Alix kept her gaze upon Philip. He, too, was part of the dance, lightly holding Marguerite's fingertips as they followed the intricate steps and flowing music. He saw Alix watching him, and he, too, kept his gaze in her direction. To Alix, it seemed they drew hope from each other in that dance, as if to look away was to lose each other. She could almost smile then, feeling his strength, and her own strength gathering force to match his. She didn't care if anyone else saw them looking at one another; she couldn't tear her eyes away.

When the dance ended, Philip returned Marguerite to her father, spoke briefly, then approached the other betrothal couple.

"I would like to wish you both the marriage you most desire," he said in a smooth, confident voice. Alix noted he did not wish them a happy marriage together, as all others had done. His meaning was intoxicatingly clear to her. He had not given up!

Julian did not issue any good wishes in return;

he said nothing in response to Philip.

But Philip was undaunted. He continued speaking as if his company were highly welcomed. "It has been a long and tiring afternoon, Julian. Perhaps Demoiselle Alix would like to retire early. After all, it isn't often a woman's betrothal is announced, and it might be exhausting for her to be part of the center of attention at so large a feast."

"That is certainly true," Alix said, before Julian could reply. The fact that the sun still brightened the late afternoon sky did not make her hesitate. She heard Julian's intake of breath, as if bracing himself for an argument with his brother, and she hurriedly mediated. "I do feel quite weary, Julian."

Philip spoke quickly. "Yes, Marguerite said as much, too. I intend escorting her from the hall very soon."

Then Alix knew the meaning behind Philip's words. Somehow, she thought to herself, Philip meant to be alone with her, away from their respective betrothal partners. She had to plead fatigue, and free herself from Julian's company.

"I am quite capable of seeing to Demoiselle Alix's desires without your intervention," Julian said coldly to Philip.

Philip bowed formally. "Perhaps you are," he said easily, but Alix heard the confidence in Philip's voice—and she knew he would never allow Julian the chance to find out if he could indeed satisfy her desires. Then Philip smiled at Alix before excusing himself and walking away, stopping to say a few words to Simon before continuing toward Marguerite. Moments later, Philip led Marguerite from the hall. Simon, Alix noted, disappeared soon after.

And Alix had every intention of doing exactly the same!

17

Alix watched Philip leave the hall. His sudden disappearance with Marguerite was noticed by all, it seemed, for there were whispers from every corner about how quickly the two had decided to be alone. Only Alix knew, if there was indeed a lovers' tryst, it consisted of Simon and Marguerite. She knew it had been Philip's idea to see that Simon followed when he took Marguerite from the hall. No doubt Philip would soon be waiting for Alix. She wondered where they would meet. In the garden? In his tower?

It was time to make her own escape.

"Do you find it stifling in here?" she asked. In truth, smoke from the two hearths was thicker than normal, and her eyes were beginning to sting. Though it was only late afternoon it was already quite stuffy in the hall.

Julian did not need any further words to rush to do her bidding. He'd heard those around him whispering about how quickly and easily Philip had gotten his betrothed alone, and, not to be outdone, he was eager to do the same.

He placed her hand on his forearm and led her, smiling, from the crowded hall. Anyone who happened to see them pass cast them a conspiratorial grin or glance, as if their leaving together was amusingly expected. Julian found himself answering those grins with one of his own, glad the entire time that his homecoming feast had turned into a betrothal celebration—with such a beautiful and desirable woman for his own.

He knew this day would have come sooner or later; not that he had expected his betrothal feast quite *this* soon, however! But he would make no protest. Though he knew so very little about his betrothed, what he did know—and what he could see—was gladly received thus far. But there were a few things he would learn about her, first and foremost being why she would want to leave a feast before the sun had even set. Alone with her, he could get to know her—something he was very eager to do.

Outside, the sun was still high in the western half of the sky. The villagers caroused with such merriment Alix was sure more than half of them would awaken the next day with a sore head from the amount of wine consumed. Cheers rang out as she and Julian passed by, and from every direction came wishes for their happy union. News of the double betrothals had obviously traveled quickly to this other half of the Chateau guests.

"Tell me, Demoiselle," Julian asked as they reached the inner bailey gate. "Why is it you have not enjoyed today's feast? Is it every feast you detest, or simply the one in honor of me?"

Alix looked at him with surprise. She'd thought him too concerned over his own good time to see that she wasn't enjoying herself.

She shrugged. "I do not like feasts," she admitted, adding, "But you do, I could see that."

He nodded, then said, "A minor difference between us, I believe. It is good, don't you think, that we will be able to get to know one another before our wedding and final vows?"

Alix said nothing.

"Come with me," he said. "I know a place we can talk, where no one will disturb us."

He started to lead her outside the Chateau gate, but she held back, not wanting to follow. "I thank you for taking me from the festivities, Sir Julian, but I do not wish to go anywhere with you. I would like to go to my chambers, to be alone for the remainder of the day."

Julian laughed easily, taking both her hands in his. "But it is right for us to be together," he said, then surprised, he said, "Your hands are cold! And here it is May already. The sun is warmer than any damp Chateau chamber. Stay with me, Alix. I only want to talk to you."

"Sir Julian—"

"Please, Alix, just Julian," he said, still smiling. Alix was becoming tired of that smile.

"Julian," she began again. "I truly do wish to return to my chamber. My head fairly bursts with pain, from all the smoke and noise of the feast."

"Then it is fresh air you need, Alix!" he said with assurance. "And to rest on a soft cushion of new green grass."

"My father does not wish for me to go outside the Chateau," she said in a final attempt to escape.

But Julian laughed. "I'm sure he would approve if I accompanied you. Besides, the entire populace is enjoying my feast—there is no one left outside the gates to accost us. Come," he said with his hand at her elbow, beckoning her to follow. Alix knew there was little she could do to dissuade him. He was friendly, that was certain, and obviously happy with their betrothal. She would at least be flattered he found her a fitting bride-to-be. Yet he was so overly persistent it would have been easy to snap at him.

She did not snap at him, however tempted she might have been. She followed, thinking all the while as he talked and talked that she should find a way not just to rid herself of his company, but rid herself of this betrothal. She had no intention of marrying any de Saines but Philip. And as they walked she looked in every direction, knowing Philip was waiting for her somewhere.

To her poignant surprise, Julian took her to the brook where she'd happened to meet Philip that one morning . . . that morning he'd kissed her so passionately. But Alix did not listen as Julian spoke of himself and his childhood; she was remembering Philip. Philip's skin had felt so cool and smooth, still damp from his swim. And his kiss . . . How vividly she remembered his lips on hers, warm and at first gentle, then so urgent the passion had erupted quickly between them. Why had they stopped that day? she lamented now. Why hadn't they loved one another then, without delay? Perhaps Philip would have spoken to her father then, that very day . . . before it was too late.

But it wasn't too late! she scolded herself. She couldn't simply give up her love for Philip, and marry his brother without the truth known. She loved Philip! She'd given herself to him! Would Julian want a woman who'd surrendered her purity to someone else—to his brother?

"Sit beside me," Julian invited, after laying out a blanket he'd taken from the gatehouse before leaving the outer Chateau walls.

Silently, Alix did as he bade, though upon the farthest corner of the woven material. She looked at Julian curiously, wondering what he would do if she simply told him the truth, here and now. That only hours ago she'd lain with his brother, letting him teach her all that passion entailed. Would he become violent? Would he run to his father, and announce to all present that Lord Geoffrey had betrothed Julian to a woman drenched in sin?

That thought sobered her, not because she minded being labeled a woman of sin. Rather, the scandal would no doubt touch Philip. How could it not? And while it would certainly see an end to the two unacceptable betrothals announced today, she could not deny it would create a deeper rift between Philip and his family. Could she be responsible for that?

How tempting it was to blurt out the truth, but Alix knew she could not. She must first talk to Philip, to ask what he intended doing about this whole horrible matter. Surely he would not accept what their fathers had done; he'd made that clear already.

Her thoughts returned to how she could escape Julian's company and search for Philip, knowing that by now Philip must certainly be waiting for her. Somewhere.

"I used to swim here as a child," Julian told her.

"See that rock?"

She nodded, looking in the direction he pointed. The rock was on the far side of the pond, jutting out like a crooked nose on the bank opposite them.

"It doesn't look very high from here, but from on top—especially as a child—it was like being among the clouds. We used to jump into the water from there. And," he added with a glance that seemed too intimate for simply recalling childhood memories, "we used to sun ourselves there in the afternoon. We had to carry a pouch of water up there to drench the rock, because the sun made it too hot to lie on without any clothes."

She didn't blush even though Alix was sure that had been his intent.

"Didn't you do anything like that when you were a child?" he asked. "Like swim without any clothes on, and let the sun touch you . . . everywhere?"

"No," she told him, refusing to look him in the eye. She would not let him see that his words, his tone, his very manner, were beginning to embarrass her—just exactly what he wanted! "The Church disapproves of disrobing—except in bed—and my uncle is the Bishop." Her tone was intentionally prim.

"Then perhaps," he said, obviously undaunted by her demure behavior, "after we are married," he moved closer, "we can swim here together . . . and I can show you just how hot that rock can get."

She knew he was going to kiss her then, and if she didn't move away she was afraid he would have his way. Not that she was willing, but she'd learned already he was a very persistent man, and undoubtedly strong as well. She had little doubt he would try forcing himself upon her unless she made it known she was not in the least bit agreeable to his intention.

She scrambled to her feet, going to the water's edge. "I swam here once," she said over her shoulder. "Last summer, when I first came to the

Chateau. It was so warm, and the water felt so cool . . ."

But Julian hardly heard her. Annoyed, he stared at her turned back and wondered if there might be something wrong with the woman. Why hadn't she let him kiss her? He knew without doubt she'd guessed that had been his intention. They were betrothed—and even if it *was* sudden and still new, there would come a time, and soon, he hoped, that she would be unable to resist his kiss. Why not test the waters of their lovemaking? What difference would it make if they didn't wait for their wedding vows? By heaven, he would not wait!

He stood, approaching her. He halted quite close behind her, and placed his hands upon her shoulders, all the while straining for gentleness. But it was hard not to take her right then and there. Julian had never before practiced tolerance and patience, and that combined with the fact of her beauty and the obvious right he had as her betrothed made it exceedingly difficult to contain his passion. Then he whispered into her ear.

"Do not be afraid of me, Alix. Or of what will happen between us. I can see you are an innocent, but can you not see what you've done? How can I resist you, as beautiful as you are, knowing it won't be long before you're mine?"

He turned her around then, and though Alix pushed at his massive chest, all she saw were his lips descending upon hers. His mouth seemed to devour hers, forceful from the start, as he pressed himself upon her and thrust his tongue between her constricted lips. She wanted to cry out, but only a moan escaped her—one of repulsion and anger. How dare he use his strength against her! How dare he take advantage of his male brawn simply because she was the weaker of the two! She hated this feeling of helplessness, knowing there was nothing she could do against his bulk. If he wanted his way, what could she do to stop him? Words were her only defense, and if he never lifted his mouth from hers, how could she defend herself at all?

At last he did part his lips from hers, and, after gasping for air, she pushed at his chest once again.

"Sir Julian! Let me go!"

"There is nothing to fear, Alix," he said coaxingly. "Can we not take just a taste of what our wedded bliss will be?"

"I'll not wed you!" she blurted, unthinking. "I'd sooner spend my last breath in a nunnery!"

He laughed, holding her even closer. "You are as nervous as a rabbit before the hawk, my lovely Alix. If you would only let me show you . . . I'd wager to say you'd prefer your breathing in my bed than a lonely nun's bed."

His mouth came down on hers once again, and this time Alix used more than her meager strength to push against his brawn. Her fingernails, long and tapered, would not prove as effective a weapon as her dagger, but—blazes!—she'd not worn her dagger at her belt today. She reached up, squirming her hand between them, and reached his face. Then, finding her mark, she sunk her nails into the leather-like flesh of his cheek, all the anger welled within from this entire day lending potency to her attack.

"Damnation!"

Julian thrust her away so roughly she landed on her back and half in the water. But Alix hardly minded; the cool water was far preferable to his heated embrace—or the anger that appeared, as quick as wildfire, upon his face. She saw the damage she'd done, and for a moment regretted her action. Surely she'd given him more pain than she'd intended! Blood ran free down his cheek, a triple red stream flowing to the collar of his doublet.

But any remorse was quickly forgotten when he reached down and savagely grabbed her arm, pulling her to the grassy bank. Then, either uncaring or unaware that despite his effort their legs still dangled half in the cool water, he lay atop her and let his mouth consume hers once more. At

226

the same time, his hand released hers and traversed the length of her to her breast, where he pulled away the green satin and with a ruthless lack of tenderness fondled a nipple that only last night had known such wonders.

Alix kicked and tried to claw at him once again, but, having learned what damage her nails could inflict, Julian grabbed her hands and imprisoned them above her head in his mighty grip. She writhed beneath him, but none of her struggles mattered to Julian. His lips were relentless upon hers, his free hand merciless upon her tender skin. Surely he bruised her with his cruel caresses.

Suddenly, as if by some sort of godly intercession, Alix was free. But then she saw this was no miracle; Philip was there, holding Julian by the seat of his pants, and proceeded to throw the young brother into the cold water of the river.

Julian might have been brawnier than his older brother from his daily knighthood training, but even from her seated position, Alix could see the bloodlust upon Philip's face. Never would she have imagined such a look in Philip's eyes, he who would not fight. But fight he did, once Julian emerged from the river. It was fortunate, Alix knew, that neither man was armed with dagger or sword. She had no doubt a weapon would have seen the death of one of them.

Philip's powerful fist connected resoundingly with Julian's cheek—the very cheek with three scratches already gracing it. And though the punch sent Julian to his backside once again, he was up in less than a moment, sending a return blow to Philip's jaw. Philip barely flinched, although the thwacking sound made Alix wince. Blow after blow, neither gave in, until Alix feared they would kill one another, even without a weapon. She stood, trying to intervene, but was ignored and at last shoved away, by whom she did not know. It seemed both combatants were crazed with a hatred that went beyond what had started this fight.

"Stop!" she pleaded, but her voice went

unheeded.

At last Philip was knocked to the ground, and Alix went to him. But firmly, he took her shoulders and sent her away from him, resuming the fight with as much vehemence as ever.

It was obvious she could not stop the fight herself—and if she let them continue, they truly *could* do fatal damage to one another—she saw that in their eyes. There was only one thing to do: go for help. She would find Simon, or Sir Oliver or Sir Hugh; any one of them had the strength needed to part these two adversaries. Before they killed one another.

She ran as fast as she could, fear for Philip's life giving each step she took urgent speed. It seemed forever before she came to the Chateau gates, first the drawbridge and then the inner portcullis. The festivities went on as before, and her frantic behavior went unheeded until she found Sir Hugh. He sat at one of the trestle tables, wine in hand, watching the others with a contented look. But seeing her eyes wide with crisis, he pushed aside his wine and listened as she spoke.

"Come with me, Sir Hugh!" she urged. "It is Philip and Sir Julian—they'll surely kill one another!"

Although she hadn't meant to attract more attention than necessary, her father was nearby and overheard Alix's words. She saw him frown, then called her to his side. But she had no time to spare. She waved at him, then led Hugh—running —from the hall.

Before they'd even emerged from the trees to the river's edge, Alix could see that the battle continued. How long had she been gone? It seemed longer than any two people could possibly have the stamina to endure a fight, no matter how much hatred the hostilities stemmed from. She could see from the difference in the power behind each blow that they had lost some of their vigor, and from the bruises upon both faces, she knew much damage had already been done.

But what appalled her as she neared was the

intensity upon Philip's face. Now that she was in full view of the fight, she could see it was Julian who suffered the most in this fight; his blows no longer had the strength that Philip's did, and if Philip could only see without the blood lust tinting his gaze, he would know, as Alix did, that the fight was over. At least for Julian. He could no longer defend himself. Nonetheless, Philip did not give in. One punch after another landed upon Julian's face, until Julian almost collapsed against his older brother. But still Philip did not stop. One backhanded blow would have sent Julian sprawling again, but Sir Hugh stepped in between, holding Julian and Philip at arm's length like a couple of unmanageable children. And though Alix was assured of Philip's welfare, she couldn't help but breathe a sigh of relief that it was finally over.

"What's this?" Sir Hugh said reprovingly. "Two brothers only just united and already squabbling?"

Both brothers, breathing heavily, eyed one another with malice. Julian looked the worst of the two, but he'd regained his senses remarkably quickly and was now standing on his own power.

"It's none of your concern," Philip said to Sir Hugh.

"That's right," Julian said, then added to Philip, "And what was going on here before you came was none of *your* concern."

Philip reached for him once again, but Hugh, stronger than both of them at the moment, held them farther apart.

A moment later the sound of voices reached them through the trees. Giles, followed quickly by Sire Geoffrey and Lady Eleanore, approached. Alix watched with a twisting heart when Eleanore went to Julian's side, moaning over what had happened. Alix wanted to go to Philip, but held back when her father came to her side.

"I want to know what happened here," Sire Geoffrey demanded, directing his question, and the blame, too, it seemed, at Philip.

Philip squared his shoulders, looking directly at

229

Julian, who was being fussed over by their mother. "A difference of opinion, that is all." His eyes smoldered, as if in silent warning to Julian to keep silent about the real reason for their fight.

"Well, now that it is over, I trust the two of you will settle your disputes on the tourney ground, not at a family feast. That is," he added with disgust aimed only one place, "if both of you will ever attend tourney grounds again." All present knew he referred to Philip, who would have no business at a tournament without a sword.

"Are you badly hurt, my son?" Eleanore asked of Julian. "I will apply a plaster to ease the pain of those welts."

"No," he said, adding with a glance from Philip to Alix, "if you don't mind, I'd like Alix to tend my wounds."

Only for the barest moment did Eleanore's countenance reveal the disappointment she felt at her favored son's request. But she said, "It is fitting. Let us go back to the Chateau. Alix."

Alix followed, with one last glance toward Philip. But he'd already turned away, heading toward the cool water to bathe his bruised face. Would he have no one tend his wounds?

To Alix's surprise, Lady Eleanore beckoned her elder son.

"Come home, Philip. I will see to your bruises."

Alix guessed what his answer would be before he'd even spoken. Philip pressed a new, fallen leaf dipped into the cool water against his purplish cheek as he spoke.

"No, Mother," he said, gently but firmly. "My bruises are not severe enough for any plasters. Help Alix see to Julian."

Though Lady Eleanore's aid had been rejected by both sons, she seemed almost relieved to be free to watch over Julian. She had never left his side, despite the fact that he had asked for Alix's help, and now Lady Eleanore urged him forward. She led the procession back to the Chateau, and Lord Giles pressed Alix forward when she might have lingered. All she could do was cast one last glance toward Philip, who had once again turned back to the cool, soothing water of the river.

Sire Geoffrey and Lord Giles returned immediately to the feast, while Lady Eleanore and Alix went to the kitchen entrance rather than the hall.

Cook had one look at Julian's damaged face and uttered, "Ah, God help you! Who should welcome young Julian in such a way?"

Cook received no reply. Lady Eleanore issued orders for a plaster to be mixed, using herbs and mustard, and while Cook hurried to do his Lady's bidding, he continued to fill the silence.

"Such a fight it must have been, Sir Julian!" he said, taking a large wooden bowl from the shelf, at the same time calling one of the scullery maids to retrieve two pouches of herbs kept in the dry, cool stone pantry. "I have not seen a face covered with such bruises since the day you left . . . and young Lord Philip's as well. God's breath! how the two of you fought that day—"

"Cook, that is enough of your tongue," Lady Eleanore said. "See to the plaster in silence."

Cook did so, an expression of suspicion forming upon his face. Alix knew, soon enough, it would be widely known that Philip had beaten Sir Julian on the day of his homecoming. Hardly the type of talk that would do his already tarnished reputation any good.

When Cook finished, Lady Eleanore sent him and the two scullery maids out of the kitchen. Then, alone with Alix and Julian, she handed the bowl of healing plaster to Alix.

"I'll say one thing on this fight, and one thing only, Julian," Lady Eleanore said. "Heed your father's words: if you want to fight with your brother, do it at a Tourney. I'll not have you fighting with Philip at your own home, to be the source of all manner of talk."

"You also heard what else Father said," Julian countered, his bruised mouth twisting bitterly, "he knows I'll never get Philip on Tourney grounds."

"Then you must find another way to settle your disputes—whatever it is you two have found to fight over after not seeing one another for so long."

Alix said nothing, knowing the blame was hers. How could this have happened—she never would have wished for Philip to fight over her! How she wished to go to Philip, to see to his wounds. For if they were anything like Julian's he was in need of help.

Alix was troubled by one particularly deep cut along Julian's cheekbone. The skin had split and blood continued to flow—she feared the blow had been so close to the scratches she herself had inflicted that the wound was made worse. At the very least, the blood flowed much more freely.

Eleanore looked on, and said no more about the strained relationship between her sons. "I fear that one will leave a scar," Eleanore said with concern.

"I cannot stop the blood," Alix admitted. "There is but one thing to do, close the wound with a stitch or two."

Both Eleanore and Julian looked at her as if she'd suddenly sprouted a tail. "I've seen it done," she assured them. "Father Fantin has shown me how he helped a small child who'd fallen and cut her skin, much worse than this. It is done as if to a garment, only upon the skin instead, and leaves only a minor scar. Shall I call Father Fantin?"

"Do the physicians practice such a method?" Eleanore asked.

"I do not know," Alix answered truthfully.

Eleanore helped Julian to his feet, though he looked as though he felt uncomfortable being treated as an invalid. "Come, my son. Father Fantin left the feast earlier, and will be in his chamber. We will go to him and have him do this stitching on you, if it will dimish the possibility of a scar."

She kept an arm about Julian's waist as she led him from the kitchen. Then, over her shoulder she said, "Alix, you are free to return to the feast. But please say nothing of this fight between my sons. Rumors shall start soon enough without any help."

Alix was only too glad to have Lady Eleanore assume the nursemaid ministrations to Julian. She knew Father Fantin's stitching would close the wound on Julian's face, and probably leave nary a scar as evidence of today's fight. And so, without further thought to anyone but Philip, she left the kitchen. She was free at last to go to him.

Alix went first to the river, hoping Philip was still there. But the small clearing was empty and, with growing concern, she retraced her steps back to the Chateau, first going past the garden, then, finding that empty as well, found her way to Philip's tower.

The afternoon had passed quickly and the sun was already beginning to set. Philip's tower was in a lonely corner of the crowded Chateau, and for that she was grateful. No one saw her entering the dark tower.

Once again she climbed the winding stairway with only diminishing light to show her the way. But, halfway to the top, she called Philip's name, and a moment later his tall shadow filled the doorway.

"Stop, Alix."

Her first impulse, to run to him, was squelched with that command.

"Did anyone see you coming here?"

"No; it grows dark."

"You shouldn't have come."

Alix ignored the words he spoke to keep her away; instead, she followed every instinct inside her that bade her to touch him. Without faltering, she walked the rest of the curved stairway and stood directly in front of him, then, boldly, put her arms about his neck.

"I had to be with you. Don't you know that?"

If Philip had any thoughts to resist her, they were lost once contact was made. His arms went around her, almost desperately, and he kissed her as if they'd been separated far longer than mere

233

hours. But how long it seemed, he thought to himself, since last night. It seemed ages ago.

There was much to say, and surely they should not remain there, in his tower, where discovery would mean not only scandal but scorn from both their parents and all the Chateau inhabitants. But such sense did not penetrate the haze of longing stirred so quickly between them. Philip could not contain the passion, despite warnings flashing in his mind. How could he command her to leave, or take her back to the feast where she belonged, when his arms held her tight, his lips clung to hers, his very loins cried out for the sweet depth of her?

There was no leaving when, seductively, Alix parted from him and backed away, but only toward the bed. So many images had haunted Philip since leaving the river's edge; memory of what he had done, how he had felt, when fighting his brother. Vivid recollections of nearly killing the brother he'd once loved so much—and still loved—had sent shivers of self-loathing coursing down his spine. How could he have done it? How could he have beaten him, when he'd vowed violence was no longer a part of him? Hadn't knighthood taught him violence was not for him?

But all those thoughts, all those horrible visions of Julian's discolored and lacerated face were swallowed up in a whirl of desire as Alix's nearness, her kiss and caress filled his mind with other images. Quickly, they shed their clothes, knowing each other with such intimacy they could have been lovers far longer than only a day.

Alix had learned much about herself last night, and much about Philip as well. She had learned the depth but not the bounds of passion, and trembled anew that Philip could so quickly and effortlessly bring it all back, as exciting and fresh as it had been last night. And she knew the delight she received from his caress was matched by the delight her touch brought to him. She heard his breathing, unsteady as her own, and a gasp of pleasure when she explored and found the

234

evidence of his ready passion.

They were eager, more eager than last night, for the emotions of the day—the hopes that turned to desolation, the anger that resulted in pain—all welled within to create a desperation between them in this time together. Tonight, Philip commanded no sensual delay in this coupling; rather, as unrestrained as they were, each touch, each caress, was intensified and Philip had no power to slow the arousal between them. He was as desperate as she, as in need of fulfillment as she—and now. His fingers touched but did not linger, his kiss pressed to her lips, her ears, her throat, her breast, but traversed with a path that led quickly, desperately, along her body.

Alix's skin, so sensitive to his touch, sprang to life under his touch. How she wanted him! She thrust her hips upward, impelling his entrance, and before she could send further invitation he'd done so, but satisfaction was hardly achieved. A white-hot passion erupted between them at their joining, one so great Alix felt sure the very earth beneath them trembled along with her. With a quickness that matched each plunge, she moved beneath him, and for one moment before a kiss, their eyes met. Passion reflected passion, need and desire and fulfillment all passed between them as they soared ever higher, joined as one.

And then, when the movement between them suddenly ceased, their passion spent and in its wake leaving only exhaustion, they gazed at one another once again. One element alone remained.

"I love you," Philip said, his voice trembling as it mirrored the love he saw in Alix's eye. "And nothing, no one, will take you from me."

They held each other, and Alix let go only when she realized her own breathing came ragged. Philip lay by her side, the entire length of her still touching him. One hand lay gently at her breast, caressing her gently, not to stir renewed passion but only in a form of reverence, as if he could not resist touching her beauty.

"Philip, what are we to do?" she said at last.

But he didn't answer her question. That single question restored all of the images only their passion had made him forget. He raised himself on to one elbow to look down at her, and took her hand, pressing her palm firmly into his. Then, urgently, he asked, "Did he hurt you? Did he . . . touch you before I came upon you, just before the fight?"

She shook her head, squeezing his hand to reinforce her words. "He would have, I've no doubt of that. But you came in time to save me from that . . . that beast."

Philip laughed, ironically, and laid back once again, this time barely touching her. Only their legs still met, somewhere beneath the cover he'd carelessly thrown over them. "I fear Julian isn't the only beast."

"What do you mean?"

"Can't you guess? I could have killed him—my own brother! If you hadn't gone for help . . . perhaps I would have."

Alix remembered how Philip had continued to pommel his brother, despite Julian's obvious fatigue. But she said, "You were justified in your anger! He was forcing himself upon me. What would any man do, if the woman he loved were being attacked in such a way?"

He smiled with self-scorn. "A civilized man, or me?"

"But you *are* civilized! Truly so, far more civilized than . . . than even me! Me with my vengeance-wish toward the Montforts, and all the others with their bloody swords. Only you, Philip, are beyond us in this. That is why this fight sits so ill with you. Do you think Julian regrets one blow? Do you think he would have regretted raping me, simply because he and I are betrothed?"

Philip was thoughtful for a moment, then gave her a lopsided grin. Gently, he touched her face. "I'm glad you're here with me now. Do you know, that is part of the reason I threw down the sword? Because I thought it uncivilized to kill another human being?" He gave a half-hearted laugh. "My father has told me nearly all my life that we, as nobility, are here to civilize our country. The serfs are here to work, the clergy to teach and edify, the knights to protect and defend, the king to unify. And nobility is here to civilize the whole of France. But is it civilized to kill another human being? Is it civilized to fight my own brother?" He shook his head at his own words.

Alix gazed at him, thinking with awe—and not for the first time—what an unusual man he was. And how she loved him! There was but one way for her to show him . . .

18

"What will we do?"

Although Alix had to ask the question again, and Philip knew she had to, Philip did not want to answer. Would *could* they do? He doubted Lord Giles would allow Philip to wed his daughter, even if the other two betrothals were miraculously dropped. The thought gave him little hope. Would the truth make a difference? If Lord Giles knew his daughter shared the bed of the man she loved, knew that at this very moment they lay so intimately together, would it make a difference in his decision of whom his daughter would wed?

"What do you think your father would do if we told him, privately, that you and I have already been lovers? If I brought him evidence of our love, that it was I who took your virginity, and you have known only me?"

Alix knew her father well enough to guess that the truth would make little difference to him. It would have been hard enough to convince Lord Giles to let her wed Philip without the match set up between herself and Julian, a match Lord Giles obviously welcomed. She didn't want to voice her hopeless answer.

"Perhaps we should talk to my mother first," Alix suggested. "She has a way with my father . . . Perhaps she could convince him we would be happy together."

Philip smirked, and the bruise on his cheek deepened in color under the light of a pair of brightly burning candles. "I think your father believes he knows what is best for your happiness." Then Philip's arm, still holding her close beneath the blankets, tightened around her. "Do you think he would force you to marry Julian, regardless of what has passed between us?"

"I . . . do not know." Then she said, "But I do know that I am not the only one betrothed to the wrong person. What of Marguerite?"

Philip dismissed that thought with a wave. "For that, I will enlist the aid of one interested party by the name of Simon Beauchamp. I'm sure your brother will be only too willing to convince the Marquis that his only child will be happier wed to someone other than a de Saines."

"I only hope this will all work out so easily!"

Much later than both had intended, Alix and Philip dressed and Alix slipped from Philip's tower. He insisted on returning to the main keep at her side, fearing not only that she might be discovered leaving his chambers, but also any lingering revelers from the daytime feast. Sounds of the merrymaking still echoed from the hall, but Philip saw Alix to the kitchen entrance and Alix hurried up the stairway to her chamber.

Blanche was nowhere to be found, but Alix didn't mind. No doubt the servant was still enjoying the day's celebration. Alix stripped off her clothes and slipped into her bed, all the while thinking of the morning. There was only one way Alix could think of to change her father's mind about Philip, and that was through Marie. With that thought, she had convinced Philip to speak to Marie rather than Lord Giles, and so in the morning they would seek her mother to have a very private, very important conversation. Alix knew her future happiness depended upon this conversation, and all must go well. It must! Marie was their best hope.

Alix had not wanted to voice her fears to Philip, but in truth she thought it would take more than her lost virginity to convince Giles to allow her to marry Philip. And she knew there was but one alternative should that fact be learned: being despoiled, she could not possibly wed. That left only one future for her: the convent. She shuddered to think of it. But indeed that was the only alternative to marrying Philip, even in her own mind. Her father certainly would not have her marry another man having already given herself to Philip—and she would not allow that, either.

Pray God her father's choice would be for her happiness—and Philip's!

Sleep was not to be had, Alix knew. With such worrisome thoughts of her future, there would be no rest for her this night. But not long after she'd covered herself a knock sounded at the wooden door. Reaching to the table at her side, Alix lit a candle, calling to the doorway.

"Blanche?" Then, receiving no answer, she called again. "Hugh? I am abed."

"Demoiselle Alix."

Julian's newly familiar voice was vastly unwelcome. Clinging to the blankets for covering as well as to still her trembling fingers, Alix watched, wide-eyed, as the door swung wide. She was not afraid, she insisted to herself, despite the fact Julian had forced himself upon her earlier. She would not let him make her afraid.

To her great relief, Sir Julian was not alone. Marie Beauchamp stepped in behind him.

"Alix!" Her mother's voice sounded both relieved and reproving at the same time. She came to her daughter's bedside, taking Alix's bare shoulders in a gentle shake. "Where have you been? We've gone through the entire Chateau

239

looking for you."

Julian stepped to the end of the bed. "I was concerned today's unfortunate fight with my brother might have distressed you. When I couldn't find you with your mother, I feared you might have gone off upset."

Even in the dim light, Alix could see his eyes resting not on her face but on her shoulders and the top of the blanket. She held the covering even closer, all too aware of her nakedness. She knew Julian was very observant of that fact himself.

"I—I've been here. I was tired."

"But we came to your room earlier, searching for you," Marie said. "And you weren't here."

"Oh . . . earlier I was . . . in the garden. Alone."

"The garden!" Julian repeated. "It's a disarray of overgrown bushes!"

"I like it," she said most assuredly.

"Alix goes there often," Marie said, somewhat slowly, not taking her eyes from her daughter. Then she stood, facing Julian. "As you can see, Sir Julian, Alix has come to no harm. I think, given the hour, and despite the fact of your recent betrothal, you should return to the feast or to your own chambers."

"Of course," he said smoothly, casting a smile first at Marie, then another lingering one on Alix. "I will see you tomorrow, Demoiselle. Good-night."

He was gone after that, closing the door behind him. Heavy silence filled the room with his absence. Alix hated to lie to her mother. But she could hardly have spoken the truth, there before Julian! Even so, the falsehood put a weight upon her shoulders she was unsure she could hide, regardless of the single candle barely lighting the room.

"I went to the garden earlier," Marie said quietly, still seated on Alix's bedside. "And you were not there."

"The center is very hard to reach . . ."

"The stone bench was empty."

Alix felt her pulse quicken at being found out.

240

There was nothing to do now but admit the truth. It was not so bad, she assured herself, to tell her mother the truth. After all, she had intended doing this very thing in the morning. But somehow it would have been far easier with Philip at her side!

"I will tell you, Mother," Alix said slowly, trying to muster the courage. At last she raised her gaze to meet her mother's. "But promise me one thing before I do. You will think before you give your reaction. Think of me . . . and my happiness."

"I will," Marie answered, after only the briefest pause.

Alix drew in a deep breath. Then, knowing the only way to admit the truth was to be blunt, she said, "I was with Philip. In his tower."

Marie sat, completely unmoving. Perhaps she was doing as Alix bade, and thinking of her daughter's happiness. But she hardly looked as if she welcomed the news. She looked down at her lap, hiding her eyes, and a frown wrinkled her forehead. Slowly, she stood, and turned her back on her daughter.

"I knew," she whispered, over her shoulder. "I knew."

Alix raised her eyes in surprise. "But how . . . ?"

Marie faced her again, and stared at her so intently Alix felt her mother knew her very thoughts. "I just knew. Perhaps even before it happened. Perhaps that first day . . . the day I saw how you looked at him when you returned together from that one early morning ride."

Alix threw a blanket over her shoulders and stood, barely feeling the cold stone floor beneath her bare feet. "Then why did you allow today's announcement? Why did you let Father betrothe me to that . . . that . . ." Her search for words ended futilely, but Marie knew to whom she referred.

"I didn't know!" Marie insisted. "Today's announcement was as much a surprise to me as to you. But," she added firmly, "there was nothing—*nothing*—I could have done. And there is nothing I can do now."

241

"But surely *something*—"

Marie was already shaking her head, and it incensed Alix. She stepped closer to her mother, barely inches away, her knuckles turning white as she clung angrily to the blanket covering her. "I *gave* myself to Philip! I am a maiden no longer! In my eyes, in Philip's—and in God's—I am wed to Philip already. You cannot force me to wed another!"

Marie shook her daughter once again, this time more firmly. "I told you before . . . I warned you . . . Giles will not approve of Philip as son-in-law. I've heard him say as much, and nothing will change his mind."

"Then I will run off with him! I will go off with Philip and live outside this country!"

But Marie was shaking her head. "Philip is Geoffrey's heir; he will never let him go. Never."

Anger filled Alix, because she knew Marie was right. She trembled from head to foot, feeling the frustration almost bursting within her. "Then . . . then I will tell Julian what I've done. He won't want a woman who gave her virginity to another man—to his own brother."

"From what I know of their current relationship, knowing Philip wants you will only make Julian want you more. They have no consideration between them, Alix. And anyone with eyes can see Julian welcomes you as his betrothed."

The dam burst behind Alix's eyes. Frustration coursed through her, pain sprang forth from a bottomless well. And the tears streamed down her cheeks unheeded, knowing too well how true each of her mother's arguments would prove if tested.

She threw herself onto the bed, her shoulders shuddering with unchecked sobs. "I won't marry Julian . . . I won't . . ."

Marie went to her daughter's side, gathering her into her arms. She stroked her hair, shushed her cries, soothing her as if she were a child who had just lost a toy. And Alix did not welcome such comfort.

Alix stood once again, brushing away her tears

and forcing steadiness to her voice. "Did you hear me, Mother?" she said, looking Marie in the eye. "I will not marry Julian."

Marie returned the gaze with a new intensity. "Then there is but one thing to do, isn't there?" she asked, her voice low and serious. "Change your father's mind . . . and Sire Geoffrey's."

Alix grasped at the hope her mother offered. "Do you . . . do you think we could?"

Marie stood, frowning once again. "It will not be easy, that is certain. And there will be a price to pay. I know your father, Alix, and there is only one way to convince him Philip is suitable for his family. And that is if Philip takes up his sword once again."

Alix was silent, and waited for her mother to continue. Such a plan offered little hope, but if that was the only way . . .

"If Philip could do something to bring on the end of this feud with the Montforts," Marie continued, "perhaps lead Sire Geoffrey's men in a battle that conquers the Montforts for once and for all . . . It would not only convince your father of Philip's suitability, but it would also mend whatever damage now exists between Philip and his own family. And you know, you will need their approval as well if you wish to turn your back on their favorite son in order to marry the other."

Alix bit her bottom lip, and her knuckles whitened once again as she clung to the blanket around her. But her eyes were filled with determination. "I believe you are right, Mother," she said firmly, not even looking at Marie. "This is the only way." And God help us, she thought to herself. For to get Philip to take up his sword again will take no less than divine intervention, she was sure of that.

The next morning, Alix entered the hall with eager anticipation. It was early yet, she knew, but she had to find Philip and tell him of her discussion with Marie last night. Then, together, they would plan how best to conquer the Montforts.

243

She had lain awake most of last night, wondering how to convince Philip this was the only way. But at last she'd put aside her worry. After all, Philip wanted to wed just as desperately as she did. If he knew there was no other way to gain her father's approval—and certainly there wasn't!—then surely his resolve not to touch the sword again would be set aside, at least for a time.

But the hall was empty except for a myriad of servants still cleaning up after yesterday's feast. No one spoke, for it was an ominous task to clean the debris of such a boisterous day. Alix left the hall quickly, going outside but finding only more peasants cleaning the Chateau grounds. It seemed everyone but the servants was still abed.

Alix wanted to go to Philip's tower, but feared detection with so many people cleaning up the area. So, thinking it too early to wait in the garden for Philip to come to her, she walked the length of the high parapet wall that bridged the rear of the Chateau. From there she could see the green hills that led the way to Paris, beyond the horizon.

She was plagued by her thoughts. One moment she was convinced Philip's sword was the only answer, the next she fretted this was too much to ask. She knew how deeply went his vow not to pick up the weapon again. Could she ask such a thing? To renounce that vow which meant so much to him?

But she must! She must! There was no other way; talking with her mother last night had convinced her of that.

Alix spent the morning between the high wall, the garden, and the great hall. And nowhere could she find either Philip or Sire de Saines. As the morning waned and she had no word or sight of Philip, she fretted something had happened. Surely he would have come to her as soon as he was able, knowing they intended to speak to Marie that morning. Where was he?

At last, too anxious to wait any longer, she approached Philip's tower once again. But there were many peasants about, and she knew she

could not be so bold as to enter without surely
having the news spread throughout the Chateau.
So, seeking out Blanche, she sent the servant to
Philip's tower, to see if he was there, perhaps ill or
still asleep.

The servant asked no questions and did Alix's
bidding without delay. And though only a few
minutes had gone by, it seemed far longer before
Blanche returned. Lord Philip's tower was empty.

Alix frowned at the news, although part of her
was relieved Philip did not lie ill upon his bed. But
where could he be?

She went to her parents' chamber, hoping to
find Marie. But once there, Elda, Marie's servant,
shooed Alix away.

"But I wish to see my mother," Alix told the
servant.

"She is with your father, in the Sire's inner
chamber."

"Is something wrong?" Alix persisted.

Elda said nothing, just closed the door of her
parents' chamber in Alix's still frowning face.

Part of Alix wanted to go straight to the de
Saineses' inner apartments, sure she could find
Philip there as well. But she held back, knowing
even as Julian's betrothed she had no right to go
there unless beckoned.

So she waited. She paced her own chambers, she
went back and forth to the hall in hopes the
secretive audience with the Sire had ended. At
last, too restless to stay indoors any longer, she
found her way out the kitchen and headed toward
the stables.

The sun was bright, almost blinding after the
darkness of the Chateau. In every direction of the
bailey evidence abounded of Philip's organiza-
tional skills upon the Chateau. Philip's orders to
renovate the Chateau had stopped short at the
overgrown garden; Alix smiled as she remembered
how several servants, scythes in hand, had been
commanded away from the garden to perform
other duties—it was more important, Philip had
said, to trim the overgrown grasses surrounding

the chapel. But Alix knew the real reason behind his order; the garden was their only private retreat. Neither of them wished to have it taken away by the slice of a gardener's scythe, trimming back the rosebush walls that provided such intimacy only to those willing to find the garden's center.

As she approached the stables, Alix was surprised by the amount of activity. Men called to one another, peasants ran to and fro, even James, the Marshall of the horses, was out in the midst of the melee. Alix neared him.

"What is the fuss about?" she asked once those surrounding James had disappeared to carry out their orders. It seemed she was ignorant of every happening at the Chateau today, from the meeting within Sire Geoffrey's chamber to the reason for this present commotion.

James raised his eyes heavenward, and ran his hand through his thick, wiry hair. "The master has ordered a complete inventory of horses immediately. He intends sending one of his sons to buy whatever we shall need for the knighting ceremony being planned for week after next."

Alix lifted her brows. "Oh? I hadn't heard. That is," she added, "I knew there was to be a knighting, but I didn't know the de Saineses ever bought horses. I thought you raised them all here."

James gestured in annoyance. "That I do, and usually more than necessary. But with so many being knighted because of that Montfort family stirring up trouble, the Sire needs more than ever."

Alix knew it was the custom to bestow a prime charger to each newly knighted man, but now her thoughts ran to what James had said earlier. "Will you be going with whomever goes . . . Philip or Julian?"

"Of course, Demoiselle. Need you ask?"

"Then do you know which brother will be going?"

James shook his head. "I did not speak to the

246

Sire himself; the messenger simply said one son will be sent and I am to go at his side. He said no more."

"When will you be leaving?"

"As soon as this list of horseflesh is compiled." He motioned to the parchment in his hand. "This afternoon, perhaps, or tomorrow morning."

Alix, now determined to find out which brother had been given the order, wanted to waste no further time finding Philip. She turned on her heel, but James called after her.

"If you wish to ride Morivek, Demoiselle, I will have her readied for you if you only name your chaperone."

"No, James," she called back, already several paces away. "I'll not interfere with your count."

"But it is no trouble . . ."

Alix paid no heed; quick steps took her rapidly to the keep. She went to the hall, determined to wait there until someone emerged from the upper de Saines apartments. Surely even Philip, on his way out, would pass by and see her there.

But upon entering, she saw Philip and his father seated at the far end where the servants had already cleaned. Philip sat across from his father, his back to the entry at which Alix stood.

"Come hither, Alix," Geoffrey called. "Soon you will be a member of the de Saines family, and you should hear what we discuss."

Alix approached, eyeing Philip with one stolen glance. He looked her way as well, but she could not tell from that single, brief exchange if it had been him or Julian who had been ordered on the horse-purchase expedition. She did see one glimmer of happiness in his eyes, but dared not guess why it was there. If Julian was to go on the horse-buying trip, that would at least leave Philip and Alix time together. But was that what the de Saineses had been discussing all morning? It seemed unlikely, particularly since the discussion had included Alix's parents.

"Good-morning, Demoiselle," Philip greeted. Even his voice sounded free of worry; perhaps

Julian *had* been the one ordered on the trip.

"The keep has been very quiet this morning," Alix greeted them both. "It seems most are slow to rise after yesterday's feast."

Sire Geoffrey laughed heartily. "Most have sore heads, from all the wine consumed. Julian as well, if it is he to whom you refer. I suppose you've been looking for him this morning?"

"I . . . Yes," she lied, not knowing what else to say.

"He should be well recovered by this evening, Demoiselle. He was up feasting until early this morning." Then, after one brief pause, the Sire spoke again, this time in a more serious tone. "In two weeks' time there shall be a knighting ceremony," he announced. "We shall be knighting fourteen of our squires, and for that purpose we require several more chargers. I have asked Philip to do this bidding, to go to the northwest of our country where horses are bred the finest, and purchase as many as we need."

Alix felt her heart sink with disappointment. She dared not raise her eyes, fearing Sire Geofrey would guess the sadness caused by the thought of Philip's absence. She knew she could not hide the unhappiness this news brought.

Sire Geoffrey continued. "But there are reasons for sending Philip on this mission. After yesterday, I think it wise to separate my two raucous sons for a time. Then, when Philip returns, perhaps they will greet one another in a more civilized manner." He added in a deeper voice, one of conviction, "God help them if they don't."

"That is only part of why it is better for me to leave, at least for a short time," Philip said at last. He had seen how Alix did not raise her eyes, knew the pain their separation would cause, and wanted to offer what good news he had. It might make the idea of two weeks apart a little easier to bear. "My betrothal to Marguerite de Boigne has been broken."

Alix's gaze shot to Philip's, her eyes wide with happiness. "Oh?" she said. She felt her hands

248

tremble and held them in tight fists upon her lap. She dared not say more, knowing her voice would quiver as well.

"It seems Marguerite prefers your brother, penniless as he is," Sire Geoffrey said, adding quickly, "Now I know how Simon is favored in your family, Alix, so do not rush to his defense because I have called him penniless. I only speak the truth."

In fact, Alix had not intended to say a word; she was too happy that at least some of the obstacles between herself and Philip had been removed—and so easily! What joy if all other obstacles could be removed as well!

"I took no offense," Alix replied to Sire Geoffrey, adding, "because you do speak the truth. I will be glad if Marguerite and my brother find happiness."

The Sire took one deep breath, then said, "It will be a good enough match. You and your brother come from an old and noble family. Marguerite's dowry will no doubt help restore the Estate, although Philip has already told them he will continue renovation until the task is complete, to show all there are no harsh feelings."

Sire Geoffrey stood then, telling them he was off to the training yard to see how the young squires were doing in their quest for knighthood.

Sire Geoffrey left the hall, and Alix did not move from her seat beside Philip. Once they were alone, comparatively alone, for the servants still working in the hall were far away in the opposite corner, Alix had the almost uncontrollable urge to put her arms about him. But she held herself back, settling instead for a smile that came from her heart to touch his.

"Alone," he said, returning her smile.

"Almost," she replied, glancing briefly at the working servants.

"As alone as we'll ever be within this room."

Then Alix frowned. "I saw James at the stable. He is to accompany you on this expedition to purchase more horses. How long do you think you'll be gone?"

"I must return within two weeks," he said. "That is when the knighting will be."

"Will it take so long?"

He nodded. "It'll be days of travel, to and fro. And to select and purchase at least as long."

Alix bowed her head, feeling tears threaten her eyes and not wanting to show such weakness to Philip. "I wish it were Julian, not you, who must go."

Philip gave a brief laugh, and dared to reach across and gently, quickly, stroke her cheek. "So do I."

Then Alix surprised them both with a spontaneous smile. "But I am pleased about the news of Marguerite."

"The Marquis obviously prefers his daughter's happiness to increasing his own wealth. A wise man, I think. Do you think your father is as wise?"

"I spoke to my mother already," Alix told him. "She came to my room last night . . . She had guessed where I was."

"She knows?" Philip asked, frowning.

Alix nodded. "I did not have to tell her. She knows me well, Philip. She guessed long ago, only by the way I look at you."

He seemed pleased by that, but only momentarily. "Did she offer any hope?"

"She said there is but one way for you to gain my father's approval. That is if you return to knighthood . . . at least long enough to do something about this feud with the Montforts that so troubles the land."

Philip stiffened, so visibly Alix thought he might refuse, before even considering what she asked. But he sighed, and though his voice was calm, she saw how his hands gripped the arms of his chair. "I'll not raise the sword again, Alix. I cannot."

"But you must!" Alix cast away all caution and reached for one of his hands. He took hers in both of his, and though he looked into her eyes as she spoke, Alix had little hope her words moved him. "Do you not see? If you do this, if you gain not only my father's approval, but your own father's, how can they deny your wish to wed me, particularly if it is what I wish as well? As it is now, Julian is your father's favorite; he can do no wrong. But if you only tried to end this feud . . . to show him you are willing to be the son he wants, and the knight my father wants, if only temporarily—"

"No, Alix." The two words were firm and sure, and split into Alix like a knife.

"You'll not do this, not even for me? If it is the only way to wed me?"

"I'll not take up the sword again. Not for my father, or yours."

"But I don't ask you to do it for them! I ask this for myself—so we may be wed!"

Philip gazed at her, silently. At last he said, "You don't know what you're asking me." His voice was low, almost a whisper. "To raise the sword again, after I swore it would never cross my hand again . . . I cannot do it."

Alix stood, her hands clenched into fists at her sides. "Is this vow you made to yourself more important than marrying me? Doesn't your love for me go as deep?"

Philip stood as well, forgetting the presence of the servants and placed a hand on each of her shoulders. "There must be another way, Alix. You know I love you. I'll not let you wed Julian, you must know that. I'll find another way to convince your father and mine that I am a fitting husband for you."

"But there *is* no other way! You've already offered to rebuild my father's home. You're providing a home for my brother and his new bride. Your wealth means nothing to my father, don't you see that? Nor does my happiness, if I went to him and told him my wishes."

"I'll find another way," Philip told her.

"There is no other way," she said again, this time quietly. "If you do not do this, then I shall be forced to marry Julian." She gazed at Philip, desperately resorting to arguments she would have preferred never to have uttered. "Could you bear to see me wed to him, sharing his bed? He's already stolen your parents' love—will you let him steal me, too?"

Philip breathed deeply; Alix saw him stiffen. "Julian has stolen nothing." Then, still standing rigid, he said quietly, "How convenient of you to find a way for me to please your father that also happens to satisfy the one wish for vengeance you have. To avenge the Montforts who destroyed your home."

Alix took a step backward, away from him, her eyes wide, a pain in her middle so fierce she felt as though his words were tiny daggers, each striking her heart. She could see on his face he believed his accusation, and it struck her as no physical blow could have. She wanted to cry, but refused to allow herself such comfort. Instead, she stood straight and tall, and felt her eyes narrow as she said, "If that is what you believe of me, then perhaps we have been wrong in wanting to marry."

"Perhaps," he said, just as quietly as before.

She breathed deeply, then, though the words were painful to say, "Make no haste in your time away from the Chateau. Perhaps what we need most is to be separate, to think on what we have said just now."

Then she turned away. Every part of her wished he would come after her, take back his words, but there was only an empty, desolate silence in her wake.

19

From the window of her chamber, Alix could still hear the commotion in the inner courtyard below. Although only a few men would accompany Philip, just James and three pages, the entire Chateau seemed to be participating in preparations to see them off. She heard some of the young squires tease James about seeing that the master bought only the best horses, no matter what the cost. It would be them, after all, the horses would be given to.

From her window ledge, Alix watched for Philip. She'd spotted him once, coming from his tower with a bundle, probably clothing, which he hurled toward one of the pages to add to the pack horse. Then he disappeared in the direction of the stables.

Would he leave without seeking her out, without a word of farewell? After their last words, she knew the answer already. But how could he think so ill of her? He once thought her bloodthirsty because she did not agree he should offer shelter to a Montfort. Surely now he thought her devious as well, if he truly believed she'd asked him to end this feud for any other reason than making their betrothal possible.

Remembering her anger, she turned away from the window, taking a seat at her dressing table. Such a possibility had never even entered her mind, that Philip might think she would ask him to take up his sword just to satisfy her own vengeance. She picked up her hair brush, and with angry strokes attacked her hair. Did he think so little of her love? That her love was so shallow she could ever use it for selfish purposes?

Blazes! Let him remain a swordless knight, she thought savagely. She knew what the other knights said of him, that he was a coward. The kinder knights spared him such names, but she knew they all hoped for a full scale battle with the Montforts. And why shouldn't they? It was the sole way for a knight to earn money, through prize and booty. Perhaps Philip had no need for booty, but other knights did. Was she so uncivilized for understanding that?

But it wasn't for the booty that Lord Giles wanted Philip to fight, Alix knew that. Her father, perhaps more than anyone else, believed Philip a coward. She remembered too well the sincerity in her father's voice when he'd told her Philip was not a fitting escort beyond the safety of the thick

Chateau fortress.

Why hadn't Philip believed her? She knew her father well—at least well enough to know that having Philip take up his sword again was the only possible way to have Lord Giles accept Philip as son-by-law. Was this so great a request? Didn't his love go deeper than his own vow to put down the sword?

She shook her head, her thoughts so jumbled she wished to free herself of all her burdens. Then, realizing the commotion outside had subsided, she flew to the window.

They were gone! The courtyard was empty, the pack horse and palfreys waiting to take Philip and his companions had already vanished from below. He *had* left without seeking her out.

Alix's feet carried her swiftly from her room. She paid no heed to thoughts warning her she would be the fool if she ran after Philip and threw herself at him. After all, hadn't she been the one who said a separation might do them both good? But he was leaving! And with this anger still unresolved between them! Her feet barely touched the steps leading her down to the kitchen, then, without a word spoken in response to Cook's surprised exclamation at her haste, she ran to the front courtyard only to see the portcullis already closed.

Not to be cheated out of at least a single glimpse of her beloved, in spite of the hurtful words and the ire that still touched her heart, she raced to the stone stairway that led to the upper walkway. From there, where she'd stood just hours ago, she could see the road to Paris. For they would have to take that road east, as far as Rennes, then turn northward if they intended going to the horse-markets of the north country.

Breathless, she reached the top of the parapet. Leaning between the battlements, she could see the small, departing troop. They were too far to hail a farewell, too far to send a last word. And though Alix waved, none turned round to see. Not even Philip. They soon disappeared beyond the trees and hills below.

Alix struggled to keep her mind on the pegged board in front of her. The intricately carved wooden pieces before her seemed to blur into one; she knew she was losing, and losing badly, but she hardly cared. Julian seemed very pleased to show off his prowess at the complicated game.

They were in the de Saineses' inner chamber, the Sire and his lady still seated at the small trestle table that had been erected for the immediate family to share a private supper. Alix had endured the meal well, even managing to laugh at some of Julian's more witty comments. He was, she found, sometimes clever. But none of his lightness penetrated beneath the polite facade she managed to uphold for Julian and his parents. Inside, she felt withered.

"Succumb, Demoiselle Alix," Julian said, somewhat softly. "There is no way for you to win."

Startled from her faraway thoughts, Alix looked from Julian to the gameboard. In truth, he was correct. There was nothing for her to do but capitulate.

"Do not let this victory go to your head, my son," said Sire Geoffrey. "I have seen Alix play a far craftier game than tonight. She must have let you win, wanting to spare you the humiliation of losing to your betrothed."

Julian smiled Alix's way. "Is this true? Have you spared me?"

"No . . . truly, I did not."

Julian took one of Alix's hands in his. "It doesn't matter," he said. "I would have been moved if you had."

Uncomfortable, Alix slipped her hand away. Then she stood, going to stand before the fireplace as if to rid herself of a chill. "Are there any preparations to be made for the knighting ceremony?" she asked, hoping to keep the conversation open to all four occupants of the room. "Can I be of any help?"

"That is kind of you, Alix," Eleanore said. "And

as Julian's future wife, I'm sure we should be bestowing some duties upon you. But it is early yet; the servants still have not entirely cleaned the debris from Julian's homecoming feast, nor have the hunters replenished our supplies. I think it wise to give them a few days before preparing for the next."

"Of course," Alix agreed, then said, unable to keep her thoughts from Philip. "The horsemarkets are far away from here. Do you think Philip will be able to return in time for the festivity day?"

"If he does his duty quickly, he'll be back with a day or two to spare."

At that Julian laughed, a low, mysterious laugh that sent all gazes to him. "That is," Julian said, "if he returns at all."

"What do you mean, Julian?" Eleanore asked.

He laughed again, as if he had some private joke with himself. "I suppose I can tell you all now, now that it's too late to call him back."

"Tell us what?" Geoffrey asked, impatient. "Blazes, son, stop playing this word game and tell us what you refer to."

"Only that Philip might find some diverting company in Bayeux. Rachel la Trau is there. She has been ever since that scandal erupted with Philip."

Alix felt as if her heart had been wrung from her chest. Her palms felt suddenly damp as she clutched her hands into fists. Hiding them behind her back, she breathed once, slowly, to calm herself. She did not trust herself to speak—not yet.

Julian went on as if the news were pleasant. "Charles has been buying horses for the King for more than a month now. I was camped not far from there and heard about the whole scandal from him. He said he was sending for his wife, despite the contrast of life in Bayeux to life in Paris. He wanted her out of trouble—even if she will miss the splendor of court life."

Sire Geoffrey frowned deeply. "You should have told us, son. Hasn't the rest of France enough reason to talk about the de Saines family without rekindling that scandal, which has barely been forgotten?"

Lady Eleanore did not look worried. "If Rachel is with Charles, there is nothing to fear, Geoffrey. Surely there will be no further opportunity for scandal with the girl's husband there."

But Geoffrey's frown did not ease. "It isn't Rachel I fear. Just how do you suppose that swordless heir of ours will defend himself should Charles decide to confront him?"

Alix spent a sleepless night. She twisted and turned in her bed, one moment imagining Philip with a beautiful woman named Rachel, the next moment seeing Philip lie bloody, swordless, upon the ground with Charles la Trau standing triumphantly above, the sword in his hand dripping with Philip's precious life. Like Sire Geoffrey, she feared what Charles might do if he learned Philip was nearby, within his reach. After all, his jealousy prompted King Jean himself to banish Philip from Paris for his own protection. It was clear to anyone who knew the facts that Charles hated Philip—and might do anything, even kill an unarmed man, just to get his revenge.

And, also, Alix had to admit, though Sire Geoffrey might not have reason to fear Rachel la Trau, Alix did. How could she easily dismiss a woman who blatantly desired the man Alix loved? A woman who so obviously wanted Philip in her bed?

How she wished Sire Geoffrey had sent a messenger to call Philip back, to spare him from whatever lay ahead. Not just because she feared the temptation of Rachel's desire, but because she knew, perhaps better than anyone else, that Philip would never lift his sword to protect himself should Charles challenge him. But Geoffrey would not call his son home; he knew how it would look to the rest of France, that his son, the very son who already seemed a coward, would come running home once he learned of the dangers ahead. By the end of the evening Sire Geoffrey had even smiled, along with Julian, although for different reasons than the rivalrous Julian. The hope Geoffrey carried was clear: perhaps, if pushed far enough, Philip would be forced to take up the sword again and restore his reputation. Surely he would do that before allowing Charles to harm him.

Alix was not so sure. How, she wondered, would she survive the next two weeks without going mad with worry?

For the next few days, Alix felt as if in a haze; she was only half aware of all that went on around her. Always, inside, she wondered what Philip was doing at that very moment. And though she tried to push the less welcome thoughts from her mind, she could never entirely dismiss her fears. She remembered too well how angry Philip had been just before he left her that day, how even now he must still believe the worst of her. Thinking so ill of her, it wouldn't be Alix's memory that kept Philip from Rachel. It was that thought which added to her burdened thoughts through the days.

Alix's meals, each and every one of them, were spent with Julian. They shared the cup and trencher, and she fed him with her fingertips as was the custom. And though he remained polite, not forcing himself upon her as he did that first day, there was always that hint, in his smile or his glance, that told Alix he looked forward to the day he could bed her. More than once, he invited her to the northfield to see his hawks and falcons, but each time she refused, coming up with some excuse, usually involving her mother. She had no desire to go off on a ride alone with Julian—and certainly not to see his hawks.

Marie was Alix's only comfort. She knew her daughter preferred not to be in Julian's company, and so always upheld whatever excuse Alix gave, either that she needed Alix to sew with her, copy books with her, or accompany her to chapel. And though Marie tried to coax Alix's thoughts away from Philip, both knew her efforts were wasted.

Almost a week had passed, and though Alix still

worried over Philip's welfare she was glad for one thing. With her mother's help, she had managed to spend very little time with Julian thus far. She only hoped luck would stay with her through the second week!

After the late meal of that day, however, Julian offered to escort Alix on a walk in the courtyard. "The air is warm," he said persuasively. "And the stars and moon shine bright."

Alix might have liked to walk under the stars, remembering Philip's interest in astronomy. Perhaps, even at that moment, he might be looking at the same stars, recording their travels through the skies. How she wished she were with him!

"I believe Father Fantin is celebrating a special Mass this evening," Alix said. "Perhaps we should—"

But Julian was already shaking his head. "I no longer believe your pious facade, Alix." Though his lips were smiling, his eyes were serious.

"What do you mean?" she asked with surprise.

"I saw you this morning, riding Morivek like lightning to the trees. Did you hope to spare detection by riding so swiftly to the cover of the forest?"

"I—often ride Morivek," she defended herself. "Does that make me less pious?"

"It does," he responded, "when you told me you would be at Morning Mass instead."

Alix felt herself blush, and she looked down at her hands which were clasped in her lap.

"I intended going . . . but the sun was bright . . ."

"And so are the stars tonight," he whispered. "Wouldn't you rather walk with me than go to another Mass?"

"My mother is expecting me to go with her."

Julian let out a sigh, obviously annoyed with her answer. "All right," he said at last. "But tomorrow, after Morning Mass, I intend taking you to the north field with me. I shall speak to your mother tonight, to inform her of our plans so that she may not demand your company."

"But—"

Julian held up a hand to halt her protest. "I admire your devotion to your mother, Alix," he said. "I, too, love my mother and enjoy spending time with her. But surely Lady Marie will understand that I, as your betrothed, desire your company as well. Now, I will take you to your mother."

He stood, offering her his arm. Lady Marie sat farther down the trestle table beside Lord Giles.

"Your daughter, Lady Marie," Julian said, bowing politely. "I trust you will both enjoy this evening's Mass."

Lord Giles sputtered at that. "Mass? This evening? Marie, you wanted to retire early to-night—"

"No, Giles," Marie said quickly, somewhat nervously. "I'd forgotten telling Alix about this evening's Mass. It is a special Mass Father Fantin called at Lady Eleanore's request. Alix and I must go."

Though Alix felt Julian's gaze upon her as surely as his arm still beneath her fingertips, she did not glance his way. How could she, when guilt seemed to seep from every pore?

Julian sat beside Alix the next morning in the Chapel, never letting her out of his reach. And after Mass, when everyone, including Marie, headed back toward the inner keep, Julian steered Alix in the opposite direction.

It took less than a few minutes for them to walk through the courtyard, around the side of the inner keep and past the stables toward the mews. Julian spoke all the while.

"There is one hawk I'm particularly proud of. I call her simply Hawk, because she is such a supreme example of her species. She's a peregrine, and the finest hunter I've ever had."

"A female?" Alix asked. She knew nothing of falconry, due to her fear of the birds, and was surprised to learn females were used rather than males.

"Of course," he said easily. "Males are smaller and not such great hunters."

The mews were in a wooded area set off to the rear of the Chateau, still within the outermost fortress walls. Alix hadn't been there since that day, years past, when Julian had so frightened her with his falcon. She doubted he remembered the incident, and had no intention of reminding him.

The mews consisted of several blocks, waist high to Julian, upon each of which a tethered bird sat. They were far enough apart to allow room for their ample wing spans, and when Julian neared, cooing a few words, many of the birds showed just how far their wings could spread. It seemed as if they were all eager to show Julian how powerful they were.

Julian left Alix's side to go to a long-winged, dark-eyed hawk in the center. Alix stayed back, for even though she knew the birds were tied and thus harmless, she felt her heart beat wildly within and her hands tremble at her side. How she wished she could have convinced Julian to take his mother with him instead of her!

From a pouch Julian had carried over his shoulder, he took a thick gauntlet and slipped his left hand into it. Then, also from the pouch, he took a dark hood, which he slipped over Hawk's head. The bird calmed immediately, soothed not only by the darkness of the hood but also by Julian's tender words. He spoke as if the hawk were a child, or perhaps a lover, endearing words about the hawk's beauty. But Alix hardly listened; all she could hear were the flapping wings of the other birds, and she only wanted to be away from them all. She feared some tried so hard to be free, their tether rope couldn't possibly hold.

Julian approached her with a wide smile upon his face, obviously totally at home in their surroundings. "This, Demoiselle, is Hawk. Say a few words, so she comes to know your voice."

Feeling utterly foolish, for her voice trembled somewhat and she hardly knew what to say to a bird, she said quietly, "Hello, Hawk. You

261

look . . . very large indeed." She eyed the bird's sharp talons resting upon the thick gauntlet, praying Julian would keep a tight hold, though she saw he barely held the rope tied to the bird's claw. "Shouldn't you tie her to you? Won't she fly off?"

"Not blinded, silly," Julian said, as if she were now the child. "Come, let's get the horses and ride up to the North field."

Morivek and Arab, the half-Arabian white horse Julian rode, were waiting for them outside the stables as they approached. Julian mounted easily, still using his left wrist as a perch for the hooded bird, while a blond-haired page assisted Alix astride Morivek. As they rode out, the page mounted his own horse and followed, carrying two small cages, one containing a rabbit, the other a quail. A greyhound tagged along as well.

The air was cool for the season. Above, the sky was cloudless, leaving a seemingly endless area for the bird to fly. Alix steered Morivek a few paces wide of Arab, and the horse pranced beneath her, sensing her unease.

If the horse detected Alix's anxiety, Julian did not. He continued to talk in soothing tones to the bird at his side, and his pride of the hawk was obvious in every word. And though Alix felt a bit safer on Morivek's back, knowing the horse would skitter away faster than she could if the bird came too close, her heart continued to beat a bit harder than usual.

"Do you see how calm she is, Alix?" Julian asked, looking at Hawk. "It is because she is with me. I've had her since she was an eyas—right from the nest." He laughed, adding, "I think she believes I'm her mother." Then he cooed at the bird as if he were indeed just that.

They came upon the field and Julian took the hood from the bird's head. Alix took one look at those dark eyes, the fearless stare, the sharp beak, and it almost sent her running. How well she remembered another bird, perhaps not so large as Hawk, but as it swooped down at her out of nowhere it could have been as large or larger than

262

Hawk. The sound of the wings flapping, the high-pitched whistle before it landed... She shuddered to think of it, even now, and shook her head, eyes tightly closed against the vision.

With one command from Julian, whose attention was utterly absorbed by Hawk, the bird was free and it soared away, flying high and seeming to float up above in a wide circle. Alix breathed a little easier then, seeing the bird so far away. From up there, she looked smaller, and so graceful she seemed harmless.

"We'll give her a few minutes to enjoy herself," Julian said. Then they just watched, all three of them, Alix, Julian and the blond-haired page, as Hawk swooped and dived, doing aerial acrobatics as if to impress her master.

Before Alix was even aware of it, Julian had issued the order to free the rabbit. Though Alix had guessed the purpose of the two caged prey, preoccupation with her own fear had preempted her fear for the two animals. And now, the furry little creature was being sent to its prearranged death.

"No, Julian!" Alix cried, reaching out as if to call back the doomed animal.

But it was already too late. As the rabbit scurried away, eyeing or sniffing the cover of forest far ahead, Alix watched in fascinated repulsion as the dog pointed out the prey to the bird up above. Then, in an instant, the bird plummeted downward, striking a blow so swift and sure that the rabbit lay motionless before the bird had even resumed any height in the air. Then Hawk swooped down once again, lifting the dead rabbit and heading in Julian's direction. She landed nearby, the prey still beneath the bird's sharp talons.

Julian was off his horse and at the bird's side in a moment. Praising Hawk, he took the quarry away, then the bird flew off again. Smiling with pride, Julian turned back to Alix—who promptly slipped from Morivek and approached him, her back stiff, her steps hitting hard upon the ground.

"Of all the horrible sights!" she shouted. "How dare you bring me here to witness such a killing! Do you think I *enjoyed* that?"

Julian tossed the carcass to the waiting page, then, without even wiping his hands, he took her by the shoulders. His face, first a vision of anger at the tongue-lashing she gave him, suddenly became one of astonishment.

"You're frightened!"

Alix turned on her heel, heading back to Morivek. But Julian caught her wrist and forced her to face him once again.

"Alix, wait," he said. "I cannot believe you are so incredibly stupid that you didn't know what the sport of falconry entails. Why should you be angry?"

She bristled under his insult, retorting, "It is you, Sir, who are so incredibly stupid. Can you not guess now why I have always resisted your invitation to see your falcons?"

"But it was only a rabbit," he said. "It's what hawks do . . . by nature."

"I don't care!" she told him. "Must I be a witness to it?"

Still holding her wrist so she could not flee, he offered a lopsided grin of apology. "In the future I shall ask why it is you refuse me, so I may avoid this sort of thing."

Julian assisted her on Morivek then, and called to the page while he mounted Arab.

"Take the quail back, and the dog. Hawk has had enough sport for one day."

Then, with a shrill whistle, he called to the bird, who instantly responded. Arab did not even flinch as the hawk swooped down and landed keenly on Julian's wrist. He placed the hood over the bird, and they headed back toward the Chateau.

"Does your brother not practice falconry, or your father?" Julian asked.

Alix shook her head, her eye still cautiously on the bird. Her unease must have at last been visible to Julian, for he halted his horse and gazed at her intently.

264

"It isn't the killing, is it?" he asked quietly. "It's the bird. You're afraid of the bird."

Alix said nothing, but did not hold Morivek back so Julian could examine her more closely. She just kept the mare at a steady pace, and Julian quickly followed.

20

After three days of traveling in rain, the sun at last appeared just as Philip and James approached Bayeux. Because of the mud-soaked roads, they needed an extra half-day; it was now late afternoon, when they had expected to arrive at early morn.

Rather than stay at one of the ill-kept, crowded inns, Philip told James they would call upon a man by the name of Jacques Berry. He was a shipping merchant Philip had met at Court several months ago—one of the few men of peasant blood the flamboyant King welcomed into his Court.

The Berry Chateau was on a high cliff, overlooking the Channel. Philip remembered the huge chateau had once belonged to a nobleman's family, but they, like so many, had succumbed to the Black Death. Jacques Berry had been bequeathed the Estate by the last surviving member, the Lady of the Manor, before her death—most said Jacques and the woman had been lovers, despite the woman's husband, and Philip did not doubt the story. Jacques, though not handsome, was as fascinating as fire—and as dangerous to a woman's heart. Or so Jacques Berry boldly claimed.

When the King learned Jacques Berry had been given the Estate by the Lady, who in fact had no legal right to do such a thing, he was amused and intrigued. He knew the Lady of this particular Manor, and her reputation of being like ice around members of the opposite gender. King Jean wanted to meet the man who had melted that reputation, and when he did made him a wager. If, for one year, Jacques could uphold the Estate in its present condition, prove he was capable of managing such a place, then it would indeed become his.

Jacques did not lose that wager.

Philip and James waited inside the courtyard while a servant announced their arrival. Surrounding them was a profusion of color; white, fragrant lilies, tall red tulips, and a border of blue forget-me-nots. Thick, green vines had grown up almost to the very door of the manor, but were neatly trimmed away from the three wide stairs and the door itself. And interspersed everywhere were sprigs of sweet basil.

A loud commotion sounded from behind the wood-carved door.

"I'll have you thrashed for making them wait outside!" came a thundering, familiar voice. But there was an undeniably light edge to his tone.

"And who would you have do the thrashing? Me?" Philip recognized the servant's voice who only moments ago had rather priggishly made him wait in the courtyard. "I do everything else in this Chateau!"

Then the door swung wide and Jacques Berry's somewhat short, muscular frame filled the doorway. "Philip!"

Philip smiled broadly at Jacques and said, "It is good to see you, Jacques."

Standing on the second step, Jacques reached and grabbed Philip's upper arms in a hearty welcome.

"And you, my friend! Come inside—this poor servant of mine doesn't know who you are." He paused before the manservant, who held wide the door. The servant was smiling, obviously confident his master had no intention of carrying out his initial threat to have him thrashed. "This is

Philip de Saines!''

In instant camaraderie, sensing the friendship between this servant and master, Philip bowed and said, "You must be the sole survivor who hasn't heard the stories of me since I was banned from Court."

"It is only by the grace of God, Sire," the servant said with a formal bow but laughing eyes, "that Monsieur Berry has not been banned as well."

"Ha!" Jacques laughed. Then, urging Philip beyond the wide entry hall, he patted Philip's back. "You must forgive Emile—a full year I have had him here, and still he does not know his place."

"A year?" Philip said. "Isn't that how long you've lived in this Chateau?"

Emile, who quite boldly followed them through a wide arch to an antechamber off the hallway, said, "Yes, and before that, Sire, I was his steersman at sea. Now he calls me his steward. Either way, he cannot do without me. And most certainly he would have lost this place and been back at sea in a month if it hadn't been for me."

Jacques shook his head, then sent his eyes heavenward before pouring four drinks in wide-bottomed mugs. "He still takes credit for winning that wager with the King. Even though all know I owe this . . . ," with a wave he referred to their opulent surroundings, "to my own irresistible charm."

Now it was Philip who rolled his eyes skyward.

"Enough of this," Jacques said. "Introduce me to your friend here, and tell me what business has brought you to Bayeux. You should not be here, my friend."

"I was banned only from Paris," Philip reminded him, "not from the rest of France."

"That is not what I meant. What business brings you here?"

Philip accepted the mug from Jacques, at the same time introducing James. "This is the de Saines marshal, James Sicot, who will be aiding me in my business. We're here to buy horses for a

267

knighting we're holding in a few days time."

James, who thus far had looked quite uncomfortable being treated like a guest of equal importance to his master, bowed somewhat stiffly.

Jacques laughed, taking pity on him. "I can see by your manner, James Sicot, that you are not accustomed to my household ways. Be at ease man! I am no nobleman—King Jean can attest to that, so why should I treat others like me—like you, like Emile—any differently?"

Still, James said nothing, only glancing from Jacques to Philip and then back again.

"Shame upon the de Saineses!" Jacques said after taking a long swallow of wine. "For being like all other noblemen and treating their servants like servants!"

"James is more at home in the stables," Philip said. "Now, were this conversation to take place there, we would have a different man among us."

Jacques approached Philip's stiff-backed stablemaster, calling to Emile at the same time. "Then show this marshal to where he will be more comfortable, Emile." He said to James, "You are welcome here, James. Emile will acquaint you, so you'll not feel so out of place."

"I would like to see to our mounts," James said at last. "We left them to the pages, and they have no notion how to make a horse truly comfortable after so long a journey."

"Very well," Jacques said. "Emilie, take James to the stable."

Once they were gone, the door closed soundly after them, Jacques turned to Philip. He'd lost his smile and was openly frowning. He resumed a conversation with Philip as though nothing had interrupted them.

"Then you'll not be here in Bayeux for long?"

"Anxious to be rid of me already, Jacques?"

Jacques laughed, approaching once again the table in the center of the room which held the rose-colored wine. "It is not I, my friend, who feels that way. You may want to leave when you know

268

who also resides in Bayeux, at least since last month.''

Philip raised questioning brows.

"The King banned you from Paris to prevent you from seeing both Rachel and Charles la Trau. When I first saw you, I wondered if that is the reason you have come.'' He sighed heavily. "But I see you still wear no sword, and so I know this business of buying horses is true. They are here, Philip. Both of them.''

"Charles is here? In Bayeux?'' Philip felt stupid, asking Jacques to repeat himself, but he felt compelled to, not believing the fates would be so unfair as to bring him to the same city as the man who hated him—and without true cause.

Jacques nodded. "And when he learns you have come, he'll undoubtedly think it is to settle more serious business than buying horses. Who would imagine the de Saineses actually buying horses? You've always had the stock to raise your own.''

"How long did you say Charles has been here?'' Philip asked, his thoughts going to Julian rather than remaining on Berry's words. His brother had been in this land only days ago, and had no doubt known of Charles being there. And said nothing.

"Almost a month. He sent for Rachel when talk of the scandal reached us. He heard Jean banished you and knew there would be little point in going to Court to issue in person the challenge he made public once he heard the stories. But I believe Charles is pleased to have Rachel here—he said Rachel will find no diverting men out here to attract her eye. Of course,'' he added with a grin, "she doesn't yet know I reside here.''

Frowning, Philip set his cup of wine upon the table. "I wouldn't try for that one, friend,'' he said distractedly. "She is as ugly inside as she is beautiful on the outside.''

"From the stories being told, it is you who would know,'' Jacques teased.

But Philip shook his head. "I never touched the woman. Thank God. If the tales had all been true, I couldn't have avoided Charles. And one of us would be dead."

"But Charles should know this! If he has been duped by his own wife, surely he has no quarrel with you."

But Philip put a hand up to stop Jacques' protest. "He doesn't believe anyone but Rachel. At least," he added, "so I've been told. I haven't seen Charles since before all of this began. As soon as Jean heard of Charles's threat, he sent me away before I could even confront him. And I do not doubt Charles holds only malice for me now, despite the fact we were friends once." He hesitated, looking deep in thought. "Charles loves Rachel—like an obsession. If he thought he might lose her, he would try to destroy whatever threatened to take her away."

"Then I suggest, Philip," Jacques said, "that you tend to your business with haste, and return to Brittany without delay."

Philip smiled, bitterly. "That should add nicely to the tales of my cowardice."

"Then, blazes! Fight the man!"

But Philip did not rise to Berry's sudden passion. Calmly, he looked at Jacques and asked, "If Emile believed a falsehood of you, and wanted to kill you for it, would you fight him? Knowing if you didn't die, then perhaps he would? And all for a lie?"

Jacques saw his logic. "Then talk to him. Tell him the truth. He deserves to know his wife is a liar."

"Perhaps I will," Philip said slowly. "Perhaps I will."

"Lise! Where is she? That lazy girl! Lise!"

Rachel la Trau sat before her dressing mirror, the light from a tall, glassed window nearby dispelling all shadows from her reflection. She had been about to take a bath when her young servant simply disappeared, leaving Rachel clad in nothing more than a linen towel. How was she to wash her own hair?

270

Rachel eyed the huge tub of hot water, sitting on its rollers in the center of her chamber. Beside it stood a stool to aid in climbing in, but she knew she couldn't manage all by herself. Where was that girl!

Rage threatening to erupt, Rachel marched toward the door, thinking she would scream down the mighty walls of this hellishly cold chateau. That would bring Lise running. But just as she was about to lay a hand to the brass handle of the thick wooden door, it opened and Lise stood, wide-eyed, before her.

"If that's fear upon your face, girl, you've every right to feel it," Rachel said, turning back to the bath. "How dare you run out on me like that, when I've need of you. Now help me into this bath!"

"Yes, madame," Lise said primly, as she rushed to do her lady's bidding. "But I have news, Madame Rachel. That is why I was gone so long—and oh, I've forgotten the heated towels. It is the news ... It has made me foolish."

Rachel dismissed the silly servant's excuses with a wave of her hand. She slipped into the hot, soothing water and leaned back, closing her eyes. "Just go and get the towels, Lise. And hurry. I want you to wash my hair today."

'Yes, madame ... but do you not wish to hear my news?"

Rachel did not open her eyes. "I want you to get the towels and then wash my hair. I don't care about your news."

Lise started to turn away, but hesitated. Then, smiling confidently, she said, "But it concerns you ... and Philip de Saines."

Lise received the response she expected. Rachel's eyes opened wide, and she sat up straight. "What did you say?"

"My news, Madame. It concerns Philip de Saines."

"What is it!" she demanded, too anxious to hear what the servant had to say to be angry with her.

Lise continued smiling, and hesitated as long as she dared, enjoying the frustration her mistress was plainly feeling. "He is here, in Bayeux. He arrived at the home of Monsieur Jacques Berry only this afternoon."

Rachel leaned back again, her cheeks warm, feeling as though the water she sat in was far hotter than it actually was. Philip. Here. But why? Had he reconsidered? Had he actually come all this way to see her? To be with her? But he must have! Certainly he hadn't come to see Charles! She doubted Philip would ever pick up his sword again, even though she knew Charles would challenge Philip if ever given the chance. She had seen to that.

"He is staying with Monsieur Berry?" Rachel asked. She hadn't known Jacques Berry lived in Bayeux; she'd heard, of course, of the outrageous way he'd been bequeathed an estate, but she hadn't known it was here.

Lise nodded. "He says he has business in the horse markets . . . but isn't it true, Madame, that the de Saineses raise their own horses?"

Rachel laughed outright. Such a thin veil upon Philip's real business—to see her! He was not so clever, that Philip de Saines . . . but oh, how handsome! And soon, Rachel thought, she would have him after all.

"Hurry, Lise. Wash my hair. And then set out my bluest gown." Blue, she thought, like the color of her eyes, and his.

Soon Rachel sat before her mirror once again, clad only in her underrobe. She let Lise twirl her hair into plaits, coiling them intricately on each side. Then she used a mixture of sheep fat and chalk to whiten her skin, and rouge to tint it in just the right places. Finally, she dressed in a tightly fitted blue gown, bordered with pure white pearls along the very low decolletage and down the center of the bodice to her slim waist. She pulled at the bodice and underrobe until satisfied her full figure was enhanced to its best, then, inspecting herself one last time, smiled at the results of the afternoon.

"Now let us see where Monsieur Berry resides,"

272

she said, more to herself than to the servant beside her.

She left her bed chamber on the second floor of the town manor house, going quickly to the head of the stairs. But there she stopped, much to Lise's surprise. Then, Lise heard what Madame Rachel already had. The conversation of two men floated up the stairs.

"When do you expect him to return?"

"Before sunset, Sire," the manservant replied to the visitor at the door.

Rachel smiled to herself upon hearing Philip's voice. So, she did not need to go to him. He'd already sought her out, and was asking when Charles would return. Before sunset . . . that did not give them much time alone.

"Is that Sire de Saines?" she said, taking the steps slowly, confidently. She halted on the bottom stair, letting Philip take a full look at her before approaching any closer.

Still standing in the doorway, Philip bowed at Rachel's appearance. "Madame," he said.

It was hardly the greeting she'd anticipated, but, mindful of the servants surrounding them, she said nothing of her disappointment. Secretly, she wished he would have swept her up into his arms, telling her what a fool he'd been for delaying so long what he must have longed for all the time, ever since she'd been the bold one to tell him how she felt.

"Come in, Philip," she invited. "Have a cup of wine. Surely you are weary from your travels . . . I was told you arrived just today."

Philip hesitated, still just outside. He eyed Rachel closely. Philip could see her assurance, her certainty were as strong as they had been that day, not so long ago, when she'd first told him she wanted him. He almost shook his head at the memory, still stunned at her bold overconfidence. She'd been so sure he would want her. And when he hadn't . . . that was when all the trouble began. He knew the most sensible thing to do now was turn on his heel and leave, seeing that look in her eye once again. What manner of trouble would she stir this time? But, he told himself, he'd come to get himself out of the trouble she'd started and he'd be damned before she sent him away like the coward many believed him to be.

Philip took one last look at the sky above. Sunset, he guessed, was no more than twenty minutes away. Surely he could bear her company that long. So he stopped inside the small hallway of the manor house, still feeling he was making another mistake with this devious woman. But, he thought, if he could end this scandal, talk sensibly to both Rachel and Charles, it would have one advantage he needed very badly. It would clear his name of this scandal, without a sword lifted, and that would satisfy both himself and Lord Giles. Lord Giles would have one less reason to refuse Philip; it would no doubt ease the way toward Alix becoming his. The thought of Alix made him shake off that feeling of unease as he followed Rachel into a room set opposite the stairway she'd just come down.

The room was warmly lit by a fire in the hearth, and cluttered with heavy furniture. A polished desk shared the wall with a huge fireplace, above which hung a pair of glistening metal swords secured to the stone chimney. There was a deeply cushioned couch directly in front of the fireplace, but Philip chose to stand even though Rachel sat in the very center of that couch.

Rachel looked over her shoulder once, and watched as the manservant disappeared into the inner rooms of the manor house. "We are quite alone, Philip," she said with a smile. "Please, be at ease."

It was a blatant invitation to sit beside her, Philip knew, but he had no intention of doing so. He smiled down at her and said, "I am quite at ease, Rachel. It was good of you to invite me in. I wished to see both you and Charles as well."

Rachel laughed. "Charles? Whatever for? He really quite detests you, ever since I told him about us."

"That, Rachel, is precisely what I intend talking to him about."

Rachel stood, her confidence still evident. "So you did come all this way because of me. And they say you were interested in some silly horse purchases!"

She stood very close to him, and Philip gazed down at her. She was a striking woman, he had to admit. Large, blue eyes were set wide on a heart-shaped face, with a soft, sensual mouth smiling so eagerly at him. But there was no loveliness there, he thought. How different her beauty was from Alix's, who was pure and without deceit. He caught his own thoughts. That wasn't exactly how he'd left her that day, just before embarking on this trip to Bayeux. But there would be time to straighten that out when he returned. Surely Alix would know he hadn't meant what he'd said. And besides, if he cleared up this scandal, perhaps they could entirely forget the reason for that argument. After all, the scandal was part of the reason Lord Giles wished Philip would take up his sword again.

"I did orginally come to Bayeux to purchase a few horses," Philip said. "But I am glad my business here can settle the differences between your husband and me."

One carefully arched brow raised in doubt. "You wear no sword, Philip," she reminded him. "Surely you haven't come to see Charles. It is only I who welcome you swordless."

"I did not come to challenge Charles. You should know, Rachel, there is no need for that. Nothing happened between us that Charles need fight over."

She laughed. "But he doesn't know that." She placed her hands on his chest, pressing herself close to him and gazing up into his eyes. "You must know, Philip, why I told him the tale of our lovemaking. Because I *wanted* you . . . and you—you wanted me, I know you did. I saw the way you looked at me at Court. That's why you've come here today, isn't it? To make all those tales

275

come true.''

Philip shook his head, taking her hands and pulling them away from his chest. ''No, Rachel,'' he said gently. ''I have no wish to hurt you; I never did. But I told you then, and I tell you now, I'll not take the wife of my friend.''

''Friend!'' she repeated. ''Charles wants to kill you!''

''Only because you will not tell him the truth. You must, Rachel. He deserves to know.''

She turned away, all trace of eager passion gone from her face. ''You didn't come here to see me, did you?'' she asked.

''No, Rachel. I came to settle this matter with Charles. I must clear my name . . . in order to marry another.''

Rachel cast a wide-eyed gaze in his direction. ''Marry? You're getting married?''

He nodded.

Suddenly she laughed, long and hard, settling once again into the couch and staring blindly at the fireplace. ''And you expect me to help you? You're really quite mad, Philip! Did you think I would help you?''

In truth, Philip did not. But he'd let her know, without doubt, that he had no intention of bedding her, now or ever.

Then, her laughter dying, she gazed up at him once again. She looked small and helpless and, for the first time, actually pretty. But the vulnerable attractiveness did not last long. Her eyes once again turned cold. ''Haven't you figured out why I told everyone we bedded, even when we have not?''

''I assumed it was to hurt me, through Charles, for rejecting you.''

''Precisely. Now why should I settle for anything less just because you want to marry?''

Philip said nothing. He could have guessed, had he given it thought, this was how such a conversation would end.

Rachel stood once again, just as close to Philip as before. The passion had rekindled upon her face. "Compare me," she said, her eyelids heavy, her mouth moist, "to this woman you wish to marry. Does she have lips as willing as mine?" Boldly, she took his hand, and placed it on her cheek. "Surely she isn't as pleasing to look upon as me." She moved his hand lower, to rest upon her breast. "And is her body . . . filled with the same passion I could give?"

Philip pulled his hand away, offering only a cool, crooked, smile. "She has passion, Madame, you could not begin to know."

But Rachel was undaunted. She did not move back, just leaned even closer, putting her head against his chest and breathing in the scent of him. "But you haven't truly compared," she asked huskily. "At least give me an equal advantage to show you my passion."

Philip did not answer, though if he had it would have been only to reject her bold offer. But he had no chance to speak, for they were no longer alone.

Hadn't he known, hadn't he guessed, with that first feeling of unease as he followed Rachel into this room, that he would regret it? For at the entryway now stood Charles la Trau, a glare so intense Philip felt his hatred as surely as the heat from Rachel's body.

21

For one long, tense moment, only silence filled the room. Then Rachel, taking just one step away from Philip, faced Charles, her chin held high, her eyes sparkling as if with some sort of victory.

"So you've found us together," she said, without a trace of hesitation or cowardice.

"Charles," Philip said, his voice calm. But he knew if he allowed Rachel to say another word, she would only add more lies to those she'd already spread. "I came to see you, not Rachel. I wish to speak to you about the stories you've been told."

Slowly, Charles stepped farther into the room. He stared at Philip without flinching and said, "You have come into my home like a thief. Leave before I strike you down as one."

But Philip did not move. "Not until I've had the chance to tell you the truth."

"I'll tell you the truth!" Rachel exclaimed. "He came to Bayeux to see me! He's really quite besotted with me, Charles. Just now, he asked me to marry him! Despite the fact I'm already wed. He wants me to run off with him."

Charles hadn't taken his eyes off Philip. "There is but one way for you to take my wife, Philip. And that is if you kill me. Yet I see you still play the coward, without sword or dagger at your side. Did you think I would send you off together without a fight?"

"I do not want to fight you, Charles."

Charles smiled, but without humor. "Perhaps you would like me to bless your infidelities with my wife?"

"Your wife may indeed be guilty of infidelity, but not with me. There has been nothing between us—except the lies she's told you."

Slowly, Charles walked past them, nearing the fireplace. Above, the hilts of the crossed swords shone like long icicles in the steadily dimming light of the room. The sun had disappeared quickly, leaving behind only the dancing firelight to fill the room with ever-changing shadows. Charles stood stiff, tall. He was no more than three paces from Philip.

"I find it hard to believe you've no wish for challenge, Philip, especially given the fact you are here—days away from your home, where the King sent you to protect you like the coward you are."

Suddenly Charles reached up and grabbed one of the swords, and threw it toward Philip. It landed with a clatter at his feet, where Philip let it lie. Neither man moved.

"Pick it up," Charles said, quietly. He clutched at the jeweled hilt of the sword that hung at his side, with not one hand but two, as if he could not wait to face Philip with arms.

Still, Philip did not move.

"Are you such a coward?" Charles taunted. "Has my lovely wife indeed fallen in love with a mouse?"

"We trained to be knights together, Charles," Philip softly reminded him. "We fought together. Do you really believe me a coward?"

"Then fight me." He took his sword from his belt, and touched its tip to the fallen sword before Philip. "Pick it up," he said again.

Anticipation tingled up Philip's spine. He rubbed his thumb along his fisted fingers, vividly remembering the touch of a hilt. How tempting it was to pick it up, he thought as he stared at the scornful face of a man who had once been his friend.

But Philip did not succumb to that temptation. It would have been so easy, he thought to himself, just to fight Charles and have done with it. But doing so would not only have been senseless, it would, in Philip's mind, be an admission of guilt. And more, it would have been exactly what Rachel wanted. So he held back, his spine stiff against any rash wish to bend and pick up that sword as Charles asked.

"I have no desire to spill your blood over tales that have no truth to them," Philip said, his gaze not wavering from Charles.

Charles, for one mere moment, looked confused. His brows moved, ever so slightly, his hand, holding the sword, trembled. He looked from Philip to his wife, and seeing her, with bloodlust so clearly written upon her delicate features, that moment of indecision disappeared.

"Damn you to hell, Philip de Saines!" he cried.

In a flash, he lifted the sword to strike, and Philip knew there was no time to defend himself, unarmed as he was. If he reached down to retrieve

279

the sword on the floor, surely his life would be over before even reaching the weapon.

A low moan, almost a sigh, escaped Charles. His face was a mass of emotion, his dark eyes darker than ever, his fair skin splotched red with pent-up frustration. His mouth was set in a scowl, twisted like a grotesque smile. The battle Charles waged was inside himself, Philip saw as he watched. He felt only overwhelming pity—and disgust, but not aimed at Charles. The disgust was for Rachel, who looked on with confusion at her husband's odd behavior. For Charles stood, barely moving, until he slowly, harmlessly, lowered the sword. It was plain this was hardly the action Rachel had expected.

"Kill him!" Rachel's words, certainly no surprise, fell upon her husband without the impact she hoped. Instead of doing as she bid, he dropped his sword and it hit the other one with an empty clang, there before his feet.

Philip wanted to touch Charles, to put a hand upon his shoulder in remembered friendship—for surely that was what had saved him—but couldn't. He knew Charles wanted nothing from him, not even to let a glance pass between them. Charles did not lift his eyes from the two swords between them.

Philip quietly left the manor house.

Outside, the evening was quiet. It seemed so tranquil, with the town streets empty, friendly lights beaming from cozy manner houses. Outside the gate of the la Trau home, Philip stood still. He put a hand to the back of his neck, rubbing it when he realized his tension. Then, ironically, he gave a short laugh. For a moment he'd believed Charles might have severed that neck. Philip looked back at the house. What had made him stop, he wondered? Certainly not Rachel. If it had been up to her, Philip would lie dead on their antechamber floor. He resisted the shudder about to run up his spine.

Philip took a deep breath, and shook off the unease he'd felt since first entering that place. He started walking, briskly, down the street, back toward Jacques Berry's home. He tried not to recall just how close he'd been to sparring with Charles; he tried not to think of any part of the encounter he'd just come from. But nonetheless, one point could not be ignored: he hadn't settled the scandal. If anything, he'd made it worse. He had no doubt Rachel would see to that.

Because he could not help it, or because it kept him sane, Philip let his thoughts go to Alix. It was obvious settling this clash with Charles would not be solved quickly, and he'd not gotten any closer to making their betrothal possible. If not by the sword, then time must allow this scandal to wear thin upon everyone's memory, most especially upon Lord Giles's. Fighting Charles would not have been the answer, even if others might think so. Philip knew, if he had indeed picked up that sword, than either Charles or he would be dead at this moment. And only Rachel would be the victor then.

There was but one avenue left, and that was one Alix had spoken of before he left. If he couldn't squash this scandal attached to his name, perhaps he could direct the attention of Alix's family elsewhere. To the feud with the Montforts. Perhaps ending that feud was indeed the only answer now.

Philip's steps slowed as plans and schemes filled his mind. Was there a way, he wondered, to solve this feud peacefully? He grimaced, thinking himself foolish for having such a hope, even for a moment. Hadn't he hoped to end that scandal peacefully? And look what it had brought; only a deeper rift between Charles and himself, and Rachel armed with more fuel to add to the tales she'd spread already.

But Philip was determined. He would find a way, he thought to himself, of ending the feud and still, he prayed, without breaking that vow he'd made to himself.

"Hold the lance higher! Higher!" Julian yelled at the young boy atop the huge destrier. The boy looked as if he could barely sit straight, with heavy chain mail causing his shoulders to droop, a massive pot helmet much too large for his small head tilting to one side, and the long lance he struggled to keep under one arm.

"He's just a boy, Julian," Alix said in young Louis's defense. "He can barely hold all the paraphernalia required."

"He's nearly thirteen, Demoiselle," Julian said firmly; his tone had barely softened from what he'd used toward the boy.

"And small for his age."

"Do you know how many boys are knighted at age fourteen? A mere one year difference from him?"

"I'm sure a great many," Alix replied. "But that does not mean Louis should be knighted at that age."

But Julian had already returned his attention to the failures of Louis. "If you cannot carry the lance, you have no business at the quintain!"

The quintain, a chain-mailed dummy perched upon a post, was set at the opposite end of the track Louis rode upon Julian's huge destrier. If a man, or boy, could not excel at spearing the quintain with lance or sword, he certainly had no business thinking of becoming a knight.

Then, to Alix, Julian said, "I was smaller than Louis when I was taught to wield a lance. If my teacher had given up on me, as you seem to think I should do with Louis, I doubt I would be a knight today."

"Perhaps your teacher was wrong to expect so much of you."

"My teacher," Julian said, a glint in his eye of such admiration Alix could not mistake it, "made few mistakes." Just then Louis charged at the quintain, missing the dummy by several lengths. "No, no!" Julian said, shaking his head, then left Alix's side to run toward Louis, enumerating Louis's mistakes all the way.

Gustave, who also watched from the edge of the training yard, neared Alix. "He has the energy of a great teacher, that one," Gustave said toward Julian's back.

"The energy, perhaps, but I believe he could use a bit more patience." As Alix spoke, Julian pulled the boy from the horse, jumping astride and grabbing the lance. He then proceeded to show Louis, one more time, the proper way to hold, maintain, and charge.

"But he does have patience, Demoiselle," Gustave assured her. "At least as much as he needs—to go over, again and again, the correct way. He is teaching as he was taught. Relentlessly."

"Julian mentioned his teacher several times while standing here with me. It seems he still holds the man in extremely high favor. Did you teach him, Gustave?"

Gustave shook his head, a slow smile covering his face. "He was closer to his teacher than most . . . He loved him a great deal, and his teacher loved him. Perhaps that's why he taught him so well. Better, in fact, than I could have done."

"Who was he?"

"His brother."

"Philip?" Alix said, surprised. "But I thought . . . That is, they seem so . . . ."

Alix nodded. "So like enemies today?"

"It is because Philip taught Julian all he thought necessary; how to be the best knight, the bravest, the most skilled. And then he renounced it all. I do not believe Julian will ever forgive Philip for that. They were closest when they were knights together, even though Julian was a few years younger. Now, they hold no common ideas."

Alix was thoughtful, realizing for the first time that Julian did not really hate his brother as he wanted everyone to think. How could he, when he obviously still held the memory of what Philip used to be with such respect?

Soon, Julian was back at her side, and Louis tried again to best the quintain. Alix watched Julian rather than Louis; she had just discovered something which she knew, instinctively, Julian would have wished was still secret.

22

One last hill between him and the Chateau. Philip could not help but spur his weary horse to a quicker pace. He felt hot and dusty, thirsty, hungry and in great need of a bath. But it wasn't the promise of comfort that made him want to force himself and his beast into a full gallop toward home. The ache in his loins made the other discomforts pale in comparison; what he wanted more than anything else was sight of Alix, and to blot out entirely those harsh words that had passed between them when they'd seen each other last.

It was late; the sun had set long ago. More than likely, the entire Chateau was already abed. James had suggested they stop for the night several hours back, but Philip had stubbornly refused. He was for home, without delaying another night. James, mindful of the horses, might have argued, but Philip's silent determination to go on had been clear enough.

And now, seeing the tall shadow of the Chateau, even James was glad they hadn't delayed.

James called out to the sentries posted on the high walls of the Chateau, and soon after he identified who they were, the drawbridge creaked across the Chateau moat. Hooves of a dozen horses in tow sounded loud in the night, Philip thought. Loud enough to wake Alix? Part of him hoped so.

Philip left the care of all the horses, including his own, to James and the others in the stables. Then, with one glance up toward Alix's chamber and seeing it dark, he made his way to his tower. Perhaps it would have been better to ride easy coming home, he thought. It looked as though he would not be able to see Alix tonight anyway.

He considered going to Alix's room, but remembered Hugh, who kept his pallet at the foot of her stairs. Hugh was an old man, Philip thought. And, if sound asleep, Philip might even step right past him without detection. But somehow he doubted Hugh could sleep quite so soundly, or else his very position there would be nullified. So Philip continued on to his tower, his feet moving slowly, his body giving in to the weariness.

"Philip."

Had he imagined his name being called? He paused, looking around. Between him and his tower far ahead there was nothing, no place for a midnight visitor to hide. He must be daft. The voice had even sounded like Alix's; no doubt his desire for her was making him hear things. He continued walking.

What made him turn toward the garden, Philip did not know. But then he did, passing the forebuilding of the keep, beyond the sight of Alix's window. And then he knew he had not imagined Alix's voice, for beyond the tall shadows of the ill-kept garden she waited. Once he, too, was under cover of the thorny vines, she reached out. In an instant they were in each other's arms, without a word more spoken.

"I didn't think you could hear me," Alix said at last, in her eyes a joy so obvious that Philip held her even tighter. "I called three times, afraid everyone but you could hear me."

"James and the others are as weary as I. Do not fear they would pay attention to any voices in the night."

Her brow creased. "Are you so very tired? Should I let you go straight to your bed? Alone?"

Her concern displaced all his weariness, and he held her close, whispering into her ear, "You should let me go straight to my bed, but not alone.

285

Never alone."

She laughed huskily, her breath tickling his cheek. "I've missed you."

There was so much more that she wanted to say, to ask, to tell, but she said nothing, wanting only to enjoy being within his embrace once again.

Suddenly he held her at arm's length. "You may have missed me, Demoiselle, but I am quite sure you cannot enjoy welcoming me when I am in dire need of a bath."

Smiling seductively, she said, "It is the custom in many great homes, Sire, that the lady give the lord a bath. Perhaps I could volunteer for such a service?"

"Come with me," he said.

They hurried into the night, the danger of being discovered only adding excitement to their chase. The drawbridge was still lowered, and from within the gatehouse, they heard the sentires arguing over a board game they played. With Alix clinging to Philip's hand, the two lovers made their way silently over the drawbridge, running to the privacy of the trees.

They did not stop until at the water's edge, some distance down river from where Philip had come upon Julian and Alix that day of the feast. Once there, as if of one thought, they raced each other free of their clothes, and splashed into the water in childish abandon.

Alix, neck-high in water, laughed when Philip disappeared beneath the surface, only to rise moments later just inches away. Immediately his arms encircled her, and he kissed her. Then, his face still close, he whispered, "I love you," and kissed her again.

Though it could hardly be called a bath, neither seemed to care. They almost floated back to the grassy bank, half-in, half-out of the water, and the whole time Alix's hands were as inquisitive as Philip's. Philip couldn't wait, he couldn't hold back. Alix's obvious eagerness only intensified Philip's longing; this unexpected reunion released all the passions he'd only dreamed of while parted from her. At that moment, Philip's need to be with her, to be joined with her, was desperate—as if their separation had been years rather than days.

The full moon peeked in and out from behind gossamer clouds up above, shedding a silvery light upon them and transforming the water clinging to their bodies into shimmering pearls reflecting here and there. They were oblivious to everything but each other, which was the reason they did not hear the one who had followed all the way from the Chateau.

Julian de Saines turned away, having seen too much already. He hadn't meant to watch even this long, for he'd guessed their relationship the moment he spied them running from the Chateau, hand in hand. But he'd followed anyway, speeding down from his perch on the high wall. It had taken a moment to catch up, and they'd been in the water already when he arrived. And now, seeing their passionate reunion, he did not need to see more. He returned to the Chateau, neither hurt nor glad nor even surprised. Hadn't he guessed, still feeling the worst of the bruises upon his cheek, that Alix had stirred something in his brother?

He returned to his chamber in the inner Keep, all the while wondering how best to use what he'd just learned.

"There aren't many stars tonight," Alix said, her voice lazy and content. They lay in each other's arms, she dressed only in her chemise and he in the loincloth he wore beneath his hose.

"The moon is too bright," he told her, before pressing a kiss to her temple.

"Do you think the drawbridge will still be lowered?" she wondered. She supposed the thought should have concerned her, but oddly, she didn't care. It was hard to be distressed when in Philip's arms.

He laughed. "I doubt it. We'll have to wait until morning."

"Perhaps we'll be found out," she said in a low

voice.

"Hmm."

"Shouldn't we . . . be worried?"

Philip leaned up on one elbow, looking down at her with anything but unease. "I do not think you'll be betrothed to Julian much longer," he said confidently.

Her eyes sparkled as she gazed up at him. "Oh?"

"After the knighting ceremony I plan speaking to your father about our own plans to wed."

Alix sat up, the sparkle in her eyes changing from happiness to anticipation to intrigue. "But you know he doesn't approve of you, Philip, despite your name and title." She frowned. "He is happy with my betrothal to your brother."

"You said before I left for Bayeux that if I could bring about the end of the feud with the Montforts, that would gain the approval of both your father and my own. I intend doing that."

She lifted her brows, but before long a frown brought those brows together. "You will do battle with the Montforts?" For all her old dreams of revenge, the actual thought of Philip at war made her shiver.

But he shook his head. "I have an idea to end the feud another way."

"How? Surely the Montforts will only listen to might."

Philip sat up, the earnestness of his plan lending excitement to his voice and a glimmer to his eye. "What is it the Montforts want? Why have they attacked all the nobles in the land—and issued so many insults to the de Saines name these past two years?"

Alix was thoughtful, for she'd never before given such a question any consideration. "They want to prove their own increasing strength."

"Strength that matches any noble's," Philip elaborated. "With their hired mercenaries, they've boasted they are more powerful than the de Saineses—that even King Jean himself would be hard pressed to put them back if they advanced. And they've the numbers, so I've heard, to make such threats. But why is it they are so eager to prove this strength?"

"Everyone says they've petitioned both King Jean and England's King Edward for ennoblement. Obviously their loyalty is to themselves before France."

"Then why not give them their noble title? Let Henri Montfort become Lord of his estate, if that will end this feud."

"But Philip!" That Alix was appalled was vitally clear in those two words. "Reward Henri Montfort with a title? What has he done but add to the bloodshed in France?"

Philip was not set back. "You are too covetous of a title. What price is it if the feud is ended? A small one, I think—except for Henri Montfort himself. I've no doubt King Jean will make him pay dearly in gold for a title."

Alix shook her head. "They do not deserve to be titled after all they've done."

"What exactly have they done?" Philip asked, some of the excitement gone from his voice.

"The d'Aussy . . ."

Philip shook his head, and raised a hand to end her reminder. "I have asked about, Alix. It seems the attack on the d'Aussy land that day was not the Montforts' idea. In fact, the battle began on Montfort land, where d'Aussy men-at-arms attacked first. The Montforts chased them all the way home, and burned and looted the house in conquest."

Alix stared at him, accepting the news with wide eyes. It was clear she had trouble believing his words. "And what of my home? We did not provoke the Montforts, yet my home lies in ruins."

"You have no proof . . ." he began gently, but when he saw tears fill her eyes just before she turned away, he stopped.

"I *know* they did it," she said, somewhat weakly, over her shoulder.

Philip went up on his knees, stooping in front of her and, finally, taking her into his arms. "There is no doubt the Montforts are the cause of much bloodshed here in our County. If they were not so blatant about their lack of loyalty, they would not stir such ire in the land. But if we gave them reason to be loyal, there is no doubt it would bring us peace.''

"But why should King Jean title them?'' she asked, a hard edge to her tone. "They are peasants who did nothing more than steal the home of the family the Black Death claimed.''

He laughed lightly. "You sound as priggish as your father, Alix. And I know it is only bitterness over the loss of your home which makes you speak so harshly. But believe me, if I can get King Jean to listen to the Montforts' case for ennoblement, we shall see peace in this land—and isn't that what we should all want, after losing so many to the Death?''

She nodded, trying desperately to agree with his words. But part of her, perhaps that part he'd correctly identified as bitterness over the loss of her home, still nagged at the back of her mind.

"The King is in Tours,'' Philip said, "I will leave the day after the knighting for Vannes, and travel by boat down the Bay to the Loire. Perhaps, even knowing just the reason for this mission, the Montforts will act in peace.''

"Why not take Henri Montfort or one of his men with you?''

"I would, if they would come. But good faith must be shown first; they have little reason to trust a de Saines. And, a year ago when they offered to pay for ennoblement, their plea was turned down because it was learned they had bargained with Edward as well—should he be the victor in any battle. But now, with a truce between Edward and Jean, and perhaps the Montforts' willingness to deal with the English forgotten, Jean may listen, this time. But I believe it will be enough to show good faith from a de Saines.''

Although this was not exactly the way she had imagined the end of the feud with the Montforts, Alix could not deny this would indeed help in silencing the tongues which continued to wag over

Philip's scandal. Which reminded her of all the worries she had suffered during his absence. She did not know how to broach the subject, but now there was another worry tugging at her thoughts. Had he seen Rachel la Trau? She guessed he had not seen Charles; if he had, surely some violence would have come of such a reunion. For that, she was grateful. But the thought of Philip seeing a woman who so obviously desired him did cast a frown upon her brow.

"I will hate to see you leave again after only just returning from Bayeux," she said, her pulse quickening with the question she wanted most to ask. "Did you ... get all the horses your family will need for the knighting?"

Philip eyed her closely, seeing that she avoided looking at him squarely and stared at her own hand as if she'd just sprouted a sixth finger. He knew then that Julian must have told her who was in Bayeux.

"Yes, I bought all the horses we shall need," he answered. Then, after the briefest of pauses, he said, "Julian told you, didn't he?"

Her gaze flew to his. "You knew? Did Julian tell you before you left?"

He shook his head. "When I arrived in Bayeux and found Charles and his wife had been living there several weeks, I assumed Julian knew they were there, since he'd just left that town not long ago. But no, I did not know they were there when I left here."

"And ... did you see Charles? I so worried he would confront you and perhaps challenge you."

"That he did." Philip let out a scornful sigh, aimed only at himself. "I was fool enough to think I could talk him through the lies his wife told—to tell him the truth and actually have him believe me over her." He laughed bitterly. "It seems living with Rachel has driven him to harbor a hatred of me that forgets what friends we used to be."

"He would not believe you?"

Philip shook his head. "The circumstances were less than favorable. Rachel told him I'd come to

Bayeux to be with her."

"Then Rachel was there," she said, trying to keep her voice devoid of emotion. She did not look at him, fearing he would read the blatant possessiveness she felt for him.

"Yes, I saw her, too."

The fact that he did not expand on that, tell her all she wished—or perhaps did not wish—to hear, made her turn an exasperated glance in his direction. "And? Did she . . . does she still want you?"

"I thought you didn't listen to rumors." There was an annoying little curve at the corner of his mouth, as if he were trying to suppress a full smile at her obvious unease.

She said nothing, not enjoying his teasing.

Gently, he shook her at the shoulders, every trace of that teasing smile now gone. "How could you think, even for a moment, that I would be untrue to you? I never wanted Rachel la Trau; that hasn't changed. But now no woman appeals to me, except you. How can you doubt that?"

She put her arms about his neck, pulling him close. "I didn't doubt you—I believe in your love. But I think it must be hard for a man to resist a woman who wants him, especially if she is beautiful. Is she?"

"Is she what?"

Alix sensed he was teasing her again, but went on anyway. "Beautiful," she said.

He was silent for one agonizing moment, as if contemplating, but when he laughed Alix was sure he'd meant to make her suffer with his delay. "Oh!" she said, exasperated, and stood, heading for the rest of her clothing.

Philip chased after her, taking her underrobe away when she would have slipped it over her head. She tried to snatch it back, but he held it past her reach. Then, seriously, he spoke,

"I'll help you," he said. "Don't you have a servant to dress you? Let me be your servant for tonight."

It was hard to be cross when he gently lifted the

garment above her, and quite tenderly pulled it in place. There were tiny buttons down the bodice, and his fingers, she guessed intentionally, touched beneath the garment he was buttoning. Through her thin chemise where contact was made, her skin tingled, and she felt as though he were undressing rather than dressing her. In a moment, she knew, that was what she would prefer him to do.

When each of the buttons were secured, Philip's hands moved to her waist, pulling her against him. "Alix," he said her name in a low voice, void of all teasing. "There is no woman to compare with you. Don't you know that?"

His lips came down on hers then, and when he felt the fire he'd stirred in her while tending to her underrobe it was barely a moment later that he was unbuttoning the very buttons he'd just fastened.

Before dawn, the two weary lovers headed back toward the Chateau. Surprisingly enough, the drawbridge was still lowered; Philip had thought they would have to wait until morning when it was sure to be in place above the moat, but it seemed there had been no need to have waited at all. Someone must have forgotten to lift it from late the night before. Odd, Philip thought. As far as he knew, that had never happened before.

23

The day of the knighting arrived. Once Philip returned, final preparations had been made, and now nothing was lacking. Fine white clothes of pure silk had already been stitched for each of the knight-aspirants, while the blacksmith and his attendants had hammered out shimmering swords, glistening helmets and double-woven mail shirts to protect the armed knights in battle.

The excitement of the day gave the knight-aspirants great energy, despite the fact they had spent the previous night in the chapel, purifying their souls before God. In the morning, a bath was prepared for each of them, to cleanse their bodies as their souls had been cleansed. Afterward, they dressed in the colors of their sponsor, not yet ready to don the white clothes for the ceremony. After a full, early meal, the entire company of knights, aspirants, lords, ladies and guests, moved to the courtyard for the ceremony to begin.

Alix stood beside her mother. Julian, along with other knights who would be sponsoring their squires into knighthood, stood in a long row beneath bright red banners and flags that waved in the wind. They awaited the knight-aspirants who were in nearby tents at last dressing in their fine new clothes. Though Alix looked eagerly for Philip, he was nowhere to be seen.

Not that Alix was surprised; it was assumed by all present that since Philip no longer wore his own sword, he would not approve of others wearing one. But, foolishly, Alix hoped he would attend the ceremonies anyway.

Trumpets blared, and every eye turned toward the tents especially erected beside the training yard. The aspirants emerged, dressed entirely in white; even their robes of soft ermine or miniver were like pure virgin snow. Each looked resplendent and proud as they headed toward the dubbing ceremony welcoming them into nobility.

A huge red carpet had been spread over the ground on which the knights, and now the aspirants, stood. Young squires came forward to take the robes from those to be knighted, and to help them don mail shirts, helmets; and finally, after the aspirants kissed the hilt, a sword was girt at their side.

Then, one by one, the knights were administered the Colee, an open-handed buffet to the side of the head, along with admonition of bravery and holiness, and boldness in the face of enemies.

Though Alix could not hear all of the knights as they spoke, she had attended enough of these ceremonies to guess the content of their vows. But she was remembering a ceremony long ago; she'd been a child then, no more than six years old. One knight-aspirant, though he was only fourteen, stood out from the rest. He was tall for his age and handsome, and held his sword as if he'd been born with it. His blue eyes shone with the pride of that day, and she'd clearly heard his claim, "So shall I be brave and upright, with God's help!" just before his father had dubbed him. And, from that day, he'd been a knight—until two years ago, she thought with a strange mixture of gladness, respect, and a bit of remorse.

It was silly to even think about that now, she told herself. In truth, she was happy Philip wore no sword. It meant she would not have to share him with battles and wars, or worry each time he left the Chateau that someone's sword might be the death of him. And it wasn't only that. Though Philip had never told her all the circumstances which led him to renounce the sword, she did know him well enough to believe his decision was noble.

"May I accompany you to the games, Demoiselle?"

Alix started, for she had been far away in her thoughts and even the cheering voices around her had not stirred her from her reverie. But Julian had touched her arm, and she could not help but be brought back to the present.

"The games." He motioned toward the training yard. "They're about to begin."

With silent consent, she followed Julian to the platforms set up around the yard. As she took a seat, she tried not to think of Philip. It was impossible to truly enjoy a festival her beloved might not approve of. She wanted to go to him, to show Philip that, while part of her did not fully understand his decision against the sword, she at least respected him. If she were already his wife, wouldn't her place be at his side?

The new knights galloped about on the chargers they'd just been given. Quintains were set up for the knights to show off their prowess with the lance, and later, there would be mock fights between individual knights. The training yard was decorated with banners of the de Saines dragon; that, coupled with the knights in their fine clothes, some of them with festive plumes attached to their helmets, made it truly look like a glorious day.

"I've learned already you do not enjoy large feasts," Julian said, eyeing her closely. "Does that include ceremonies like this?"

Alix brushed away a stray strand of hair the wind had blown out of place. She sent Julian a half smile. "Just because I am quiet does not mean I don't enjoy myself."

"It seems to me you're quiet a great deal of the time when in my company, Demoiselle Alix. With me, your betrothed."

Her gaze shot to his. There was something in his tone, the way he'd called himself her betrothed, as if he needed to remind her of the fact. But when he returned her gaze, there was no hint of the sensuality he'd aimed her way so often before. Just a rather cold, detached look that bewildered her. He didn't seem angry, yet, somehow, he seemed very different.

"They look pristine and pure, don't they?" Julian said as he watched the knights, his tone the same as before, confident and steady, as if she might find a deeper meaning behind his words. "Like brides to knighthood, in a way. Since they have not yet drawn blood, they are like virgins."

Once again, Alix stole a glance his way. Such strange words!

"But of course they will not have the witnesses we shall have on our wedding night," Julian went on. "When they perform the rite of knighthood, they shall be in battle, with every knight too busy looking to his own sword to see the blood others may draw."

Alix watched the knights in the yard, feeling an

uncomfortable twinge at the base of her neck at Julian's mention of the witnesses they would have of their consummation. She told herself that night would never come, that it would be Philip with whom she would share a wedding night, but nonetheless Julian's manner was extremely hard to tolerate. He was so quietly confident, as if he knew his words were affecting her and chose to speak in this way regardless of her unease.

"Your comparison is a very . . . unusual one," she said.

"But effective, don't you agree?"

Alix did not agree; she was silent. She wondered if she could leave without causing any concern, thinking she would much prefer finding Philip than staying here at Julian's side.

But she would not have had to look far, for she noticed Constance, seated upon the bench before her, looking avidly in a direction opposite the knights in the yard. Following her gaze, Alix saw Philip as he approached from the keep. He paused at the side fence of the training yard, watching the knights for a few moments. Then, seeing Alix was seated near his parents, he made his way toward them.

He greeted his mother and father, nodded almost imperceptibly toward Julian, then smiled cordially at Alix. She smiled back, wondering if she looked as cool and detached as he. Couldn't anyone see, she wondered, that her heart trembled at the mere sight of him? She had seen so clearly the obvious infatuation Constance had for Philip. Was she as transparent as Constance?

"I am surprised to see you, brother," Julian said as Philip took a seat. His words reflected Alix's thoughts. "I thought you disapproved of knights and their ways."

Philip only smiled. "I am not such a dreamer, Julian, to believe France is ready to go on without knights."

Julian was plainly amazed at his older brother's words. "But the very fact you hold no sword—"

"Means I no longer wish to add blood to my

297

hands," Philip finished. "And though I may wish others would tire of killing, as I have, it does not mean I expect it."

"You have a very high-minded son, Sire," said Sir Oliver, who stood behind Geoffrey. But his tone and the stare he sent Philip's way belied the compliment of his words.

But Philip hardly cared what Sir Oliver thought of him; Philip's gaze stayed upon Julian, for he still looked surprised by Philip's words. "You have never looked beyond your own scorn of me to see that I do not hold scorn for those who still wear the sword." He might have gone on, saying it was only himself he had scorned for all the killing he'd done as a knight, but thought he had said enough. It seemed, for the first time, Julian had actually listened to what Philip had to say, and he did not want to press him to listen to too much.

Alix was not much less surprised than Julian at Philip's words. Since their argument before he left for Bayeux, they had hardly discussed his refusal to wear a sword; it was as if Philip feared Alix truly did not understand. And perhaps she didn't, remembering the remorse she felt with thoughts of the beginning of his knighthood so long ago. Though she felt no scorn toward Philip, as his brother and father—and even her father—so obviously did, perhaps she was guilty of something else. Of ignoring, and in a way denying—at least to herself—Philip's decision not to wear a sword. Yet she respected that decision, she told herself. She loved Philip, every aspect of him, and that included his decision to give up the sword.

The day passed quickly for the entire Chateau. Alix, Philip noted, spent much of her time with her mother, leaving Julian to watch the festivities with his men-at-arms. And when nightfall came and the last of the games were played under the light of several lamps, Philip watched Alix bid good-night to those around.

She kissed her father and Sire Geoffrey, then stood before Julian and offered him her hand. He kissed her fingertips but, strangely enough, glanced Philip's way before doing so. Then Alix, Lady Marie, and Philip's mother disappeared beyond the shadows of the keep.

Philip stayed outdoors with his father, brother and several of the men-at-arms. He had no wish to return to his lonely tower, and had every intention of watching Hugh, Alix's old sentry. If Hugh continued to drink as much as he had throughout the day, it would take nothing short of the crumbling walls of the Chateau to wake him . . . and though Philip was growing tired of this sneaking about to be alone with Alix and longed for the day they would be man and wife, the ache in his loins was too strong a drive for his pride to ignore.

But there was one more reason, other than watching Sir Hugh, that Philip chose to remain outdoors with his father. He had not yet told Geoffrey of his plan to petition the king to hear the Montforts' case for ennoblement. And though he did not anticipate hearty approval, he knew he must make his intentions known.

The subject of the Montforts was a popular one, for just the day before, the men had returned who had been sent to learn of the numbers of Montforts had at their disposal. Today's knighting had been a boost, for the Montforts had a huge army of mercenaries at hand—more than even Sir Oliver had imagined. But with the added number of de Saines knights, plus the peasant foot soldiers Geoffrey could attract from his villages, the de Saines still had the advantage.

Philip and Sire Geoffrey sat comparatively alone, for Julian, who by now was somewhat drunk, was with the other men-at-arms in the training yard. They caroused with the game weapons, swords and lances which had been dulled so as to be harmless for Tourneys and knightings like today's.

"I will be leaving the Chateau again, Father," Philip said, and Geoffrey's gaze shifted from those in the yard to Philip at his side. "I plan traveling to Tours before weekend."

"Tours? Isn't that where the king is?"

Philip nodded. "I intend seeing him about this problem with the Montforts."

Geoffrey's brows raised. "What does he care about the Montforts? He has his hands full with true nobles disgusted with his reign, without adding the Montforts to his troubles."

It was true, ever since Jean had had Comte d'Eu, Constable of France, executed for supposed treachery, the sometimes vindictive King had grown exceedingly unpopular with many nobles. And with the Montforts living so far from the king's rule on the westernmost coast of Brittany, they had been easily overlooked for some time now. But Philip intended to change that.

"It is my belief that if I could return with a petition from Jean recognizing Henri Montfort as Lord of his estate, this unrest in our county would cease."

Geoffrey frowned at his son in evident, and quite expected, disapproval. "What deed has Henri Montfort done to warrant becoming Lord of an estate he simply usurped?"

"He has upheld the estate in as much—greater—splendor than the Villon family before him. Why shouldn't the king recognize him? It is why the Montforts fight so hard today—to be recognized for their power. If they no longer have need to prove this through might, the unrest would end."

"And you would go to Tours—on behalf of the Montforts?" His father was plainly aghast.

Philip nodded. "Yes, Father. I think it necessary to save our County from this continued threat."

Geoffrey continued to frown. "If the Montforts wish to renew their plea for ennoblement, let them do it on their own."

"I doubt they could even get to see Jean, let alone make him listen to their plea. At least there, I could help."

Geoffrey waved a hand in disgust aimed at his son. "I'll not stop you, but I wish you no luck in this venture of yours. The Montforts have done nothing to warrant the help of a de Saines."

Philip stood. "I will leave on Friday."

Then, seeing Hugh fast asleep beneath a huge tree in the corner of the training yard, undoubtedly the victim of too much wine, Philip realized Alix's chamber guard would hardly stand between them this night. Philip soon left his father and headed toward the keep. Friday, he thought, would come all too soon; leaving Alix behind once more would not be any easier this time.

24

Philip barely knocked at Alix's door before it was opened to him. And upon seeing each other, they embraced before the door was even closed behind him.

The room was dimly lit by a pair of candles, one beside the bed, the other at Alix's dressing table. Philip could see her clearly as she smiled that seductive smile she saved, he knew, only for him.

"I sent Blanche away for the night," Alix told Philip. "Where is Hugh?"

"Deep in a wine-sleep outside."

"Then no one will disturb us," Alix said, still smiling.

But Philip resisted her kiss. "Didn't you say your mother often comes here to see you?"

"She is abed," Alix assured him.

However, instead of taking her back into his arms, Philip led her to the chair before her dressing table. He sat upon the chest beside it, still holding her hand, but obviously attempting to cool the passion that was so strong between them.

"I came to talk to you."

"Talk?" Alix repeated. Then she laughed at her own surprised reaction. "I'm sure you must think I'm shameless, to be so quick to bring you to my bed."

He smiled crookedly. "That, Demoiselle, is one of the reasons I love you so much." He leaned closer and kissed her briefly, then sat back, letting go her hand, as if even such innocent contact as hand-holding could lead to passion he could not control. "I leave on Friday for Tours," he said. "And when I return, no matter what the outcome—whether I am successful or otherwise—I intend speaking to your father about our betrothal."

Alix could not contain her happiness. She left her seat, which suddenly seemed too far from him, to sit upon his lap. She put her arms about his neck, and caressed his cheek with one gentle touch. "This time when you leave the Chateau, I shall send you off properly," she promised. "And there will be no doubt in your mind just how much I shall miss you."

"And I'll miss you," he said, kissing the fingertips caressing him. "But it's necessary that I go, you know that. If I am able to do something about this feud, your father will be more receptive to what I have to say. Once our intentions are known, I doubt your father will force you to marry Julian."

"No, I do not believe he would do that," Alix said slowly. "And if he did, I would petition the King for divorce because the wedding would be against my wishes."

"Your father knows that is within your rights," Philip reminded her. "There would be little point in forcing you to wed anyone you did not wish to wed."

"There is the possibility my father wouldn't believe the King would grant a divorce—especially from a de Saines, even if he is the second son, not the firstborn."

"There is no reason for such worries, Alix!" Philip assured her. "We'll be married by midsummer."

But Alix had not told Philip of her greatest fear. Though she did not wish to worry Philip unnecessarily, she could not stifle the thought that bothered her most. "My father would not force me to wed, perhaps, but he might do something else."

Philip did not looked concerned. "What else could he do?"

"Force me into a nunnery; you know that is within his power—he has always had close connections to the Church, with my uncle being a bishop. And how would I escape such a fate, if that is what he decides to do?"

Philip shushed her worries, and kissed away her frown. "He couldn't do that without opposition from every front—even my own father wouldn't approve of that. Anyone who knows you would hardly think you would be happy cloistered away."

Alix was eager to believe him. "You will be successful in ending this feud with the Montforts, and that will be enough for my father to know you are a fitting husband for any woman, despite your lack of a sword."

She hadn't meant for the tactless words to slip out, to refer to Philip's decision to put down the sword as anything shameful, and immediately she looked at him with slightly widened eyes.

Philip hesitated before responding. "Alix," he began slowly. "Your words did not offend me. It is fact that I do not wear a sword, so to say it can hardly be wrong. I have accepted giving up the sword as the right decision for me; have you? Can you?"

"Yes, Philip!" she said quickly—too quickly? But what else could she say? She loved him!

She bent her head and kissed him then, trying to wipe away the frown forming at his brow. That he was not entirely convinced was obvious, and she had only one way to prove her true love for him.

"We have talked enough," she whispered into his ear. "If you intend leaving for Tours in just two days' time, I intend showing you now all the ways I shall miss you."

Friday came all too quickly. The entire Chateau knew of Philip's mission and the reason for it, and while many did not approve, there were several men-at-arms hoping to accompany him. A chance

303

to meet the King, even with only a remote possibility of gaining his attention, was more than enough reason for an ambitious knight to make the journey with Philip. Philip chose four knights to accompany him, along with their pages.

Once again, Alix watched from her window as preparations for Philip's departure were made. He would be gone longer this time, perhaps as long as a month, and as each bundle was added to the packhorses, Alix's spirits grew heavier. How she wished she could accompany him, she thought. But she comforted herself with one promise: this would be the last journey Philip would make without her. Upon his return, their love would be known to all, and she could travel with him wherever he went forever after.

It was early morning and she knew there would be few people in the hall. But Alix didn't care; she had no intention of letting Philip leave without seeing him once more. Alix had not been alone with Philip since mid-week, the night Hugh had been so drunk. Since then, Hugh had been a most vigilant watchdog, perhaps feeling guilty over leaving her unprotected for one night. Alix had no doubt this single-mindedness would pass, but certainly not soon enough. After Philip left, there would be no need to sneak out of her room.

Only those accompanying Philip were in the hall when she arrived. Sir August-Caron was there, a young knight who was never without a smile. When he saw Alix, he approached her with a courteous bow.

"May I be of assistance to you, Demoiselle? You look quite serious for so early in the morning."

"No . . . I often take a ride at this hour; I find I cannot sleep past dawn."

August-Caron laughed. "I have been on campaign with Sir Julian, Demoiselle. And I will tell you a secret about his habits that might help you in your coming marriage: he detests morning! So move softly when leaving for your ride once you are wed—your husband-to-be is like the dragon of his name if awakened."

Alix smiled, at the same time thinking she was glad she would have no need of such advice once Philip returned from this journey. Nonetheless, she was warmed by Sir August-Carson's friendly advice. "Thank you, Sir August. I shall remember your warning."

Just then, over Sir August-Caron's shoulder, Alix saw Philip enter the hall from outside. Though it was barely light outside, the hall was lit by many torches along the walls, and Alix could clearly see the smile Philip greeted her with when he first saw her.

"Demoiselle," he said politely, then nodded in the young knight's direction. August-Caron bowed, then left to join the other knights who waited to depart.

Though they could not touch, even briefly, for it would have been improper and also much too difficult to break away, the silent message that passed between them with one mere glance said enough.

"You will be in my thoughts every moment," Alix whispered, her gaze spellbound by his.

"This will be the last good-bye."

"I shall hold you to that promise, Philip," she told him.

"It will be an easy one to keep. I do not intend leaving you again."

Then she said, "When you reach the last rise outside the Chateau, turn round and look at the battlement. I'll be there, watching you."

He nodded, then they both knew he must go. To prolong their farewells would no doubt have been viewed as odd by the others; the fact that Alix had arrived so opportunely for her morning ride was already pushing coincidence. Besides, a longer good-bye would only make the moment of separation that much harder to bear.

She followed them outside, but said no more to Philip. She headed toward the stables, because that was expected, but once the departing group was beyond the portcullis she hurried beyond the stables, going to the narrow stone stairway leading to the high wall. From between the battlements she peeked, and, exactly as anticipated, she waved at Philip when they could see each other best, once he approached the last, highest rise just outside the Chateau. He did not wave in return, and she knew it was because he did not wish to call attention to their secret farewell. But assurance that this was indeed their last good-bye made this parting somewhat easier to endure.

As the days passed, Alix's promise that Philip would always be in her thoughts did indeed come true. She went about her activities as usual, beginning with Morning Mass, then the first meal of the day, followed by embroidery or stitchery or other such domestic functions with her mother and other ladies of the Chateau. But always her mind went to Philip, and she failed to uphold her end of various conversations more than once.

By the end of the first week, Alix noticed something very unusual. Because her thoughts had been elsewhere, she hardly noticed Julian had paid her scant attention of late. She did not miss his company but, when her mother mentioned that Alix seemed to have no need of her to ward off her betrothed's company, as Marie had the last time Philip was away, Alix realized Julian had barely said more than a dozen words to her all week. They still shared their meals, though on several occasions Julian had sent his page, begging Julian's excuses, and Alix had supped alone. And while Alix was relieved not to have to avoid his company, she could not deny she was puzzled by his behavior. He'd been so persistent—up until recently! What had changed him?

She had no intention of questioning him, however, for she was only too glad he'd obviously lost whatever interest he might once have had in her. It would make their broken betrothal just that much easier; he hardly behaved like a betrothed any more.

It was late at night; after taking her supper alone in her chamber, Alix had spent much of the evening in the garden, then slipped past the snoring Hugh and followed the stairway back to her chamber. Because Julian had been such a stranger lately, her life had gone back to much the way it had been before either of the de Saines brothers had returned—except for one difference. She missed Philip so terribly she felt lonelier than she ever had before knowing him. What a fate, she thought to herself, having found such happiness only to have that very happiness also teach her what true loneliness was.

She brushed her hair, then slipped out of her clothes. It was a warm night, so she did not bother to keep on her chemise. Naked, she lay on the bed, covering herself with only the thinnest coverlet. She was quite drowsy, and she knew sleep would not be long in coming.

Just then, she heard the footfall of someone outside her door. Perhaps she had awakened Hugh after all, she thought sluggishly, and waited for the steps to pass. But for a long moment she heard nothing at all, and wondered if she might have imagined the footsteps. Snuggling against the softly scented mattress, she dismissed the sounds as her imagination.

No sooner had she relaxed than the door swung open and the light of the hall torch spilled into the room. One tall shadow, much taller than Hugh, was formidably outlined. For a brief, sleepy moment she thought it was Philip; then, realizing such a hope was impossible, she sat up stiff and straight, clutching the suddenly much-too-thin coverlet around her.

The darkly clad figure staggered into the room with amazing quiet for so unsteady a stride. For a moment he simply stood there, unaccustomed to the dimness of the room—long enough for Alix to reach for her discarded chemise and hurriedly slip it over her head. But the movement, or perhaps the light fabric of the garment, caught his eye. He tottered to the edge of her bed, where he unmistakably swayed. The light from the hall shone on Julian's countenance, and Alix had seen enough to know he was drunk beyond control.

"Get out of here," she told him calmly, feeling more confident now that she had at least a meager covering over her body. Besides, Julian was obviously so drunk he would be unable to put up much resistance.

But instead of obeying, Julian sank to the bed, sitting so near her she could smell the wine on his breath.

"I want you," he told her, his words slurred but the meaning too horribly clear. "Not because you're beautiful . . . even though you are . . . not because everybody in this chateau thinks you'll be my wife one day . . . I want you," he repeated, trying carefully to enunciate properly, "because *he's* had you."

Slowly, Alix slid away from him. Her heart pounded with the realization that somehow her relationship with Philip had been revealed. That certainly accounted for Julian's behavior during the week. But her present worry was not what she could do about this revelation; she needed to find a way to get Julian out of her room. Yet, how would she do that without having him tell the whole Chateau what he knew? In his present condition, subtlety was beyond him.

"Julian," she said, her voice hushed, almost friendly, "I'm going to put on a bedrobe and help you to your chamber—or at least as far as the hall. You can find a pallet there to sleep on for the night."

But Julian shook his head, his droopy eyelids widening ever so slightly. "I'm sleeping here. With you."

Alix ignored his words. She found a flint and candle, and lit the wick. She hadn't used a bedrobe for quite some time, and needed the light to search through the clothes in the chest near her dressing table. Her mistake was in turning her back on her midnight visitor.

Quicker than Alix would have thought possible, Julian came up behind her, grabbing her round the waist with one arm. With his free hand, he touched her face as she turned to him—his fingers brushed her gently, as if he were almost afraid he might hurt her.

"It isn't as if you're a virgin," he whispered. "And it isn't as if you haven't already had a man without the blessing of the Church."

Alix pushed him away, angrier than she should have allowed herself to be. But the truth of his statements made her forget Julian hardly knew what he was saying.

"Leave here, Julian, before I call Hugh."

That made Julian laugh. "That old man couldn't even throw *you* out of a room." But when he finished that statement, his eyes skimmed her, seeing through the skimpy garment. He still held her with both hands now at her waist, and his thumbs began to move suggestively, in a rhythmic motion up and down her hipbones. "I can bring you pleasure, Dem'selle. Just as much as Philip. I was only thirteen when he took me to my first woman. And before I had her, Philip gave me a bit of advice I follow to this day: let the woman pitch first. The sword I carry to battle isn't the only shaft my brother taught me how to use."

Alix, amazed and appalled at the blatantly coarse words Julian flung at her, was still for the barest moment. Then she pushed hard at his chest, and perhaps because he wasn't prepared for the sudden assault, he fell back, almost losing his footing. But he remained standing, and when she headed toward the door, he caught her wrist.

"Are you miserly with your favors, Alix? Or is it just me you don't like?"

She slapped him then, and felt no remorse even as she heard the loud sting and saw the imprint of her fingers several moments after withdrawing. Julian, however, hardly seemed to feel the pain. He just grinned at her, swayed once and regained balance, then stood straight.

"I don't know who you think I've bedded with," she lied, thinking total denial was the only way out, "but you're mistaken. Now leave here or I will scream for Hugh—and tell him to bring help, if necessary."

"You're lying about not bedding with Philip," Julian said, ignoring her threats. He dropped her wrist, turning away but without heading toward the door. Instead, he walked to the chair at her dressing table and sat down. "I knew when he found us that day—and beat me nearly to death—that he cared for you. It wasn't only that he thought I was molesting you; for that he would have booted me back to the Chateau and that would have been the end of it. But because it was you...he nearly killed me. That's when I guessed." He gave a short laugh. "Do you know how many beatings I've taken for that cowardly brother of mine?"

"He is no coward," Alix said.

Julian shrugged. "He didn't used to be. But now he won't fight...that's what everyone calls him. A coward. I hated him for that. For teaching me how to be the best knight, and then by his actions telling me it's wrong somehow."

"He never said it was wrong for anyone else to be a knight—he never said it was wrong for you to be a knight." Alix spoke gently, forgetting, for the moment, that her main concern was to get Julian out of her room, not continue a conversation with him.

"So he said," Julian admitted, "that day at the knighting."

Alix stepped closer. "Julian, please go. You came here tonight to hurt Philip, not me. Because you're still angry he won't fight. That's why you wanted me—to get back at Philip because you think it might hurt him. Isn't it?" It was hardly a question; they both knew her words were true.

Julian stood, but the fact that he was still very drunk was obvious. He looked at her again, from head to foot, his gaze lingering here and there. He grinned. "But you are a beautiful woman, Alix. I could want you for other reasons, too."

"Go, Julian," she told him firmly.

And he did, to Alix's great relief.

25

All the pomp and splendor of the King's high court followed Jean to Tours, from the leading nobles and their families to administrative councilmen of various ranks. The King was there seeing to business with the French mint, located in the center of Tours. Because funds of the royal treasury were low after years of the plague, it was King Jean's idea to simply recall the coins already minted and produce more coins with less actual gold and silver content, thereby replenishing his diminished supply with the surplus squeezed out of the recalled gold. The fact that the new coins were worth less did not seem to concern the King whatsoever.

The city was bustling with activity when Philip arrived. It was a populous, wealthy city, and an important one to King Jean for the revenue brought in from tolls on the bridge over the Loire which connected northern and southern France. It was also a pilgrim's city, for many still journeyed from far reaches to visit the shrine of St. Martin, where miracles were purported to have happened. If all else failed, Philip thought wryly, perhaps he would pay a visit to the shrine himself. It might just take a miracle to free Alix from the betrothal her family was so happy with.

Philip had sent a page ahead to inform the King of his coming, knowing there was always room at Jean's court for another nobleman. Philip's relationship to the King was odd, even Philip himself thought so. Because Jean had been trained more like a knight than a king, Philip had once believed

Jean would uphold the charge of treason called against Philip when he laid down his sword. But the King had not. Jean, always honorable, had been one of the few to respect Philip's decision. Perhaps some part of this King, though known to be eager for battle, realized the hope of his country was not in bloodshed. In any case, he still held Philip in affection even after Philip gave up the sword.

Philip and the knights he traveled with arrived in Tours at late morning, after several days of travel. As he approached the huge Chateau owned by the King, Philip could not deny the doubts that had nagged at him since the inception of his idea to petition Jean on the Montforts' behalf. No doubt it was the King's Grand Council the Montforts had petitioned for ennoblement last year; that was where they had been turned down. Perhaps those noblemen sitting on the council at the time of the Montforts' petition had not favored the *nouveaux riches*; many nobles did not, Philip knew that. The fact that any man, regardless of his heritage, could buy his way into their aristocratic status had been a contention with many nobles since it was first practiced.

It was Philip's idea to carry the Montforts' wishes directly to the King's ears; perhaps, if Jean learned of the strife in the land, he would call Henri Montfort to his Court to hear his petition. That alone should be enough to appease the Montforts, having gained the King's attention. Why else did they stir trouble in Brittany, except to win the notice of the nobles and, ultimately, the attention of the King himself? But coupled with the fact that a de Saines had made possible this meeting would, in Philip's opinion, settle the Montforts' wish for bloodshed. Whatever happened, Philip thought, he knew he must at least try to end this feud in his county. And seeing the King appeared to be the wisest choice.

But during his first hours in Tours, Philip did nothing more than settle himself and his knights at the royal Chateau. He had little hope he would be summoned to the King immediately, and so did not wait for any quick reply to his message requesting an audience with the King.

Late that afternoon Philip and his companions made their way to the great hall of the chateau. Crossed swords, shields, banners of every color graced the stone walls. The high ceiling was supported by thick oak beams, darkened with age and the grime from many fires in the center fire pit. There was only one window in the entire room, just behind the platform at the opposite end from the entry. The towering glass was stained with rich blues and greens, reds and gold, in the image of the city's patron saint, Martin.

The King sat in the rainbow light shining through his window from the setting sun. Jean was dressed splendidly, as always, in brocade doublet, dark chausses and leather boots. He looked merry, as always, as he was entertained by brightly dressed tumblers performing in the center of the room. A lavish meal was in the process of being served, and though Jean noted Philip's arrival with a friendly wave, Philip had no further chance to speak to him.

It might have been easy, once, for Philip to be caught up in court life. Hadn't he been, when serving on the King's council two years ago? He knew many of those who had accompanied the King to Tours and was approached by several acquaintances, both men and women alike. If they remembered the scandal Philip had been involved in—and certainly they did—they made no mention of it before him.

But by the end of the evening Philip was already tired of court life. He had left behind a chateau almost as crowded as this one—and it was only Alix's company he had enjoyed most. He was tired of the conversations that had double meanings, both for power and pleasure, tired of the over-indulgence of nobility with their food and wine; he wanted to attend to his business and return home.

The second day in Tours he went to the city markets, looking for some trinket to bring back to

Alix. He settled on a brooch, in its center an emerald which reminded him of her eyes. By the time he returned to the King's Chateau, the evening meal was in full din; there would be no summons from the King this day.

It was an entire week before Philip received an answer to his request to see the King alone. Philip was aware he was the only one of his traveling companions eager to be about the business at hand, for it was plain to see the knights enjoying themselves between the luxuries of the King's court and the many damsels who graced his tables. August-Caron already wore the favor of one lady's color upon his sleeve, a delicate lace kerchief which proved she'd chosen August-Caron as her champion—at least while he stayed in Tours. Philip knew, the longer he and his knights stayed at court, the harder it would be for his companions to leave.

So it was with a great deal of relief that Philip was asked to join the King in his inner chambers, set in the very center of the Chateau, it being the most easily defensible spot in this city fortress.

Philip was brought to the chambers by a young page. When Philip passed through the guarded doors, he found the King alone, seated before a chess table.

Jean greeted Philip with a broad smile.

"I've missed your game, Philip," Jean said, beckoning him closer with a wave of his hand. "Sit down."

Philip did as he was bid, pleased he would have the King's company for the long length of a game, yet slightly dissatisfied their attention would obviously be split between the strategies of chess and the business he wished to discuss.

"I did not expect to find you in Tours," Jean said.

"It was I, Sire, who found you in Tours," Philip explained as they adjusted the gamepieces to their satisfaction. "I sought you out on purpose."

"And not for a game of chess, I wager," Jean replied, looking at Philip rather than the gameboard between them. "You've a very serious face when you want, Philip. When you served on my council I knew if I watched that face of yours I would hardly have to listen to the boring rhetoric of others; if your face looked as it does now, I knew the matter should be attended to. What has made you seek an audience with me? Anything to do with Charles?"

"No, Sire," Philip said. "I am hopeful that all involved in that tale will think it best forgotten."

"There will be other tales to take its place," Jean said. Then the King paused, continuing to eye Philip. "I thought perhaps you came here to ask me to set up a Tourney in which you might confront Charles."

"As you can see, Sire, I still wear no sword."

"No guests do, in my chambers," Jean laughed. "Except my guards." Then, more seriously, he said, "In truth, Philip, I would have been very surprised if you had come here asking for a match with Charles. I know why you do not wish to fight him; I remember when you were friends. And it is noble of you to suffer the stories—for it's you, my friend, who have been called the worst of the names, not this supposedly cuckolded husband."

"Charles has enough punishment being wed to Rachel," Philip said easily. "I would not wish to add more to his unhappiness."

Jean laughed out loud. "There are few men like you, Philip de Saines. Most would have forgotten any vow not to kill again and taken up the sword again posthaste. But not you—you are a man who does not easily change his mind. It is an asset, Philip—but it has worked against you this time."

"I shall survive the stories, Sire. And as you said, there will soon be another tale to replace the ones about myself."

"Now tell me what has brought you to Tours; it is a fair journey from Chateau de Saines."

"It is a local matter in my home county," he replied, glad they were getting to business at last; the chess game had been forgotten. "Do you recall the name Henri Montfort?" he asked.

Jean was thoughtful a moment, rubbing his chin absently. Then he shook his head. "Refresh me, Philip. Why should I recall such a name?"

"Henri Montfort petitioned you—or your Council—for ennoblement a year or so back; he has taken ownership of the Villon estate in western Brittany."

"By conquership?"

Philip shook his head. "The family died from the Plague; the Montforts simply took control of the estate when it lay empty. No one ever bothered to oust them, and now they've built up their own personal army so that few could cast them out even if it were attempted."

Jean held up a hand, saying, "Ah . . . I do remember now. The matter was brought to my attention. But surely they have not continued to be so successful? I expected them to return to their peasantry before I needed to reexamine that estate for the crown."

"They prosper," Philip assured him.

Jean cast him a puzzled frown. "Then they have earned money anew since they petitioned for ennoblement."

"Tales were spread you refused to grant any title because of their petition to Edward. It was said, if Edward won in a battle against France, the Montforts would side with Edward and he would grant them titleship."

Jean laughed lightly. "That would have been far more noble of me, I fear. In truth, Philip, at the time the Montforts petitioned me, the treasury was in sad need. That is why the Council brought this to me to begin with; they knew I would have welcomed selling a title for a hefty sum. And I would have sold the Montforts a title, regardless of their possible treason, if they'd been able to supply the one hundred thousand livres I asked."

"One hundred thousand . . ." Even Philip was amazed; it was indeed a hefty sum!

"More than usual, I admit," Jean said with a shrug, absently fingering one of the pawns before him. "But they did speak to Edward; for that, they must pay. And from what I recall of that estate, the sum would not have been insurmountable if they'd run it successfully."

"They must have that amount, Sire," Philip replied. "The army they support boasts of vast wealth. If they can afford such a legion, surely they could afford even a high price for ennoblement—if they wanted to gain the title legally."

Jean shrugged once more. "The price still stands at one hundred thousand livres. For that, I shall welcome the Montfort family, even at my Court."

Philip was thoughtful; this was news indeed. If the Montforts had the money, and it was their wish to be accepted as nobles, then why did they not just buy the title and be satisfied? Wasn't the reason for the strife they caused to gain the King's attention, to show all in the land they were as powerful as any noble and should be treated like one?

The fact that they had the opportunity to gain what they wanted in a peaceful manner started many questions in Philip's mind. And he meant to have answers. But for now, the King was eager for the chess game; Philip's plans would have to wait.

Sir August-Caron, for all of his merrymaking and evident frivolity, was nonetheless a cautious man. His ambitions ran deep, as well as his loyalties to both his lord and country. Therefore when he found himself falling in love with a woman who was not only far above his station but also one who had never, and would never in all likelihood live in Brittany, he found himself in a quandary. And the best thing to do, he decided, was to leave the lady's company.

But of course while she was within reach during the time of his stay at court, it was impossible to stay away from her. And though he wore her favor upon his sleeve, he knew it was just a sign of the many games being played at Court. Once August-Caron returned to Brittany, the widow Comtesse Genevieve le Jeune would no doubt allow her favor to be worn by another knight of her choosing. And he knew tarrying at her side would only instill her into his memory that much more deeply. His cautious nature warned him he was headed only for pain if he stayed much longer in her company.

Therefore when Philip requested to see him, August-Caron had mixed feelings. The cure to this malady Gen le Jeune had inflicted within him lay in escape; yet the very thought of leaving at Philip's command gave August-Caron an empty feeling of loss—even before his actual departure. Was there no answer, no way to avoid the pain?

August-Caron met Philip in an antechamber off the main hall, where the King's business was often discussed. Today, however, only Philip was there. August-Caron was surprised he alone had been summoned; he had expected Philip to inform all of the knights who had traveled with him of their imminent departure. The fact that only he had been called made his pulse race just a bit; had someone guessed his intentions toward Gen, that they were more serious than the usual chivalric games of court? Undoubtedly, for a landless knight to harbor any notions of wedding—or bedding—a woman so far above him would be more than frowned upon. But how had anyone guessed his thoughts? He'd done no more than kiss the lady's hand!

"You've been loyal in the de Saineses' service many years, August-Caron," Philip said, after preliminary greetings and both men had been seated comfortably. Each of them had a cup of wine before them.

"Yes, Sire," August-Caron replied. "Since my knighting, when I was a boy of fourteen."

"And how old are you now?"

"Twenty-nine."

"You are not married?"

August-Caron shook his head. Surely, with such odd questions, Philip had learned of his wayward thoughts about Gen! Why else would he ask of his marital status?

"Have you ever been?"

Again, August-Caron shook his head.

"What about family? Or bastard children?"

"None to my knowledge, Sire."

Philip paused, and took a long drink before going on. "I have a request to make to you then, Sir August-Caron. Not a command, but a request, for it may prove dangerous."

August-Caron's pulse stopped racing; his secret was safe. But he listened with interest, for serving his lord was his duty.

"I would like a man to go to the Montforts' chateau, establish himself there as if in their service. This man must prove to be a good liar, August-Caron, for he must fool the Montfort men that he is loyal to them. At least to the extent of finding out certain information."

"Sir Oliver has already sent men to find out the numbers of their army," August-Caron pointed out.

"Their numbers are obvious," Philip said. "And so, it would seem, is their wealth. It is that which I wish to learn more about. How is their Chateau run? So efficiently their revenue is great? Are their men paid lavishly? I need to know their financial state, August-Caron. And anything else you might happen to learn, of course. If they've been in contact with Edward of England. If their men are well-satisfied, and what they know about the Montfort family. Does Henri Montfort still wish to become recognized lord of the Villon estate? They have wrought havoc in our county, and I wish to know the true reasons—if not to prove their power in the land, that they should be ennobled, then why?"

"Then you wish for me to spy, Sire?"

"Exactly."

"And how would I send my information to you?"

"I do not care to risk many lives," Philip assured him. "Therefore I want you to gather what information you can, and when you have sufficient answers to certain questions—key ones being of the financial state of the Montforts—you may send

319

word through your page. After that, whatever other information you learn you may bring to me yourself. You should have no trouble deserting their army. Of course, you would never be able to return there, but if you do a good job of gaining information, there should be no need for you to go back. I am willing to put my faith in you that you could do this job. Are you?"

August-Caron stood and dramatically placed his right hand over his heart. "I am, Sire."

Philip stood as well, and extended his hand to clasp August-Caron's. "I wish for you to leave immediately; the King has asked me to stay on a few days more, after that the others and I shall return to the Chateau. You are to go directly to the Montforts."

"As you wish." He bowed, then left the room. Closing the door behind him, he realized he would not see Genevieve again, and that feeling of emptiness he feared rose with more strength than he anticipated. It was his duty, he reminded himself, to follow the wishes of his lord. And, he thought with a heavy heart, perhaps the fact that he would be leaving Court ahead of the others was a sign from God. Surely even God did not approve of the thoughts he'd carried of Gen. If only his heart would follow God's will!

26

The small council of men surrounding Sire Geoffrey dispersed just before noon. Geoffrey, with Giles Beauchamp at his side, had heard reports from each of his stewards and bailiffs. It was a more common sight ever since Philip had first begun rejuvenating the Chateau and organizing the men; these councilmen were eager to tell Geoffrey how well their work progressed.

Marie and Alix entered the hall and approached Giles, who left Sire Geoffrey's side to stand near one of the fire pits with a cup of wine in his hand. Sir Hugh, beside him, was drinking as well. Dinner would be served before long, and many of the Chateau guests were beginning to arrive in the hall.

"Alix, where is your betrothed?" Giles asked. His tone was gruff, and Alix knew her answer would not please him.

"I do not know," she told him truthfully.

"Madame," Giles said to his wife, "what do you know about the scant time those two spend together? I've hardly seen them together at all for the past weeks. Do you still allow Alix to stay at your side like some suckling child?"

Alix spoke before her mother had a chance. "I am always available to the visits of my betrothed, Father. But I have seen little of Sir Julian lately."

"What have you done to displease him? When your betrothal was first announced, he seemed happy enough. What has changed?"

"I do not know," Alix said, though secretly she had a very good idea. Somehow, Julian had learned of her relationship to Philip and had every right to be "displeased" with her.

"I shall see to it that you spend more time with him," Giles said with assurance. "You'll be wed soon enough; you should get to know one another. Geoffrey and I demand that all goes well with this betrothal, Alix. I will not have our family involved in another broken betrothal—it was enough of a scandal to have your brother involved in the mishap with Marguerite. I'll not stand for any more wagging tongues flapping about the wedding plans to come."

Alix exchanged a glance with her mother, but neither said a word. They'd been lucky to be spared much gossip about Simon and Marguerite; the couple had returned to Burgundy with the Marquis and so their absence had stilled many a wagging tongue. They would be wed in Burgundy,

Alix knew, and return to Brittany once the Beauchamp Estate was ready for them to live in.

Just then the trumpets sounded for the meal to begin, and they went to their places. Alix, ever since her betrothal was announced, sat in the seat near Julian's. He had missed more meals than he'd attended of late, and so she did not expect him today. However, before the cupbearers had even finished serving the wine, Julian arrived.

He bowed formally before Alix, but his gaze never reached her eyes. "Forgive me for being late, Demoiselle." Then he took his seat, and for the remainder of the meal not another word was exchanged.

But there was plenty of noise to fill their silence. Geoffrey, pleased by the good tidings his councilmen had brought that morning, was in high spirits. No one was more boisterous than him during that meal, and afterward, when dancing began, he led Eleanore to the center of the mosaic floor for a rare dance with the lady of the manor. With lord and lady so obviously enjoying themselves, it was easy for the rest of the Chateau to partake in this jubilance.

Even Julian cheered when his father swung Eleanore into an embrace before all, and kissed her soundly upon the lips.

"Soon they will be cheering for you and your bride."

Both Julian and Alix turned to see Lord Giles standing behind their chairs.

"Julian," Giles continued, looking at the younger man, "why not join your parents in this dance? Alix is a fair dancer."

Julian glanced at Alix, then back to Lord Giles before answering. "I'm sure she is. However, I must pass. I'm afraid I had too much wine yet again last night, and my head still pains me."

Giles hardly looked pleased, but accepted the answer. "It is plain to see you have enjoyed yourself since coming home, Julian. I'm sure having my daughter named to be your wife only adds to your spirit of celebration."

Julian said nothing, and an awkward silence followed. But Giles was undaunted. He leaned closer to the two seated side by side, and took one hand of each of them and bid them to stand. "Alix, you should see to the discomfort of your betrothed. The noise here cannot be welcome. Take him to the antechamber and bid him lie down until the ache passes. And stay at his side."

Like two children, they did as Lord Giles asked, though Alix was not pleased to do so and neither, she guessed, was Julian. He truly did look as though his head pained him, but she wondered if she, rather than too much drink, had been the cause.

Julian closed the door of the small antechamber. From within, the music could still be heard, but was muffled by the thick, tapestry-covered stone walls and heavy wooden door. There was a daybed along one wall, and two chairs near a table in the center of the room. Julian went to the daybed, sinking down as though relieved to be out of the crowded hall. Alix stood near the table, not relaxed enough to take one of the seats.

"Can I get you . . . anything? Water? A cool cloth for your head?"

Julian grinned up at her. "There is no need for you to play the concerned wife-to-be, Alix. At least without an audience."

"But I am concerned," Alix said.

At that Julian laughed. "As you would be over a sick lap dog, I'm sure."

Alix gazed at Julian, who was no longer looking her way. He leaned back on the heavily-padded daybed, covering his eyes with an arm over his face. But she was not willing to simply sit quietly while the farce of their betrothal continued.

"Julian, if you are so sure that I have no compassion for you, then why do you continue our betrothal? I have little reason to believe you have any kind thoughts toward me. If we are both unwilling to wed each other, then why should we continue letting our families think we will go through with it?"

At that Julian stood, approaching her slowly. He stopped before her, and he rested his hands on her shoulders with a smile that showed no warmth. "But we have every intention of going through with this wedding, Alix. Why should you think otherwise?"

Alix turned away, out of his reach. Over her shoulder, she said, "Because you avoid me at every chance of late; you barely speak to me when you are in my company. You do not like me, and I . . ."

Julian finished when Alix's voice dwindled away. "You do not like me, either." He neared her yet again, but did not touch her. "You are wrong, Alix. I do like you. You are a beautiful woman and will make a very fine wife. Didn't my father pick you out?"

"Yes, and he picked Marguerite for Philip. And that did not work out."

"Ah, Philip. So his name rises in this conversation after all. I did not think you would bring up his name."

"Why shouldn't I?"

He laughed. "I thought you might feel a bit of guilt in front of me. After all, you should come to my wedding bed pure, Alix. But my brother has seen to stealing that away from me."

"Philip stole nothing."

Julian laughed again, this time louder. "I've no doubt of that. You looked perfectly willing the night I saw you together. So do not deny the relationship you have with my brother, as you did the night I came to your chamber."

Alix looked down at her hands, folding her fingers together. "I did not think you remembered that night. You were quite drunk."

"Not drunk enough, it seems. I should have had my way with you then."

But Alix shook her head. "If you had tried, I would have made such a ruckus the whole Chateau would have come to my rescue."

"Which would only have sped our wedding day, to have your father find us alone in your chamber

324

together."

"If you think my father values my purity so much, perhaps all I need do is tell him about Philip and me, and he will speed to wed me to Philip rather than to you."

"I do not think so," Julian said. "My foolish brother has earned little respect from your father since he gave up the sword. And this business with Rachel has only made Giles detest Philip even more, despite his wealth. He knows, even though I am the second son, I shall have land ceded to me, and wealth to make any woman happy the rest of her days. Why should he want you to marry Philip, a man for whom he has no respect, when I am available—and quite willing—to wed you?"

"You don't even know me, Julian, so you cannot harbor any hidden feelings for me. You've had every opportunity to know me better in the last weeks since Philip has been gone, yet you've avoided me. So why is it you want to wed me?"

"As I said, you are beautiful. You come from a noble family."

Alix shook her head. "No, Julian. You want to wed me for the same reason you wanted to bed me a few weeks ago. Because it would hurt Philip." Julian said nothing so, very quietly, the dulled music from the hall almost making her words impossible to hear, she said, "You love him very much, don't you, Julian?"

That question riveted Julian's gaze to hers, but he laughed it off. "Love him? He's a fool. He didn't even defend himself in that scandal with Charles and Rachel. Your father is a wise man, Alix. He has no respect for Philip; neither do I."

"For someone to have the power to hurt you as Philip must have done can only mean you love him."

"He didn't hurt me—except to sully the name I share with him."

"Julian, you are a very stubborn man," Alix told him. "But your wish to marry me is not as great as my determination *not* to marry you. And I won't let you use me to retaliate against Philip for becoming your fallen idol."

"He was never my idol!"

Alix ignored his denial. "It doesn't matter what you say, Julian. I'll not marry you, no matter what your reasons are for wanting me."

"You wound me greatly with your rejection, Demoiselle," Julian said without a trace of sincerity in his tone.

"Then perhaps you would feel better if I left you alone; I'm sure even the noise of the hall would suit you better than discussing this any further."

"No, Demoiselle, I do not wish to return to the hall. What I wish for is some fresh air; but do not feel compelled to join me. If your father sees me leave alone, tell him I no longer desired your company. That is, after all, the truth."

Then he left the room, not bothering to close the door behind him. He knew he had to leave before another word was spoken. How he would have liked to strangle that lovely neck of hers! Calling Philip his idol!

The bright sun just outside the keep burned his eyes and for a moment he stood still in indecision. In truth, his head was beginning to pound—blast the woman. But even as he blamed Alix for the pain, he knew he, too, was responsible. It was hard to suppress the desire to pommel someone. And it wasn't Alix, but rather Philip, whom he wanted to punch. Fallen idol, indeed!

He went to the stables, deciding to ride alone rather than taking Hawk. He'd half a mind to take the predatory bird, but didn't want to take the time to go to the mews. Instead, he saddled Arab himself and within minutes was out of the Chateau gates.

Julian rode fast and hard, as if to battle, and part of him wished he was headed for a fight. He felt as though something was bottled up inside him, and only a good joust would set it free. He considered visiting Abigail, a merchant's daughter he'd seen several times since returning home, but decided against it. That wasn't the kind of passion he was feeling just then.

Fallen idol. Why did the words keep haunting him?

At last, after following the water's edge far downriver, he came to a halt. He let Arab drink at leisure, then, dismounting, he bent to his knees to the water swirling over some rocks to take refreshment for himself as well. Afterward, he sat back, watching the rushing river and trying to blot out all thought.

But it didn't work. He knew Alix was right; he *was* using her to hurt Philip. And if she got hurt in the bargain . . . well, innocents always suffered in war, and this was practically the same thing. It was the only kind of war he could fight with a man who wouldn't touch a sword.

Julian took the rein of his horse and started walking; he headed in the direction of the Chateau, although he had no intention of returning to the hall. He walked slowly, for even though it was a fair distance back, he was in no hurry.

After a while, he mounted once again, but let Arab take a slow pace. It was not much farther and he wasn't certain he wanted to face anyone just yet.

But as he took the rise of one of the many hills in the area, Julian spotted a group of riders headed in the same direction. For a moment he held back, mindful of the strife of the Montforts, until he could make an identification. It was a small traveling party, and they did not look heavily armed.

Julian recognized his brother's horse before Philip himself. Cedric was an Arab, like Julian's horse, and because their breed was highly valued, Julian spotted them easily even among many others of their species. Julian did not move forward, he simply watched, although as the party neared him, he knew he'd been spotted. And when Philip separated from the others with a wave telling them to go on, Julian had half decided to welcome Philip home the way Philip had welcomed him all those weeks ago. It would be good to land a fist hard against Philip's jaw. But when Philip halted his mount before Julian's, Julian remained still.

"It is good to see you, Julian," Philip greeted him. He did not smile, but he held his brother's gaze intensely.

"Was your mission successful?" Julian asked without salutation.

Philip shook his head. "But it was interesting. I learned the Montforts could have ennoblement at any time they wish, if they are willing to pay for it."

Julian gave a brief laugh. "Does that prove anything to you, dear brother? That the Montforts have bloodied our county for no good reason? There is only one way to settle this feud—and that is with the sword."

"No, Julian," Philip replied. "There must be another answer than adding to the blood that has already been spilled."

"Damn you! Won't you pick up your sword for any reason?"

Philip said nothing, but it was answer enough. Julian pulled the rein on Arab, turning away from the direction of the Chateau. He hadn't wanted to go back anyway.

27

"You should have accompanied Julian outside, Alix," Lord Giles said to his daughter.

"I was not invited."

"Invited!" Giles repeated. "If I had waited for an invitation to your mother's bed, my dear, you would not have been born."

Marie, seated at the table between Giles and Alix, laughed. "Giles, you know that isn't so. You've always been welcome in my bed."

"Not when we were first married," he reminded her. "You were so shy of me you slept in your underrobe for a week."

"It takes time to get to know one another, Giles. You must give Alix and Julian time as well."

"They've had time! It seems to me our daughter was eager enough to be alone with Julian's brother. I haven't forgotten that ride she shared with Philip after he'd only just arrived. So it isn't simple shyness of the male species that has Alix avoiding Julian's company."

"Father," Alix said, "hasn't it occurred to you that Julian might be avoiding *me*? I told you earlier—"

"Until you give me a good reason for his change in attitude, I will not believe this is Julian's doing. Unless you've realized what you've done to change his attitude toward you?"

Alix said nothing, looking down at her hands, folded in her lap.

Marie patted her husband's arm. "I'm sure you worry too much, Giles. Let Alix be."

The three settled back in their chairs to watch the pastime games and entertainment. Lord Geoffrey had invited a new poet to his hall who was about to give a recitation. In respect to the artist, the hall quieted.

Alix hardly listened to the flowery words the poet recited. Instead, she thought of what Julian had said to her earlier, that he had every intention of marrying her regardless of all the reasons not to. There would be enough opposition to her intentions to marry Philip without Julian adding to it! It would take fierce persuasion to change her father's mind.

But change it they must. How she longed for Philip's return; she knew when Philip came home he would not delay in making known their intentions to wed. And even if it would take time to change Lord Giles's mind, at least her love for Philip would no longer be a secret.

As if all she had to do was but wish for Philip's arrival home, he appeared at the hall entryway.

329

When Alix caught sight of the movement there, she sat up straight in her chair and felt her heart race. Philip! He *was* there, come home at last. Behind him were three of the knights who accompanied him, and they were all deferentially quiet until the poet finished his tale.

When the center of the hall was clear, Philip and his companions made their way across the room to Lord Geoffrey. Philip bowed respectfully in greeting.

"The King sends his salutations," Philip said as he straightened. But his gaze went to Alix after he spoke, seated down the table. Alix smiled, unable to hide her happiness at his return.

"Be seated, son," Geoffrey said to Philip, then called for a steward to bring food for Philip and the others. "We did not expect you until next week."

"The King granted me early audience," Philip replied.

As Philip and his knights were served, entertainment in the center of the room began again. Alix could barely hear the conversation between Philip and his father, but hardly cared. It was enough just to see him again.

"And what did Jean say about the Montforts?" Geoffrey asked. "Will he offer them ennoblement?"

Philip nodded. "For the right price."

"Then your mission was a success," Geoffrey said, though his voice hardly sounded as if he were proud of his son's possible achievement.

"The Montforts won't pay it," Philip stated bluntly.

"What! Isn't that what that family wants—to be one of us?"

"The sum Jean asked was one hundred thousand livres—it is possible they won't pay because the sum is an insult. Few people have ever paid more than twenty thousand."

Geoffrey laughed. "Jean is smarter than I have given him credit for. He wishes to make the Montforts pay for talking to the English, does he not?"

"Exactly. Which is of course understandable."

"The Montforts should be happy to even be considered for ennoblement under any circumstances—they should be happy Jean does not oust them from their estate."

"I confess," Philip admitted, "I do not understand why the Montforts have refused to pay."

"Then nothing has changed," spoke up Giles. "And the Montforts will continue to harry the land."

Philip said nothing; he could not deny that was true.

"It would appear, Sire," said Sir Oliver, who had come forward to listen to Philip's report, "that Lord Philip's mission was not a success, after all."

"It would appear so," Geoffrey conceded.

"Then might I suggest we go ahead with the plan I suggested weeks ago, after the d'Aussy land was attacked?"

Geoffrey frowned. "I do not like the idea of starting more bloodshed. We have heard nothing from the Montforts for several weeks now; perhaps they have had their fill of unrest as well."

"Sire—" Sir Oliver began.

But Geoffrey held up a hand. "The de Saineses have no outright cause to attack the Montforts. They've done nothing against us directly except call us a few names. I'll not attack unless commissioned by the King or in self-defense."

Oliver bowed. "As you wish." Then he turned on his heel and departed from the room.

Alix leaned forward, looking past those between her and Philip. He caught her eye, and smiled.

"Perhaps you might go and look for your betrothed," Lord Giles said to Alix quietly. Alix doubted anyone other than herself and her mother had heard his words. She knew he had seen the brief smile she exchanged with Philip and that was the reason she was being sent from the hall. But she didn't care if her father did suspect her feelings for Philip; it wouldn't be long before he knew the truth.

She stood, casting one last glance Philip's way, then left the hall. She was confident, once Philip saw that her direction was outside, it would not be long before he followed.

Alix found her way to the garden. She had no intention of seeking Julian; in all probability he was out with his hawks and she certainly had no wish to find him if that were the case.

Because there had been such progress in restoring the Chateau to its full beauty, the garden had, at last, succumbed to the scythe. But Alix was happy to see that, as spring progressed, the neatly trimmed bushes grew thick and offered almost as much privacy as before. Of course, now that the garden was no longer a jungle of unkempt weeds but had been transformed into neat rows of flowers, shrubs and fresh-smelling herbs, she was not the only one to frequent its center. Many of the ladies of the Chateau liked to bring their embroidery out under the sun; she herself had joined them several times with her own stitchery. It was pleasant, she had to admit, to be outside on sunny days rather than within the thick walls of the Chateau, so she could not blame the women for being glad the garden had finally been restored.

But today, because there were games in the hall, no one was in the garden despite the fair weather. No clinging boughs or branches touched her skirts as she found her way to the stone bench. The roses were just beginning to bloom, so colorful and fragrant, and the honeysuckle smelled as sweet as ever. A gentle breeze rustled the leaves, and she sat down, breathing deeply and turning her face upward toward the warm sun. She hadn't felt so happy since before Philip left. And soon, she thought with a leaping heart, he would come to her.

Alix did not have to wait long. When she heard the leaves rustle again but felt no breeze, she knew someone approached. Philip was walking the path, his height far above the neatly trimmed garden. In his hand, he held a rose that matched the small red dragon stitched on the cuffs of his black doublet.

"Demoiselle," he said, bowing formally as he handed her the flower.

Alix took it, put it to her lips and kissed it, and never once took her eyes from Philip. "I missed you."

He sat beside her. "And I you," he said. Then he smiled. "I've missed you at night, beside me. And at meals, seeing your smile. And I've missed talking to you."

She laughed at his recitation. "Remember your promise, Philip," she said, almost urgently. "We'll never be parted again."

He eyed her with love in his gaze. "I remember." Then, at last, as if mindful they might not be alone, he looked around. As he did, he said, "There have been changes since I left."

Alix nodded. "The garden could not be spared attention any longer," she said. "Your mother gave the command for the scythes to be taken to the garden, and before that day was over, the garden was . . . like this."

"It's as it was years ago," he said. "That should have made my mother happy. She must come here often."

"Yes; this is a very popular place now. We'll find no privacy here, as we did before."

They sat very close on the small stone bench, and though they exchanged such innocent talk, the contact between their bodies with their legs pressing against each other and their hands holding one another said far more. Alix's fingers rubbed against his palm; it felt cool and hard, the skin slightly rough from days clutching the rein of his horse. He must have stopped to bathe before arriving home, for he smelled of soap rather than saddle leather. He was cleanly shaven—and how she longed to touch his face. But she dared not; the garden was no longer their secret place.

There was much to tell him; of Julian and his knowledge of them, of her fears that Julian, as much as her father, would stand in their way. But she had no desire to speak of anything but Philip himself; she wanted to hold him, to feel his arms around her. It had been so long!

"Last time," she said, her tone slightly breathless from her wayward thoughts, "when you came home, I was able to welcome you as I wished. But now ... here ... in the daylight ..."

Philip clutched her hand tighter, daring to put his arm about her waist. "You tempt me, Alix! I am almost willing to take the risk of being discovered here with you."

Alix could not resist pulling him closer for the briefest moment. She kissed him, letting her fingers touch his face as she'd wanted to do before. Then she separated from him, knowing they were not yet free to do as they wished.

But Philip did not break contact. He put one finger below her chin, turning her face to his. "I intend speaking to your father tomorrow morning, Alix. My mission to the King was not as successful as I would have wished, but that can no longer matter. I do not intend waiting for everyone to know you will be my wife."

"Will you tell him how close we've become? That I gave myself to you?"

"Only if I have to," he said. "I hope to keep that between us."

Alix frowned. "My mother already knows ... and so does Julian."

Philip's brows lifted in surprise. "You told me your mother knew before ... but Julian? How did he find out?"

"He claims he saw us together. Perhaps on the night you returned from Bayeux; I do not know for certain."

Philip was thoughtful. "And he still intends to marry you, knowing you will come to his wedding bed after having given yourself freely to me?"

Alix nodded. "I think this knowledge only makes me a better prize," she said, somewhat bitterly. She knew she was merely a pawn in Julian's game against his brother, and the certainty of that hardly improved her hopes to clear all obstacles between herself and Philip.

"Do no worry over Julian," Philip told her. "He will not hold you to this betrothal, I promise you that."

Alix wanted to believe him, but doubts still nagged her. "He is resentful of you, Philip. To the point he nearly hates you."

"I did not live up to his expectations of me."

Alix hesitated before saying, "I do not know Julian well, but I believe his expectations might have been unreasonable. I think, when he was younger, he must have worshipped you as the perfect knight. Then, when you gave it up, his image of you crumbled."

Philip smiled slowly as he listened to Alix's words. Then he dropped a brief kiss on her lips. "You have a gift, Alix, of discerning the truth even if it is not obvious."

"But I fear it will take time for Julian to think of you as his brother rather than a fallen idol. More time than I am willing to give; my father would like to see me marry Julian at mid-summer."

"I will speak to Julian," Philip said. "Tonight."

"Tonight?" she repeated, then smiled, stroking his hand. "I hoped you would spend tonight with me."

"I will see Julian in the evening," he told her, his face very near hers. "Then I will come to your chamber."

But she shook her head. "It is safer if I come to you. Hugh might hear us."

He frowned, annoyed with the circumstances. "I will be glad once all of this secrecy is done with."

Alix leaned closer as if to kiss him, but her hand felt something small and hard stuck in the fold of his doublet. "What is this?"

Philip pulled a box from its place of concealment. "This is for you. I almost forgot about it."

Alix opened the lid, and a brilliant emerald winked from the center of the gold brooch. "Philip! It's lovely. I will think of this as a wedding gift."

But he shook his head. "A betrothal gift," he said. "For tomorrow we shall announce our betrothal.''

Julian de Saines groaned out loud. The morning sun was much too bright. Why couldn't a cloud or two appear to spare his sun-blinded eyes?

He rubbed his chin, itching for a shave. He looked back at the merchant's house. No need to go back there for a shave; Abigail would probably just as soon slit his throat as administer him any help. After last night, he hardly expected any kindness from her.

He knew he'd been harsh with her, even as he was doing it. He called her names he never would have done had he any hope of continuing their affair. Affair! It was a business arrangement, and always had been. She'd been fairly paid for each of his visits, even though she'd never charged him. Not that she had such a business arrangement with anyone else, he knew. Abigail was a merchant's daughter and hardly needed to be paid for her services to Julian. But nonetheless, he knew their relationship for what it was: she satisfied his loins the way any whore might, and so he felt obligated to pay.

And last night he'd told her exactly what he thought of their relationship. She'd laughed! Oh, she knew she'd been used by him, and that's what disgusted him. He'd taken out all his anger on her in their lovemaking; he might have hurt her, he didn't care. He'd left her bed this morning before she'd even awakened.

Is that what women are for? he wondered to himself. To be used by men like him? He'd used Abigail for weeks now; there was no tenderness there, no love that made his body want hers. She was a pretty wench who knew how to please him. That was as far as his concern for her went.

And what of Alix? He might not have used her body, but wasn't he using her for another purpose? And she knew it, just as Abigail knew she'd been used. But the difference was Abigail accepted the truth; Alix was unwilling to be used—no matter what the price, he could guess.

Suddenly it all seemed so ridiculous. He didn't

really want to marry Alix, he knew that. And she knew it, too. Did he really want to bind himself to a woman who wanted his brother?

Philip. *He* was the cause of all this self-recrimination. But was he? For the first time, Julian wondered if Philip's decision to lay down the sword had been so wrong, after all. Did that truly make him a coward, just because he didn't care enough of what others thought to make him go against what he really believed in? If he was tired of bloodshed, why should others make him kill? The day of the knighting, Philip had told Julian he'd been too scornful to notice Philip was without scorn for those who still carried their swords. If Philip wasn't going to judge others, why should Julian?

But Julian still remembered all the talk at the various camps he'd been in during the last two years. Everyone snickered, sometimes boldly, sometimes not. But the fact was that most people believed Philip had laid down his sword because he was a coward—and Julian had tried more than once to prove it didn't run in the blood. He'd started fights, he'd been rash in battle—he never backed down, not ever. Because he knew he had to prove himself. And none of that would have been necessary if Philip had only lived up to his vow of knighthood.

Julian rubbed his neck. He was tired of all this contemplation. He'd tried to forget it all last night, but even deep inside Abigail, he couldn't put Alix and Philip far from his mind. Everything Alix had said yesterday kept running through his thoughts; he couldn't forget that she believed he actually loved his brother, that's why Philip had the power to hurt him. Well, perhaps she was right.

He was well outside the village by now, with only a few more hills to traverse before coming to the Chateau. He could see the highest tower, the one that supported the de Saines flag. He would have to go back, Julian thought to himself. He knew what he wanted to do: free Alix from their betrothal. It didn't mean he loved his brother, he thought, remembering too many beatings and too much foolish behavior to go that far. It only meant he would not use another human being if he wanted to take revenge against Philip for all those times he'd defended the de Saines name because of him.

He didn't relish the thought of telling Alix she was free of him; he knew she would be grateful and happy, but blast! it was like admitting she'd been right, and that did not sit well with him at all.

A bird overhead caught his eye, having flown from a high branch from the cluster of trees up ahead. Perhaps he would go hawking today, he thought.

Arab took his time up the slight incline toward those trees, and Julian did not spur him on. He was not anxious to go home; though Alix might welcome their broken betrothal, Julian knew his father would feel differently. To have both the betrothals he'd set up run askew would undoubtedly jar his pride.

Without warning, the trees he approached seemed to come alive with black shadows. From a low ditch, darkly clad men scrambled forward and before Julian had even deciphered they were foe not friend, he was pulled from his horse and a sack was thrown over his head.

"Tie him tight!" one male voice said at his side. "He's worth a fortune."

"What should we do with his horse?"

"Let him go; he'll have no use for him."

"What is this?" Julian demanded, struggling against his captors. "If you do not free me this instant I'll have a thousand men hankering to kill the lot of you."

Julian's wrists were tied behind him, and the sack was bound around his waist, covering the entire upper half of him. It was black, and he could see nothing through the thick, coarse material. One man who felt twice as wide as Julian himself thrust him over a saddled horse like a sack of flour, then mounted as well.

"Do you know who I am?" Julian asked, finding

it difficult to speak while gasping for air from his tethered position.

The man he shared a horse with laughed. "Of course. You do not think we would go to all this trouble for anyone but Philip de Saines, do you?"

"Philip? What has he to do with this?"

It seemed many laughed at that, and Julian was irate. To think he was considering forgiving his brother!

But the words of one of his captors confused him. "No need to play the fool, Philip de Saines. Your father will pay well to have his heir restored to him."

"I am *not* his heir," Julian assured them. "I am Julian de Saines—and whoever you are you had best see fit to release me or you'll pay with your lives."

There was silence, and Julian felt the horse beneath him come to an abrupt halt. "Olivier, come here. Take the sack off him and get a closer look."

In a moment, Julian felt the sack cut away, and he stared straight into the eyes of a short, stocky man who looked as if he were seeing a ghost.

"It is true, my lord," the man said. "This is not Philip de Saines—but the second son, Julian. What shall we do? We just can't let him go—they'll know what we have in mind."

The burly man who held Julian captive in front of him paused before answering. Then, spurring the horse onward he said, "We'll take him anyway. He should be worth as much to his father."

28

Despite her lack of sleep, Alix was in high spirits as she readied herself for the day. Philip had taken her back toward her chamber just an hour earlier, after a full night reacquainting themselves with an intimacy born of their love. Surprisingly, Hugh had not been at his pallet when they arrived at Alix's stairway, so they had shared one last kiss, then parted.

After her bath, Alix chose an underrobe of pale rose with a plunging neckline. The surcoat of deep blue dasmask had an equally daring decolletage, with the edges of the underrobe peeking out. The full sleeves were slit down the middle, also showing the rose material beneath. She wound her hair in one long, neat braid, intertwining it with a ribbon of the same rose hue as her underrobe. She wanted to add the emerald brooch Philip had given her yesterday, but knew it was too soon to show everyone. Her father would undoubtedly see that it was a new, costly piece of jewelry, and would ask where she got it. Better to tell him the truth after she and Philip were formally betrothed.

She left her room, unable to hold back a smile. Today, she thought, the love she shared with Philip would be known to all. Nothing would stand in their way. Hadn't Philip assured her of that last night, in so many ways?

It was well past dawn, much later than Alix usually entered the hall for the first time during the day. But even so, she did not expect to find so many people present. Morning Mass would begin soon, and it was the custom to spend time in the chapel praying well before the actual service began.

It did not take long to discover something was amiss. Everyone was speaking in hushed tones, and there was nary a smile to be found. Geoffrey and Eleanore sat at their places on the raised platform at the end of the room, Eleanore with a kerchief in hand and Geoffrey looking as if he was barely aware of those around him. The frown was deep in his face, the worry so apparent Alix could see it even from across the huge room.

Alix made her way toward them, but noticed as

she walked that people were staring at her quite strangely. One woman even came forward, touched her hand and said, "Be brave, child. God will see you through."

Alix merely looked at the woman, saying nothing. Such an ominous warning! The entire company filling the hall acted as if someone had just died.

Her eyes flew around the room—Philip was nowhere to be seen! Had something happened to him, even in the short time since he'd left her that morning? Her pace picked up speed, and she found her way to her parents' side, spotting them speaking to Sir Hugh and several others.

"What is it?" she asked her mother. "What has happened?"

But Marie had no chance to answer. With her mother on one side and her father on the other, they led her near the Lord and Lady of the manor.

"Alix," her father said as he offered a chair to her beside Lady Eleanore, "your place is with the de Saineses now, to share in their concern."

Alix's heart pounded so heavily she barely heard her father's words. Where was Philip? She felt her hands tremble, and clutched them into fists.

"Has something happened to—"

Marie did not let her daughter finish. "It is Julian, Alix. His horse returned riderless just after dawn. Julian is nowhere to be found."

Alix felt as if her insides might collapse; her pulse had raced so fiercely it seemed to fill every vein to bursting. Now, knowing it was not Philip, the relief sank in slowly and she felt as though she might faint for the first time in her life. Her shoulders slumped, and she bowed her head, glad she was seated rather than standing. At last, able to move again, she looked at the others around her.

Neither Geoffrey nor Eleanore spoke, in fact Lady Eleanore looked as if she could not speak. Her eyes were red and swollen, her face pale and drawn.

Marie spoke again. "Philip is out searching for

him, Alix, along with many of Sire Geoffrey's men."

Alix was grateful her mother knew her needs; she alone knew exactly why Alix was so powerless to speak. It might have been expected for the betrothed of the man missing to be so overcome, but, she realized with belated shame, she had not yet spared one thought for Julian.

"There has been no sign of him?" she asked. "No clue to what happened?"

Geoffrey spoke up at last. "No, Alix. The saddle was still properly fastened, so if there was an accident, that was not the cause."

Eleanore turned her gaze to Alix, as if noticing her for the first time. "His manservant said he had not come to his room all night," Eleanore said, her voice trembling. She looked at Alix with wide, tear-filled eyes. "I must ask you, Alix, did you see him at all last night? Did he come to you?"

Alix shook her head. Though she knew there was little possibility of Julian even entertaining the thought of coming to her room, she nonetheless felt a twinge of guilt that she'd been with his brother at the time of Julian's disappearance.

Just then men entered the hall, their battle armor jingling an announcement of their approach. Alix looked eagerly, but Philip was not among them. However, they did escort a visitor. A young girl, perhaps Alix's age or a few years older, walked in the center, her red-gold hair standing out starkly from the helmet-clad men-at-arms.

Sir Oliver led the woman to stand before Lord and Lady de Saines. She stood tall, buxom as evidenced by the tight-fitting bodice of her gown, and was smiling saucily. Though she looked like a prostitute she did not wear the colors required by law to identify her as such.

"This woman is Abigail Duval, Sire. She is the last person to have seen Sir Julian."

"That is true," the woman announced. "Julian was with me all night."

The news spread quickly through the hall with whispers and gasps. And, inevitably, all eyes went

342

between the bold woman and Alix. It was not difficult for Alix to pretend indifference to the news; indeed, there was no pretense at all.

But the red-haired woman spotted Alix and must have guessed who she was, for she stared at Alix openly. "Are you the one he is to marry?"

Alix nodded, seeing no harm in answering the woman's question.

"Perhaps we may talk privately somewhere, Demoiselle," she said with a confident grin. "I can tell you what he likes best so you can please him in your wedding bed."

Though Alix said nothing and took little insult, Sire Geoffrey stood. His mouth was drawn into a tight line as he said, "Get this woman out of here. If she doesn't know where Julian is now, she is no use to us."

Sir Oliver did Geoffrey's bidding without delay.

"God forgive my son and bring him home safely," Alix heard Lady Eleanore whisper.

Alix took the older woman's hand, squeezing it gently. "He will be found unharmed, my lady."

Alix's solace only compounded Eleanore's tears. "Then you will forgive him for that . . . that woman?"

Alix nodded. "Of course."

Eleanore leaned forward and embraced Alix, saying, "You are good, Alix. I am well-pleased you will become my daughter in the eyes of the law."

Alix patted the bereaved woman's back, looking over her shoulder at her own mother. If Eleanore only knew . . . How could Alix blame Julian when she herself was just as guilty of such disloyalty to her betrothed? Marie knew, but she gave a smile of encouragement to Alix. There was no judgement there.

Minutes passed like hours. Lady Eleanore said no more; Lord Geoffrey was just as quiet. Those guests and family still filling the hall were somber; they offered their presence, their sympathy, and their prayers, for Father Fantin arrived and said the Mass in the hall, as had been the custom years ago before the Chapel was finished. It seemed appropriate this morning; the entire Chateau seemed to move in sympathy to Eleanore and Geoffrey. Everyone knew how well-loved Julian was.

Just after noon, a second group of men-at-arms entered the hall, this time led by Philip. Alix's gaze went to his. He looked tired and travel-dusty, and as somber as anyone else present. She knew, despite the differences he had with Julian, there was still much love between the brothers, even if neither one had admitted such love lately. Alix wished she could go to him, offer him solace, and tell him she knew he loved Julian. If anyone else doubted that, she herself did not. Perhaps he even felt the same guilt she did, having been secretly together when Julian disappeared. She wanted to put her arms around Philip and hold him close, and wipe the worry away from his eyes.

He had not shaved that morning, she noted as he neared, and had on the same clothes he'd worn earlier when he left Alix at her room. When he looked her way, he did not let his gaze linger. She couldn't read what he felt just then, whether or not he would have welcomed her solace if she'd been able to give it.

As Philip approached he held up a rolled piece of parchment. From behind him among the men-at-arms he pulled forward a young boy, dressed as a page. Alix did not recognize the dark-haired boy. "He is from the Montforts," Philip announced. "He was carrying this note when we found him headed our way."

Geoffrey took the note Philip offered, and while he read it silently Eleanore impatiently begged Philip to tell her what news it contained.

"It is a ransom note," Philip said gently. He came closer to his mother, taking her hand. "Which means Julian is safe. He's valuable enough to warrant the best treatment, I assure you of that."

"The Montforts have abducted Julian," Geoffrey said, still reading. Then, suddenly, his brows raised and he gasped. "One million livres!" he shouted.

"The ransom amount?" Giles asked in horrified surprise, standing beside Alix's chair, and Geoffrey nodded.

"One million!"

The sum was echoed in every direction, for never had a ransom been set at such a price. Even the de Saineses, with the Plague so recently over and having drawn on their resources, could not possibly have such a sum. Everyone present guessed that much.

Alix looked at Philip, but he was still gazing at his mother. Then, as Geoffrey handed the ransom note to Giles, Philip spoke up.

"I wish to speak to you privately, Father. You, and Sir Giles and anyone else you wish to discuss the best action to take against this matter."

Geoffrey nodded distractedly. "We'll go to the antechamber."

A page was sent to fetch Sir Oliver, and Geoffrey led the way to one of the small rooms off the hall, motioning to Sir Hugh to join them. Eleanore stood as well, taking hold of Alix's hand. Giles and Marie followed behind. Once inside the antechamber, they all took seats around the table, and before long Sir Oliver entered.

Philip spoke first, his tone and face serious but seemingly uneffected by the grief so evident on his parent's faces.

"One thing is obvious," he began. "We cannot pay the ransom."

Sir Oliver, the only one who had elected to stay standing, spoke up eagerly. "Sire Geoffrey, let me lead your men to storm the Montfort stronghold. We can save your son and be rid of the boil known as the Montforts all at once."

Geoffrey looked at Sir Oliver, and though he might have spoken, Philip did not give him the chance.

"If we send an army against them they might kill Julian before we even have the chance to rescue him," Philip said.

"It seems to me," Giles spoke up, "there are only

two options: pay the ransom or storm the Mont-forts, as Oliver has suggested. And since we cannot pay . . .''

"There is a third option," Philip said to Giles. "I have a man in the Montfort army. After I spoke with King Jean and learned of the Montfort's refusal to pay for ennoblement, I wanted to learn about their state of finances. I sent August-Caron to find out what he could; he is still there. Having help from inside, we could possibly set Julian free with the minimum of bloodshed."

"I hardly see how one foot soldier in the Mont-fort army could be of any use," Oliver said snidely.

"August-Caron did not join the Montforts as a foot soldier," Philip told him. "He is a knight, fully armored and possessing a fine mount. The Montforts will hardly send a man of his means to the outer camps with the foot soldiers. He was most likely accepted as a Chateau man-at-arms upon sight, given his skill and weaponry."

Giles rubbed his chin thoughtfully. "Still, he is only one man. How would we communicate with him?"

"I am expecting word from him; he has with him a page who is to send a message to me secretly."

"If he isn't caught," Oliver mentioned.

Philip's silence conceded that was true. Then he said, "There is one more option."

Geoffrey raised his brows. "Which is?"

"Negotiations. We can offer to pay for their ennoblement—"

"No." Geoffrey's answer was firm and clear, and by his tone Philip, who had not carried much hope in this final option even upon his own mention of it, chose not to pursue it any further.

"We have a third more men than the Montforts," Geoffrey said, as if thinking out loud. "But still, they have the advantage of their stronghold. It would take more men on our side of the balance to penetrate with any quick conquest. And perhaps months of siege if that is what we are forced to do—months we do not have, for my son's sake."

"I beg to differ, Sire," Oliver said. "True, they

346

have the advantage of their Chateau, but their army is a diverse group of mercenaries hired from all over Europe and England. Our men, on the other hand, are highly trained Frenchmen and can work together as one force. We have a finer army, and that, combined with our greater number, should guarantee us victory."

"No victory can be guaranteed," Philip said quietly. "I have been in battles our troops were sure to win . . . only to barely escape total annihilation. We cannot truly know the ability of our enemy until in the actual battle—and then it may be too late."

Philip heard his mother's low whimper, followed by his father's warning. "Your doom-saying is not welcome, Philip. But I must agree with you. August-Caron is an able knight; we shall try it your way first. What have you in mind?"

An odd sense of well-being settled on Philip, almost gratitude that his father still had the ability to trust his judgment. And he knew what he had to do. "I would like to take a small troop of men to the outskirts of Montfort land. No doubt Henri Montfort will be fully aware of our arrival and be confused by it—but my presence there will be known, so August-Caron will know where to send his page to contact me. All we need is help in two areas: access into the Chateau and directions to where Julian is being held."

"Aren't you depending on just a few miracles, Sir Philip?" Oliver said. "First, that August-Caron's page will want to contact you and then have the means to, and then that August-Caron will even be in any position to help us inside—not to mention knowing where Julian is being hidden."

"Any chamber in the Chateau which is heavily guarded will undoubtedly house Julian—anyone with eyes that see could find that out. As for his page contacting me, of that I have no doubt. August-Caron is a worthy knight; I would trust him with my life."

Giles stood. "Tell me one thing, Philip," he said.

"If you plan to lead these men to save your brother, will you wear a sword?"

All gazes, including Alix's, went to Philip.

"Yes, Lord Giles. I will carry a sword."

29

In the silence that followed, Philip looked from Giles to Alix. He saw her gaze, as intense as anyone else's present, but without the surprise so obvious on every other face. She looked at him with pride, as if she fully expected such an announcement. She knew, he thought, that this was the only decision he could have made. Because Julian was his brother; because Philip loved Julian—and even if no one else believed that, even Julian himself, Alix did.

But there was one other reason, one that entered his mind without welcome. He had to save his brother, he thought. If only to prove to himself he truly was the chivalrous man he believed himself to be. For if he didn't . . . if he let Julian die, without trying to save him, how could he know he hadn't just used this to be rid of a major obstacle between himself and the woman he loved? How would he know he hadn't used his vow to avoid the sword as an excuse, because he had no desire to save the brother who might steal away the woman he loved?

"Choose the men you shall need," Geoffrey said to Philip. Then he stood, placing his hands on Philip's shoulders. "And when you go, I will give you my sword."

Philip managed a slight grin. "Then perhaps you should give it to me now, Father. I shall need time while the men are chosen to reacquaint myself with the weapon in my hand." Then he turned to

Sir Oliver, once again serious. "I know you do not approve of this plan to rescue my brother. But you are my father's castellan, and as such you know his men and their abilities the best. I will trust your loyalty to my family, Sir Oliver, to outweigh your disapproval of this. I want you to choose the men who will accompany us to the Montfort land. Bring me your choices day after tomorrow; we shall leave after that."

Then Philip turned and left.

Alix moved instinctively to follow, but Marie, seated next to her, took hold of her wrist and held her back. "I think it would be wise if we joined the rest of the people now, Alix. Eleanore, I will ask your family and guests to accompany us to the chapel. If God is on our side, surely Julian will be returned to us safely."

Eleanore nodded wearily, and followed Marie and Alix to the chapel.

The chapel was dark, cool and damp, very much like the innermost chambers of the Chateau. Alix knelt beside her mother, her head bowed in prayer. There was silence all around, except for an occasional cough, a rustle of material as someone shifted, and, at times, a sniffle from those who still cried over Julian's fate.

Between Alix's supplications to God, her thoughts strayed to Philip. She prayed for him, too, for she knew how dangerous this mission was to save his brother. And for all the times she wondered if she fully upheld his decision to ignore the sword, she wished now that he had no need to take it up once again. What if taking up the sword again carried him to his death? He might regain her father's respect, but what good would it do if he were dead?

She knew where he was now. On her way to the chapel, she had seen Philip head toward his father's chamber, no doubt to retrieve the sword Sire Geoffrey offered. He might have smiled when he said it, but she knew he was serious when he told his father he needed time in the next few days to know once again the feel of the sword in his hand.

In just two days he would be leaving her yet
again . . . after he'd promised her at his last
departure there were to be no more good-byes
between them. A turmoil of worry welled inside of
her; she couldn't let him go so easily this time.
This time he was off to risk his life, not simply to
purchase horses or negotiate with the King.

She wished she could leave this somber and
quiet Chapel, and go to his side. How she wished
she could spend every last moment with him—she
would follow him closer than his own shadow, and
never let him out of her sight. She couldn't let him
go off to a battle without the thought more than
simply crossing her mind that he might not return.
Wasn't that what drove some women to become
camp followers? True, she knew many of the
women who followed the troops were prostitutes
just looking for the gold they could earn, but some
of the women were wives. Peasant women who had
no home apart from their foot soldier husbands.

As the thought took hold, taking on meaning,
Alix felt her heart beat faster, and her piously
folded hands tremble. She would go with Philip.
Who would be surprised if that is what she set out
to do? Certainly not her mother, knowing how Alix
felt about Philip. Nor should Geoffrey or Eleanore
or even Giles—they believed Philip was off to
rescue *her* betrothed. Didn't she have a right to
follow after? It wouldn't mean she went off to
battle with them; camp followers were just that:
they stayed in the relative safety of camp while the
men did actual battle. But it would mean she
would be there at Philip's side, spending all the
time she could with him . . . and she would know
just that much sooner how he fared in this mission
of his.

She would not be in the way, she decided. At
least not any more than any other camp follower.
Philip loved her, didn't he? He might even
welcome her. After all, they *belonged* together.

Suddenly she could not stay in the too-quiet
chapel. She would not tell Philip just yet what her

350

plans were, but she knew she must see him. She fled from the chapel, knowing her mother would stay with Eleanore.

Alix found Philip in the training yard. Gustave was there, helping Philip refresh the skills he'd taught him as a youth. Philip was not using his father's sword, but rather a training sword with a dulled tip. And though Gustave was obviously trying his best, his age was making it difficult to withstand the kind of training Philip demanded. Alix saw Gustave ward off one mighty whack of Philip's sword, and though he did not waver, Gustave held up a warning hand.

"I thought I could help you, Philip, but I am too old for this, after all," Gustave said, the sword in his hand now weighing down his arm.

Philip patted his shoulder. "You taught me well. Stay and talk me through then. Tell me like you used to what I am doing wrong."

"You will need a partner then," Gustave said.

"Who is the best? I am more than rusty, Gustave."

Gustave was thoughtful a moment. "That would be Oliver."

Philip shook his head. "I've assigned him to choose the men who will accompany us. Who else?"

"August-Caron . . . but he is not here. I will call Roger; he is young, but strong."

Just as Gustave summoned a nearby page to find Sir Roger, Philip caught sight of Alix. He approached with a smile.

"I am not at all certain I welcome you watching me," he said, teasing. "If I weren't certain all of Gustave's swords are dulled, my life would be in serious jeopardy."

"The time you spent as a knight far outweighs the time you spent swordless," she reminded him. "I believe you are not so rusty as you think."

Her encouragement was welcomed, as evidenced by the warmth that touched his smile. Then he said, more seriously, "I'm glad you came here. I wanted to thank you."

351

She raised her brows. "For what?"

"For not being surprised, as my father was, when I said I would take up the sword again in hopes of saving my brother. It was obvious to me then that you are the only one who truly believes I love Julian—and that I'm not too much of a coward to try doing something to save his life."

"I never believed you a coward," she told him.

"There is another reason I must save him, Alix," he said.

She looked at him closely. "You love him; that is reason enough."

But Philip shook his head. He started to speak, but both were distracted by the sound of someone nearing them from behind Philip.

"Sir Philip," intruded a young man, breathless from his hasty approach, "Gustave says you have called upon me to be your training partner. I am honored."

Both Philip and Alix turned their gazes to the sound of the eager boy behind them. He was tall and muscular, with light blond hair and a wide face; his neck was corded with muscles and his chest looked as wide as a horse's. He did indeed look strong, as Gustave had promised.

"You must be Roger, is that correct?"

The boy nodded.

"We will begin in a moment."

Roger bowed, then left to stand with Gustave, several paces away.

"I will come to your room tonight," Alix whispered.

"I'll be late."

"I'll wait," she assured him with a smile. Then he turned back to Gustave and Roger.

Alix stayed as long as she dared, watching him retrain his body in the balance and quickness of a knight. He was as strong as ever, the physical labor he continued doing at the Chateau having kept his body in fine condition. Though he looked as if the agility and prowess with the sword came to him naturally, Alix heard him swear with frustration several times over an ineffective thrust or a parry that was too slow. But despite his own dissatisfaction, Alix enjoyed watching him. His lean body was a great contrast to Roger's more bulky one, and she let her gaze linger lovingly over his broad shoulders, quick steps, and long, muscular legs so pleasantly outlined in the tight, dark chausses. For a moment she felt like a child again, the same one who had seen him on his charger and fallen in love with the knight of her dreams. She smiled, knowing her love was more real than any childhood infatuation—but, more importantly, Philip's love was real as well.

As the sun sank lower in the western sky, Alix knew she had already stayed too long. The evening meal would be served soon, and she doubted Philip would attend. He might even continue past sunset, under the light of several lamps.

When Blanche came to fetch her, having been sent by Alix's mother, Alix knew she had no choice but to leave. She consoled herself with the thought that she would see Philip later that night. But with one last glance over her shoulder, seeing he continued to work at the various training tools alone—having sent a tired Roger away more than an hour ago—she wondered if he would have even enough energy to carry on a simple conversation. Even now, he was before the great pole that held two man-size sacks suspended from the top. As it twirled round, Philip dodged and thrust, killing the two inhuman aggressors many times over. Yes, she thought, he would be exceedingly tired when she saw him later tonight.

It was almost midnight when Alix walked stealthily up the stairs of Philip's tower. She had waited until Hugh found his pallet and fell asleep, and because of the continued upheaval in the Chateau caused by Julian's kidnapping, he had stayed longer in the hall.

Alix hoped Philip was already abed, for his own good. If he was asleep, she told herself resolutely, she would not waken him. He needed rest more than he needed her, at least tonight.

But Philip was awake when she entered his room. He must not have heard her approach, for at first she thought he had not yet returned. Then she caught sight of him on the balcony, seated on the cool stone with a candle at his side and parchment in his lap. Quietly, she watched him. He gazed up at the stars, then made an entry on the page in his lap. He looked at peace, she thought to herself; the determination which had been so apparent upon his face that day while training was now gone. In its place was a tranquility she almost envied. Where were his thoughts? In the stars, she knew. She wished it had been her to bring him that peace—he'd found it even when there was so much turmoil around and ahead.

"You should be sleeping," she told him, her voice low.

Philip glanced up in surprise. "I didn't hear you." He abandoned the tools of his astronomy, then came to her side. Putting a hand on each shoulder, he drew her close for a kiss. "I was waiting for you. I knew Hugh would be late tonight, and that you wouldn't be able to get away very soon."

"You were in the hall? I would have stayed had I known."

Philip shook his head. "I went to the kitchen for a late supper; Hugh was just going to his pallet."

Alix stood on tiptoe and kissed him. "I told myself that if you were asleep I would not wake you. It's sleep you need tonight, Philip, not me."

"I need both," he assured her.

They went to the bed, and lay down fully clothed.

"If I truly loved you selflessly, I would insist you go right to sleep," Alix said, snuggling into his arms. "But I must be selfish instead; I want to stay."

"I wouldn't let you go anyway," he said. "I wanted to talk to you . . . before I make love to you."

Alix ignored what he said; she kissed his lips, teasing him with her tongue. Then she kissed his cheek, his ear, his jawline, his neck. And despite what he said, Philip kissed her back without any resistance. Talk, at least for now, was forgotten.

They undressed each other, making it part of their lovemaking. Philip's kiss followed his fingertips as he slowly peeled away her garments. Alix, eager to feel him against her, slipped her fingers beneath his doublet and lifted it over his head. In a moment, after discarding the rest of their clothes just as eagerly, Alix felt his skin was cool pressed against hers. He must have swum or bathed after his day of training, for though his hair looked dry it was still slightly damp at the back.

They loved one another as they always did: slowly yet eagerly, the passion between them making every caress like the crest of a wave of desire. And, when the final culmination came, the zenith soared within them like an ocean in a storm, wild and untamed and beyond their control. They rode the wave to its pinnacle, together as one, until slowly, gradually, the tempest brought them back. Back from that place they had shared as one, where no other force could intrude.

But reality did return. And though they delayed it as long as possible, with a kiss, another caress, a whispered word of love, Alix knew they would have to talk.

"I'm going with you," she whispered, one finger tracing his jawline from ear to chin.

"Where?" he asked, concentrating more on the corner of her mouth than the words she spoke. He kissed her softly, letting the tip of his tongue outline the tiny curve of her half-smile.

"To western Brittany, to the Montforts' land."

Philip raised his gaze from her delectable mouth to her too-serious eyes. Was she insane? He did not move, thinking he surely misunderstood. "You want to go with me to retrieve Julian?"

Much to his dismay, Alix nodded without hesitation. She was even smiling!

"Alix—"

She sat up, seeing his answer before he even spoke a word. "Wait, Philip. Let me remind you of a promise you made to me just a few short weeks ago. Before you left for Tours, you said that was to be our last good-bye. So do not expect me to say good-bye again to you now. I won't."

Philip sat up as well, every bit as determined as she seemed to be. "That promise certainly didn't include going off to possible battle with me, Alix. How can you even think I would take you along on such a mission?"

"You sound as though no woman has ever followed her husband off to other lands. I'll hardly be the first."

"No, you won't be. Do you know the sort of woman who follows men to battlegrounds?"

"I admit I've never met such a woman, but—"

"And it's doubtful you ever shall. No woman of nobility has ever done such a thing."

"I don't care," she said, all too easily.

"I won't allow it, Alix. It's too dangerous."

"Why should it be dangerous?" she asked. "I promise to stay at camp; I won't be in the way because I'll do whatever you tell me; I won't try to manage things because I've never interfered in battle strategies. I won't even eat—much. I'll simply be by your side, where I belong."

"No, Alix."

She ignored him. "And who would be surprised to find that I've gone after you? Everyone will think it's concern for Julian that has made me be so rash—"

"Then you admit it's foolish to go."

She shook her head. "I said rash, Philip, not foolish. Is it so foolish to want to be with the man I love, especially when he might not return?"

"I admit my skill as a knight is in question since it's been so long since I've been in battle, but I hoped you had some faith in my abilities, Alix. You said this afternoon that I was not as rusty as I thought—didn't you mean that?"

"Of course I did! But how can you deny the danger you'll be facing?"

"I don't; but that doesn't mean you have to start digging my grave already."

Suddenly Alix laughed, and threw her arms about his neck. "Oh, Philip. Of course I believe in you! How can you doubt that? I want to be with you because I love you—and I refuse to be parted from you. I intend holding you to the promise you made never to say good-bye to me again."

"It didn't include matters like this; women of your status do not follow their men to battle."

"Why not?" she challenged. "Simply because of the hardships of camp life? I promise not to complain—even if I can't bring Blanche and several trunks of clothing."

"There, you see? Of course you couldn't bring—"

"I was teasing!" she laughed. "I wouldn't have even considered taking Blanche."

"It isn't only lack of a servant," he told her. "Camp life is anything but pleasant."

"I've been to several Tourneys, and my family has camped at them many times."

"With wagonloads of niceties, I'm sure," he said, then counted, "A portable bed with twenty cushions, food that King Jean himself would be proud to serve, servants at every turn, huge tents with inner tents enough to keep out the wind. That's hardly any comparison, my love."

Alix was undaunted. "My place is at your side," she told him stubbornly. "I won't let you leave me again."

"And what if I'm unsuccessful in retrieving Julian from the Montforts?" he asked. "What if I and every man with me die trying to save him? Then what will you do?"

She threw her arms about him again, this time tighter. "Don't say such things! Do you want to frigthen me?"

He pulled her away. "Alix, it is a possibility, as much as I hate to admit it. A moment ago you admitted it's possible I might not return. And if I am killed, my men conquered with me, there is also the possibility the Montforts will raid whatever camp we leave behind, looking for spoils. And you, my beautiful, Alix, would be precious winnings in such a battle—too precious for me to risk leaving behind."

Alix said nothing. Philip eyed her, knowing he hadn't convinced her, fully aware his words had hardly made any impact thus far. But he'd be damned before he let her go with him!

"This morning," he said slowly, "when I told everyone I would pick up the sword again, you looked at me with pride. Do not make me regret my decision, Alix."

"What do you mean?"

"If I sent someone else to rescue my brother, then you would remain here, safe."

Alix shook her head. "But you won't change your mind, Philip. I know you won't. Not even if you knew for certain I would go along."

The bluff had not succeeded; not that Philip thought it would have. Alix was too smart for that.

"You are right," he admitted. "I cannot change my mind . . . and you are part of the reason, Alix."

"Am I? I thought you did this for the love of your brother."

He nodded agreement. "That is true, but also because I love the woman he is betrothed to."

"You cannot mean to save him for me!"

"No," he said. "But if I do not—if I let him die, as surely the Montforts would do if they do not get their money or hear from us in the three month time limit they've set—then how would I know I didn't let Julian die on purpose—so that you would be free for me to marry?"

"Philip! You are not so cold-hearted and devious as to think that way."

He shrugged, although her instant belief in his valor was welcome. "Perhaps not, at least not outwardly. But even if it isn't true, won't that be what is generally believed once our betrothal is announced? Won't everyone—including your father and mine—believe I simply used my vow to lay down the sword as an excuse to do nothing to save my brother? I've learned not to care what others think, Alix, but in this I must. If your father believed that of me, I would have no chance to

358

marry you. So I must do all I can to save Julian, not only because I love him. It's what I wished to tell you earlier, so you'll know I do not deserve all of your pride in me. Part of the reason I choose to help my brother is purely selfish."

"But you do deserve my pride!" she told him. "Not only because you love your brother and will risk your life to save him, but because you are *not* the devious man some others might be; you won't tolerate even the most remote possibility that temptation might be great to hope Julian never comes back. After all, it would be logical for us to marry if Julian were to die. It would bind our two families as our parents are eager to do. But you won't allow such a possibility—and for that, you truly are the civilized man your father always wanted you to be."

He remembered having told Alix about his wish to be civilized; that idea, instigated by his father, had played an ironic part of his decision to lay down the sword. He smiled cynically. "Isn't it strange," he said, "that to prove I am civilized I must take up the sword once again?"

30

It was well before dawn and the sky was still dark; Alix had slept very little, even though she had spent the night alone. This was the morning Philip would depart for the western coast of Brittany, and she had more in mind than an early-morning good-bye.

Alix's satchel was already packed. She'd chosen to take only the barest essentials: a change of clothes, a hair brush, her jeweled dagger and one other item she thought she might have need of. She'd added the emerald pendant her father had given her long ago; it was a pretty trinket but one she could give away without too much heartache. And it would take something at least this valuable to bribe her way into the back of the weapons wagon. A silent mouth was a costly purchase—but one she knew this trinket could afford.

Alix was dressed for the journey. She wore her oldest gown, which clung to her figure and would prove less cumbersome than underrobe and surcoat. Her hair was tied out of the way in a thick, single braid. She wore leather shoes—although they were soft, they were her sturdiest. And finally, she added a light shawl over her shoulders to ward off the morning chill.

Alix folded the note she'd left for her mother. It said, in very brief terms, that she'd followed those who went after her betrothed. She left it on her dressing table, then quickly snatched up her sack of belongings and left her room.

At the base of the stairway, she saw Hugh still asleep. He was snoring loudly, and so she had little fear of detection. She stepped past him confidently, holding the skirt of her simple gown high out of the way so not to disturb him with a careless swish of material. She was out of the kitchen within moments.

The only sounds outside came from the direction of the stable; sticking to the shadows, Alix headed that way. Once the stable was in sight, Alix hesitated. Though the men seemed too occupied with the tasks at hand to notice her, she nonetheless did not care to take any chance of being detected. It wouldn't do to have Philip discover her—until it was too late to send her back.

A dozen horses stood ready and waiting. Several men, also waiting, stood nearby. The greatest flurry of activity came from just outside the stable, where a wagon was being loaded with camp supplies: folded tents, clanking cooking utensils, sacks of food, extra weapons such as bows and arrows, several longbows, and one Ribaud. The Ribaud was a small cannon Alix had seen demonstrated at a Tourney once; most believed it was of little value since its projected bolts could not possibly penetrate the thick walls of any Chateau. And Alix knew Philip shared in the skepticism about the weapon; she'd heard Philip and Sir Oliver discussing the weapon at one evening meal. While Philip thought the concept of the weapon intriguing, he'd said it would be of no real practical value unless it could shoot bolts much larger and faster. As it was now, the power within the weapon served only the enemy because of its ineffectiveness. Philip had cited several times during battle when men had spent so much time re-loading that the enemy had gained the advantage. Alix was surprised to see the weapon being added to the cargo wagon now; no doubt it was Sir Oliver who insisted upon bringing it along.

The departing party was to leave just after lauds, which Alix was sure was swiftly approaching. Three more hours till dawn; by then they would all be well away from the Chateau. Once the sun brightened the land, she would be less worried if she were discovered—they would be too far gone to make her turn back all alone. And surely Philip would not spare one of his carefully chosen men to escort her all the way home.

Soon the wagon was fully loaded and Alix knew she must make her sprint. This was, she realized, the most crucial part of her journey. If she were discovered here and now, the only place she would be going was back to her chamber—Philip would make sure of that.

She spotted Philip just then, coming from inside the stable. He was between Sir Oliver and Sir Roger, but no one spoke. She leaned back in the shadows, waiting until their footfalls took them past the wagon. Then, peeking round the corner, she saw them go to the horses. Luck was with her in the placement of the wagon; its rear was toward her, and the knights and their mounts opposite. And when Philip approached the others, Alix took full advantage of the attention he created. The knights had been waiting for him, and now that he was there, they knew their mission would begin.

Alix held her bundle close before her and ran quickly and silently, thankful it was a dark and moonless night.

Breathless, she reached the wagon. The back panel was already secured with a rope, and she was surprised at how high it looked at close ground vantage. She threw her sack over the back, glad when it landed softly. Alix dared not waste time wondering how best to follow that sack; boldly, she reached up and grabbed hold of the panel with both hands, then, quite without dignity or grace, she heaved herself up and swung one leg, then the other inside. She did not land quite so softly; the barrel of the Ribaud was just beneath her, and the cold, unyielding iron wedged into her rib. But she did not cry out; she simply shifted her weight and pushed the weapon away to make room for herself. Then she waited; if she'd been spotted, it wouldn't be long before she'd be ousted.

But no one came. The only sounds she heard were of men as they mounted their horses. Then the wagon jiggled as a driver climbed aboard. Alix kept low, unmoving, barely breathing for fear of being discovered. But at last, when the wagon pulled forward, she allowed one huge sigh. There was nothing to do now but wait until morning. It looked as though she had no need of her emerald bribe, after all.

Philip mounted his horse, glancing around as he did so. His gaze went several times to the dark window of Alix's bedchamber. Was she there, he wondered, perhaps still sleeping? They hadn't said good-bye. Not really, anyway. Last evening, just after supper, she'd come to stand before him and graciously wished him safety and God's blessing as he went forth on this noble deed to rescue her betrothed. Then, with a smile that could have been meant for a brother—the brother that all present believed he would be to her once she married Julian—she had excused herself for the evening and he hadn't seen her again. He'd gone to the stairway leading to her chamber twice; both times

Hugh was there, fully awake. No doubt the old man wondered about Philip's odd behavior; and so he didn't go back a third time. He waited in the garden, watching her window for a light. But it remained dark, as if she'd gone immediately to sleep. Was that public good-bye going to suffice?

He'd finally gone to his tower and tried to sleep the hour or two until his departure. He knew he would not see her in the morning. He'd made it clear they would be leaving at the hour of lauds, three hours past midnight. No one would be seeing them off. But still, as they loaded the wagon and readied the horses, he'd watched the outbuilding of the keep for some sign of her.

Now, as he led the party of knights past the raised portcullis and across the drawbridge, he couldn't help glancing back a few times more. Is that how she would keep him to his promise, he wondered? He'd said there would be no more good-byes; did that mean she would simply not see him for a proper farewell? He was half tempted to turn around, jump from his horse and run to her chamber, despite Hugh's presence at the base of her stairway. No good-bye was certainly not the answer; he wanted to see her again, just once more.

But he kept going; once past the drawbridge he did not look back. He would see her again, he promised himself. This rescue mission wouldn't take longer than a few days . . . and then he would come home to her.

Alix might have slept; certainly she was in need of it, having had barely an hour's rest last night. But the jouncing wagon beneath her was hardly as comfortable as her bed, and she had not thought it possible to find any amount of rest. But when the wagon hit a particularly hard bump in the road, she was jarred from a half-slumber and was surprised to find the sun shining brightly through the wagon's canvas top.

She wondered how far they had come, and dared to lift her head above the wagon's back panel. But quickly she lowered her head again; there were four or five men bringing up the rear of their party just behind the wagon. Had they seen her? She wondered again how far they were from the Chateau; in her brief glimpse she'd seen little more than the mounted knights. She hadn't recognized any of the surrounding landscape. If she were caught too soon . . .

"What are you doing?" a male voice called from behind.

Alix's heart pounded, matching the hard hoof-beats of a horse so close to the back of the wagon she could even smell the leather and hear the creaking of the saddle. But the questioning voice had come from farther away. Alix said nothing, pulling the shawl up over her head and lying as still as possible in the bouncing wagon.

"I thought I saw something moving in here." Alix recognized the voice; it belonged to Sir Roger . . . and he was extremely close!

"It's this road," the other called back. "Everything in the back of that wagon has been bouncing around since we left the roads of de Saines county."

Alix breathed a deep sigh of relief to hear the hoofbeats of Sir Roger's horse carry him away. At least she knew they were outside de Saines county. That meant they'd been traveling at least three hours, perhaps four. Montfort land was not far away, which meant they would stop soon to set up camp. Before long, she thought, her presence could be discovered and it wouldn't matter.

"The town of St. Autiers ahead, Sir Philip," Alix heard someone call.

"Continue on," Philip replied. He sounded so near, as if his horse were just beside the wagon.

"No sense warning the Montforts of our arrival," said another voice close by. It sounded like Sir Oliver. "Why not skirt around the town? There are sure to be Montfort men there."

"Exactly what I hope for, Sir Oliver."

"To warn the enemy, in total daylight, that we've arrived?" Then he added, "I knew we should have left an hour earlier. We could have set up our

364

camp outside Montfort land under cover of darkness. And now you want to announce that we're here?"

"I want August-Caron to know where to send a message to me," Philip said. "The only way to do that is to let the Montfort army know where we are."

"Don't you think you're taking a mighty chance just for the hope of a single man inside their stronghold? If they see an army approaching, they'll have us outnumbered and conquered in no time."

"No, Sir Oliver. Their only hope of the ransom money is through us. We'll be free to set up camp anywhere nearby; they'll wait for us to contact them about the money."

Soon Alix felt the wagon slow and the quality of the road become much better. Alix heard sounds of a village; more horses, merchants peddling their wares. St. Autiers was the last village before Montfort land. Alix had never been there before, but she'd been told the village had prospered after the Black Death. Many serfs had fled their homes in search of freedom and because St. Autiers, like a small city, was not owned by any nobility, the town was a likely choice for men to find that freedom. It certainly sounded like a bustling town, far busier than those Alix was accustomed to in de Saines territory.

Though they rode slowly through the town, Philip's party did not linger. Alix wished she could have picked her head up and watched; she would have liked to put faces with the names of those who called out to the passing knights. Because they were so obviously wealthy, the merchants saw them as prime customers. And not only merchants saw an opportunity to add to their gold; Alix heard more than one bold invitation coming from women. Alix didn't have to see their clothing to know the voices belonged to women of prostitution.

Not long after they left the limits of the town, Philip called the others to halt. Alix shifted position uncomfortably, feeling suddenly like a coward. For the first time she wondered how Philip would react to her presence. He would not be pleased, she thought to herself, at least not at first. But what did he expect? She'd warned him, hadn't she? Told him—quite clearly—that she intended coming along? Did he really think she would let him leave after the good-bye they'd said at dinner last night? He should have guessed then, when she wished him good luck before all and quietly left the hall without a private word spoken between them. That was hardly a good-bye for either of them to be satisfied with, especially when he was leaving for such a dangerous mission.

But Alix's fears did not have long to fester. A moment later, the back of the wagon was pulled open and she had no choice but to sit up straight and grab hold of the sideboard, else she might have tumbled to the ground.

"Demoiselle!"

Alix stared straight into the surprised eyes of Sir Roger, who stood still holding the rope that released the back panel. He seemed thunderstruck, standing there gaping at her. Alix took control of herself, ignoring those unpleasant thoughts of Philip's possible anger at her discovery.

She slipped from the wagon and stood tall, chin held high. "Sir Roger," she greeted him with a slight nod. "You may close your mouth; I assure you, I am quite real and not a vision to be gaped at."

Roger shut his mouth firmly, but a moment later opened it again. "Does anyone know you're here?"

"They're about to find out."

Alix was amazed that her limbs carried her so calmly. From the cramped position she'd been forced to endure during the ride, she would not have been surprised if her legs gave out on her without having the added burden of facing Philip. But she walked toward his turned back without hesitation, and halted just two paces away. He was issuing orders to a page to see to his horse, then glanced in front of him as if deciding where best to erect the tents.

"Philip."

He did not turn immediately; in fact, it was that hesitation that allowed Alix's demeanor to waver, ever so slightly. Was he too angry to face her? She took a deep breath. Perhaps he hadn't heard her.

"Philip, I am here."

He swung around then, on his face bare surprise, wonder, happiness, and finally reserve. The other knights were gathering round.

"Demoiselle Alix," he said stiffly, "what do you think you're doing here?"

"I've come to be as close as possible to this mission to save Julian," she told him. "I found I could not wait back at the Chateau, so I decided to accompany you."

Philip cleared his throat as if struggling to control what words he used. "Your concern for . . . your betrothed . . . is understandable. However, this is hardly the place for a woman of nobility."

She looked around. "I think this is a lovely spot for camp. I'm quite used to camping, you know. My family has attended many Tourneys."

Sir Oliver stepped forward, scowling. "This is hardly the same thing, Demoiselle. You should not have come."

"Nonetheless, I am here. And now that I am, I intend on staying." Her tone was firm, leaving no doubt she was serious.

"Roger," Philip called. "Take my page and my horse and accompany Demoiselle Alix back to the Chateau."

"Philip!" she spoke his name reprovingly. "I'll not go back."

"Perhaps not willingly," he said, walking past her and taking over the task of resaddling his horse from his page.

"May I speak to you . . . alone?" she asked, coming up behind him.

Philip hesitated indecisively. He wanted to crush her to him, glad to see her once again after having been cheated out of the intimate good-bye he'd hoped for last night. And he wanted to shake her. Did she think this was some great picnic they were on, camping here on the border of Montfort land? He knew, if he allowed himself to be alone with her, it would only be harder to send her away. Besides that, there was no privacy to be found here. They were far from the trees where possible mercenaries might hide; far from every rock or bush or hill that might be used against them. If anyone approached their camp, they would be spotted before any damage could be done.

Philip led her out of hearing distance from the others. Much to his dismay, when he stopped she made a move toward him, as if she would embrace him. But at the last moment, perhaps seeing the warning in his face, she held back.

"You cannot send me away, Philip," she told him. "If you do, I'll just find another way to return here to you. And you cannot spare Sir Roger. If August-Caron gets word to you today, you will have to act immediately without waiting for Roger to return."

"We'll have to go on without him then."

But Alix shook her head. "I told you I was coming, Philip. And no matter what you do, I won't be put from you again. It was you who promised we would never have to say good-bye again. I only intend holding you to that promise."

"That promise had nothing to do with going off to do battle."

"It had only to do with you leaving the Chateau," she insisted. "And that you've done; so I followed. And if you insist on having me brought back, I will just find a way to return here. You know I will, Philip. I want to be with you every moment, don't you see? How could I stay behind, especially when I had the perfect reason to follow? Everyone thinks it is concern for Julian . . . and while I am worried about him, it's concern for *you* that has made me want to be here spending every last moment together."

"Last moment?" he repeated. "Are you digging my grave again, Alix?"

"Philip!" she said, exasperated. "You know this mission is dangerous. Who knows what will happen. I only know I want to be with you every moment . . . especially now."

"Why especially now?" he asked curiously.

Alix didn't know why she had chosen those words; but they did best describe how she felt. She only knew that she could not, would not, be parted from him. No matter what.

"I'm not leaving," was all she said, so stubbornly all Philip could do was stare at her for one long moment.

He sighed. "All right—" He saw her eyes light up and held up a hand before she jumped to the wrong conclusion. "You don't have to go back to the Chateau, but you will have to return to St. Autiers. There is an inn there; I will send with you two pages we can spare."

With that spoken, he turned his back on her to head toward the men huddled near the wagon.

"But, Philip—"

Alix stopped, seeing the impenetrable anger on his face when he turned to her. "Say nothing, Alix. I'll not give in. Choose where you care to go: the inn or Chateau de Saines."

She hesitated, but knew any battle she waged against his decision would be fruitless. Finally, she said in a low tone, "The inn."

Once Philip's horse was resaddled and the two pages were ready, Philip aided Alix astride. A third page would accompany them to return with Philip's horse.

"Will I hear any news?" she asked. What she wanted to ask was if she would see him, but she dared not say so before the others. He must truly be angry with her, she thought, otherwise he would accompany her to the inn.

"When it is safe."

He swatted the back of his horse then, and she

let the mount follow the page in front of her. She wanted to look back, but her pride did not allow it.

31

Philip sat before the campfire, stick in hand. He had sent his page as one of the two ordered to remain with Alix at the inn, and though he could have "borrowed" one of the dozen or so pages who had accompanied other knights, he chose to tend his own fire. Sir Oliver's page had cooked for both Philip and Sir Oliver, but once he had taken his fill, Philip excused himself to start his own fire before his tent. For this evening at least, he preferred keeping to himself.

The sun had set more than an hour ago. They were too far from the city limit to see even a speck of light from any town lamp or home, but nonetheless Philip's gaze kept turning in that direction. After the surprise of having Alix follow him from the Chateau, Philip half expected Alix to come boldly riding up to their campsite insisting she would not stay at the inn another moment.

He pushed a half-burnt log further into the center of the small ring of fire. No doubt she was angry with him for sending her away. But God's teeth! What else could he have done? Let her stay? Impossible. One woman in a knight's camp would have created havoc—from divided attention in the purpose of their mission to silly court-like behavior when the knights would inevitably vie for Alix's favor.

And that wasn't all. Though Philip fully intended their mission to succeed, there was always the possibility that it would not. If they left for the Montfort stronghold never to return, that would leave Alix in a battle camp with the scant protection of the pages left behind. At least at the inn she remained an uninvolved bystander, able to return to the Chateau de Saines without being hindered should the Montforts choose to raid their camp if a loss on Philip's part made such a raid possible.

Philip shook off such thoughts. Blast the woman! She had succeeded in dividing his attention from the purpose at hand despite the fact he'd sent her away. He should be thinking about Julian rather than Alix. But with a sigh he realized St. Autiers might be beyond the horizon, yet it was much too close to eliminate Alix from his thoughts. He knew she was just a short ride away, and despite his anger with her for following him so foolishly, his greatest desire was to go to her.

He knew that was impossible. If they did not hear from August-Caron by morning, Philip intended sending word to Henri Montfort. Philip would let the Montforts believe he wanted to negotiate Julian's release; it shouldn't be difficult to convince them of that, considering the limited number of men Philip had brought with him. With any luck, the Montforts would allow Philip and a handful of his men inside their stronghold. And that, Philip was confident, was all it would take. With a bit of cunning and six of his best fighters, Philip was sure they could escape the mercenaries Henri Montfort had hired. It was only the high walls of their stronghold Philip knew he could not penetrate; but let him inside and he could fight his way out.

"A rider approaches, Sir Philip," called Sir Oliver. Oliver came from the edge of the camp, his hand already resting upon his sword as if ready to draw. "He was spotted from the direction of St. Autiers."

Immediately Philip's thoughts went to Alix and he said, "Identify the rider before taking any action."

"It's a boy."

"One of my pages?"

Sir Oliver shook his head. "No, Sir Philip. The horse is not one of ours."

"Bring him to me."

A few moments later, Sir Oliver and two other knights escorted the boy to Philip. He was not more than fourteen years old and dressed in simple but finely tailored clothes. He looked like a merchant's son, certainly not a poor serf or peasant, and not wearing the colors of a knight to identify him as a page or squire.

Philip stayed seated, still holding the stick and twirling it in the fire. The boy eyed him closely, with an arrogance surprising for a younger stranger in an armed camp. Philip almost smiled; this young stripling gazed at him as though he were assessing Philip—and Philip was coming up far short of whatever the boy's expectations were.

"You are Philip de Saines?" the boy inquired.

Philip nodded. "Does that surprise you?"

The youth folded his hands behind him and boldly circled the campfire to stand closer to Philip. His gaze went from Philip's face to the sword still connected at his hip. "Yes, it surprises me," he told Philip. "They said if you wore a sword you would be like a madman; they say you gave it up years ago because you could not control your bloodlust."

Philip laughed. "How do you know I am not a madman?"

"You look like a page, sitting there tending your master's fire."

Philip laughed again, this time much louder. "Who are you, boy?"

"My name is Christian Bernier." He bowed formally, though the look on his face never wavered from cocky self-assurance. "I am come from Sir August-Caron."

Immediately Sir Oliver stepped forward. "What news have you, then?"

But Philip held up a hand. "This is not August-Caron's page," he said. "How do you know August-Caron?"

The boy smiled a lopsided grin, and clean white

teeth shone under the firelight. "Only through his gold."

"You are part of the Montfort household, then?"

Christian shrugged, noncommittal. "At times. When it serves my purpose."

Philip smiled. "Sir Oliver," Philip said, not taking his eyes from the boy, "have your page bring Christian a hot meal." Then he said to Christian, "Sit down, boy."

Christian obliged, seeming as unconcerned about possible damage to his clothing as Philip was. Philip had not offered a pallet, nor did he use one himself.

"Tell me what your connection is to August-Caron," Philip asked as a page handed Christian a bowl of steaming beef and fresh bread and a cup of wine. "He has hired you to seek me out?"

Christian nodded, at the same time devouring the food before him as if he hadn't eaten in days. He wiped his mouth on the cuff of his tunic before replying. "He couldn't risk coming himself or sending his page for fear of discovery. So he hired me."

"And just how did he make contact with you? What is your 'sometimes' relationship to the Montforts?"

Christian laughed despite the fact he stuffed bread between his teeth. "Are you looking for some kind of loyalty in me? Either to the Montforts or to your August-Caron?"

"Yes," Philip said slowly, pleased by the boy's wit. "I suppose I am."

"You won't find any. I serve myself—and anyone who's willing to pay me. And I'm not alone in that; August-Caron has picked other men just like me out of the Montfort lot; he can spot the true loner. Not that they're hard to find in the Montfort camp."

"Then August-Caron has people in his trust inside the Montfort stronghold?"

"I wouldn't call it trust," Christian said. "It's more like . . . employ. He pays us well—much better than the Montforts ever could."

"How many of you are there?" Sir Oliver asked.

"Four, counting me. But not counting August-Caron himself and his page."

Oliver rubbed his chin, saying, "So there are others beside August-Caron we can count on from within. That is good . . . better than I expected."

"Is that what August-Caron sent you here to tell us?" Philip asked.

Christian nodded. "He knows you are here with some sort of plan to rescue Julian. None of the Montforts think you'll pay the ransom, even if you might have come with your small army to negotiate. They never expected you to pay to begin with."

"I thought as much," Philip said, "given the ridiculous amount they requested. Do you know what they intend settling for?"

"Not just money, I can tell you that," Christian told him.

"What do you mean?" Sir Oliver demanded, obviously impatient with the boy's manner.

Christian spoke to Philip, never even looking up at Sir Oliver as he replied. "August-Caron told me you sent him to the Montforts to find out about their supply of money."

"That's true."

Christian smiled mysteriously. "They don't have any."

"What!" Sir Oliver said. "How can they have no money and sustain an army the size of a wealthy baron's?"

"They did have money," Christian said. "When I first came to work with them they had plenty. But Henri got a bit too ambitious with that army of his. Hired more than he could afford. Now he pays them with promises . . . the promise of taking over the de Saines Chateau and all its wealth by right of conquest."

Sir Oliver sputtered at that. "And he expects to get away with such a ridiculous plan? It's outrageous. King Jean would never allow him to the right of conquest over one of his most loyal nobles."

"Jean would have to stop him . . . and he won't have much time to do that if he's occupied with King Edward of England."

Philip spoke up, having taken the news of the plot for the de Saines demise thus far in silence. "Henri Montfort has been dealing with the English again?"

Christian laughed confidently. "He's never stopped dealing with them. He knows how badly Edward wants men for his cause right here in France. And the Montfort estate is placed so conveniently close to the western edge, allowing easy access for Edward to set foot on the continent. If Jean ever raises his army against the Montforts, Henri assures us all Edward himself would rally to save Montfort men."

Sir Oliver paced once, as if too eager for battle to stand still a moment longer. "I told you we should have brought the whole of our army and crushed the traitors here and now!"

Philip stood, knowing Oliver's attitude could spread too easily among the men if not squelched immediately. "And have my brother killed in the bargain."

"Then let's save Julian in whatever manner you choose, Lord Philip, and follow it with a battle to oust these traitors once and for all. I can send word back to the Chateau and have the rest of our army here by tomorrow night—"

Philip shook his head. "No, Sir Oliver. You are too hasty into battle."

"And you are too eager to avoid it! Madman, indeed!" he scoffed. "I would like to see a bit of blood on your sword—it might remind you what a knight is honor-bound to do when faced with traitors in our land."

Oliver's words were bold—so bold everyone nearby waited in silence for Philip's response. Even Christian watched closely, hesitating for the first time since given the food to take another bite.

But Philip gave no response. Instead, he turned once again to Christian. "Can you get word back to August-Caron?"

Christian took a quick swill of wine, surprised to have the attention focused on him when he'd been sure Sir Oliver had been about to be chastised. "I do not think I was spotted coming here, but I hadn't planned taking the chance of returning to the Montforts. There is a boy at the inn waiting for word; I am to pass it on to him, and he will take any message you have to August-Caron."

"We need access into the stronghold."

"August-Caron guessed that much. He has sentry duty on the south wall; he'll let you approach without calling attention to you."

"We'll need more than that," Philip said. "Is the Montfort chateau surrounded by water?"

"No; it's on a hill with walls so thick and high there is no need of a moat."

"Then we'll need a rope dropped from the battlements to let us inside. Do you think August-Caron can manage that?"

Christian pushed away the empty bowl of food, and stood. "The hardest part will be getting a rope long enough to allow you to scale the wall. But anything can be bought in the Montfort stronghold . . . for the right price." Christian smiled slyly, adding, "I wonder if August-Caron has enough money to pay such a price?"

Philip eyed the boy the barest moment before reaching inside his doublet for a small but heavy pouch of coins.

"You're not actually going to trust this wretch!" Sir Oliver was astounded, guessing what Philip was about to do.

Philip never took his gaze from Christian's. "Yes, Sir Oliver, I am." He handed Christian the entire pouch. "This will cover whatever August-Caron needs."

The boy took it without hesitation, stuffing it into his own tunic before it even lost the warmth from Philip's body.

"And you know, boy, that if you desert us, you'll be deserting a source of income larger than that scant amount of gold you now carry. I do not ask loyalty to me or my family—with your avarice I do not think loyalty necessary." Then, from another pouch inside his doublet, Philip withdrew a small handful of coins. "This is for you; there will be more if you do what we ask."

Christian laughed boldly, accepting the coins and jingling them in his palm. "I will expect a pouch of my own one day, my lord."

Then he turned and ran to his horse, trotting away . . . in the opposite direction of the inn at St. Autiers.

"That's the last we'll see of him," Sir Oliver predicted sourly.

Philip laughed. "Don't be too quick to give up on him, Oliver. If he is being watched, even casually, it'll be wise not to reach his contact so quickly after seeing us or the connection might be made. He was wise in heading the opposite way."

Oliver shook his head. "This is all foolishness. I say we take the Montforts by storm . . . rid ourselves and our country of the lot of them."

"Your patriotism is noble, Sir Oliver," Philip said, "but even if we were to ransack the Montforts with our entire army, there is no guarantee we could win. And with Edward so eager to help him, we could easily be the cause of renewed war between France and England—the end of the truce between our two countries. Do you want to thrust our entire nation into renewed battle with England, when our numbers are so low from the pestilence?"

"The pestilence did not stop at England's door, my lord. They, too, have suffered grievous loss. And that boy made it sound as if it's only Jean's army the English would aid the Montforts to fight against," Oliver pointed out. "Edward would have no cause to rally against Jean if we left his army out of it."

"That may well be true," Philip conceded. "But if we cannot call on Jean's army to help us if we need it, perhaps we could not win at all against the Montforts. They have the advantage of their stronghold, and that is a great asset. I doubt

August-Caron could smuggle our entire army inside their Chateau—and that is exactly what we would need if we ever planned to overthrow the Montfort army completely.''

Philip stepped closer to Oliver, laying a hand to the other man's arm. He continued, saying, "It is wise to take Julian and retreat, Sir Oliver. If the Montforts desire to storm the Chateau de Saines, let them come to us. We shouldn't give them the advantage of letting them draw us from our shelter. That is what they mean for us to do, can't you see? Bring our army here, outside the protection of the Chateau. We would be far easier to conquer then . . . and Henri Montfort would have his right of conquest. Even Jean himself would see that, if we attacked first.''

"You speak as though we have no chance of winning outside the protection of the Chateau de Saines.''

"Perhaps that's what I believe.''

Sir Oliver clamped his mouth shut; Philip saw the struggle in Sir Oliver. The fierce knight wanted to retaliate, to espouse the might and power of his men as being invincible. But he must have guessed his words would do little good; Oliver turned on his heel and headed toward his tent several paces away.

Philip soon entered his own tent, weary from so little sleep the night before and all the day's happenings. But when he lay upon his pallet his thoughts kept him from any rest. However, before long it wasn't only the strife with the Montforts or the plans to rescue Julian which penetrated his mind. In between such serious thoughts, he remembered Alix. These were the hours Alix had meant to share with him. The tent seemed far too quiet, too lonely. And he wished he hadn't sent her away.

Philip sat up. He knew there was nothing to do until the following night. Henri Montfort would hardly approached Philip's camp; he would wait for word from Philip. Perhaps tomorrow Philip would send a page telling Henri that he wanted to negotiate; he could set the meeting for the day after next . . . long after Philip had set his real plan into motion. But at least it would assure Philip that Henri Montfort would not be sending any envoys to him asking what he was doing camped just outside his boundary. Sending word to the Montforts also had the added advantage of avoiding any suspicions on Henri's part, wondering exactly what Philip intended. If Philip simply told him what he wanted Henri to believe, Henri's mind wound not wander to other possibilities.

Yes, Philip thought, he would send a page in the morning. But that still left Philip with far too much idle time; he could do nothing until well past sunset tomorrow before attempting to rescue Julian. Philip felt restless; eager to be finished with this call to his sword, not allowing the thoughts that had plagued him since realizing he could not avoid the sword any longer. He didn't want to think of how he was breaking the vow he'd made to himself.

But that wasn't all that plagued him now. If only Alix had stayed at the Chateau! She wouldn't be such a temptation if she'd stayed too far from him to reach. God's teeth! He was angry at her for causing this dilemma in him. He needed sleep, not a ride to the inn . . . and certainly sleep would not be found in her arms.

He lay down again, thinking resolutely that it was best for him to stay where he was. Even if he would be completely idle until nightfall next . . .

With an oath aimed at both himself and Alix for being the cause of his weakness, Philip dressed and headed outside. He couldn't help himself; he called himself a fool—and a weak one at that—but it did no good. He couldn't resist, he knew that. He simply couldn't stay away from her.

Before leaving the camp, Philip left instructions with Sir Oliver of the message that was to be sent to the Montforts in the morning, letting Henri Montfort think they intended negotiations. Then Philip straddled his horse, spurring him almost immediately into a quick trot.

Alix pulled the blanket up under her chin, shifting position yet again. This is foolish, she thought to herself. She should have been asleep long ago. She was tired, wasn't she? All day, in between spurts of anger at being sent away from Philip and frustration at knowing he was so close—and yet so far—she had admitted to herself she as tired. She'd longed to go to bed, but she stayed up anyway, thinking Philip would come to her despite the anger she knew he felt.

But he hadn't come. And, when his page brought dinner to her room—a private room the page had no doubt paid dearly for and a meal that at first smelled heavenly—Alix had put aside her hopes of Philip walking through the door at any moment. It had grown dark already and she had little reason to think he would come. But when the page left the tray of food behind and Alix approached it, a sudden wave of nausea overwhelmed her. Without warning, the smell of that food threatened to make her sick, despite the fact she hadn't eaten all day. She had ordered the page to take the untouched tray away.

Was she so angry with Philip that she couldn't eat, or sleep? While she had to admit the bed beneath her was not nearly as soft as the one at home, she'd felt so tired all day that the thought of sleep was welcome. She turned onto her back, lying still and staring up at the wood beams on the ceiling of the small, square room. Dim light filtered through the shutters of the single window placed high on the wall above the bed. Besides, she thought to herself, she wasn't really angry. She even admitted Philip had a right to be angry with her . . . after all, it wasn't just a horse-buying expedition he was on. There were dangers in her being with him, she knew that. But she'd been willing to take that risk, just to let them have more time together. Time was one thing that had never been a luxury for them.

What she wanted to do was leave this inn and go

back to his camp. But she knew not just one but both of the pages Philip had sent along with her were outside her door. And they were hardly any comparison to Hugh as guards; there would be no getting past them without detection. So she stayed put, continuing to feel alternately angry and frustrated—and at times ill. But she dismissed her queasiness easily, thinking she was just worried over the dangers Philip would be facing.

Alix dozed at last, but the sound of voices just outside her door awakened her. She sat up immediately, thinking though the two pages were armed, they were not trained knights. And this was a city . . . where all manner of people frequented the inns. For the first time she realized she was not as safe as at home, and listened intently to find out who seemed to want entry to her room.

But she had little chance to wonder. A moment later the door opened, without force, and it shut quietly behind the midnight visitor. It was very dark; the visitor was tall and male, but his dark clothes blended into the shadows of the room.

"Alix?"

Philip's voice was a relief so great Alix slipped from the bed and rushed to his side, throwing her arms about him in heartfelt welcome.

"Alix," he said, holding her close, "you're trembling. Did I frighten you?"

She laughed uneasily. "It's silly, I know, but yes! I—I'm just now realizing I've never been away from home before . . . by myself, that is."

"Well, you're not by yourself any more. There's no need to be afraid."

She hugged him close. "Not with you here. I gave up hoping you would come."

He stroked her hair, pressing her head against his chest. "I shouldn't have."

"Why?" she demanded, looking up at him.

"Well, to begin with our relationship is no longer a secret." He motioned back toward the door with a tilt of his head. "Two pages now know—and though I've made it clear this is to remain between us, I've never been one to believe the tongue is an easily controlled part of the human body."

She laughed briefly, and, still arm-in-arm, they approached the bed, the single piece of furniture within the sparse room. Alix separated from Philip just long enough to light a candle, which was on the floor beside the bed.

Philip looked around at the rough surroundings; the walls, while not dirty, were an unappealing, unadorned gray; the floor had no rushes, the bed beneath them was hard and unyielding. It smelled vaguely of barley, as if the room had been used to make or store beer.

"I should have taken you to the church," he said. "They would have offered more comfortable lodgings, I'm sure."

Alix shook her head, pulling him close. "I'm glad you brought me here; I doubt you would have—or could have—visited me had I been in the care of holy sisters."

He smiled, their faces very near each other. "That is true," he admitted. He kissed her then, but laughed when he heard her stomach growl. "It seems you're hungry, Demoiselle, and not just for me. Haven't you eaten?"

She shook her head. "I wasn't hungry."

"You haven't eaten at all?"

She tried to ignore his persistence by pulling him closer once again and kissing him. "I don't want to eat."

But Philip held back. "Why? Let me have a tray brought here for you."

"They brought one earlier . . . I didn't touch it."

Philip frowned. "Aren't you feeling well?"

She shrugged. "How could I eat knowing you'll be facing danger at any moment?"

"Then allow me to put your mind at rest," he told her. "I have good news. I will have help gaining access inside the Montfort stronghold—and that, I'm sure, is all the help we'll need to rescue Julian successfully and safely. There is very little to worry about, Alix."

"I'm glad of that. Still, I won't be at ease until we're all home."

"Soon we will be home again," he promised, adding as he fingered the sword still at his side, "and I will be able to return my father's sword to him."

Alix sensed the struggle in him. "You've done the right thing," she told him softly. "You could not ignore the sword forever, no matter how much you wished to. Not when the rest of the world lives by the sword."

Philip looked at her, the frown gone but replaced by a look of surprise. "You sound as if you never thought I could have kept my vow not to take up the sword again."

Alix bowed her head, regretting her words . . . even if she did believe they were true.

"You did, didn't you? You thought I would go back to the sword eventually . . . Julian being kidnapped has just made that day come sooner."

"I only meant to comfort you," she said. "Because I know I am part of the reason you had to touch the sword again. I wish you never had to break that vow . . . and I wish I was not part of the reason. I never want to give you reason to regret loving me."

Philip pulled her to him. "I'll never regret loving you," he said. "And it's true I have to save my brother for love of you as well as love of him . . . but that doesn't make you responsible for this decision. No one is to blame—except the Montforts for concocting this whole kidnapping to begin with."

She put his arms around her neck. "I love you, Philip. I do honor your vow and will gladly welcome the day we are home and you can lay the sword down once again."

He held her close. "That day will be here soon," he said. "Once we have Julian back again, there will be peace. The Montforts won't attempt another kidnapping if this one is so easily foiled."

Alix rested her head against his chest, hoping his words were true. She prayed this kidnapping

would be easily foiled, and that both Philip and
Julian would soon be safe.

But even by the tone of his voice, Alix could tell
Philip himself did not entirely believe they would
be rid of the strife caused by the Montforts just by
outwitting their kidnapping scheme. She had an
odd feeling that though the Montforts might be
about to lose their hostage, they would not let that
end their feud with the de Saines family.

32

A fine drizzle began just as Philip, Sir Oliver and a
half-dozen other knights approached the Montfort
stronghold. Philip signalled the others to pause at
the edge of the trees; between them and the high
wall of the chateau was a barren hill which
offered no hope of camouflage. Now came the
time of trust, Philip thought—not only trust in
August-Caron, but in a newer and lesser-known
ally, Christian Bernier. Pray the boy's avarice
allowed thoughts of the future and not just the
sack of gold Philip had trusted him with the day
before.

They were too far away to see if indeed the rope
was in place; Christian had said only that August-
Caron would see that the south wall was free for
their approach. But the south wall was long, and
in the utter darkness of the rainy night, it was
impossible to see any line or shadow of what
might be a rope.

"Has anyone a flintrock?" Philip asked quietly.

One knight rummaged through a rather bulky
gipon which he wore over his chain mail. In a
moment, he handed a small stone to Philip.

"I will go to the wall," he said, "and when I
come to the rope I'll signal a spark. Join me
there."

Philip would have set off immediately, but Sir Oliver detained him with one hand to Philip's elbow.

"You should send one of us, Lord Philip. What if August-Caron was unable to free the south wall of other sentries not in his trust? You could be spotted and speared down."

Philip smiled crookedly. "Then we will know if this mission will succeed or not, won't we?"

He was off before another word could be spoken.

The ground was slippery as Philip made his way out of the safe shadows of the forest. He prayed once for a continued absence of lightning—knowing nature itself could turn against him on a night like this. But for now it seemed to be on his side; clouds hid the light of the stars and moon, and the drizzle that fell was not enough to hinder him.

Philip kept his eye on the wall before him; he did not look up for sentries, or behind him to see how far he'd come. He kept low, but speed was with him and he made it to the wall in moments and without a sound heard from the battlements above. His faith in Christian Bernier's service strengthened—it didn't matter that the impetus of the boy's help was greed and not loyalty.

There was little possibility of Philip being spotted while directly below the battlements, and so while he still kept silent, he did have the confidence of relative safety. He went left first, but found no rope. Then he backtracked, but the thought that August-Caron might not have succeeded in what Philip had asked did cross his mind. If that was so, access inside the Montfort stronghold would be impossible.

But the rope was there. Philip almost stumbled over it, he came upon it so quickly. He hadn't realized how he was speeding to find that rope; his pulse was quick, his mind a battleground of its own, part of him fearing the worst, the other part refusing to give up hope. But there it was—a thick, strong rope that was sturdy enough for the brawniest knight to scale even this tall wall. Philip

385

pulled on it once, hard, finding it secure. Then he turned back toward the knights still hidden in the shadows, withdrawing his sword and taking the flint in hand. He rubbed the two together quickly, just once. Even in the rain, a small flash like a firefly ignited for the barest moment—but it was long enough. Moments later he was joined by Sir Oliver and the others.

"I beg you to let me go up the rope first," Oliver whispered. "If this is a trap . . ."

Philip eyed Oliver once; he knew it was not personal concern for Philip that made the older knight so cautious. Philip did not call Oliver a friend—he hardly liked the man and knew the feeling was mutual—but Philip knew Oliver's loyalty to the de Saines family was great. And since Philip was the de Saines heir, it followed that Oliver wanted to do whatever possible to assure Philip's safety throughout this mission. It was no less than Oliver's duty and promise to Sire Geoffrey, Oliver's liege.

Philip nodded once, without speaking, and Oliver jumped on the rope without delay.

Philip was the third to scale the wall. Other than an occasional scrape of a sword as it brushed against the stone wall, the men were silent in their ascent.

August-Caron was on the ledge of the battlement when Philip heaved himself over the wall. The two men clasped hands once, briefly, then August-Caron whispered.

"You will blend in with all of the other armed men of this stronghold if you walk easily," he said. "I know where they are holding Julian; it is heavily guarded, but we should have no trouble overcoming them."

"You are to stay here in wait," Philip told him. "If you are seen missing from your post, it may cause unnecessary attention. Tell us how to get there."

But a familiar young voice spoke up from behind. "I will show you."

Philip and the others turned, seeing Christian

Bernier standing with a cocksure smile upon his youthful face. Philip felt laughter welling up from his middle, but squelched it; this was hardly the time for lightness. But the boy looked as if he were about to go on his first hunting jaunt, not on a mission that threatened his very life. No doubt he had a price to act as their escort, Philip thought.

"Very well," Philip said. "Lead the way."

As Philip fell in step beside Christian, the boy said, "You see, Seigneur, I will have earned that extra pouch of gold you promised."

Philip did smile then, patting the boy's back. "Indeed, Christian. And you shall have it."

"That is," Christian said, "if we all live through tonight."

So the boy did know the danger. Philip glanced at Christian marveling; for so young a boy to be aware of danger and yet look so unafraid was indeed unusual. The boy had more than his share of all the ingredients of knighthood.

With Philip and Christian at the fore, the knights traversed the ledge on the high wall, taking a narrow stone stairway to the courtyard below. Philip could hear the sounds of men from various directions; the guardhouse sounded loud and full of men, no doubt many of the sentries had gone there to be out of the rain. There was an overhanging porch roof at the base of the forebuilding to the keep, and there, too, men talked and laughed, many of them sounding as if well into their cups.

Christian did not lead them to the main entryway; instead, he took them to a doorway on the side of the keep. It led to a dark tunnelway, first down several steps past our doorways, then back up again, then down ever lower into the deep recesses of the stronghold. It was damp and dark as pitch, and their footsteps echoed dully off the stone walls. From somewhere, the sound of dripping water thumped rhythmically, as if in tune with someone's heartbeat. But not Philip's; his beat faster than usual. Visions of old battles and the feel of his blood pumping faster through his veins combined with the sense of readiness and it was as if he'd never been away from the life of a knight. It all came back more quickly than he would have dreamed—or hoped. What happened to the two years he'd ignored the sword?

From above, he could hear voices and footsteps.

"The hall is directly above us," Christian whispered. "They have Julian in the very bowels of this place—no one could find him unless they knew where to look."

Soon Christian slowed and a light shone from around the bend of the narrow tunnel. Christian motioned for the others to stay back, then he walked boldly round the curving tunnel, with a sudden and decidedly jaunty sway to his walk.

"Where's Rampall?" Christian's voice took on an unusual drawl. "I came to relieve him." Then he laughed. "Of guard duty, that is . . . This is one young boy he won't find solace with."

Laughter followed the boy's slanderous words, one loud guffaw sounding above the others. Judging by the laughs, Philip guessed there were at least four or five guards, perhaps a couple more.

"Rampall isn't here," said one gravelly voice, probably the same who'd laughed so much louder than the others. "And you'd do well not to look for him. He's had his eye on you for a month now."

"I'm supposed to relieve him of guard duty . . . somewhere. Anyone know where he is?"

A few low grumbles were the only response.

Christian spoke up again, and Philip could hear the echo of his footsteps saunter farther into the midst of the guards. "So how is our honored guest this evening, anyway? Well-fed? Comfortable? He's awfully quiet. Is he even in there?"

"Who cares?" the same man responded. "He's in there all right. He's hardly said a word since he came here—won't eat, either. Says the food is no good. Imagine that!" He coughed, then added, "There are ways to get our pompous guest quickly accustomed to life as a hostage—in fact, I showed him one way tonight."

The others laughed, and one spoke up. "I wonder how much better the food tastes to him now? Now that he'd had the comparison of a raw snake shoved down his throat."

"You made him eat a snake?" Christian's voice was surprised, but not so surprised as Philip felt as he listened. He wanted to go round the bend of the tunnel and attack his brother's tormentors without delay. But he held back, knowing it was far better to keep a tight rein on his wits and emotions.

"I was looking for a rodent, but the blasted snake must have eaten every last one of them down here."

Another man laughed. "He was a fat one, all right."

Christian spoke up. "I thought Henri Montfort left orders the prisoner was to be treated well."

"What's this? A bit of compassion from the pretty boy?" That was a new voice which spoke, one who hadn't spoken up before.

"He's a de Saines," Christian said, ignoring the insulting name flung his way.

But the other man spoke again, not responding to Christian's reminder of the importance of their prisoner. "Maybe Rampall has his eye on you for a reason?" His footsteps echoed, a shuffling sound that suggested he was a large man. "Maybe you're looking for Rampall so you *can* give him some relief . . . in the loins, that is."

There was the barest pause before a thump and a grunt sounded, and Philip and the other knights behind him needed no further reason to step forward. They moved out of the shadows as one giant force, swords already drawn.

The guards were taken by surprise. Philip reached them first, and the nearest guard could only draw a dagger in defense, the sword too slow to leave his side binding. But the dagger was little defense; with one swoop of Philip's sword, the dagger fell from the guard's hand and hit the damp stone floor with a dull thud.

From the corner of his eye Philip counted the

guards; there must have been eight or nine, more than Philip and those he'd brought. Henri Montfort was guarding this precious prisoner well—but that hardly set Philip back. He pressed on, striking down the now weaponless guard before him without delay—or remorse. There wasn't time . . .

Philip saw Christian defending himself against a great hulk of a man. He'd already drawn blood from Christian's shoulder—one more blow from the oversized man could prove fatal to Christian. Philip swung from behind, the hard edge of his sword lethal as it penetrated through gipon and chain mail of the huge guard, so great was Philip's strength.

Philip spared one flash of a smile Christian's way before turning on another aggressor—but not too soon to see Christian grin in return. He'd hardly noticed his shoulder wound, it seemed. A moment later the boy raised his sword again, this time against a more evenly matched opponent. The clanking of swords, the grunt of men as they heaved their weapons against one another, the sound echoed above all. A pained gasp came from floor all blended to fill Philip's ears—but one sound echoed above. A pained gasp came from beside him, and he turned his gaze áway from the guard he sparred with just long enough to see Sir Oliver fall, blood spewing from his chest where the mail had been pierced through.

A surge of strength coursed through Philip's veins; Sir Oliver had used caution for Philip's sake, Philip could do no less in return. In a rash fit of fury, he thrust at the opponent opposite him, somewhere in the back of his mind knowing to lose balance and clear thought in a battle was to sign his own death warrant. But for a moment he did just that; the sight of Sir Oliver falling, with his aggressor still advancing, made Philip lose the singleness of vision to keep his own defenses up. Still sparring, Philip moved sideways, and in a moment he both defended and attacked at the same time, having two guards before him now.

The one above Sir Oliver was taken completely by surprise; his sword had been lifted, as if to thrust deep into the wounded adversary he'd just sent to his feet. But with one wide swoop, Philip parried one guard's sword and deflected the other from its mark.

Both guards descended on Philip then. His sword sang through the air, quicker than either of his attackers, stronger than both combined. It was all there inside of him, he knew, the balance, the stimulant, the precision—after two years, he hadn't lost it. In the dim light from variously placed sconces, the metal swords glistened—and he saw the blood that stained the edge of his own. Blood he'd vowed never to draw again.

But he couldn't stop, despite that fleeting thought. When one attacker was too slow in raising his sword, Philip took the advantage. His sword sunk deep into the other man's gut, but did not linger. Philip raised it just soon enough to deflect another blow from the remaining attacker. Then he slid his sword along the edge of the other's, by sheer strength following the movement of his opponent. In a moment the weapon was flung to the floor, forced away by Philip as hilt met hilt and Philip's strength proved superior. Then he took the dagger from the other man's hip and with the man's own weapon, separated soul from body with one fatal cut. The man fell to the floor in a bloody, lifeless heap.

No one else came forward. One man, still fighting opposite Christian, saw he alone was left to defend himself in the battle, and turned on his heel and fled.

Christian's laughter echoed after him.

"No time to gloat over our victory now," Philip cautioned. "Let's get Julian and be away."

It took three men to remove the blockade on the door to the small room that held Julian. The door itself was wider than two handspreads, and it was not on hinges so it had to be pulled out completely from the door frame. In all, it took several minutes to free Julian from his confines, just a further safeguard the Montforts had taken to keep their pawn in possession.

"Philip!"

Julian had barely heard the skirmish outside, but once the huge door was being removed he knew something was odd. He'd never been disturbed so late at night in the past few days he'd been held. But now to see his brother standing in the light of the tunnel sconce—with sword in hand—Julian thought for a moment he'd gone mad and was imagining the whole sight.

"Time for greetings later, brother," Philip said, and so Julian knew his brother was real. Surely no imaginary vision spoke!

A moment later Philip pulled Julian from the tiny, foul-smelling room. Julian looked far worse than Philip had imagined his brother would be after only barely a week of confinement. A beard had grown to cover his chin and cheeks, surprisingly thick for so short a time left unattended, but not thick enough to hide several fresh bruises. And his clothes were soiled and torn. He wore no chains or bondage, a sure sign of the Montforts' confidence no one could penetrate their stronghold. But despite Julian's obvious weakness and all the evidence of mistreatment, Philip's younger brother smiled broadly and followed Philip from the room with surprising agility.

Philip briefly assessed the wounds to his men with a quick glance around. Besides Sir Oliver, one other knight had been wounded, but when one of Philip's men went to the other knight's side, he felt for any sign of life but found none.

"We'll have to leave him," Philip said. "Help Sir Oliver and let's be gone."

They found their way quickly back through the tunnel. Julian stumbled more than once, limping from a wound to his limbs, and Philip put an arm about him to lend assistance.

Once outside, they moved more carefully. It was raining more heavily now, with gusty winds and an occasional rumble of thunder. Lightning was bound to appear, Philip thought, making it much too easy for them to be spotted for who they were. The south wall was across the courtyard, and though it was only a matter of time before the guard who fled realized the fatal battle had not been caused by an insult but rather a plot to free the prisoner, they dared not call attention to their wounds or their identity.

The only way across the courtyard with any speed was pure boldness, Philip thought. He took the lead, and the others followed his act. With an arm still about Julian, he pretended to stagger ahead, talking loud and throwing in a belch or two. The others went along immediately, laughing as if they shared some great joke. If they were noticed, and no doubt they were, a handful of drunken men was hardly uncommon within this stronghold.

Once they reached the shadows of the high south wall, their laughter drifted away as if they were ending their festivities for the night. So close to their exit, Philip could not resist stepping more quickly once in sight of the stone stairway.

But he was too eager. From an archway leading out of a tunnel from the front portcullis a pair of armed men appeared. At first it seemed as if the men might pass by the odd-looking group of Philip's men. But something must have caught one man's eye. He looked at Philip, who did his best to sway in accomplished drunken unsteadiness, then the man looked at Julian, whose head was bent as if passed out cold.

The man grabbed Julian by the hair, pulling his head up to stare at his face. Philip knew the man recognized the prized hostage—his eyebrows rose and he was about to call out. But Philip slid a dagger from his side, the very one he'd taken from the guard in the archives of the stronghold. He thrust it into the surprised man's middle, and nary a sound was uttered as the man sunk, somewhat slowly, to the ground.

The second man seemed as if he'd just been rudely awakened from some sort of dream. He gazed at the fallen man, then up at Philip in confusion and finally horror as the truth of what had happened finally dawned. And though the dagger was still deep in the man at Philip's feet, Philip knew he could hardly leave this man alive to call attention to them and the direction of their escape.

"Kill him," Philip said over his shoulder, then pulled Julian forward, leaving the task to one of the knights behind.

They were up the stairs and on the high battlements in a matter of moments. August-Caron was still there, along with three other guards posted on the south wall who were obviously trusted.

No words were exchanged as they went to the rope. As the knights started to go down one by one, Julian and Sir Oliver were left between August-Caron and another knight. Julian was able to stand of his own power, but, Philip noted, Oliver wavered on the edge of unconsciousness.

"I can make it," Julian said.

"I don't doubt it," Philip replied confidently. "It's not you I'm worried about. We're going to have to tie Oliver to my back."

"You'll never make it down that long wall with such a weight dangling behind you," Julian said.

"We have no choice."

Oliver was barely conscious, but when they tried to tie a rope around his waist and up his shoulders, connecting him to Philip like some sort of baby to its mother, he protested.

"I can make it down on my own," he said, but even his voice sounded weak.

"I'm going to need your help," Philip said over his shoulder to Oliver. "I want you to grab the rope just as if you were scaling the wall yourself. Ready?"

Oliver did not reply. Philip climbed over the edge of the battlement, feeling Oliver's full weight for the first time. God's teeth! the man was heavy. Philip glanced down. The wall was sheer, and those who had already descended looked like dwarves in comparison.

But Philip did not contemplate for long. As if

Oliver were a backpack and he was climbing the cliffs for hawks, Philip swung over the edge. For a moment he held still, feeling Oliver's weight pulling him off balance for the barest moment. But he clung to the rope, his elbows still atop the battlement. Slowly, he eased himself downward, letting his feet aid him in carrying his burden as he slid in minute sections down the wall. He felt the coarse rope burn into his palms, but ignored the pain. They felt numb in a moment.

Halfway down the wall, just as one blinding ray of lightning pierced the dark night, Philip felt Oliver slip further down his back. "Grab hold!" Philip whispered in a fierce voice, but Oliver must have passed out; perhaps that was why he was no longer balancing part of his weight evenly across Philip's shoulders. For one horrible moment Philip thought Oliver might fall, but the rope held that bound Oliver to Philip and so, miraculously, did Philip's strength. Philip fairly flew down the remainder of the way, not caring that the skin on his palms was ripped away.

Philip jumped to the ground, and a moment later so did Julian, just behind him. Julian, along with Christian who had waited for them, helped untie Oliver from Philip's back.

"Perhaps one day you'll give your children rides like that," Julian said, teasing.

Philip grunted. "Not if they weigh anything like him," he said, then breathed once heavily as Oliver was fully detached from him. He was indeed in a dead faint, but he was breathing easily despite the wound on his upper chest near the shoulder.

Philip and Christian carried Oliver to the edge of the forest, where the others waited with their mounts.

"How bad is your shoulder?" Philip asked Christian as they walked with their burden between them.

Christian grinned. "More blood than pain; I'll live long enough to enjoy the gold you'll pay me, Seigneur."

Then Julian spoke from behind them. "Are you

camped nearby?"

Philip shook his head. "We were, but we planned to go back to the Chateau de Saines once we got you. But Oliver will never make it all the way back. We'd better take him to the inn—we have to stop there anyway."

"Why?" Julian asked.

"Alix is there."

"What! You mean you allowed—"

But Julian's surprise was cut short by a feminine voice behind them.

"No, Julian, your brother did not 'allow' anything. But I didn't intend to let that stand in the way of what I wanted to do."

Every eye present turned to the sound. No one was more amazed than Philip himself to see Alix, dressed like a page, emerge from among the horses. Philip walked directly up to her, and spoke in a voice that was sharp as the point of his sword.

"I won't ask what you are doing here; I don't intend to say anything right now or I might work myself into such a rage I could wring your neck. Get on one of these horses and don't say another word. Understood?"

Alix did as he said, though she counted a full five seconds before doing his bidding. She knew he was angry—angrier than she'd ever seen him—but she had no regrets.

Just then August-Caron, the last to scale down the wall, approached in a run and fit of gasps.

"They've discovered the two bodies at the base of the stairs," he announced. "It'll only be a matter of time before they think of looking in on the prisoner and realizing what happened. We had better make haste if we want to stay far ahead of them."

Philip spoke to Alix. "Did you come from the camp?"

She nodded. "They're ready to go—they just wait for you."

August-Caron's head jerked in the direction of the female voice. "God's teeth! It's Demoiselle Alix!"

396

"Think about that later, August-Caron," Philip
said. "Right now we've got to get Oliver to the
battle wagon. We'll have to go directly to the
Chateau de Saines, and pray God he makes it all
the way—and us too, with the devil on our heels."

No one delayed; Oliver was straddled across the
front of Philip's horse, Philip buffering as best he
could the unsteady ride of their quick departure.
But all the while he kept his gaze on the stiff,
proud back of Alix Beauchamp. Blast the
woman—if they all survived this alive, he would
happily kill her for endangering herself this way.

33

Alix rode in silence all the way to the Chateau. She
felt Philip's gaze upon her more than once, and
though she stole several glances his way, his harsh
expression never wavered. By the time the
Chateau was in view, Alix was thoroughly
drenched from the continuing rain and exhausted
from the steady pace they kept to stay far ahead
any possible pursuers.

But if the Montforts followed, they never came
within sight or sound of the rescue party. The
mission, a total success, was coming to a safe end.
And Alix guessed there would be a celebration
once the Chateau welcomed them home. Even
now, coming so close to home, the others around
her began speaking and laughing, their rising
spirits eliminating the fatigue from the night's
toilsome events and long ride back.

Philip, however, remained silent. His face did
not reflect the invigoration the others so obviously
felt. And, Alix guessed, it was not only due to his
anger at her. She doubted he would want to
celebrate the blood that had been shed this night.

397

The approaching party did not have to shout their identity upon nearing the Chateau. It was just before dawn, and though most of the inhabitants were more than likely still abed, a sentry hailed their arrival once they topped the rise of the last hill before the gateway. The draw-bridge was lowered and out came several guards and men-at-arms, pages and servants to greet them. At last, obviously hastily dressed, Sire Geoffrey emerged. And just as the troupe entered the inner courtyard, others came out to greet them, including a somewhat unkempt Lady Eleanore, dressed only in a flowing velvet bed-robe.

Lady Eleanore and Sire Geoffrey went im-mediately to Julian's side; once Julian slid from his horse, his mother embraced him and kissed his cheek, tears streaming from her eyes.

"My son, my son," Alix heard her say, and fleetingly Alix wondered if Eleanore would spare a moment for her other son, the one who had made Julian's homecoming possible.

But she had little time for such bitter contem-plation. She saw Philip walk off in the direction of his tower, but Geoffrey called after him.

"Philip!" Geoffrey left Julian at Eleanore's side, approaching Philip who had halted his departure but did not return into the crowd of others around them.

Alix, standing near Lady Eleanore, did not listen to Eleanore's welcoming words for Julian but instead watched Geoffrey and Philip. She could not hear what they said, but it appeared Geoffrey welcomed Philip warmly, with a brief embrace and a fatherly kiss upon his son's cheek.

Philip did not smile at his father's obvious warmth. He still possessed the cold, detached countenance of a man struggling to forget some-thing. And Alix knew what it was he wanted to forget. She was, therefore, unsurprised, when Philip took this earliest opportunity to draw forth his sword, slowly and without any indication of emotion. He placed the hilt in his father's hand, returning the weapon to its owner.

Then, without another word, he turned and headed to his tower.

Alix wanted to follow, but knew she could not. She might have anyway, but the sound of her mother's voice made her turn her head from the closed door of Philip's tower.

"Alix Beauchamp, I shall have you sent to the convent myself after the worry you've caused your father and me these past days!"

Alix faced her mother, but despite her words and harsh tone, Marie had tears in her eyes and a smile on her face. She embraced Alix quickly, holding her close for a long moment and sniffling ever so slightly.

Giles Beauchamp spoke up. "Alix, it was a very foolish thing for you to go after these men on such a mission. You were no doubt in the way."

Alix stepped back from her mother's embrace. She turned to her father and smiled. She could see past his gruff greeting; though she knew he would never admit it, he too had been worried over her welfare. "No, Father. When they discovered my presence they sent me to an inn. I wasn't in the way at all."

"Just as well—a woman has no place on the battlefield."

"That is true, Alix," Marie said. "You should not have followed, and not just for your own sake. You should have realized you would be a nuisance . . . and that we would worry terribly over your welfare."

Just then Julian approached, having separated himself from his clinging mother.

"Alix, I should like to speak with you alone," he said. "Later, if you wish. I have no doubt you are exhausted. What I have to say is important, but it can wait until you are rested."

Alix nodded.

"You'll have a hard time keeping her in place, Julian, once you are wed," Giles said lightly. "But I'm sure it was warming to your heart to know your betrothed cares so much for you that she wanted to be there when you were rescued."

Julian said nothing; he just bowed formally, then disappeared into the forebuilding of the keep.

Alix exchanged glances with her mother; concern for Julian had nothing to do with the reason Alix had followed the rescue party, as Marie knew so well. And, Alix guessed, Julian knew it, too.

Talk of a feast rumbled through the courtyard, celebrating the fact they'd outwitted the Montforts. But for now, sleep was what the entire company who had rescued Julian needed. The feast could wait until later in the day. Alix let her mother walk her to her bedchamber, all the while thinking she would not stay there for long. She would go to Philip's tower at the earliest opportunity.

But Marie was slow to leave Alix's chamber once she saw her daughter there. She talked on and on, about how worried they had been when they found her gone, how her father had wanted to send men after her but Geoffrey had insisted such a move might endanger the whole mission if the Montforts thought too many men were arriving at their doorstep.

Alix barely listened. She sat on the ledge of her window looking out, her gaze resting on the window of the tower opposite her.

At last Marie was silent, just looking at her daughter.

"I know you intend going to him as soon as I leave here," Marie said quietly.

Alix turned her head to face her mother. There was no use denying it; her mother knew her too well. "Does it matter now? Now that you know what we mean to each other?"

Marie nodded. "The entire Chateau thinks you went after the rescue party out of love and concern for Julian."

"They will know the truth sooner or later," Alix pointed out. "Besides, no one has seen me go to Philip before; I will be careful."

"The wedding is set for three weeks from today,

Alix. Have you forgotten?"

In truth, Alix had indeed forgotten. She'd put it out of her mind intentionally, and it seemed to have worked. But three weeks! So soon!

"I'm sure Philip will speak to Father soon," she said. "When he realizes the wedding is so close, he will remember we have no time to spare."

But still, Marie frowned. "Your father will not easily give up the notion of having you marry Julian."

"Surely he would prefer I marry the first rather than the second son, especially in a family such as the de Saineses."

Marie shook her head. "Perhaps in any other family except the de Saineses; Philip has not cleared his name."

"But he saved his brother! Surely that will outweigh any past indiscretions Father might believe of Philip."

Marie shrugged. "It is no secret your father prefers Julian to Philip; I do not think Philip's heroic act will make enough difference in your father's opinion of him to do you any good."

"I do not believe that," Alix said stubbornly. "Once Father knows it's Philip I love, combined with the fact that Philip can no longer be labeled a coward by anyone, he will realize Philip is a fitting husband for any woman."

"That may well be true ... but do not forget Philip is not willing to defend himself against one man who hates him. Your father knows Charles la Trau and his challenge against Philip will not simply disappear—and he knows Philip will never accept that challenge. Knowing he has enemies like this, will your Father want you to marry a man who will not defend himself against his enemies? He defends his brother—but not himself."

Alix stood, leaving the window ledge and approaching the bed. She knew part of that was true; she knew Philip had returned Sire Geoffrey's sword with the intention never to raise a sword again—he had no wish to raise it against Charles

401

la Trau. But she shook such thoughts away. She
didn't want Philip to raise a sword again, did she?
Of course not. She would find a way, she thought,
to convince her father that Philip was indeed the
best choice as a husband for her.

"Please, Mother, I am so very tired."

"Then you won't go to him tonight?"

Alix grinned. "It's morning, Mother. The sun is
already rising."

Marie neared her daughter and put an arm
about her shoulders. "You need sleep, Alix. And so
does he."

That much, she had to admit, was certainly true.

But once Marie was gone, Alix could not deny
her greatest desire was to go to Philip anyway. She
reined in such desires, however. Perhaps Philip
was already asleep. It was true he did need
sleep . . . and so did she. She was so tired.

Alix undressed and slipped into bed. But no
sooner had she laid down than a noise sounded at
her door. The room was light, with the sun shining
brightly now. Alix bid entrance to the person at
the door.

Philip came in without a word. He closed the
door, then leaned against it, just looking at her.
How tired he looked, she marveled. He hadn't
changed clothes; his face was rough with a day or
two of beard's growth, and his hair was an unruly
mass of dark waves. But, she thought with a light
heart, he had never looked more handsome.

"My mother convinced me you needed sleep
more than you needed me," Alix said with a smile.
"And I must admit, you do look in need of it."

He smiled in return. The anger of earlier, it
seemed, had disappeared. He approached the bed.

Alix sat up, still holding the covers demurely in
front of her although she did not know why. Then,
still smiling, she held the covers away, revealing
her nakedness and inviting him to lay beside her.

He undressed first, and Alix watched, marveling
that such passion could stir inside her when she'd
felt so utterly exhausted just moments ago.

But when Philip lay beside her, reaching closer

to embrace her, the sight of his wounded hands made Alix gasp.

"Your hands!" She held them, palms up, and inspected the torn and discolored skin. He had already put something on it, she could tell by the slight scent of herbs. But she did not doubt the pain he must feel. "It happened when you carried Sir Oliver down the rope, didn't it?" she asked. "I saw you—I knew it was you the moment the lightning lit the sky and I saw you coming down the wall. My heart nearly stopped when I saw Oliver slip, I worried for you so!"

He grinned. "My own heart skipped a beat or two, I must admit. But it's over now. It doesn't hurt anymore—at least not when I'm here with you. There are other matters filling my mind than how my hands feel."

She kissed his mouth softly, wanting to do what she could to keep him from remembering whatever pain which might still be present. Their lovemaking was gentle, and not so thorough as in the past. But even so when they joined as one nothing was lacking—they loved and shared and penetrated each other's minds and souls. Their love was complete in each other, Alix thought—and nothing, she vowed, would ever separate them.

Later, Alix lay within Philip's embrace, feeling the steady rise and fall of his breathing. She wondered if he'd fallen asleep.

"It isn't over," he said quietly, answering her silent question of whether he slept or not. But his words raised another question.

"What isn't?" she asked, then turned to kiss him. "Our lovemaking?"

He kissed her back, but grew serious afterward. "The feud with the Montforts. The killing."

"But I saw you return your father's sword to him. Surely you believed it over then?"

He breathed deeply. "I returned the sword because I remembered my vow; I was sick of killing, Alix. I vowed never to shed another's blood again." He paused, absently rubbing his fingertips along her shoulder as he spoke. "Two years ago, I was with an over-zealous knight who wanted to purge France of anyone involved with ties to England. There was a village . . . a sleepy little town just like the ones outside Chateau de Saines—with people just the same, too. Women, children, old people and young. But they were guilty of some sort of treason—of housing English vessels in their harbor, even giving shelter to English soldiers. But I did not believe annihilating them was the answer." He laughed bitterly, briefly. "He wanted us to kill them all, from the fiercest would-be traitor to the most innocent babe. I wanted to challenge the foot soldiers, peasants and whatever men they housed in a battle—a conventional battle without the presence of women and children. But Sidney Paul wanted them all punished. As an example, he said."

"Oh, Philip," Alix whispered. "It's little wonder you lost your taste for blood."

"I tried not to fight on either side when the battle began; I lifted my sword in defense—of myself and any innocent I saw about to be speared through by a knight of France. That was my crime; Philip was king then; he could have banished me from France for raising a sword against one of his knights. I don't know why he didn't—perhaps it would have been easier then, for a while. Perhaps that was my punishment; he made me stay to face all those who would call me a coward for putting down the sword. Then, when Jean became king, he requested me on his council—hardly any punishment."

"But you are no coward. And now, after saving your brother, no one can call you a coward again."

"It all came back so quickly," he whispered, as if he still marveled at the truth. "When I went into the Montfort stronghold, I knew I would have to kill again. There was no way to avoid it. And as I was fighting, seeing one guard after another die at my hands, I felt nothing. No regret, no remorse. Nothing."

"Because you did what you had to do."

She felt him shrug. "When I left there, with Julian safe, all I could think of was throwing down the sword again. That's why I returned my father's sword so quickly. But now, I fear, too quickly."

"Why?"

"I was foolish to hope—even for a moment—that this feud was over. Our outwitting the Montforts isn't enough—they'll probably try again to kidnap either me or Julian, or my father, who would never survive—or else they'll be bold enough to attack. They have an army of soldiers living on promises of de Saines wealth; they have to do something to keep those promises."

"If they attack the Chateau de Saines," Alix said, "there is little possibility of them achieving victory."

"Perhaps not," Philip said slowly. "But they might try for a siege—and perhaps succeed, with the amount of men they have. And though the Chateau is more prosperous than it was just a few months ago, we do not have the stored grains and other such necessities to withstand a siege of any length. The days after the Plague drained us of those supplies."

"Do you think that will be the Montforts' next step? A siege?"

"If I were them, it would be my choice. Unless . . ." Philip sat up, running a hand through his hair. "Unless they were offered an opportunity for one quick way to settle this."

"How?"

"The surest way to gain their interest—and the safest way to end all of this." He turned to her, the look in his eyes so focused and the tone of his voice so fervent Alix knew he thoroughly believed in what he was saying. "A tournament," he announced. "Each side chooses forty of their best men for a melee. The victorious side will indeed prove the most powerful in the land—and normal rules will apply. The winner takes the wealth."

"But the de Saines wealth against the Montforts'—it's hardly fair!"

"However necessary," Philip said. "And that is

405

the only way we'll get them to agree. This will be the end, truly the end.''

''And if the Montforts win?''

Philip hesitated, but he smiled crookedly. ''The de Saineses will have been a long and noble dynasty. But it wouldn't be the end of the de Saineses. There is room to rebuild in a country like France.''

''But is it worth that risk?''

''If we are put to siege—and I'm sure that's the Montforts' only alternative—we could lose many more lives. Others would suffer besides the men called to arms—women and children . . . and you.'' He touched her cheek briefly, a frown upon his face. But when he spoke again, there was nothing but assurance in his tone. ''And by the rules of the tourney, the Montforts will not be entitled to take all of the land; we will be left with a portion of it—that is, if we lose. I do not count on that. We succeeded against the Montforts already . . . we shall do so again.''

Philip rose from the bed, dressing quickly.

Alix guessed where Philip was headed. ''You need sleep, Philip!'' Alix admonished out of concern for him. ''Can you not go to your father later with this plan?''

''I cannot,'' he said, looking at her intently once again. ''This must be settled before the Montforts decide on attack and a siege is all they have left. Besides,'' he added, bending down and kissing her once, briefly, ''I can't expect your father to wed you to any de Saines—even Julian—while the threat of the Montforts hangs over my family.''

Alix reached up to pull him closer. ''I do not expect to marry any de Saines but you,'' she told him.

''Exactly what I intend,'' he said with a smile. Then, still clasping the belt around his slim waist, he left the room.

Alix stood with the full intention of following after him. But before she'd even donned her underrobe, a wave of nausea overcame her and all she could do was sink back into the covers of her bed. Sleep visited so quickly she had no chance to fight it away.

"It is the only way, Father," Philip said quietly while he waited for his father's reply. He'd told him all his thoughts, his firm belief that the Montforts' next step would be siege, knowing the Montforts' plan was to pay their mercenary army with de Saines money. Philip knew he must convince his father their best hope was in the Tourney. "We can even suggest *a plaisance*," he added.

"Blunted weapons? Never! We couldn't trust the Montforts to blunt their swords." He rubbed his chin. "No," he said, "it will have to be *a outrance*." Then he stood; they were in the de Saineses' inner chamber, where no one could overhear their words. "It is a sound idea, Philip. And, I fear you are correct; this is our only alternative to siege. From what you have told me now, and from what August-Caron reported to me earlier, I am convinced that Montforts' goal is to claim the de Saines fortune by right of conquest. Better to fight than to be trapped like caged animals at a circus."

"The Church will not approve," Philip cautioned.

"It is a risk we must take. I doubt excommunication will be considered for us, son. We pay the Church far too much in donations and tithes to let them want to lose us."

It was the first time Philip had ever heard his father speak the least bit disrespectfully of the Church he so loved, but Philip knew his father spoke the truth. They were indeed—at least their wealth was—far too important to the Church to fear excommunication because they held a Tourney where blood would no doubt be shed.

"We shall hold a conference with my councilmen," Geoffrey said as they walked to the door of the chamber. "And call the Tourney as quickly as possible; perhaps as a forerunner of festivity to your brother's wedding." He frowned. "Of course, if the Montforts are the victors, no wedding will be necessary. The de Saines can wed in the village chapel without a guest present—that's all we'll be able to afford."

Philip grabbed his father's upper arms and held firm. "We will be the victors, Father. I promise you that."

Geoffrey gazed at his son, a glimmer of admiration forming in his eye. He turned, going to the mantlepiece above the fireplace. From there, he took his sword, so recently returned to him, and headed back toward Philip.

"You will need this again, I fear," he said. "But Philip, I know you are no coward. You are a wiser man than I've given you credit for to resist the sword as you have. And now, when faced with the fact that it is our only hope, you have not shirked your duty. For that, you have earned and deserve my respect, as well as my love."

Philip took the sword, fingering the jeweled hilt and gazing at it with a blank expression. But when he looked at his father he smiled. "I am glad to have regained your faith in me, yet I cannot say I have earned it. I do only what I expect of myself—I cannot say I have done it for you, or even for love of you."

Geoffrey laughed. "If you had, do you think I would hold you in such respect?"

They turned once again toward the door, as Philip slipped the sword down the side of his belt.

"We will hold a council at noon," Geoffrey said. "Be there."

Philip nodded, then left the room. And as he walked the dark hallway back toward the fore-building, the sword at his side felt far too familiar.

34

By the time Alix woke she was ravenous. She was

surprised when she glanced toward the window and saw the sun was beginning to set. She'd slept the entire day away!

But she'd needed it, she thought—and deserved it. It had been days since she'd slept well. And now what she needed was a full meal.

She called for Blanche and had the servant prepare a bath for her. And while she bathed and dressed, Alix's thoughts went to Philip. No doubt he'd spoken to his father already and, if Geoffrey agreed, a Tournament would be called.

But this was one Tourney Alix would not welcome. It was true that all melees and individual jousts were not without danger—that's what made them so popular. But the melee Philip proposed was so risky—and not just because the de Saines fortune was at stake. Philip himself would certainly participate, and she had no doubt he would be a prominent target of the enemy among the forty men chosen to fight.

Once dressed, Alix left her chamber for the hall. Even before she entered the huge room, sounds of merrymaking greeted her. The feast to welcome home the victors, it seemed, was already underway.

She could not help but smile as she passed among the revelers. People danced in the center of the mosaic floor, while those who remained seated at the surrounding tables drank or were still eating from an array of foods many servants offered. The music was gay and loud, but animated voices could be heard—tales, undoubtedly, of the rescue mission.

"There she is! Demoiselle Alix!"

Alix turned to see August-Caron, obviously well into his cups, and at his side a pretty young girl; Alix recognized her as Blanche's sister, Elena.

August-Caron bowed formally, if somewhat unsteadily. "You, too, Demoiselle, are to be cel'brated here tonight. For your bravery and love . . ." He hiccuped loudly. ". . . and love of your betrothed. If I had a woman love me the way you must love Julian . . ."

Alix put a hand to his shoulder as if to steady him, seeing him sway dramatically to the side. "Elena, hold him!" she said worriedly, ignoring his words.

But August-Caron shook Elena away. "I am terribly sorry, madame . . . that is, Demoiselle Elena . . . but you are not the one . . ." Then he turned to Alix, his eyelids heavy and his breath smelling heavily of wine. "Do you know Gen? She is the one I'm looking for . . ."

Alix shook her head, getting on his other side and motioning Elena to help carry the drunken knight to the side of the room. "Do you mean Genevieve, Sire Geoffrey's niece? She's but nine years old, Sir August-Caron!"

August-Caron laughed so hard he nearly knocked over three of them. But just in time, they reached a chair at the side of the hall and August-Caron toppled into it.

"I meant Genevieve le Jeune, Demoiselle. Not little Genny de Saines." He laughed again, but when he leaned back on the large chair, his eyes closed as if he'd lost consciousness. He continued mumbling, belying his unconscious state, but it was plain slumber was not far away.

"Stay with him until he falls asleep," Alix told Elena. "Make sure he doesn't fall from that chair."

Elena giggled. "Perhaps I should strap him to it like a small child."

"That won't be necessary," said Philip from behind them.

Alix turned, a ready smile upon her face. Philip gave her a brief smile, then walked past her toward August-Caron. He lifted the man with ease, and carried him to an antechamber off the main hall where he could sleep undisturbed and no one need fear the knight would injure himself.

Elena disappeared after that, quickly finding companionship with another man-at-arms.

"August-Caron spoke of a woman called Gen," Alix said when Philip rejoined her. "He seems smitten."

Philip nodded as they walked toward the

opposite end of the room where the rest of his family and Alix's were seated. "She is a woman he met while we were at Court. A widow—a Comtesse."

"Ah," Alix said, somewhat sadly.

"Yes," Philip said, agreeing with Alix's unhappy conclusion. "A mismatch, even if August-Caron is a knight. He's landless—though after all of this is over, providing the de Saines win the melee, August-Caron should be rewarded for his part in ending this feud with the Montforts. Awarding land would be suitable."

Alix lifted her brows in interest; perhaps, she thought, August-Caron might one day claim his Comtesse, after all. She certainly hoped so, for the friendly young knight's sake.

They had no time for further discussion for Julian approached. Alix might have expected him, too, to be well into his cups, but he looked completely sober and in far better health than he had that morning. A shave, clean clothes and a good meal seemed to have eliminated any sign of his days of captivity. He barely limped, and the bruises upon his face did not seem so severe.

"I would like to speak to you—both of you," he said. "Privately."

Alix glanced at Philip, who nodded. They followed Julian out of the hall, past the kitchen exit and to the garden. It was quiet there, for all of the merrymakers were left inside. Alix wished Julian had taken them elsewhere; she still thought of the garden as her secret place, despite its newfound popularity with other Chateau occupants now that it was neatly cultivated. But to her, it was a secret place she wanted to share only with Philip. She still remembered the night he'd first found her there; it seemed so long ago.

No one sat on the single stone bench. Perhaps the two men expected Alix to take it, but she did not. She waited expectantly for Julian to speak.

"Before I was taken by the Montforts, I was headed to see you, Alix," Julian began. He neared her, and took her one of her hands in both of his.

Gently, he kissed the inside of her wrist, ignoring the fact that Philip visibly stiffened at their side.

But Alix was confused. She didn't pull away from him; she knew Julian well enough by now to guess he wouldn't try to do anything against her will with Philip standing right there. But it wasn't only that; there was something in Julian, a sort of friendly smile, not the cocky lustiness he'd shown before.

"I know it's Philip you love," Julian said quietly. Then he let go Alix's hand and turned to his brother. "And Philip, I know you return her love. That's why what I have to say should be said in front of both of you. I've decided to break the betrothal between Alix and me, so the two of you can be married."

"Julian!" Alix gasped happily, but Philip said nothing.

Then, though he was no longer standing so stiffly, and his voice was not harsh, Philip said, "You know, don't you, that Alix intended to break the betrothal if you did not? That she would have appealed to Jean, because the wedding would have been against her will?"

Julian nodded. "There won't be any need for all of that now," he assured them. "At the very least, brother, I've saved you time and trouble. Hardly a fair repayment for all you've done for me, but it's a start."

"There is no reason to feel indebted to me," Philip said.

Julian laughed. "Perhaps you think my life is of little value, Philip, but from my point of view, the fact that you saved me is reason enough to feel indebted. And it isn't only that." His tone grew more serious. "You took up the sword again—because of me."

Philip smirked. "So now that I carry a sword again, you can find at least some small reason to respect me again."

"You are making this more difficult than it needs to be," Julian said slowly. Some of the lightness had left his voice. "I didn't think you would

412

take up the sword again for any reason. And now, knowing you did that for my sake, I realize . . . well, you must love me. I knew, once, that you loved me. When we were growing up and I shadowed you and mimicked everything you did . . . I must have been quite a nuisance. But you loved me anyway. In the last two years, when you laid down the sword I thought you laid down whatever love you must have had for me because I still carried a sword. I stopped mimicking you . . . and I thought you couldn't love me any more."

Philip laid a hand on Julian's shoulder, his countenance softening from Julian's words. The two were about the same height, and he looked him eye to eye. "I didn't know . . . I never expected anyone else to give up the sword. Not you, or any other knight. It was my decision. And now, I realize, an unreasonable one. I cannot live in this world and not use the tools everyone else lives by. It just doesn't work."

Julian's eyebrows rose. "Then you will live by the sword?"

Philip paused, then finally shook his head. "No, but I cannot refuse to take it up when duty calls."

Julian stood straight and tall. "I will be at your side at the melee, Philip. We will conquer the Montforts once and for all, so you will not have to take up your sword, ever again."

Philip patted his brother's shoulder. "You sound just like you did ten years ago, when you vowed to go off to battle with me."

"But I was too young to go with you then. Now I am not."

"Perhaps not too young," Alix cautioned, "but are you up to a melee? After being in captivity?"

Both men eyed her as if she were insane, and she knew keeping Julian out of the melee would be impossible.

"Julian," Philip told Alix, "has more reason than any of the rest of us to want to see the Montforts ousted—and to try and do so with his own hands." He remembered overhearing the story about the

413

snake, and though he made no verbal reference to it, with one glance at his younger brother he made it clear he had some idea of how his brother had been treated. That had been only one incident; what else might have happened in the long days Julian had been held?

Philip put an arm about Alix. "It's time, I think, we told your father about our intentions. Let's make certain the right two people are being wed, shall we?"

The three of them returned to the hall, and all the while Alix's heart danced within her. It was time, at long last, to let the love she shared with Philip be known throughout the Chateau. She wanted to sing out the news to all present . . . but she knew they must begin with her father.

Lord Giles was seated beside Marie, watching the dancers and tumblers entertaining those filling the hall. Alix waited beside Julian while Philip approached her father and spoke a few brief words, then she smiled at Giles when he glanced her way. A moment later both Giles and Marie followed Philip out of the hall and up the stairs toward the Beauchamp chambers. Julian and Alix fell in step behind them.

No one spoke until Philip closed the door behind them all, inside the small solar beside the Beauchamp bedchamber. But Julian did not give Philip a chance to speak. He stepped forward.

"We've come to speak of your daughter's wedding day, Lord Giles," Julian said.

Alix caught her mother's quick glance at the pronouncement; she hardly looked surprised, but she did look from Alix to Giles in concern.

"Father," Alix said slowly, "it's become very obvious to Julian and me that we are mismatched for marriage. Neither of us wishes to wed the other."

Giles stared at his daughter as the words slowly took on meaning. He seemed incredulous, as if confused by such a statement. His gray eyes clouded, his brows knits together. "But I thought you cared a great deal for him," Giles said. "You

414

followed after him when he was kidnapped by the Montforts."

Alix took a step closer to Philip. "No, Father. I followed Philip. I was concerned for his safety, and wanted to spend every moment I could with him before he endangered his life."

Giles brushed off the consoling hand Marie put to his arm. He walked toward his daughter, seeing her boldly holding Philip's arm, the other hand resting on his chest as if they were already man and wife. "Step away from him, Alix."

Alix did not move. She looked at her father, confused.

"Step away," he repeated.

Marie came to stand beside Giles. "They want to be wed, Giles. Can you not see they love each other?"

"She is far too familiar with him, pressing herself against him that way."

Alix stood stiff, a hand's spread away from Philip. She was tempted to blurt out she'd been much more familiar with Philip, but held back. No sense making this more difficult than it already was.

"Lord Giles," Philip said, "Alix and I have come to care for one another deeply. Julian has agreed he has no wish to marry a woman who loves another; therefore it will be an easy matter to simply announce it will be Philip de Saines, not Julian, who will be wed in three weeks to your daughter."

Giles laughed, but without humor. "An easy matter?" Giles turned to Julian. "I chose you," he said firmly, "you, not your brother, to be a husband for my daughter."

"And your daughter chose me," Philip pointed out, causing Giles to look at him once again. "You know, don't you, that Alix could appeal to the King if you force her to marry someone else?"

"And you know, don't you, that my brother is Bishop here at your father's Chateau? He could see that Alix disappears into a nunnery so that even Jean himself wouldn't be able to find her."

415

Philip wasn't daunted. "I doubt you would do that to your daughter," he said.

Giles sighed heavily, looking at last to Alix. The fact that he'd been bluffing was obvious. His shoulders were slumped, as if he were giving in against his will. "Is this truly what you want? To marry him, instead of Julian?" he asked.

She nodded immediately.

But Giles did not give up so easily. "Think, daughter! To wed a man with a scandal attached to his name? A man who hid from another man's challenge? A man who obviously has little regard for the sanctity of matrimony if he beds another man's wife—his friend's wife. If his life is directed by his loins and not his sense of honor, what sort of husband will he make?"

Alix took hold of her father's hand. "I do not believe any of those rumors, Father. I believe Philip. He never bedded Charles la Trau's wife."

But Giles shook his head. His own words against Philip had reminded him of all the reasons he far preferred Julian as a choice for his child. He directed his daughter to the couch in the corner of the room, away from the others. He sat beside her and spoke in a whisper so only Alix could hear.

"I cannot allow you to marry him," he said softly. "I cannot. He is not a man fitting to be a husband."

"But he *is* fitting!" Alix insisted, somewhat louder than she'd intended.

"You believe he is innocent of these charges because of your love for him. And even if he is innocent, child, what manner of man would run from a challenge?"

"Doesn't that prove his innocence? He doesn't want to fight Charles because of a groundless lie."

"It proves only one thing, Alix. That he fled like a coward."

Alix stiffened. "How can you call him a coward after what he did to save Julian? He's taken up the sword again—and will fight in the melee to save the Chateau from the Montfort's greed. He is no coward."

416

Giles nodded. "I admit he acted admirably in saving his brother and intending to fight in the melee. But will he continue to ignore the challenge of Charles la Trau? The man and his challenge will not simply disappear. Even if Charles succumbed to some dread disease and his life faded away, his unmet challenge will follow Philip's name forever. And it's that people will remember of Philip, not the better deeds of saving his brother and fighting in a melee. People choose to remember the unfavorable things, Alix. It's somehow easier to think of another's faults rather than our own. And in this, Philip is at fault. Do you want to be the wife of such a man? The mother of such a man's children? And your children will be affected, Alix, do not fool yourself. Any son Philip has will have to prove himself over and again, and meet any and all challenges flung his way, even unfair ones, just to prove he is better than his father."

"But *this* is an unfair challenge."

Giles shook his head. "Not with Rachel la Trau herself vouching for the truth of it."

Still, Alix would not bend to her father's way of thinking. "The truth will come out," she said confidently.

"The only way of proof is through a challenge. The victor will be the one who speaks the truth; God himself will be on the side of the one who wins the challenge, proving the truth to all. And by Philip refusing to submit to that test, he reveals his own guilt."

But Alix shook her head. "That isn't the reason he doesn't want to fight. He doesn't want to lift a sword against a man he once called a friend. And if God is on his side—as surely He is—Philip would be the winner and Charles could be hurt, perhaps killed. Philip has no wish to kill this man, just because he was cuckolded so cruelly by his wife."

Lord Giles frowned, but Alix could not guess if her words were penetrating her father's stubbornness. Giles stood, and rejoined the others.

"I want nothing said of this for now," he told them. "The wedding will go on as planned." At his daughter's protesting gasp, he held up a cautioning hand. "The Tournament is foremost on everyone's mind for the time being. The wedding preparations will be lost in the tumult of that festivity. If on the day of the wedding it is announced you will be marrying Philip, not Julian, it will make little difference."

"But to let everyone continue thinking I will be marrying Julian . . ."

"Will harm no one," Giles said. "I will not force you to marry Julian—I could not. But let us forestall the wagging tongues for a while. Let us say nothing; I cannot condone your marrying Philip, and during that time many things could happen."

"I'll not change my mind, if that's what you mean," Alix warned him.

But Philip took her hand, eyeing Giles closely. "That isn't what your father meant," he said. "Is it? I think he refers to the melee. If the de Saines lose . . . or if either I or Julian are killed, the wedding will be altered without any scandal ever being revealed. That is what you were thinking, isn't it?"

Giles said nothing, unwilling to admit such coldheartedness.

Alix stepped closer to her father. "If you love me, Father—and Mother tells me you do—you'll pray as hard as I will that neither Philip—nor Julian—will be wounded or hurt in that melee."

Giles squeezed her hand. "I wish neither of them harm, you must know that. And I do love you, Alix," he told her hoarsely. "That is why I want what is best for you. That is why I chose Julian."

"I'm sure Sire Geoffrey chose Marguerite for Philip because he thought she was the best choice. But Simon should have taught you that mistakes are made when those being betrothed aren't consulted first."

35

Christian Bernier hauled three shields, four blunted swords, and a pair of thick gauntlets from one of the storage rooms within the high wall. He headed toward the training yard, and this being his sixth such trip, he did not walk with as much haste as he had the first time out. But then, he hadn't expected to be used as a mere servant to all of these de Saines men-at-arms.

What was he doing here? He'd been better off at the Montforts—at least there he'd been a guard, even if he hadn't been given the most strategic posts. But he was young, he knew that, and even if he was far more experienced than his years, he had accepted those inferior guard positions as part of his duty. And now, what was he? No better than a servant—not even a page or squire, which would hardly be anything to aspire to.

He had to admit, however, as he glanced around this Chateau, the de Saineses were far better off than the Montforts—or anyone else he'd ever served in his fourteen years. But even so, he said to himself as he shifted the heavy shields once again, this was absolutely the last trip he would make to the storage room. If he was sent back one more time . . . he'd simply leave. He didn't owe the de Saineses anything. In fact, they owed him. Certainly more than a job as one of the lowliest servants.

When he arrived back at the training yard, he was surprised to see Philip de Saines there. Julian was there as well, and both were dressed in chain mail and helmets and standing beside tall chargers. Christian dumped his burden with a loud clatter, having delivered what he was told, then sauntered toward the long, narrow field that was used for practice tilting. As Christian neared them, a page handed Philip and Julian long but blunted lances. Opposite them was the quintain, which would serve as their adversary during the tilt.

Christian ignored the calls from men-at-arms honing their skills at other sections of the training yard. The yard was full, more full than usual, for every knight of Sire Geoffrey's household hoped to be chosen as one of the forty knights to fight in the melee—and to be chosen one had to be seen performing knightly skills. But Christian had done enough work serving them for the day, he decided as he ignored the calls, then leaned against one of the gates and watched the de Saines brothers.

Philip charged at the quintain first. It was magnificent, Christian thought, to see horse and rider spring to such instant, rhythmic unison. It was as if they were one force: horse, rider, weapon, all together in perfect balance. The dummy hanging upon the quintain hadn't a prayer, Christian knew, and once Philip pummeled his lance into it, it swung so furiously it would be a long wait before it was stable enough for the next challenge.

The next challenge came from Julian de Saines. He was decidedly more striking than Philip. Upon his shining helmet he wore one thick red plume, and down his back a black cape billowed in the wind, making the de Saines dragon stitched there almost seem alive. The dragon was also emblazoned upon his shield, a stark red standing out so vividly against a white background.

Julian, too, had the precision, speed and balance to land a deadly blow, had the dummy been alive. The two de Saines brothers made it look so easy, Christian fairly itched to try it himself. He was handy enough with a sword, he thought, why not with lance as well? Spotting Philip coming round for a second try, Christian boldly marched up to him.

"Lord Philip!" Christian called.

Philip turned to him somewhat stiffly, encumbered by the battle paraphernalia and the limited view from the two square eye holes cut into the helmet.

"Ah, Christian," Philip greeted. "I am glad to see you. Would you mind taking this shield and exchanging it for the one there, near the gate?"

Christian clenched his teeth, biting back a harsh reply. He accepted the shield from Philip—he had no choice, really, when it was shoved in his face—and retrieved the other one which he found was a bit lighter. Before another word could be spoken, Philip was off at a second tilt.

That was enough! Christian would rather be picking pockets again rather than bowing to this sort of treatment. He was no man's servant. With a scowl, he turned on his heel—and so suddenly bumped into another person he almost fell back in surprise.

All anger, all prideful frustration, all thoughts disappeared when Christian gazed into the face of the person who had appeared so silently behind him. If he were in heaven, he thought, all the angels would look like this woman. She had wide, bright green eyes, the color of he sea. Her skin was fair, her hair reddish brown—a contrast, he thought, that made him wonder if she were delicate, like her skin, or bold and willful like the color and curl of her hair.

But then he remembered who she was, and knew the latter was true of this woman. "You are Demoiselle Alix, aren't you?" he asked softly. "I hardly recognized you."

She laughed, and it sounded like music to him. "Yes, I suppose I do look different than the last time I saw you. I haven't seen you since that night we all returned from the Montfort stronghold. Did I look so different dressed as a page?"

Christian only nodded, feeling like a fool yet so besotted no words came to him. Suddenly the thought of leaving the Chateau de Saines was unthinkable.

He stood at her side and the two of them

watched the de Saines brothers take their turns tilting at the quintain. It didn't take Christian long, however, to assume one of these brothers was vitally important to this lovely woman. After all, he thought, hadn't she followed after the rescue party when Julian had been kidnapped? He'd heard they were to be wed, but it was odd that when Christian looked at her, her gaze was more often on the other de Saines, Philip.

But none of this mattered so much. If he were a knight, Christian thought, he could be this woman's champion, even if she were married to one of these de Saines. At least he could tell her then how lovely he thought she was. How could he now, when he was no more than a servant in the de Saines household?

At last, Philip dismounted and pulled the helmet off his head. He approached them, smiling broadly at Alix.

"I'd forgotten how difficult this is," he said, much to Christian's surprise. It had looked as if he'd been born at the tilt!

"I've never seen anyone in the training yard make it look quite so easy," Alix said, echoing Christian's thoughts. But Christian said nothing. He watched Alix, thinking she looked somehow different in this man's presence. Lovelier still, if that was possible.

"Did you hear me, Christian?"

Christian turned, startled out of his intense gaze directed toward Alix. "No—I'm sorry."

"I wondered if you wanted to try the tilt? You look strong—and I've seen the way you ride a horse, capably enough. Would you like to try it?"

It had been exactly what he wanted just minutes ago. But now? With Demoiselle Alix watching? God's teeth, what if it were harder than it looked, as Philip seemed to indicate? He would hate to look the fool in front of someone as beautiful as Alix.

Philip spoke, filling up Christian's hesitation. "Christian, you would make a fine knight," he said. "I saw plenty of evidence of that the night we rescued Julian. I'd like to sponsor you—but to do that, you'll have to try out every part of battle training."

"I'm more than ready," Christian said. Mention of knighthood had brought back his senses—he'd be a fool to let even deep, chivalrous love come between them and that goal. Besides, he thought, feeling a bit of his old confidence returning, how hard could it be?

While Philip outfitted Christian, Julian approached Alix's side. He'd discarded his lance and shield, but held sword in one hand and helmet under one arm. He looked very muscular and bulky, dressed in his battle armor and cape, and very friendly as he smiled Alix's way.

"The whole Chateau is preparing for this Tourney," Julian said. "Sir Oliver and my brother will have a difficult time choosing which men will be part of the forty in the melee. Every knight is willing and ready."

"How is Sir Oliver?" Alix asked. "Is he well on the mend?"

Julian nodded. "He even wants to be one of the forty, but of course that's out of the question."

"Julian," Alix began slowly, "do you think there is any possibility of the de Saineses . . . losing this melee?"

He grinned at her. "Only a fool would deny at least the possibility. I've seen the Montfort men-at-arms. They are an unruly lot, hardly trained except for what they've taught themselves. But they know enough to stay alive in battle, and that's all it will take in a melee."

"But what will you do if the melee is lost?"

"That, Demoiselle," he said, "is an unnecessary question. If my side loses, I shall not live to tell about it. And neither, I fear, will Philip." Then he added, "Your father has a viable reason for not wanting to announce any possible changes in the wedding day to come. If neither of us live, a scandal brooked now would be needless."

"What difference would a scandal make?" she said, her eyes filling with unwanted tears. But she refrained from crying; she believed, didn't she, with all her heart, that the de Saineses would be the victors?

Julian replaced his sword in its sheath at his side, and patted her shoulder. "A scandal won't make a difference to the de Saineses, Alix, but it will to your father's household. This melee will not risk your father's land, even though he is a vassal of my father's. He will simply become a vassal of the Montfort's instead."

"The de Saineses will be the victors," she spoke her thoughts. "And Philip and I will be wed."

Julian let his arm fall about her shoulders comfortingly. "You know," he said in a light, teasing tone, "I like you much better now that we aren't betrothed. A marriage would have been disastrous between us, do you know that? How could I ever accept a wife who is afraid of hawks?"

Alix laughed with him then, but she could not eliminate thoughts of the Tourney. There was no turning back now, she knew. The challenge of the melee had been issued to the Montforts, and readily accepted, as expected. Almost immediately Sire Geoffrey had sent heralds all over the countryside to announce the coming Tournament. The entire Chateau had been in a flurry of activity ever since; besides the gaming, there would be many feasts to boast the de Saineses' wealth, and every servant in the Chateau—from bakers to hunters—scrambled to meet the needs. Already a few guests had arrived, and many more were expected, from as far away as Rennes and Auray.

A loud shout called their attention, and Alix turned to see Philip racing to Christian's side—the boy had obviously been felled from his horse in the first challenge against the quintain dummy. Alix and Julian started to follow Philip's path toward Christian, fearing he might have harmed himself, but in a moment they saw him stand, brush himself off, and climb on the mount's back once again.

"Looks like young Bernier could use the help of two trainers," Julian said.

Alix smiled. "I'll leave you and Philip to your work, then."

But before she turned away, Julian took her hand in his. "We will win at the Tourney, Alix," he whispered confidently. "Have no fear of that. And your wedding will be just as you hope—Philip wouldn't have it any other way. Believe in that."

Alix nodded, for the first time since knowing Julian truly glad of his company and comfort.

Alix did not see Julian, or Philip, again until later that day at the evening meal. Despite the added guests, it was a quiet meal, as was the custom in the de Saines household. Alix sat beside Julian—at her father's request, since they had agreed not to reveal their broken betrothal just yet, even to Sire Geoffrey and Lady Eleanore. And because Alix had not yet been given her father's permission to wed Philip, she hesitated to disobey him in matters so unimportant as who she supped with.

"When will the forty names be announced?" called one of the men-at-arms seated at an adjacent table. It was a question asked each evening, ever since the Tourney had been announced almost a week ago.

Sire Geoffrey answered as he always did. "My son and Sir Oliver will announce the names the day before the Tourney—not before."

"But surely you have some idea, Lord Philip," one man persisted. "Can you give us even a partial list?"

"I can tell you one name that won't be on the list!"

The strange voice from the hall entryway sounded above all others, and every eye in the hall turned to it. Alix watched as a dark-haired, swarthy-complected man entered the room with a flourish, a black cape swaying behind him as he strode to the center of the mosaic floor. Whispers spread through the hall at the man's entrance, but Alix did not recognize him.

"Who is he?" she asked Julian softly.

"Charles la Trau."

425

Alix's heart sunk deep within her, and her gaze left the dark intruder to go to Philip, seated a few places from her. He stared at Charles, his face placid, unmoved. He did not bother to stand and greet the man who approached; Charles la Trau stared directly at him, but the gaze Philip sent in return did not waver.

Charles turned from Philip to bow formally to Sire Geoffrey and Lady Eleanore.

"Sire Geoffrey," Charles greeted the older man. "I have come as a guest at your Tournament heralded all over Brittany. My wife," he added, glancing toward Philip, "is with me. We have set up a Tourney camp near the grounds marked off for the games."

Sire Geoffrey spoke smoothly and clearly. "I cannot offer you into my household, Charles. Not with this strife between you and my son. But I'll not turn you away from the Tourney. It is open to all."

"To all challenges?" he asked, then turned to Philip. "The countryside is ablaze with news of your melee, Philip," he said, his voice almost friendly. But his eyes were cold. "They say it was your idea—and so I had to come and see for myself. Can it be true, I wondered, that Philip de Saines—the same Philip de Saines I know—has issued a melee? Surely he will not be one of the forty to fight—on that list someone just asked about as I entered? And not even *a plaisance*, but with real weapons! Stand up, old friend, let me see if it's true that you wear your sword again."

Philip stayed seated, his eyes almost as cold as Charles's.

Charles was undaunted. He stepped even closer, his voice lower and his hand gripping the sword still within its sheath at his side. "I have come to join this Tourney of yours, Philip. Even if I have to join the Montfort family to get my try at you—I *will* fight you. Unless," he added, now smiling, "you've not only found your sword but your courage as well. Perhaps you will at last grant my wish and stand up to my challenge?"

No one spoke; Alix felt her heart pounding within her, wishing someone—somewhere—would speak. But everyone looked at Philip, with attention as rapt as her own.

Philip eyed Charles. He saw the hatred, as vividly as the last time he'd confronted Charles at Bayeux. And he knew there was no turning away. Rachel, or gossip, or something inside Charles himself had festered such hatred that Philip knew there was no more avoiding it. He'd hoped the truth would come out, and Charles would no longer have reason to hate him—but, he thought fleetingly, even if Philip never had bedded the man's wife, it must have been obvious to Charles that his wife had wished it were true. Perhaps jealousy alone would have been enough to nurture this hatred in Charles.

Slowly, Philip stood. "I've denied the charges against me before, Charles," Philip said, knowing his words were useless but giving one last try anyway. "A fight between us would be over lies."

Charles laughed. "No, old friend. A fight between us is the only way to prove innocence. Let the might of my sword prove to all that I have been a champion of my wife's honor."

Philip wanted to deny that his wife possessed any honor, but knew that would only add more cause to Charles and his wish to fight. Philip sighed deeply, his hand going automatically to the sword at his side. Was there no escaping this weapon?

"I have no wish to fight you."

Charles laughed boldly. "Still the coward, I see!"

Such an insult could not be ignored, no matter how deeply Philip might wish to. At his side, Sire Geoffrey stood as well. All eyes were on Philip.

Philip's gaze held steady upon Charles's taunting countenance. As if sensing Philip was closer than ever to accepting this challenge—for even now he was fingering the sword at his side—Charles pressed the matter further.

"You can no longer avoid me, Philip. Here I am,

in your midst—and I've insulted you before your vassals." He laughed once more as he glanced around briefly. "They all look at you, Philip—knowing you will always be the coward if you refuse my challenge."

At last Sire Geoffrey spoke, but quietly so that few, besides those at his table, could hear. Alix listened intently.

"Let it be up to God, my son," he said imploringly.

To Alix's horror, she heard her father join in the encouragement. "Your father is right. Take this challenge and let God above decide the innocent as the victor."

Philip gazed at Giles, and Alix could guess easily enough what he was thinking. Her breathing quickened along with the beat of her heart. She didn't want this! But how could Philip refuse?

"All right," he said in a low voice. "We will fight." Then he added, looking straight into Charles la Trau's eyes, "But it is all for lies."

Charles's eyes fairly sparkled. He stood straight and tall, anticipation so obvious it could not be mistaken. "You have only to set the day, Philip, not offer platitudes."

"I'll fight you after the melee—that is my first consideration."

Charles bowed his acceptance of the date, smiling a triumphant smile as he straightened to his full height once again. "Let us pray you survive the Montforts' forty, so I may have my try at you at long last."

Charles turned and strode from the room, the smile never wavering.

Philip watched Charles until he disappeared beyond the hall entryway. Then he was reseated, and slowly, the hall began to fill with chatter. He didn't have to hear any of the conversations to know it was him they spoke of. And, finally, his gaze went to Alix.

She did not smile his way; her eyes were wide, a trifle worried, he thought. Worried, he wondered, because she knew how he hated to use the sword against Charles? Or worried because she feared he might not survive a joust against a man so filled with hatred lending strength to each blow behind his lance or sword?

Alix could not smile Philip's way; she could not offer him the encouragement she should have. She knew only one thing: if Philip hadn't fallen in love with her, if she didn't have a father who insisted such battles be fought, then Philip would not have to pick up his sword one last time. She'd thought, once the melee was over, Philip could lay down his sword again and, with God's help, never have to pick it up again.

It was her fault that wish wouldn't come true. After all, she knew Philip never wanted to fight Charles. Why had he agreed to now, except that he knew Giles hesitated to let him wed her because of this scandal, this challenge that hung over Philip like a dark cloud? The moment her father spoke, convincing Philip to fight, Alix knew she must share the blame.

She bowed her head, the guilt so strong she could not look Philip's way. Please God, let him survive this added battle . . . for if he didn't, she knew that would be the end of her life as well.

36

Alix barely heard the tap at her door the next morning. Sicker than she wanted to admit, she was bent over the edge of her bed, but forced herself to sit up when her mother entered the room.

"Still sleepy?" Marie greeted her cheerily. But after a closer look at her pale daughter, she came to her side and put a caressing hand to Alix's forehead. "Are you feeling well?"

"I'm perfectly fine," Alix said quickly. She had

no idea why it was suddenly so important to keep her ill health from her mother. There would be no keeping her indoors today, she thought to herself, even if her mother did learn how very sick she felt. She would be at the Tourney field just like everyone else!

Marie accepted Alix's assurance, and helped her to dress in her fine attire for the day, a blue damask gown belted at the low waist by a silver chain. Before long, they headed outside.

Blasting horns proclaimed the start of the Tournament just as Alix and her mother took seats on the raised platform especially erected for Sire and Lady de Saines and their highest-ranking guests. Above hung a white tarp, shading them from the sun. It was a warm day with only a slight southern breeze, and the de Saines banners hooked to the four corners of the tarp barely swayed.

The sides of the field before them were marked off by other de Saines banners, affixed to tall poles. Each end of the field, however, was open. The eastern end led to the hills beyond, and to the west was the forest. Alix knew the spot had been purposely chosen for the melee. Like a real battle, the victors could chase the retreating party down, and take hostages for ransom. In this case, however, as everyone was aware, to the side with most remaining knights—alive and not held hostage— went the wealth of the family sponsoring those knights. It was a huge risk, taken mainly by the de Saineses, and so this Tourney had drawn an unusually large crowd.

Alix gazed about. Normally, she would have loved the sights she saw. People from all over mingled about in anticipation of the contests scheduled for the day: women were dressed in their finest, men at their most resplendent. There were poor, too, for the Tourney was open to all. Thieves, prostitutes and other such undersirables were in abundance, eager to use the Tourney for their own gain. The Tourney was an event where the rich showed off their wealth, the strong showed off their prowess, and everyone—both rich and poor—gambled to profit from the Tourney itself, whether in contest or by thievery. Merchants, too, benefited by such a large gathering of people. They hawked their wares, either food or trinkets, and the size of their money pouches increased as their merchandise dwindled.

But the excitement so tangible around Alix could not eliminate her own worries. She glanced at Sire Geoffrey and Lady Eleanore; the Sire looked as though this Tourney was like any other. He was smiling and talking to the Count beside him, and Alix had to marvel. For a man who might be about to lose his entire wealth, perhaps even his position in society, he hardly looked worried. Lady Eleanore, however, did not share her husband's easy manner. She was pale, her mouth drawn into a tight, fretful line, and she stared ahead at the Tourney field, as if blind to all else. The fact that she did not approve of Philip's idea for the terms of the melee was well-known to all.

Alix couldn't guess whether Lady Eleanore was worried over the risks involved with her family's wealth or the fact that her sons' lives were also at stake. But Alix herself could think of only one thing: Philip's life would be at risk not just once, at the melee, but twice. For if he survived the melee—God let him!—he would have to face Charles la Trau in an individual joust, which was every bit as dangerous as a melee. Perhaps more so; no one hated Philip the way Charles la Trau seemed to hate him.

The herald entered the field, announcing the first contest of the day. Alix knew the reasoning behind the Tourney's schedule; today would be wrestling, contests with bow and arrow, and lance hurling. Each of these was approved of by the Church—decreed civilized, for bloodshed would not result from such contests. The Sire de Saines had issued his command to begin the Tourney in this way, so that it could not be said he'd totally ignored the wishes of the Church. The fact that the melee was a thinly veiled war, albeit in somewhat

controlled circumstances, would not be overlooked. However, if some attempt had been made
to heed the Church's wish, that, too, would not be
overlooked.

Just after the contest with bow and arrow, Alix
whispered to her mother that she would like to
take a look around the Tourney grounds rather
than watch the next competition.

"Hugh will accompany you," Marie said, then
nodded toward the older knight who stood in front
of their raised platform. At Alix's frown upon
hearing she must be chaperoned, Marie shook her
head and spoke firmly. "There are too many
people here for you to be roaming about unprotected. Do as I ask, Alix."

Alix capitulated then, thinking if she disobeyed,
her father might hear of it, and for the time being
at least, she dreaded displeasing him. She met Sir
Hugh at the base of the platform and started
walking, knowing he followed close behind.

Those closest to the field were loud and
boisterous as they cheered on those of their
choice. Alix did not linger around the field;
instead, she headed toward the surrounding
campgrounds, hoping it was there she would find
Philip. The Tourney grounds were not far from the
Chateau, but most of the Sire's men had chosen to
erect tents closer to the Tourney field rather than
stay within the Chateau. The fact that Montfort
men were all around made some of them cautious,
wanting to keep a close eye on the enemy within
their midst. Philip would no doubt be found
among them, and Julian as well, for they, along
with their men, were a team and would be best
served by thinking and behaving as one force, like
those on a campaign.

Alix walked through the camps, skirting
campfires and passing colorful tents. Although
this camp was perhaps in higher spirits and better
equipped with luxuries like a wider range of
foods, more servants to see to various needs, and
the knowledge that home wasn't far away, Alix
couldn't help thinking this was not much different

from any other knight's camp. And battle wasn't far off . . . like some prearranged strategy against the enemy, it was set for the very next day. That was why she'd left the Tourney field in search of Philip; she wanted to spend every moment she could at his side.

Philip laughed just as loud as those around him at the way a clownish young tumbler balanced so precariously on a long rope strung up high between two trees. Several times the acrobat appeared nearly to fall, only to miraculously catch himself and resume his trek along the rope. Such peripheral entertainment was normally for the benefit of those who cared little for the contests within the Tourney field, which were sometimes bloody. Many mothers held their children close at hand to enjoy this merry amusement while dangerous jousts or melees were being fought within the field beyond sight. Today, however, most spectators around the outside entertainment were those bored with such mild contests as scheduled for the day.

But Philip had stopped to watch because the face of that clown looked so familiar. His nose and cheeks were covered with stripes of white paint, but beneath that paint he looked like . . . Christian! It was him, Philip was sure of it. And, when Christian ended his antics and the sound of coins clanked inside a metal cup sitting at the base of one of the trees, Philip guessed the reason behind Christian's pastime.

"Wasn't the pouch of coins I gave you enough for one so young as yourself?" Philip greeted the boy as he hopped to the ground from the dangling rope.

Christain laughed, and took a kerchief from beneath his doublet to wipe away some of the paint upon his face. "I haven't yet discovered what amount of gold is 'enough.' "

"I trust tomorrow you will leave this other job behind you?" Philip asked. "At least long enough to serve as my squire before the melee and the joust?"

Christain's eyes sparkled. "Of course! I myself will be a knight before long—I need to know how to treat my own squire . . . once I have one."

Philip might have reproved anyone else—such a romantic, silly reason to act as squire hardly declared him serious about what knighthood meant. But Philip knew better; Christian might not have had the benefit of a foster family taking him in to show him the ways of knighthood and chivalry, but his free upbringing had taught him just as much in other ways.

Philip patted Christian's back, then bent to retrieve the cup, which was now full of coins. He shook it once before handing it to Christian. "Fortune smiles on you, Christian."

Christian grinned back. "Only by sheer force of my will," he said with his usual unwavering self-confidence.

Philip smiled a farewell, then turned toward the Tourney field, for he'd been on his way to find Alix when first spotting Christian. But he hadn't even left the shade of the trees dotting the camp-grounds when a young boy stepped in front of him, impeding Philip's way.

"You're Philip de Saines?"

Philip gazed down at the little boy. He couldn't be more than nine years old, Philip thought, and obviously quite poor. Curiously, he wondered what possible business the boy could have with him. Philip nodded.

"There's a lady who wants to see you. There," he said, pointing to a wide tent, complete with guards, set up on the edge of the grounds sectioned off for visiting Tourney guests.

Philip frowned, guessing who might have sent the boy. "Did she tell you her name, boy?"

"No, Sire. Just a lady—and she's pretty. You'll want to see this one, Sire, I swear."

Philip pulled a coin out of the pouch hanging at his hip, and tossed it to the boy. The boy uttered a squeal of delight after biting the gold to assure himself of its worth, then he raced off.

Philip did not move toward the tent immediately. What purpose would it serve to see Rachel again? he wondered. He had no doubt it was she who'd hired the boy to fetch him. Who else?

His guess proved correct, for just as Philip was about to turn away, resuming his way toward the Tourney ground—and toward Alix—Rachel la Trau stepped out from behind the tent flap. It was mid-morning, yet Rachel looked as if she'd just risen—in a delectably disheveled state. Her hair, thick and free of any restraint, tumbled over her shoulders and down her back. She wore a pure white bedrobe, with slit sleeves and daring decolletage. Even from where Philip stood, he could see the fullness of her breasts straining the thin material, and the slimness of her waist where the belt was pulled tight. And, he noted, she wore nothing on her feet. There was a tarp laid upon the ground to protect her from stones or sharp needles, but that she was barely dressed was obvious to anyone looking her way.

When Rachel caught sight of Philip she smiled and beckoned him near. There were two guards standing just at the edge of Rachel's tent, and so Philip stepped forward, having witnesses to discourage Rachel if she wished to spread any lies about this meeting.

"I cannot say you are welcome," Philip told her, "under the circumstances."

Rachel's laughter sounded as free of deceit as a young, innocent babe's. "At last I have come to de Saines county and this is how you greet me? I have heard of your fair land, and it is truly beautiful, Philip."

Philip said nothing.

"Charles is off with a couple of his men . . . preparing himself for his joust with you on the morrow." Still, Philip did not reply and Rachel gave a pretty pout. "Do you have nothing to say to me, Philip? Then I will say something to you." She stepped closer, and placed one hand upon his chest. Then, with upturned face, she gazed into his

435

eyes and whispered, "Tomorrow, when you fight against my husband . . . it shall be you my heart is with. I would give you my favor to wear upon your sleeve, if only I could."

Philip placed his hands on her shoulders, gently but firmly pulling her away from him. "You are a deceitful wife, Rachel—and I will be glad once all of this is over and the stories will no longer link your name to mine."

Rachel stiffened, and she held her head high. "That is only if you win, dear Philip. For if you lose—God himself will have judged you guilty of bedding me, and your name and mine will be forever linked together."

Philip turned from her, disgusted not only by her words and the triumphant way she'd issued them, but also by the truth contained within.

But that disgust was quickly replaced by a surge of surprise as Philip caught sight of Alix, standing not far from Rachel's tent. Upon her face was neither condemnation nor a reflection of his own surprise; Philip's heart moved within, seeing only pain upon Alix's lovely face.

Philip was at her side in a moment, and took her hands in his. He didn't care how such movement appeared; he'd forgotten Rachel the moment he saw Alix. And the thought that Alix might feel some pain—either from seeing him with Rachel or if she'd overheard what the other woman said, made Philip want only one thing: to erase that crestfallen look he saw in Alix's eyes.

"Alix," he said her name gently. "Come with me, away from here."

Alix followed, saying nothing, and her silence tore into Philip like a hot knife. What was she thinking? he wondered. Had she lost trust, was she wondering how long he'd been with Rachel? Did she notice the way Rachel was dressed—or not dressed?

When they were far enough away from the campgrounds, Philip stopped, once again taking both of Alix's hands in his. He was about to speak, but noticed Hugh for the first time. The older man stood behind them, his gaze intent upon them.

"Hugh," Philip said over Alix's shoulder, "I will see that Demoiselle Alix is kept from harm. You may return to Lord Giles."

Hugh's gaze went from Philip to Alix and back again. "I will leave you both together, Lord Philip, but I shall have to tell Lord Giles it was you I left to care for Alix."

"That will be fine," Philip said, then waited until Hugh departed before turning his gaze back upon Alix.

"Alix," he began, his tone earnest, "surely you don't think I was with Rachel any longer than a few moments? I was on my way to finding you—"

But Alix, still unsmiling, shook her head. She looked at him, and though they were in full view of others milling on the outskirts of the Tourney field, Alix reached up and touched Philip's face, caressing him briefly.

"For a moment I was surprised—it looked as though you were coming out of her tent—"

Philip shook his head, starting a protest, but Alix put a fingertip to his lips.

"I believe in your love. I know you were not with her."

Philip wanted to breathe a hugh sigh of relief, but something in Alix's manner would not let him. "What is it, Alix? If you do not doubt my fidelity to you?"

Alix lowered her gaze, wishing she could put her thoughts away, forget them entirely. But what Rachel had said was true, and it had never occurred to Alix until the moment she'd heard the beautiful, spiteful woman utter the thought.

"It's true, what she said," Alix said softly, her voice trembling ever so slightly. "People everywhere, every person here at this Tourney, will view your joust with Charles as a trial by combat. If Charles should win . . . everyone will believe the charges against you are true. And in your death, Rachel will be the woman people will know in your life. Our love . . . the love we've come to know in secret . . . will only live on in my heart. No one

437

else will ever know we loved."

"It won't happen," he assured her quietly. "If there truly is such a thing as trial by combat, God will be on my side."

Alix managed a slight smile. "I've never wanted quite so much to tell others about our love as right now," she admitted. "And it's silly, really. I know you love me; that should be enough."

"I do love you—and I don't want it a secret." Then he said, with growing hope that he might lift her spirits, "I shall wear your favor upon my sleeve during the joust. Then all shall know I am your champion."

But Alix shook her head. "What of my father? And Julian?"

"I hardly care about their wishes," Philip said.

Alix was not convinced. "Suppose the favor upon your arm is rumored to be Rachel's, not mine? If she has lied before, I would not hesitate to think she'll do so again. I would rather have you fight for your own purpose, for the truth, than to open a way for Rachel to spread more lies."

Philip accepted her wishes, but as they began walking back toward the de Saines platform, he said only one thing more. "I shall not kill Charles la Trau," he told her, "but neither will I let him kill me. I'll not lose that challenge tomorrow, Alix. I promise you that."

Throughout the day, Alix held those words close to her heart. And that night, spent alone, she repeated them again and again. He would not lose, she thought. He promised. But more than once she wished she could go to him, sneak into the tent he slept in at the men's camp near the Tourney field and demand he tell her, just one more time, that he would not lose. Not just the joust, but also the melee. She wanted his assurance; she wanted to be with him. But she knew going to him tonight would serve only the enemy. For if they allowed themselves to be together, even with a firm resolution to let Philip sleep, their passion would win out. And it was sleep, not an exhausting night of lovemaking, that Philip needed most to sustain him through the next day. For if he made it through the following day, there would be many more nights for them to share.

37

"Your shield, Lord Philip," said Christian, handing him the shield which, like Julian's beside him, had the image of the de Saines dragon painted on it in bold red.

Philip, one of the forty men already mounted and fully armed, accepted the shield from Christian. Then, hearing the herald who announced the terms of the melee about to be fought, he knew it would not be long.

"Christian," Philip said, struck by a moment's worry, "do not linger here for me once the melee begins. Go to Alix's side, and stay with her until it is over. If the Montforts are the victors, their lust for blood might extend farther than those upon the field. They'll go for my father, and though he is well-guarded, Alix is seated nearby. If you see the Montforts have the advantage, Christian . . . flee with her. Take her to the Monastery, where she'll be safe."

Christian nodded, solemnly promising to do as Philip asked.

But, just as the horns blew the command for the opposing sides to take their places, Philip called back once more. "She won't want to go . . . she'll insist upon waiting for me, to see if I've survived or not. But you must take her anyway, Christian. Abduct her if you must, but get her to safety. Do you understand?"

"I will, Lord Philip. Have no worry over Demoiselle Alix; I shall protect her with my life."

"Philip!" Julian called, already prancing off toward the Tourney field. "Hurry!"

Philip followed, and once he reached the field he

never glanced back . . . not toward Christian, or elsewhere, toward the de Saines platform where he knew his family and Alix looked on.

The herald, being long-winded, was just finishing his announcement. He boasted about the noble lineage and bravery of the de Saines family, making the risk they took against the Montforts seem all the more chivalrous. The Montforts, though not of noble birth, were extolled for their boldness, their strength and their fresh energy in establishing their own stronghold. It was truly to be an exciting match.

Philip gripped the leather handle of his shield, raising it in place in anticipation of the herald's flag about to be dropped to issue the start of the battle. The forty Montfort men were opposite, each of them armed as the de Saines men were, with shield and sword and perhaps a dagger at their hip. Expectation of what was to come fairly crackled through the air, from the hushed crowd at the sides to the nervous restlessness of the horses.

Then the flag was dropped, and Philip spurred his horse forward in unison with those beside him. The other side, too, moved forward as one, and from somewhere, whether from a spectator or from one of the knights, came a battle cry loud and savage, speeding the instinctive flow of self-defensive strength through Philip's body. A part of him, primitive and fierce, felt the surge as surely as he felt the hilt of his sword pressed in his palm.

It took only moments for the opposing sides to join as one, and moments later clanking swords, human grunts of effort behind each slice, and the whinny of horses filled the air. It began evenly matched, with one man fighting one. But even as Philip raised his sword against the man opposite him, striking him down with such force the man was felled in seconds, another opponent took his place who had felled a de Saines man.

This second man was stronger than the first, and quicker with his sword. He sliced the air with his blade, and Philip had barely a moment to protect himself. The man's attack struck Philip's shield with a loud thud, but the armor proved strong. And though Philip felt the strength behind the blow, he did not hold back an answering attack. Philip raised his sword again and again, but the two were fairly equal in strength and it seemed forever that the battle between them lasted. Philip parried one attack after another, his life saved again and again by the thickness of his shield. And he was bold on the offensive as well, thrusting and advancing without hesitation, only to be held off.

But at last Philip's sword penetrated the man's defenses; the tip of Philip's sword ripped through gipon and mail, drawing blood from the enemy's shoulder. But Philip found it a small advantage. The man did not decrease his attack. Yet the sight of the opponent's blood spurred Philip on; it could not be long, he thought fleetingly, before the man lost strength. Philip's advantage would only increase with each drop of lifeblood seeping from his opponent's shoulder.

Philip's guess, made from past experience, proved correct. Soon the force behind the man's attack did begin to waver, ever so slightly. But it was enough. Armed with the knowledge that his opponent was weakening, Philip's attack increased; the number of thrusts he waged against the man grew, and the strength behind each attack mounted as well. At last, catching the man's sword with his own, Philip nudged his horse once with the tip of his foot to move closer to the opponent. Then, with the sound of metal scraping metal, Philip slid his sword along the edge of the other man's, and balanced on the stirrups to add the weight of his body behind the force of his sword. It took only a moment to unseat the other man, and he landed upon the hard ground with a groan and a thud—and did not move again.

With a glance around, Philip noted there were still many men left on both sides. This would be no quick and easy victory—for either of the opposing family names. Then he spotted Julian, in combat

with a man so quick and fierce with his thrusting
sword it seemed almost as if he were empowered
by unseen forces. Again giving direction to his
horse with a mere touch of his foot to the horse's
middle, Philip joined Julian's defense. And with
the speed of the Montforts' man, it took both of
them more than a few moments to take the
advantage. But with Julian at his side, no one man
could take them. With an old remembered
strategy learned long ago, Philip had only to cry
"Now!" and the two lifted their swords as one,
spurring their horses on at the same time. And
though the quicksilver energies of the man put up
a noble defense, he hadn't the strength to withstand the simultaneous and powerful thrust put to
both his sword and his shield. He fell back, and in
that one mere moment of weakness, Julian took
full advantage and thrust his sword through the
man's heart.

The battle was moving outward toward the
edges of the field, for many of those who had been
in the center were now defeated. Philip saw two
men wearing the Montfort colors advancing upon
August-Caron. In one swoop, too quick to allow for
Philip's approach to be of any assistance, August-
Caron was knocked to the ground. And, still with
Julian at his side, Philip advanced upon the two
men who'd sent the noble knight to his possible
death.

The two Montfort men, seeing the de Saines men
running them down, retreated toward the very
edge of the field. Banner markers were ignored as
the men withdrew ever further, and any spectator
not quick enough to move safely away was
trampled in the two men's hasty retreat. But as
Philip and Julian neared, the way was clear of
frightened spectators, although from the corner of
his eye Philip saw the shadows of those who
lingered closer than they ought.

"Be hostage or die!" Philip called toward the
retreating pair of men, and one, even before
turning round to face his attackers, dropped his
sword and shield and held out his hands in sub-

mission. The other, about to raise his sword to fight, saw that he was alone, and he, too, called himself hostage. He threw his weapons to the ground.

Philip wasn't sure what warned him, whether Julian's outcry or the gleam in one of the surrendered men's eyes as if he welcomed something from behind Philip. Philip turned, instinctively moving his shield alongside—but he was not quick enough. He saw the shimmer of a blade, and heard it hit the edge of his shield. But because he was turned away and in too odd a position to defend himself from someone behind, the man had the advantage upon his withdrawal. A moment later the sword came down again, this time without meeting the edge of Philip's shield. It struck him in the side, and immediately Philip felt the warm rush of blood. With an oath more from anger than pain, Philip raised his sword in useless defense, knowing he would be dead in the next instant from this faceless enemy behind him.

But the fatal blow never came; Julian was quicker than the man's lifted sword, and he had the advantage of fighting the man face to face. By the time Philip had turned to face the two men, the opponent had fallen to the ground, blood staining the shield he still clung to his chest.

Philip spared his brother a lopsided smile. "Well done, brother."

"Just like you taught me," Julian replied, then the two of them directed their horses back toward the field.

But the end was quickly drawing near. There was no one in the center of the field, just a few remaining men on one end, chasing down those who were retreating. But it was the Montfort end of the field, which spoke clearly which side had withdrawn. The entire field belonged to the victors, the de Saines men-at-arms.

Cheers rang out and before even the number of wounded or hostages could be counted, the field filled with joyous spectators. Philip stayed upon his horse, replacing his sword to its sheath and putting a gentle hand to his wounded side. Julian stayed close by.

"You should return to the Chateau to have one of the leeches tend you," Julian said.

But Philip shook his head, his gaze scanning the area for sign of Alix. He would see her first.

"If not back to the Chateau, at least go to the leeches tent," Julian persisted. "You're losing blood."

"They have others to tend to," Philip answered absently. Then he added, "Why don't you see to August-Caron? I saw him go down."

Julian was not about to leave his brother's side. "That isn't necessary," Julian assured him. "August-Caron left the field by his own power—something I'm not at all sure you'll be able to do if that bleeding isn't stopped."

Philip waved away his brother's concern, then drew his fingers against his forehead and wiped away fresh sweat caused by his fight with pain. Still looking about, he saw Alix at last, and his face brightened. Julian's gaze followed Philip's, and he did not appear in the least bit surprised when Alix ran to Philip's side.

"You're hurt!" she exclaimed, reaching up and pulling Philip's bloody hand away from his wounded side. "Let me help you."

Philip grinned, sliding from his horse. But he was still pale, and Julian could see he stood unsteadily. Philip spoke to Julian over his shoulder. "Now who would want to see a leech when God has sent an angel to tend my wounds?"

Julian dismounted as well, knowing Alix would need help getting Philip to a tent. He'd lost so much blood, he was in a visibly weakened state. Philip would need to be carried in a moment!

The leech tent, one of many, was busy, just as Philip had predicted. But the Chateau was too far to have Philip walk back, and Alix insisted she tend him immediately. She searched through the bag of one indignant leech, until finding the ingredients she needed for a mustard plaster.

Alix said nothing as she removed the gipon and

444

chain mail over Philip's head. Julian helped, then
thrust the stained armor aside. Alix removed the
tunic as well, carefully peeling the blood-soaked
garment away from the wound. It was not a deep
slash, she was relieved to learn, but nonetheless
he had lost an alarming amount of blood.

"Lie back, Philip," Alix commanded when he
remained sitting upright.

"I'm all right, I tell you," Philip said. "You
needn't use any remedies on me."

"It should be cleaned, and purged with a
mustard plaster."

"Alix is right, Philip," said Julian. "Do as she
says. I will take these soiled clothes and bring
something fresh."

But Philip was slow to do their bidding. He
would do as she said, he thought, but only when he
was ready. Bending closer to her, he kissed her
soundly upon the lips. He didn't care if Julian,
who was retreating with Philip's clothes but still
in full sight, watched, and he was just as oblivious
to the leech and his two patients on the opposite
side of the tent.

"We've won, Alix," he whispered. "It's almost
over now."

Alix spared one quick smile, but his playful
manner did not detract from her goal to minister
to his wound. "We will celebrate later," she
promised. Then, hearing the tent flap close behind
Julian, she pressed Philip back and began mixing
the herbs and water to apply to Philip's side.

Sounds from outside the tent penetrated easily,
and most sounds were paid no heed. But Alix
heard Julian's voice just outside, and the tone
used made Alix listen with interest.

"Yes, he's in there. But I wouldn't see him if I
were you. There is no reason for you to be here,
Rachel."

"But is he all right? Those clothes . . . they're so
filled with blood. Are they his?"

"Yes."

That was all it took for the tent flap to open in
one hurried swish, and Rachel la Trau stood there

looking like some glorious noblewoman in her sable-trimmed satin gown, intricately styled hair and jewels glistening at her throat and nearly every finger. Her eyes sparkled, too, Alix noted, with unshed tears.

"Get out of here, Rachel," Philip said, as if she were some wayward child. He seemed annoyed, but not overly so.

Rachel stared at Philip, but seeing him sitting up and obviously in much better condition than she feared, Rachel smiled. "I only wanted to assure myself you will still be fighting my husband this afternoon."

"I will," Philip said firmly, not looking up at the other woman.

But Rachel did not retreat. She took a step closer, her gaze resting on Alix.

"This is the girl I saw you with yesterday, Philip," Rachel said, as if they were speaking of Alix's portrait rather than within her actual presence. "She's rather pretty."

"Why don't you find Charles, Rachel?" Philip asked. "You can assure him I'm well enough to fight."

"Sending me away when I've only come out of concern for your welfare?" Then she added, "But I see this little maid is tending your wound quite nicely. Tell me, Philip, is she part of the family or one of your father's serfs?"

Alix stood before Philip could reply in Alix's defense. She took two steps closer, confronting Rachel. "Who I am is none of your concern, Madame. Anyone in Philip's life is none of your concern."

Something in the way Alix issued the words, almost like a threat, must have affected Rachel. She remained standing where she was, but her brief laugh was decidedly unsteady. "You have yourself a little spitfire, Philip. Surely she is not the one you wish to wed?"

Philip did not move, knowing Alix had defended herself quite nicely without his help, and proud of her for doing so. "As she said, Rachel, it is none of your concern. Now why don't you do as I said and find your husband?"

"That won't be necessary," said another voice from the tent flap. Charles la Trau entered, his face dark and unsmiling. "You see, Philip, I know where to look for my wife when you are around, so there is no need for her to search for me."

Alix stepped back, standing beside Philip. He tried to stand, but she held him down. "Lie still!" she commanded.

"Do not think that small wound will spare you from today's challenge," Charles said.

Rachel spoke up. "Do not worry," she said smoothly, "Philip has no intention of backing down now. But you, my dear husband, will have a decided advantage, wouldn't you say?"

Charles faced his wife. "I would say, my dear," he repeated the endearment with as little warmth as she'd used, "that you should not let your blood-lust show so blatantly. His innocence is showing through you, *my dear*."

"His innocence!" Rachel repeated, aghast. "How can you say such a thing? He bedded me— forced me—"

But Charles shook his head. "I might have believed that, once. When I loved you, you could have convinced me of anything, even to sell my soul to the devil. But with every ounce of your vengeance against him, I knew you were the slighted woman. Every time you spoke against him, you made me realize it was only vengeance you wanted—through me."

"And just when did you come to this startling conclusion?" Rachel asked, still confident.

"Several weeks ago."

Rachel laughed. "I do not believe you. You just challenged Philip days ago—for *my honor*."

But Charles shook his head, and the conversation went on, totally ignoring the onlookers. "No, Rachel. This battle will be for my honor, not yours."

Alix could not keep silent any longer. "Then you still intend to fight, even though you know Philip is innocent of bedding your wife?"

Charles turned to Alix for the first time since entering the tent. He eyed her closely, but must have guessed not just by her dress but also by her concern that she was someone important to Philip, more than just a maid tending his wounds. "Philip may well be innocent of that," he said. "But he is guilty of something else. My wife loves him . . . it's because of him I've been ridiculed by others, taunted by my own wife, and have not known a moment's peace since all of this began. After all, it's quite obvious to all of France that Rachel prefers his bed to mine—even if she's only known it in her imagination." He smiled, and let his gaze fall to Philip, still seated on the pallet on the floor of the tent. But though he looked at Philip, he spoke as if he weren't there. "I shall enjoy killing Philip de Saines, if only to regain my own sense of honor—certainly not to win back my wife."

Then he left, without another word to Rachel. It was all too clear that he hardly cared what she did any more.

Rachel glared at Philip, hatred so obvious Alix thought she might want to strike. But instead, she turned away without a word, following in her husband's wake.

Alix knelt at Philip's side, imploring him. "You can convince him not to fight, Philip," she said. "He already knows you're innocent. If you talk to him, tell him that a challenge over lies is ridiculous, you can change his mind."

But Philip was shaking his head before Alix even finished her last statement. "No, Alix." He stared at the tent flap, as if still seeing Charles standing there. "We're both trapped. If he doesn't fight, everyone will know him as the man who didn't defend his lair—whether the attack upon it was real or not. And if I don't fight, it would be an admission of guilt. I wouldn't care, except that now . . . loving you, I cannot tolerate the snickers, the scandal—and the disapproval of your father. It would be there, between us. This must be settled. And a fight is the only way."

"But it's all for lies! Rachel is the one who should suffer for what she's done, not you and Charles. This is a fight to the death!"

"I will not kill Charles."

"But he will kill you, if he has the chance."

"Perhaps."

"And you'll go through with this?"

Philip caught her hand in his, and gazed into her eyes. "There is no other way. I see that now. Charles is right—we fight for honor."

Alix wanted to deny it, to remind him of his wound, to tell Philip that her father's disapproval meant nothing to her, that it would never come between them, that he had honor already without fighting Charles . . . anything to convince Philip not to fight. But she knew such words would serve no purpose. There would be no deterring Philip's intention to fight, Alix knew that beyond a doubt.

38

The sun was still high in the western half of the sky when the herald entered the field. Alix, seated once again upon the de Saines platform, was now joined by Julian at her side. And when he took her hand out of concern and only to comfort her, she did not pull away. She knew it would be viewed as tenderness between a betrothed couple, but while she worried so fiercely over the coming event, she didn't care what others thought. She knew Julian was worried, too.

"He lost so much blood . . ." Alix whispered.

Julian squeezed her hand. "Philip is too strong to let something so minor inconvenience him. He'll be as hardy as ever, I promise you that."

"You are as quick to make promises as your brother—promises you might not have the power to keep." She hadn't meant to sound harsh, but nonetheless her tone did contain a hint of irritation.

Julian took no offense. "You will see, Demoiselle," Julian said confidently. "God Himself will favor Philip."

For one quick moment Alix bowed her head, offering up a silent prayer. But the words of the herald called her attention.

"On this day, four days past the day of St. Benedict in the holy year of our Lord thirteen hundred and fifty-two, a trial by combat will be fought. Charles la Trau, knight of our blessed King Jean, issues challenge against Philip de Saines, heir to the noble dynasty of de Saines. To the victor goes the honor!"

Alix gripped Julian's hand, seeing Philip upon his huge, powerful steed as he entered the field. She knew it was him immediately, seeing the easy way he sat upon his horse. But others might have recognized him by the star constellation Draco he wore upon his chest, or the dragon painted in red upon his shield. His helmet was already in place, and so Alix knew his vision to the side of the field where she sat was impaired. He did, however, turn her way and salute to the family platform. It was a confident, bold gesture, and cheers rang out from all around.

Charles arrived at the opposite end of the level field. He, too, wore a helmet, but with a tall black plume waving in the wind. He looked quite stiff upon his horse, and even Alix could guess he was anxious to begin.

Alix watched the herald urge his horse to the neutral center of the field. As he did so, two others joined the knights on the field. Alix recognized Christian, acting as squire for Philip. He held three lances, and once the herald raised the flag, signalling the squires to arm their knights, Christian offered the first long lance. With one hand Philip held the shield, with the other he accepted the weapon; the horse beneath him would be directed by familiar nudges to the flank, as if in battle.

Alix continued to stare, transfixed, knowing the joust was about to begin. The herald had only to drop that flag . . . and Philip would begin a battle everyone expected would be to the death. Suddenly part of her wanted to flee, a cowardly impulse to run and hide, and not witness the man she so loved risk his life. But she couldn't move, couldn't flee. Her bones seemed like the branches of willow trees, and she knew they wouldn't support her.

Then the flag dropped, and the riders spurred their horses on in one quick instant. Alix had no wish to see the moment the two challengers met, but as if bewitched she stared ahead with wide-eyed, morbid fascination. She would feel what he felt, she was there with him, as if they were one . . . knowing if he were pierced through, she would be too.

The loud thump as lance met shield was heard all around. Alix sucked her breath in at the sudden impact, for both lances had found their mark, nearly unseating the two riders. But though the blows were solid and square on target, neither rider seemed to feel the whack. They rode around the sides of the field, coming to their original places for a second try.

Christian handed Philip a new lance, assurance against possible damage which might have been done to the first lance. And again, with the drop of a flag, the riders were off.

"They're going faster," Alix whispered.

"They were just testing each other the first time," Julian told her. "This time . . ."

But he had no chance to finish his statement before the two challengers collided once again. This time Philip was visibly slammed, and though he remained seated, he nearly met back to back with his horse for one quick instant.

And Charles showed the blow as well; Philip's lance had not landed square in the center as Charles's had. Instead, Philip hit to the inner side, and Charles nearly slipped from the horse. But his foot caught on the stirrup, and though he lost both lance and shield, Charles was able to cling to the leather saddle and right himself from an almost upside down position. A roar from the crowd resounded, seeing such prowess.

It took a few extra moments for Charles's shield and lance to be removed from the field while another was brought by his squire. Philip, too, was armed with yet another new lance, and once again they charged each other. Neither rider showed any indication of fatigue; their lances were held high, right on the mark. And once again they clashed.

"He's down!"

Alix had no idea who spoke the words, but before Philip had even been unseated, his fate was guessed. Alix flew from her seat, seeing nothing but Philip laying there on the field. She would have flown to his side had not Julian forcefully held her back. The blow had been so sudden, so quick, Alix hadn't been prepared for it to happen—she hadn't believed it could.

Alix stared, her chest pained for air but unable to breathe past the lump in her throat. She pressed against Julian's restraint, almost crying out.

But then Philip rose, and a sob of relief escaped her.

"He was stunned for a moment, that is all," Julian told her. "It isn't over. Look—Charles challenges him with his sword."

It was true. Charles had leapt from his charger, throwing down his lance and reaching Philip just in time for Philip to pull out his sword and lift his shield against an attack. The blades sounded loud as they struck edge to edge, and neither gave quarter. One slice after another, the whistle, then the clang, like the sound of a peaceful smith hammering out his wares. But this was no pastime; this was a battle deadly as any. And Alix caught her breath each time sword met sword.

"He's on the defense, isn't he?" Alix whispered to Julian. Though she'd seen less than a dozen individual combats, she could not mistake the fact that Charles seemed to be the one advancing, and Philip the one defending.

"Charles has more hate behind his sword," Julian said. "He's already been bested by Philip in his wife's bed, so it's thought. He won't tolerate being bested on the Tourney ground as well."

Never before had Alix prayed for hate, but she whispered, "Hate him, Philip! Hate him and best him—and have this done!"

But still the battle waged. It was as if they were both trying for the other's exhaustion, knowing their opponent was bound to give way sooner or later. And with each swing, Alix prayed silently, *Let him survive one more . . . one more.*

Alix's worst fear was realized with one loud whoosh from Charles' sword. He swung from the side, one sweeping movement meant to behead his opponent. And though Philip was quick to try and duck, Charles' sword hit hard, catching the upper part of Philip's helmet. He fell to the ground in a crumpled heap—unmoving.

Charles was quick to raise his arms in victory. Too quick, for in that moment of triumph he was taken unaware. Philip slipped his foot upward to the man's knee, knocking him backward to the ground. Philip tried to regain his footing in that time, but before he was standing, Charles kicked the shield from Philip's grip. Then, still with sword and his own shield's protection, Charles advanced.

Philip was clearly at the disadvantage. But still he dodged each threat, a new quickness saving his life, keeping him out of the deadly path of Charles's sword. And then, with Charles so confident of his win against a man without a shield, he let his own shield slip just a little. But that was enough. Philip saw the opening and took the advantage. He thrust past Charles' shield, and in one blind moment of pure self-protection, he thrust his blade deep into the chest of his opponent.

Charles stepped back in surprise; his brows rose, as if he'd been taken totally unaware . . .as if

453

he hadn't realized Philip's sword was real until the moment it pierced him. Then he fell back, hitting the ground hard as if he'd been thrown from a high ledge.

But Philip did not raise his arms in triumph, as Charles had too hastily done just moments ago. Instead, looking down at the immobile body before him, he dropped his sword and went to his knees. Alix watched, crying Philip's name, knowing that bloodlust had never been his aim. She saw him reach out, slowly, and touch the bloody chest of his opponent. Then he recoiled, as if the blood had burned him.

Philip did not look up. He stood, pulling off his helmet and throwing that to the ground beside his discarded shield and sword. Then, without a glance behind—either toward the felled man nearby or toward the surrounding spectators, Philip strode away. If he heard the cheers that greeted him as he passed through the crowd, away from the field, he gave no indication.

And Alix watched him go. He'd walked toward the opposite end of the field, away from Charles. Away from her.

Alix felt numb. She watched several men race out toward Charles and carry him away. She had no idea if he was alive or dead, although the sight of several crimson-robed physicians made her suspect he still lived. But, unmercifully, she felt no relief. She wanted to find Philip . . . even if he didn't want to be with her.

"I'm going after him," she said to Julian, and before he could respond she started walking. Julian followed close behind.

Though Alix searched the surrounding area, going immediately to the spot she'd last seen him, Philip was nowhere to be found. They went to the campground where he'd slept last night; they went to the leech's tents, thinking he might be waiting there to see about the condition of Charles. And last, they went to the Chateau, searching the courtyard, the hall, and finally his tower. Philip was nowhere to be found.

Exhausted, Alix walked back toward the hall. The evening meal would be served soon, no doubt a huge, triumphant festival to celebrate the day's victories. Perhaps he would show up there.

By the time Alix and Julian entered the hall, it was already full of merry guests. People from every direction, half in their cups so soon, greeted them with cheers of welcome. A few bold men approached Alix and twirled her about, and more than a couple of women greeted Julian with a kiss. Alix had never seen the hall so full, nor heard quite so much noise. And never had a feast been so unwelcomed by her.

"He isn't here," Alix said. Her voice was low, but Julian heard her for he squeezed her hand in response. They found their way to the raised table at the end of the hall, where Alix's parents sat with the Sire and Lady de Saines. The four were surrounded by other guests, and each of them were so obviously as happy as the others filling the hall that Alix had no desire to draw any closer.

"I don't want to stay here," she said. "I'm going to my chamber."

"No, Alix," Julian said, not letting go of the hand he held. "What will you do alone except fret? Stay with me."

But Alix shook her head. "I cannot stay here."

Without another word, Julian led her toward one of the antechambers off the hall. He had to open the doors to three chambers before he found one unoccupied—although none of those couples sharing the private rooms seemed to even notice his brief interruption. The empty room, too, showed evidence of having been used, for they found empty mugs and a woman's scarf and a man's forgotten hood discarded on the floor. The Church scorned Tourneys, holding that such gatherings always encouraged three terrible sins: bloodlust, overeating, and a blatant overindulgence in the carnal senses. No one disputed that was true, but neither did anyone follow their urging to stop Tournaments altogether.

But after Julian removed the tokens of what had

gone on in the room before they'd arrived, Alix sat upon the padded couch and stared ahead, as if seeing nothing.

"I know why he didn't come to me after the challenge," Alix said quietly. "He wanted to get away from . . . everything. Including me."

Julian sat beside her, placing an arm about her shoulder. "It was because he wanted to get as far away from the Tourney field as possible," Julian said softly. "He wanted to get away from the Tourney, not from you."

But Alix shook her head. "It was my fault he had to fight that joust. If he hadn't loved me . . . he told me himself it wouldn't have mattered—the scandals or the snickers behind his back—if it hadn't been for loving me. And for my father." She laughed bitterly. "Philip knew he couldn't marry me unless my father was satisfied—and to satisfy my father, Philip had to accept Charles's challenge. Even though he didn't want to."

"He would have had to meet Charles, sooner or later," Julian assured her. "It was easier to do once he'd broken his vow not to touch the sword again—and he broke that vow because of me. Should I blame myself for being kidnapped, and feel responsible for Philip taking the sword to save me?"

Alix laughed again, but it was a tormented sound. "Don't you see? Philip saved you for more than just love of you. If he let you die at the hands of the Montforts, he might never have known why he couldn't have raised his sword to save you. Because of the vow? Or because he wanted the woman you were betrothed to?" She held back a sob, swallowing hard. "He loves you, Julian, and wanted to save you . . . but I am part of the blame for his taking up the sword again to rescue you. He had to, if he was ever going to rest easy with the love he holds for me."

"I knew that," Julian whispered, pulling her close. "I knew he loved you, and while I was held at the Montfort stronghold, I knew letting me rot would have been an easy solution to breaking our betrothal so you would be free to marry him. But do you know, even though Philip and I have barely spoken to each other for the past two years, I never doubted he would come for me? And he would have, Alix, whether or not you gave him added reason. It's part of him, to right a wrong . . . He couldn't have let me rot. He just couldn't have."

Just then the door to the antechamber opened unexpectedly, and Giles stood there, cup in hand. At the sight of the two seated so close together upon the couch, he raised his brows. "I suppose I should not be surprised," he said, "considering you are still betrothed in the eyes of almost everyone. But, God's teeth, young daughter, I thought you wanted to marry Philip? Where is he? And what are you doing in here with Julian?"

Julian stood, motioning Giles into the room and closing the door behind him. "Philip is gone, Lord Giles. He disappeared after the joust with Charles."

"He's the victor!" Giles said. "He should be here celebrating with all of us. I was even prepared to announce the change in wedding plans. He's proven himself innocent of the scandal, and he's acted well in the last few weeks, not only in saving Julian from kidnapping, but in organizing and taking part in the melee that ousted the Montforts."

Alix stood, approaching her father. "I'm not at all sure there will be a wedding, Father."

Giles's brows met in a frown. "It was you, Alix, who told me of the love you share with Philip. That you would marry none other. Have you changed your mind, in favor of Julian?" The latter words had an unmistakable tone of hope attached to them.

Alix shook her head. "It's Philip . . . I fear he's changed his mind."

But Julian rushed in before Giles could respond. He took Alix's shoulders in a firm grip and shook her once, gently. "He's coming back, Alix. Perhaps even now he's in his tower dressing for the feast."

"I'll send someone to look for him," Giles said, watching his daughter. That she'd never looked unhappier was obvious. Nonetheless, he said, "Alix, if he has indeed disappeared, I think you should count yourself blessed. Perhaps he has no wish to marry."

Then he left the room, and Alix stared at the closed door behind him. She didn't cry, though part of her wanted to; she didn't deny her father's words or defend her own belief in Philip's love. His words merely added to the fear she already had.

But Julian remained hopeful. "He'll be back before nightfall."

"Another promise?" Alix said bitterly.

"I kept the last one, didn't I?"

Alix didn't respond. She merely walked from the antechamber, and Julian let her go, knowing she headed to the solitude of her own room. He couldn't force his company upon her any longer, and certainly not in her private bedchamber. But as he watched her walk through the crowded hall, his gaze fell upon Marie Beauchamp. Believing Alix better off in the company of someone else, he headed Marie's way.

Alix woke with a start, feeling the warmth of another body lying beside her. She sat up quickly, thoughts of Philip and the previous day's events flooding back.

Her sudden movement awakened the person beside her. Marie Beauchamp looked at her daughter in alarm.

"What is it?"

"I—I thought . . ."

Marie looked at her, a questioning gaze still upon her face, but Alix did not finish. She pulled the covers away, seeing the sun was shining brightly through her window. Perhaps Philip had returned during the night. How could she have slept through the long hours? She stood, but was suddenly struck by a now-familiar wave of nausea. She sank back on the edge of the bed.

"You needn't hurry off to see if he's returned," Marie said, getting out of bed from the other side. "I asked Blanche to come with the news immediately, no matter what the hour." Then, straightening her underrobe, Marie glanced at Alix. Upon seeing her face, ashen white, and her hands trembling in her lap, Marie approached and sat at her side. "You shouldn't make yourself so ill over this, Alix. I know he loves you. He'll be back."

But Alix hardly heard her mother's comforting words. She rushed to the bedpan, succumbing to the illness coursing through her body.

Marie was at her side in a moment. "This isn't just concern over Philip," Marie said, holding her daughter and wiping away the perspiration dotting Alix's face. She led Alix back to the bed, and bid her to lie down once again. "You are truly ill, Alix. I will send for one of the physicians."

But Alix shook her head. "No, Mother," she called weakly. "I'll be fine now. I've been suffering such mornings like this for days . . . but it always passes once I empty my stomach."

Marie frowned, then suddenly her eyes widened and her brows rose in surprise. "Alix," she began slowly, "when was the last time you bled?"

Alix seemed perturbed by such a question. "I—I don't know. Why?"

"This sickness you've been feeling. It comes only in the morning?"

Alix nodded.

"And have you been feeling . . . different? Does your body feel somehow changed?"

Annoyed, Alix brushed away the question with a wave of her hand. "I haven't noticed. I've had far too many other things to be concerned over." Then, seeing the earnestness upon her mother's face, she softened her tone and added, "I suppose I have felt different . . . I've never been sick in the morning."

"I suffered the same strange illness, Alix, long ago. Twice, in fact. Just before Simon was born, and again, when I carried you."

Slowly the truth dawned, and Alix's eyes

widened just as her mother's had only moments ago. "You think I'm . . . I might have Philip's child within me?"

Marie nodded.

The smile upon Alix's face grew slowly, and her hand went to her middle, as if her own body was something new and precious. She had never worried that such a thing might happen . . . she knew she would welcome Philip's child. They were to be wed . . .

Suddenly she sat up. "I must find him," she announced, "and tell him. If he knows, surely he won't delay—"

Then she stopped, both her speech and all movement. She turned to Marie, hot tears stinging her eyes. "What if he doesn't come back?"

Marie pressed her daughter back into the soft bed. "Why would he stay away, Alix?" she said, as if the notion was ridiculous. "He loves you, and knows that at week's end you will be wed."

"But he looked so devastated when Charles fell . . . and Charles! I haven't even spared a thought for him . . . yet if he dies because of the wound Philip gave him, how will Philip ever forgive himself? He vowed not to kill him."

"He had little choice," Marie said. "If he did not kill Charles, Charles would have killed him."

"Have you heard, then?" Alix asked, though she dreaded to hear the answer. "Has Charles died?"

Marie shook her head. "I do not know. He was taken by his men-at-arms to be tended away from the Chateau. I do not know where they took him, or if he survived."

"Suppose Philip is with Charles?" Alix guessed. "Wanting to know if he lives or not?"

Marie looked thoughtful. "It is a fair notion," she said. "Perhaps you are right. I shall find out where they've taken Charles, and send men to look there for Philip."

Marie left before Alix could call her back. In truth, she wasn't sure if she wanted Philip brought back if he wasn't ready to return. But Marie seemed almost as anxious to find Philip as Alix was, now that there was suddenly a babe to consider. And though she wished she could coddle herself with dreams of how wonderful it would be to have Philip's child, Alix's thoughts were too full of other worries just then.

Suppose they couldn't find Philip before the scheduled wedding ceremony? Surely Alix's father wouldn't insist she never marry Philip, just because Philip had left her at the altar once? She knew her father well enough to guess he would use any excuse he could to keep Alix from marrying a man he truly did not approve of.

But it wasn't as if this wedding had been theirs all along . . . as if they'd planned it and looked forward to it, knowing it would be the day of their union. It had been so uncertain . . . even to the point of the joust. How could Philip know for sure he would be returning to their wedding tomorrow? He'd won the joust, answered the challenge against his name, and by all rights should know he'd gained her father's approval. Yet their betrothal had never been announced, actual approval had never formally been given to Philip himself by Lord Giles. Perhaps Philip wasn't even sure he would be returning to his wedding if indeed he came back.

But, Alix admitted to herself, she was suddenly more than anxious to be wed. For a babe to be born too close to the wedding day could serve no purpose but gossip. And for Philip to return posthaste, he would have to learn of her pregnancy. In his mind, there was no reason for speed . . . he was full of remorse over the blood he'd shed—perhaps he even blamed her for her part in his need to face the challenge Charles issued. And perhaps he could not tolerate the thought of his own wedding while he still suffered the penitence of breaking his vow, maybe even killing Charles when he'd made it so clear to her he had no intention of fighting the joust to the death with the man who had once been his friend.

Alix rubbed her eyes, feeling an ache behind them. If Philip truly did blame her for forcing him to take up the sword again, was it right to bring him back for their wedding because of the babe she carried? Would their marriage begin only because of the babe? Perhaps he would prefer to wait, at least until he could forget any resentment he might feel toward her for her part in forcing him to take up the sword again. Would he resent being hurried? She hated to think of the beginning of their life together with anything but love between them.

Alix could not sit idly in her chamber waiting for news of Philip. She dressed and went to the hall, finding it full of guests still lingering after the Tourney. There were not as many people present for the morning meal as had been present yesterday for the feast, nonetheless it was quite different than the usually quiet near-dawn meals. Geoffrey and Eleanore were not in attendance, and neither, Alix noted, were her parents. She took her seat, and immediately a servant brought a small portion of bread and cheese for her. She ate, tasting nothing, hardly responding to the conversations around her about the exciting Tourney. Someone mentioned the wedding—her wedding —and Alix looked up. One of Geoffrey's cousins was looking straight at her.

"Word has it they're searching for Philip de Saines quite frantically," said Richard de Saines. "Now why, I wonder, is it so important for him to be at your wedding to Julian?"

Alix said nothing. She returned his stare with confidence she didn't feel, finishing her meal without a word in response. She was, however, more than relieved when a page summoned her to her parent's inner solar.

Marie and Giles were both standing when she entered the room. Giles was near the fireplace, Alix's mother behind one of the couches. The air was decidedly tense, and with one glance, Alix knew her mother was quite agitated over something.

"Is something wrong?" she asked, becoming alarmed. "Have you any news of Philip?"

"No—" Marie began. But Giles interrupted her.

"The wedding is planned for week's end," he reminded her unnecessarily. "I admit I was prepared to allow you to wed Philip—but blazes! the man you wish to serve as groom has disappeared, for no reason! He was victorious at the Tourney yesterday, and should be more than proud of not only wiping the Montforts from this land—dispersing their army of mercenaries with barely a horse or lance between them—but also clearing his name and establishing his innocence in that scandal with the la Trau woman. It's quite obvious he's disappeared because he wishes to miss his own wedding—and who will be the wiser that it was he, and not Julian, who left you at the altar? We told no one it was Philip you were to wed, so he'll not take the blame when the bride—my daughter—is left alone at the altar." Giles stared at Alix intently, his tone so serious Alix could not doubt his sincerity. "The man is truly a coward, Alix. I'll not have you wed him. It's obvious you won't be able to get him to the altar unless you drag him there."

Alix stiffened, and held her head high. "I do not wish to discuss any of this until Philip has returned and gives you his own reason for leaving."

Marie neared her daughter, and put an arm about her waist. "You've already guessed why he's left, Alix. And I agree with you. I think you were right about him following Charles, to see if he survives or not. Soon word will reach him, and he'll return in time for the wedding."

"You'll not wed him!" Giles pronounced. "Any man who leaves you—knowing you'll be wed—does not truly want to marry. He will have to marry sooner or later, to provide an heir, but he can be cursed before I'll allow my daughter to wed him."

Suddenly Alix laughed, loud and almost merrily —except she didn't feel merry. But her father's words struck the truth, the truth that she hadn't realized until that moment. This child within her

463

was heir to the great de Saines dynasty—Philip's heir. "He already has an heir," she said, her eyes filling with tears of laughter.

"Alix—" her mother's voice warned, but Giles had heard the words and now, seeing his wife's worried face and his daughter's oddly happy one, he would not let it pass.

"What do you mean?" he said to Alix. "Where has Philip an heir?"

Alix couldn't keep the news within. After all, she reasoned, he would find out sooner or later. Having a child was something one just didn't keep secret! "Right here," she said, her hands resting upon her middle. "I carry his heir inside me, Father."

Giles Beauchamp stared at Alix as if she'd suddenly gone mad. Then his gaze went to Marie. "You knew about this, didn't you?"

Marie nodded. "We just learned of it today."

"We?"

"Alix wasn't even aware she was with child," Marie explained.

Giles turned away, facing the fireplace instead of his family. He was suddenly thoughtful, as if calculating what was the best course of action. "You're sure?" he said, over his shoulder. And when Marie nodded, he stared into the crackling fire in front of him. "Take Alix back to her room, Marie. And keep her there. I don't want anyone knowing about this just yet."

Alix laughed again, though she had sobered somewhat upon seeing her father become so suddenly pensive. "Oh, Father, the babe is hardly visible yet. I don't need to hide."

But he didn't reply. He merely stared ahead, and Marie stepped forward to do as her husband commanded.

Alix let her mother pull her from the room, but with one last glance toward her father, she felt her heart sink inside. What could he be thinking?

39

Sounds echoed dully through the wide, dim halls of the monastery. Philip heard his footsteps as if they'd come from someone else, as if there were more than just the sound of his own footfall. But he knew he was alone. This part of the cloister had been heavily used by the sick and dying who suffered from the Plague just a few years ago; now, however, the sick rooms were empty but for one. And he did not suffer from the plague. Philip found the room without difficulty, and reentered quietly. A dark-caped monk sat beside the patient, and Philip took a seat as well. Waiting in silence for some sign that Charles la Trau would respond to the holy man's ministrations.

It hadn't been easy, at first, to convince the men-at-arms who had taken Charles from the Tournament grounds that Philip had any kind intentions toward Charles. When Philip had first spotted them taking Charles away sprawled upon a horse litter, he could scarcely believe they took the road headed for Paris. Although Philip had not inspected Charles's wounds closely, he doubted the man would survive such a journey, and he made haste to make his opinion known. The chief man-at-arms was reluctant to agree when Philip suggested the monastery only a few leagues ahead. He'd been given orders by Rachel la Trau to bring her husband to Paris; she herself had gone ahead to prepare a sick bed for him. But there must have been some evidence that all was not well between husband and wife before the Tourney. When Philip suggested none too gently that Rachel la Trau would probably welcome her husband's death so she would not be cut off from his funds should he survive long enough to do so, the knight at last agreed to have Charles cared for immediately.

Charles had shown little sign he was responding to any of the monk's remedies. The wound was deep, and he'd lost much blood. They had stopped the bleeding with a mixture of lemon and shepherd's purse weed poultice, but Charles had cried out agonizingly when the stinging mixture was applied, falling into a deep, unnatural sleep. And during the night, he grew hot with fever. Two monks soaked his body in cool water steeped with sage, then periodically helped him drink the juice of crushed red berries diluted with water to help diminish the fever. Philip had looked on helplessly while the monks administered to Charles, all the while wishing more and more there could have been another way of settling the scandal between them. Did the sword have to be the answer?

He doubted Charles even knew Philip was there. Charles had barely opened his eyes the whole time since Philip had first caught up with his party. And though Philip knew he was of no real use at Charles's side, he couldn't bring himself to leave. He had to know . . . he had to be there until he knew if Charles would live or die. For if he died . . .

Philip resisted such thoughts. He *wouldn't* die, Philip said to himself. He'd vowed not to kill Charles in that joust—he'd had no intention to even spear him at all. But that moment, that last second before he'd pierced him through, Philip knew it was the only way to defend himself. He'd seen the opening, knew he could thrust his sword deep into Charles's unprotected chest—unprotected for one quick instant, long enough to save Philip's life. And perhaps end Charles's.

Silently reliving that instant, he cursed himself. He certainly was no good at keeping the vows he made. Thought of that brought Alix to mind. She knew he'd broken this pledge—a second promise he'd made to himself. What value would she put upon the troth of marriage he longed to take with her? Knowing he'd broken vows as important as the two he'd taken, would she have any trust in him at all? Did he have any trust in himself?

Week's end was supposed to bring their wedding day. That is, he thought, if Giles Beauchamp was satisfied. Philip frowned grimly. He should be satisfied, Philip thought to himself. Hadn't Philip used the sword for what it was intended—to kill?

Still, Philip wondered if Lord Giles would allow Philip to wed his daughter. He was no fool; Philip knew Giles would search for any reason to keep him from marrying Alix. And how could he blame him, really? First Giles believed him a coward, and Philip had done little to renounce that insult. For the past two years of his life he'd been happy to live without caring what others thought of him. When he'd come home to the Chateau, he continued that sort of thinking—he'd worked like a peasant, freed the serfs, disdained the daily life of the aristocracy—ignoring what other nobles thought of him. And he'd been more stupid than that; he'd ignored as well the threat of the Montforts until his brother was taken captive. Philip had taken up the sword only when it was forced upon him to do so . . . And, seeing Charles lying upon his deathbed because of Philip's sword, he knew, despite the fact that some might believe Philip would use his sword freely henceforth, he would do all possible to avoid ever using it again. Couldn't Lord Giles guess that easily enough?

But what of Alix? He wondered, fleetingly, his eyes still upon Charles, what Alix thought of his disappearance. He should have spoken to her, told her where he was going. Surely she would understand his need to know if Charles lived or died. But he couldn't have stayed . . . he couldn't have faced her. When he walked from that Tourney field he hated himself more than he'd ever hated before. How could he stand before someone he loved, knowing he deserved nothing in return?

Now, as Philip continued to watch the unmoving

form of the man who had once been his friend, he wished foolishly that none of this had ever happened. He wished Charles was lively and well, he wished he didn't feel this lingering self-reproach. He wished Alix was there at his side, that he'd taken her with him, so he could share these thoughts and doubts, and feel her love. That's what he needed most of all, he thought, to know Alix still loved him . . . even when he hated himself.

Alix stood outside the door to the solar her father had summoned her to. She had paced the corridor for several minutes, knowing they were waiting for her but dreading to go in. Her father had barely spoken to her since yesterday, when he'd learned she carried Philip's child. And the silence between them was heavier than any other silence. She knew her father's concern was justified—after all, while every noble court of France upheld chivalrous love, having a child out of wedlock was not part of that code. The scandal would be great, particularly since the father of the babe was none other than Philip de Saines—a man who, of late, never seemed far from the center of most people's attention. And if Philip did not return soon the scandal of the child growing within Alix's womb would be impossible to conceal.

When her father summoned her just a short while ago, Alix had lost what little courage she'd clung to in the past few days. She felt so uncertain of every thought, every hope regarding Philip. He wasn't there to assure her of his love, and without that, far too many questions and doubts arose. The existence of the baby she carried seemed to change everything between them—what she needed most was to be assured of his love, to know they would still be wed. But she couldn't deny her own doubts about that. The guilt would not leave her, knowing it was she who had sent Philip to that Tourney field to fight Charles to begin with. Would resentment over that fester between them . . . especially if Charles did not survive? Alix had received no word of Charles la Trau, only that Marie had sent men after them and they'd headed toward Paris. Rachel la Trau had headed there to prepare a sick bed for her husband, who followed at a slower pace. Paris was a fair journey from there . . . no doubt it would be more than the usual two days before they reached the city with such a slow pace for Charles's sake. Alix's only hope was that the men Marie had sent would catch up to them, tell Philip the news of her babe, and he would return posthaste so not to miss their wedding. But if he stayed with Charles . . . traveling to Paris, it would be impossible for him to return to the Chateau by week's end. And, Alix realized with a heavy heart, she was not at all sure he would choose to return to her rather than staying at Charles's side. For the babe, he might . . . But she didn't want him to return solely for the sake of the scandal caused by their babe! She wanted him to return to her.

At last Alix pushed away her ominous thoughts and put a hand to the solar door latch. She stepped inside the room quietly; it was dim, the only light coming from the fireplace and a few candles on a small table between the two padded couches opposite one another before the crackling fire. Alix approached, hearing nothing but the spitting and snapping of the burning wood in the hearth.

She saw her parents first; they were seated on the couch facing her. She was surprised to see Julian there as well; at first his presence had been concealed by the high back of the couch. But when he saw her he looked oddly uncomfortable, then stood to make room for her upon the couch. Giles quietly told her to be seated, and once she did so, Julian took a seat beside her.

Giles eyed his daughter. "I'll not meander around the point of this meeting, Alix," he said. "I've just had a rather interesting discussion with Julian. Do you know, daughter, that the last time Philip threw down the sword it was two years before he gained the courage to return home to face his father and family? Two years . . ."

Julian spoke up, explaining to Alix. "Philip threw down his sword in battle off the coast—"

"I know about that battle," Alix said. "His reasons for becoming disgusted by the sword are strong."

"He did come home after that," Julian clarified. "But only long enough to tell us he'd given up the life of a knight. It was two years before he returned—just a few months ago, as you know."

Alix didn't look at anyone. Why were they saying this? Why remind her of all this now? "I know all that," she said unsteadily. "He went to Court; he was favored by the King . . . He served as an advisor to Jean—"

"Nonetheless, it took him quite some time before he returned home," Giles said. "Don't you see, Alix? He's disappeared again just as suddenly; he'd obviously thrown down the sword one more time, and who can guess how long it will take before he is able to face his family this time? Two years again? Or longer?"

Alix stood, shaking her head and feeling as if all three of them—even her silent mother—believed all the evidence and had given up on Philip already—given up on the love he held for her. Given up on him coming home, at least until it was too late. Time was one thing she no longer had; the babe inside her left her no such luxury.

"He's coming back," she assured them, more confident than she felt.

Marie came to her side, and patted her shoulder comfortingly. "Of course he is," she assured Alix.

Giles, however, was not assuaged by the faith of the two women before him. He spoke up in a steady, careful voice. "It no longer matters whether or not he'll return. The wedding is set for two days hence. Julian has not formally broken the betrothal, therefore—"

"No!" The single word came from not one mouth but two as both Alix and Julian spoke up in unison. Julian stood, and in a moment so did Giles, and all four of them let a long, awkward silence pass before anyone spoke again.

Giles broke the silence. "Julian," he began, "you agreed to wed Alix once before; I thought, at the time, you were satisfied with the choice your father and I made for you."

Julian laughed briefly. "Do you think I wish to marry a woman who loves another? Especially if the man she loves is my own brother?"

Giles waved away his protest. "This nonsense will pass," he assured Jullian. "Once she is wed to you, marriage will make her forget all about Philip."

But Julian shook his head. "I sincerely doubt that could happen, Lord Giles. I think it best to just postpone the wedding until Philip returns."

This time the objection came from Giles. "The wedding is set for week's end," he said. "And I'll not have that day changed. My daughter will be wed, whether or not you agree to be her husband. I believe you have a cousin of marriageable age?"

Julian looked perplexed. "You would wed her to a man she doesn't love just because the wedding day is drawing near? What harm is there in waiting until Philip returns?"

Giles spoke up quickly, before either Marie or Alix could respond with the truth. "I'll not have it known my daughter was left at the altar by any man. I've never been one to allow a scandal attached to my name—and with Simon behaving the way he did so recently, I've had the Beauchamp name on too many tongues already. She will wed at week's end, as planned."

But Julian shook his head slowly. "It makes no sense."

Giles tried one more time to change Julian's mind. "You were happy enough to be betrothed to her before," he said. "If you marry her, she will forget this brief fondness she held for Philip. But, if you feel so uncomfortable living within the same walls as Philip once you wed Alix, you could always live at the Beauchamp Estate. It'll be finished for Simon and Marguerite before long; it could certainly be a comfortable place for you to live until the de Saines lands are divided for your inheritance."

Julian looked at Giles intently, obviously puzzled. "You are too eager to have Alix wed—and soon. Why, I wonder?"

"I'll tell you," Alix said boldly, pulling away from her mother, who tried to hold her back.

But Giles would not let her speak. "I'll hear nothing from you, Alix. Be silent, do you hear?"

Alix stared at him defiantly. "Why? Don't you think Julian should know what you're trying to force upon him? Not just a wife but a family?"

"Say no more," Giles warned. "Or you may find yourself searching for your lost purity in the halls of the most remote abbey my brother can find to hide you away in."

Alix laughed. "There, you've given it away yourself, Father. My lost purity. Surely Julian should know that if he weds me he will also be getting his brother's heir." She laughed again, bitterly. "At least the babe will have his father's name your way, Father."

Julian was plainly shocked. "You—you are carrying Philip's babe?"

Alix nodded, holding her chin high despite the fact her father would no doubt prefer she show some amount of shame.

Julian was silent for a long moment. Then, nearing Alix, he took both her hands in his. "Men are scouring the countryside all the way to Paris for my brother," he told her. "But if they cannot find him by week's end . . . perhaps he doesn't want to be found just yet."

"What do you mean?"

Julian sighed deeply. "Only that if Philip struggles with the blood he shed upon the Tourney field—Charles's blood—the way he struggled with the bloodshed upon that battlefield two years ago, it could be a long while before he is ready to return home—even to you. If he finds no forgiveness for himself, how can he expect you to still love him?"

"But he knows I love him!"

"I am only saying that it may take time for him to realize he still has your love—more time than you have. My brother has never been one to act too hastily. If he cannot forgive himself for wounding, perhaps killing Charles, it may take him more time than you have for him to believe he deserves your love."

Giles pounced on the meaning behind Julian's words. "There," Giles said. "Julian agrees with me. Even he realizes Philip may not return in time to acknowledge that child within your womb."

"He'll be back!"

"But when?" Giles asked. "As soon as that babe begins to show growing within you it will already be too late. You must wed now, Alix—or go to the cloister of my brother's choice, where your sin will be hidden."

Julian had not let go of her hands. "Perhaps your father is right, Alix. Perhaps it would be best if we wed. I do not want to see you subjected to the scandal of a child not sanctioned by matrimony. And," he added with a contemptuous glance directed Lord Giles' way, "the cloister is out of the question. It would be a hellish way to spend the rest of your life . . . and who can say what would happen to the child there? A child of sin would not be loved and raised by the sisters of any cloister whose goal is to hide your sin away."

But Alix turned away, looking to her mother. "I will wait for Philip," she said stubbornly.

Marie spoke up at last, glancing at Julian briefly first. "Julian has offered something far more precious than it might sound, Alix. He's offering you a free life—and you know your father has the power to send you to this cloister. I could not stop him to save you. How could I let that happen? Never to see my own daughter again, or her child? Marriage truly is your only other choice—and marriage soon, so those counting the months when the babe is born will not come up too far short."

"But the babe can be a secret for months yet! I swear I haven't missed more than two bleedings.

473

Surely we can wait for Philip to return—even if it's a couple of months!"

"Haven't you listened, Alix?" Giles asked harshly. "It's already getting late, every day that passes is one less day you have before the child is born. As it is now, it will be seven, not the full nine months everyone expects as the very least amount of time after the wedding for a child to be proper born. If you are wed immediately, it will merely be called an early birth—and pray God it's a small child to enforce our lies."

Alix said nothing; she just stood stoically, a stubborn set to her jaw. Even her mother had given up on the love Alix shared with Philip. She wanted to run away, to find Philip. How she needed him! But, drawing in a long breath of air, she told herself she believed in his love. He would be back, he would. That was why she couldn't possibly marry anyone else—even Julian, whose only intention was kindness, she was sure of that.

Julian whispered to her. "Come with me for a while, Alix. Let us talk alone about this."

The prospect of leaving her parents was an inviting one; to leave behind her father's judgmental stare, and her mother's pitying one. But there was nothing more to say. She would not marry Julian—nor would she go to the cloister her father threatened her with. Surely there was a way to escape her father's two alternatives.

She followed Julian out of her parents' solar, down to the first level of the Chateau, past the hall and outside through the forebuilding. But when he headed for the garden, Alix stalled. She didn't want to go there with Julian . . . nor with anyone, except Philip.

"We can talk here," she told him, halting in the center of the busy courtyard.

"Don't you think the garden would be more private?" he asked.

She shook her head. "It's used quite often by the women of the chateau—they like to sew there." That much was very true, although not at all the reason she was eager to avoid going there.

So Julian went instead to the side of the inner bailey, where several tall willows grew. The branches of the first tree they passed swept the floor like a curtain of lacy leaves, and he held several branches aside, inviting Alix to the relative privacy offered by the huge tree at its hidden trunk.

He spoke lightly. "This seems an appropriate place to ask a woman to wed," he said. "We're alone—"

But Alix shook her head. "I cannot believe you are willing to wed me, knowing I carry your brother's child."

Julian sighed, staring at her. "I'm a bit surprised at that myself—I never considered myself especially chivalrous. But it is the only way, Alix. It's either me or my cousin—and I assure you, after being on campaign with the young man, he snores. You wouldn't get a good night's sleep for the rest of your life if you married him."

Alix was not like the flexible branches surrounding them; she could not bend to Julian's wry humor. She stood, stiff and tall, and said firmly, "I'll marry no one but Philip."

Julian frowned. "And if he doesn't return by week's end, you'll be going to a cloister instead."

Alix shook her head. "I'll find a way to stay here, to wait until Philip returns."

Julian put a hand to the back of his neck, rubbing once. Then, suddenly, he smiled. "You know, Alix, there is a way to wait here for Philip without fear your father will send you away."

She raised her brows. "How?"

"Marry me," he said, quickly raising a hand to halt her forthcoming and fully expected protest. "But annulment is not unheard of. If we do not consummate our wedding, we can ask for annulment so you can be free to wed Philip once he returns."

Alix looked hopeful, then desolate in one quick instant. "Just how are we supposed to convince the church we haven't consummated our wedding when they learn I'm already pregnant? If I marry you now, everyone will think the babe I carry is yours."

Momentarily taken aback, Julian did not respond immediately. Then, just as confidently, he said, "There have been annulments based upon infidelity."

Alix's hopes rose—however uncautious it was. "Of course! I can simply be quite bold about my feelings for Philip—and you can petition the Church for annulment." But then her hopes fell as quickly as they rose. "Aren't we forgetting something? Once I marry you, my father can still stop me from marrying Philip. If he challenges Philip as my brother-by-marriage, the church will not allow us to wed by issue of our family relationship."

"Only if he exercised that right," Julian reminded her. "Surely your father would allow you to wed Philip if he was here, and made it clear he wished to marry you?"

Alix frowned with worry. "And have a scandal? You must have guessed by now how eager he is to have the Beauchamp name untarnished by ignoble behavior," she said scornfully. "He may indeed take issue with any possible marriage plans for Philip and me, once I am wed to you."

"But Philip is the father of your baby!"

Alix laughed unkindly. "I hardly think that matters to him, as long as the child still has the correct name attached to it."

"It can still work," Julian insisted. "Tell your father there is only one way you'll wed me at week's end—and that is if you will be allowed to divorce me should Philip return and still want to wed you." Then, realizing how cold those words sounded, he added, "Which of course will happen."

Thoughtful, Alix paused before speaking. "It could work," she said. "But, Julian, are you willing to give up so much for me? To become the deserted husband?"

He shrugged easily. "I am the second son, Alix. What I do is not so important as what Philip does. Besides," he added with a familiarly cocky grin,

"I've never been wanting of female companionship. I doubt having been divorced will spoil too much for me."

Alix held out her hand to seal the pact. "Then it's agreed," she said. "I will wed you at week's end."

Julian accepted her hand, and brought her palm to his lips. "Agreed," he said. "Have no fear, demoiselle, this will work."

40

The smell of roses permeated the air. Alix breathed deeply, her eyes closed against the changes in the garden. How she wished it were still the wild, untamed place it had been before. The roses would still be as fragrant, she thought, and their boughs would not be cut back and stunted, but free and unhampered by man's hand—the very hand that stole their lovely buds. Free, the way she wished she could be.

Unwittingly, her hand went to her belly. It was still as flat, though she knew it wouldn't be long before the babe inside would grow and make her swell. She smiled, though at the same time marvelling that she could still want this child so very much when it was its very existence which caused so many of her troubles. But it was Philip's child, the child of the man she loved so desperately she fairly ached for him now. She wanted this child, there was no doubt about that. And while it might have been easier had she gotten with child once she was wed to the man she so loved, she could not deny the very thought of this babe sent a smile to her face and a warmth coursing through her being.

It was a rare moment of peace to be sitting there in the center of the garden she'd shared so often with Philip. The past two days had been nothing short of hell. Her father had made sure the entire Chateau was as eager for the wedding ceremony as he; for the past two days she had been responding to kind wishes, various advice from matronly women, and the added burden of knowing it was Julian, not Philip, whom she would wed.

More than once she doubted the success of the pact she'd made with Julian. Though they had gotten her father's word that he would not stand in their way when they petitioned for annulment, she couldn't resist nagging doubts that when the time came—and she had no doubt it would—that Philip returned intending to marry her, her father would still stand in their way.

The church bells rang again, startling Alix from unpleasant thoughts. The sound shouldn't have made her flinch; the bells had been ringing each hour, for today was the wedding of the de Saineses' son. The entire Chateau was prepared for a day of festivity; Alix herself was already dressed in the ermine-trimmed blue damask her mother had given her that morning. Around her neck sparkled a large diamond, a gift from her father which had once belonged to his mother, saved so he said for the happy day of her wedding. Alix had said nothing when her father presented her with the costly gift. She could not bring herself to look her father in the eye.

She had seen Julian earlier that morning; they'd exchanged a few brief words, but Alix's unhappiness must have been obvious to him, for he avoided speaking of Philip.

But Alix could not keep her thoughts from Philip. More than once, she'd gone up to the high wall, searching the horizon for some sign of him. There was still time, she had thought to herself—time for him to come back—time for him to be the one standing beside her when the bishop spoke the marriage blessing. But now those hopes were dwindling away. The wedding would begin within the hour—her mother would be coming for her soon, to take her inside the church. And she would have to go; she'd made a pact with Julian, she'd given her word to her father. It was either wed Julian, or go to the cloister—never to see Philip again. At least with her pact with Julian, there was hope for a future.

That is, she thought, her spirits so low it hardly mattered if she allowed desolate visions to spring up, *if* Philip returned. Obviously even Julian, who knew his brother well, had some reason to believe it might be some time before Philip returned. That her father believed Philip would certainly not return at all to wed her was painfully obvious.

She leaned forward, rubbing tears from her eyes. She'd been so sure . . . so very sure he would return in time for the wedding set for today. True, he had reason to doubt her father would allow them to wed, but even with only a shred of hope, she'd believed he loved her so much he would want to be there—whether or not her father had actually given his consent.

But he wasn't there, she thought bitterly. Perhaps he wouldn't return at all—at least not for her. He would come back sooner or later, she knew; this was his home, his legacy. But perhaps her father was correct in believing Philip no longer wished to marry her—that it was she, not some remorse over wounding Charles, he'd fled from that day. Did he see in her some trap, some web that would bind him not just to a wife, but also to the sword? After all, her father expected Philip to eagerly use the sword—just to make it known he was a fierce protector of his own. Did Philip think she expected him to live with a sword at his side?

She no longer knew what to think. She'd done nothing but weigh all of the reasons for his disappearance, and knew even if he did still love her, something more than remorse over Charles was keeping him away. He could have sent for her, or at the very least sent her a message, contacted her in some way so she had something to cling to, some hope that he still loved her. But there had been no word and she could only believe it was because even the love he had for her was in jeopardy; he might feel remorse at having taken up the sword again for such a purpose he thoroughly disdained, but that remorse must have spilled over to doubting his love for her. Otherwise he would have come to her, or contacted her somehow.

Alix stood, knowing it would not be long before her mother came for her. For one irrational moment she wondered what would happen if she just refused to attend . . . But she knew she was trapped. She sighed aloud, knowing time was growing short. But she was unwilling to leave the solitude of the garden. She stood there, arms folded across her chest, head bent, wondering all the while how she would stand through the wedding blessing when her knees felt weak and her head felt light. She hadn't slept or eaten properly in days, and it was taking its toll. The fact that her spirits were so low only added to her unsteadiness. But there was only one cure, she thought desolately . . . and he . . .

Just then she heard the sound of footsteps upon the stone pathway leading to the garden's center. But she couldn't face her mother; she couldn't leave for the church yet. How could she endure it? she wondered. How could she marry another man when her heart and soul cried out for Philip?

"Alix."

He said her name softly, but Alix had heard it so clearly. Yet she did not move—could not—for her limbs seemed frozen, and she was not quite so certain she had control over her body. Had her ears heard correctly? Had she indeed heard Philip's voice, saying her name? Or would she turn round and find no one—or worse, her mother, come to retrieve her for her wedding to the brother of the man she loved?

Then she heard his footsteps draw near, and he said her name again. Her heart tumbled in joyous leaps, her hands trembled uncontrollably, and her breathing seemed to stop altogether for several exhilarated moments. Alix faced him in one quick, ecstatic instant, the tears in her eyes replenishing with joy rather than the heartache which had dampened them so often in the past days.

Part of her wanted to rush to his arms, demand he hold her, kiss her, love her. She'd longed for that! She'd needed that in these past relentlessly hellish days, and now he was here before her and she wanted nothing more than to feel his love, languish in it, and let every lonely, frightening memory disappear as quickly as the flash of a falling star.

But she held back. He looked so distant for the barest moment . . . unsure, vulnerable. The uncertainty quickly filled her as well, and so she did not rush to his arms the way she wanted to. Besides, didn't she have reason to be uncertain? Had he returned only because her mother's messenger had told him about the babe she carried? Or worse, had the men-at-arms traveling with that messenger simply forced him to return?

At last, still standing several paces away, he spoke. "Alix," he almost whispered her name. How wonderful it sounded . . . "I cannot ask you to forgive me, either for staying away so long or giving us reason to be apart. I've hated myself in these past few days—for taking up my sword again in useless fighting, for nearly killing a man over the lies of a deceitful woman. And for leaving you."

Alix let her eyelids flutter down, concealing her eyes. "There is nothing for me to forgive; I knew you did not want to hurt Charles in that challenge." Then she raised her gaze to meet his, adding firmly, "But you had no choice. He was fighting for the kill."

"I meant for the fight to end without harm befalling either one of us—by sheer exhaustion bringing one of us down."

"Charles never would have surrendered. His goal was to kill you or die himself."

A smile tugged at the corner of Philip's mouth; Alix saw it there, and her heart trembled with anticipation. "I never should have left you," he said. "I've hated myself these past days, Alix, because I broke yet another vow. I vowed not to kill Charles, yet he could have died at my sword."

"Have you seen Charles since the Tourney?" She had to ask, she had to know where he'd been the last few days. She had to know if it was over yet . . . if Charles had survived, perhaps the events of the Tourney could be forgotten. But if he'd died, Alix knew it would be a long while before Philip could forgive himself—even if, as she thoroughly believed, he was innocent of any wrongdoing.

"I was with Charles," he said, confirming her guess. "I should have told you . . . sent word . . . but . . ." He ran a hand through his thick hair, and the waves sprang back defiantly once he took his hand away. "I couldn't, Alix. I couldn't face you after the Tourney, and I couldn't contact you. I knew you would come to me if you knew where I was. I half expected you to walk through the monastery door anyway, just appear miraculously the way you did at the camp when I went after Julian. Part of me hoped you would . . . the other part of me knew I didn't deserve that. I had no right to have you with me, your healing love making me forget the wrong I'd done. I needed to be with Charles, and feel each moment of remorse over what I'd done. If you had been there, your love would have made it too easy for me. Do you see?"

She nodded, though she wanted to tell him he had no true reason to want to punish himself, to feel such strong regret. He'd had no choice! But perhaps, she thought, that is precisely what he meant. She thoroughly believed in his goodness—and when he felt so utterly responsible for Charles's pain, he would not allow himself the pleasure of her inevitable and loving attempts to convince him he was blameless. "How is Charles?" she asked. "Is he . . . did he . . . ?" She left the question unfinished, suddenly at a loss for proper words.

"He wasn't responding to any of the treatments

at first. Even just this morning, the monks attending him said he could still die."

"Then . . . my mother's messengers forced you to return here for the wedding before you knew how Charles fared?" She hated to ask, she hated to think that could be true—that their wedding would take place only because he'd been forced to come back to her.

Philip looked perplexed. He shook his head. "I certainly wasn't forced to return; I knew today was the day of the wedding, and if your father agreed, I still wanted to wed you. But it was unthinkable for me to abandon Charles to go to such a happy occasion as my own wedding. I made the decision to stay at his side, to send word to you that I would return after Charles recovered or . . . once I knew for certain what would happen to him. And just as I made that decision, Charles opened his eyes. He stared right at me, and asked if I'd come to finish the task of killing him." Philip laughed. "It was strange," he said, as if he were suddenly back there at Charles's side rather than at her side, "but in that moment I knew all of the hostility, the envy, all of the hatred he felt for me in the past months was over. We'll never be truly friends again . . . there are scars besides the one my sword has left upon his chest. But it's over, truly over. He knows I had not attempted to steal his wife away, and we've both retained our honor."

Alix touched his hand, but withdrew after a brief caress. "I am glad Charles survives," she told him. "And that it's over."

She wanted to hold him, to feel his embrace envelop her, but still she did not move forward. He'd said her mother's messengers had not forced him to return; she was certainly glad that was true. She was glad, too, that he'd learned Charles would live; she even had some hope that he would have returned today anyway had not Marie's messengers retrieved him. But the fact remained that he might have preferred to wait, to postpone their wedding day until all of this unpleasantness was truly forgotten—by him if not by gossiping society. Did he feel hurried, she wondered, into marrying her just because of the baby? Would he have preferred to set another day for their wedding, one that did not have any leftover shadows looming over it?

She suddenly shook such thoughts away. He was here! He wanted to wed her, he'd said so! Whether it was because of the babe or not, he truly did want to marry her. Why must she search for problems where there were none?

But Philip had sensed her unease, for he said, "What is it, Alix? Since the moment I saw you standing here, I've wanted to take you in my arms and kiss you . . . but I sense something in you that holds me back. Yet you must have been assured I was coming back. All the way through de Saines county I heard the bells of every church announcing our wedding. And when I heard the bells I rejoiced, because you believed in our love enough to convince your father to let the wedding proceed, even though I'm more than certain he must have thought I deserted you—"

He suddenly stopped, seeing the look of pure astonishment cross her face.

She smiled, each and every worry evaporating like a tiny drop of water on a scalding desert sand. "I love you, Philip," she told him softly. "And I never stopped believing in your love for me. My faith might have trembled," she added honestly, "but it never diminished."

There was nothing between them then, no doubts or worries, and in an instant they were within each other's arms. Philip pressed his lips to hers—hard and demanding and hungry for her, she could tell. As hungry as she was for him. How she would relish their wedding night tonight!

"Haven't you spoken to anyone since your return?" she asked.

He shook his head. "There were several men-at-arms to welcome me home, but they said nothing. And the hall is empty; they are in the church, I would imagine. I went to your chamber, but found it empty. I was on my way to the church when I stopped and found you here."

Alix's hands trembled anew, confused, hopeful, even a little afraid. Didn't he know? Hadn't her mother's messengers found him, and told him about the babe? Had he truly returned without any knowledge that the wedding *must* be today?

"My father was going to have me marry Julian, thinking you would not return for me."

It was Philip's turn to be astonished. "Today's wedding was to be yours—and Julian's?"

Alix nodded.

Philip struggled to speak calmly. "How could your father force you, knowing you could petition the king for annulment if it was against your will?"

Alix took a deep breath. "I agreed," she said slowly. "I agreed to the wedding."

Philip looked as if an icy mask had slipped over his face. Quickly, Alix reached out as if to take back the meaning behind the words, knowing it cost him confusion, if not pain.

"I thought—I thought you knew," she said. "I thought my mother's messengers found you and brought you back."

Philip shook his head; for one brief moment she saw pain in his eyes. "You keep mentioning your mother's messengers—you asked if they'd forced me back here. I never saw any messengers. They didn't find me."

"They knew you were with Charles—I guessed as much while you were gone."

"Then they're probably halfway back from Paris, having followed a trail left by Rachel la Trau. She told his men to bring Charles to Paris; when I realized where his men must be taking him, I caught up to them and convinced them to take him to the monastery about fifteen leagues from here."

"I thought that was why you'd returned in time for the wedding," she said. "After all, there would be no reason for haste otherwise, unless you knew—"

"I *didn't* know," he told her. "I wasn't sure your father would still allow us to wed, especially since I'd gone after Charles. I wasn't sure he would understand why I left—or you, either. And when I heard the church bells I just assumed you'd convinced him I would be back." He laughed briefly. "Though I should have realized that would have been no easy task. He doesn't want us to wed at all, does he? He still insists you should marry Julian, and since I left you after the challenge, he must have decided I was not fit to be your husband after all, regardless of the fact that I'd fought that ridiculous joust."

Alix shook her head. "No—"

Philip ignored her. He grew angrier by the moment, and now his voice was like steel. "But you agreed? You would have married Julian today, without waiting? Did you think so little of my love for you to doubt I would return for you?"

"No! I knew you would be back, but I didn't know when—"

"So you rushed off to marry my brother?" Then he added irately, "And speaking of my brother, I thought he broke your betrothal? Has he suddenly decided he wants you anyway, even knowing what we've been to each other?"

Alix suddenly laughed. His love for her had never been more obvious: he was jealous! And so angry at the thought she would rush off to marry another, surely he loved her! She laughed harder, her eyes filling with merry tears.

Philip suddenly stopped, looking at her as if she'd gone mad. But, curiously, he asked, "By your strange behavior, I can only guess you've either lost all sense, or that I came to some wrong conclusion. What is it?" Then, before she could even answer, he said, "Did your father force you to agree to wed Julian? Has he said he won't allow you to marry me under any circumstances?"

She shook her head, still mirthful. "No," she

told him, then, at last taking control, she wiped away her tears and continued. "He'll allow us to wed—in fact, I'm sure he would prefer it was you I married today."

Philip shook his head, obviously on the brink of giving her up for mad.

"I had to make a deal with him," Alix explained. "I would marry Julian today if he allowed me to divorce Julian once you returned—whether that be one week or one year from today."

Philip waited in silence for her to finish her explanation; so far nothing at all made sense. "Then why marry him at all? Why was today's wedding so important?"

Alix stepped closer to him, putting her hands in his. "Because time is going by all too quickly," she told him. "But I'm sure my father would prefer that I marry the father of my baby . . . not the baby's uncle."

Philip looked totally perplexed by that announcement. "The father of whose—?" He cut himself short as at least some of her words began to make sense. "Your baby?"

"And yours," she told him, taking one of his hands and pressing to her still small stomach.

Suddenly he pulled her closer, smiling as broadly as she'd dreamed he would when learning of their baby. "Then that is the reason for the haste? How long have you known?"

"I didn't know until my mother recognized the symptoms. We should have a winter baby . . . a hard time to bring such delicate life into this world—"

"Chateau de Saines has plenty of wood to keep many a warm fire burning. A fire in the hearth to keep warm the babe . . . but we have a fire within us to keep us warm."

Her smile wavered between a sensual response to his words and the pure happiness this day had brought. The future was theirs, she thought, a future of promise and love—one she could welcome with each new day.

Just then the church bells rang once again. "Come, seigneur, we have a wedding to attend!"

BE SWEPT AWAY
ON A TIDE OF PASSION
BY LEISURE'S THRILLING
HISTORICAL ROMANCES!

TEMPTESTUOUS HISTORICAL ROMANCE BY ROBIN LEE HATCHER

THE SPRING HAVEN SAGA, VOL. III 2318-0
HEART STORM $3.95 US, $4.95 CAN

THE SPRING HAVEN SAGA, VOL. II 2083-1
HEART'S LANDING $3.75 US, $4.25 CAN

THE SPRING HAVEN SAGA, VOL. I 2073-4
STORMY SURRENDER $3.75 US, $4.25 CAN

THORN OF LOVE 2194-3
$3.95 US, $4.95 CAN

FOR THE FINEST
IN CONTEMPORARY
WOMEN'S FICTION,
FOLLOW LEISURE'S LEAD

2310-5	**PATTERNS**	$3.95 US, $4.50 Can
2304-0	**VENTURES**	$3.50 US, $3.95 Can
2291-5	**GIVERS AND TAKERS**	$3.25 US, $3.75 Can
2279-6	**MARGUERITE TANNER**	3.50 US, 3.95Can
2268-0	**OPTIONS**	$3.75 US, $4.50 Can
2257-5	**TO LOVE A STRANGER**	$3.75 US, $4.50 Can
2250-8	**FRAGMENTS**	$3.25
2249-4	**THE LOVING SEASON**	$3.50
2230-3	**A PROMISE BROKEN**	$3.25
2227-3	**THE HEART FORGIVES**	$3.75 US, $4.50 Can
2217-6	**THE GLITTER GAME**	$3.75 US, $4.50 Can
2207-9	**PARTINGS**	$3.50 US, $4.25 Can
2196-x	**THE LOVE ARENA**	$3.75 US, $4.50 Can
2155-2	**TOMORROW AND FOREVER**	$2.75
2143-9	**AMERICAN BEAUTY**	$3.50 US, $3.95 Can